"Nic, this is M

"Um, hello." Maya extended her hand, roaming over him, remembering him towering naked over her. Her voice cracked. "So nice to finally meet you."

Enchanté. Nic's grin slid to a dull slant as he accepted her handshake and tried to keep his face neutral. "So glad to finally put a name to a face. I am so sorry about your father."

She couldn't speak. "That's very kind."

They stared, shaking hands slowly, the air between them sizzling. The lawyer fell silent.

"Have you two met before?"

"No," they said in unison, breaking from each other's grip.

Maya sat back down and focused on her coffee, trying to ignore the fact that she'd slept with her business partner.

That it was the best sex she'd ever had.

That she was hyperaware of his every movement as he sat next to her and fixed himself a plate of food.

That he

"*Patron,*
else," a
glanced

that wo

He was the owner of the hotel.

Chloe Blake can be found dreaming up stories while she is traveling the world or just sitting on her couch in Brooklyn, New York. When she is not writing sexy novels, she is at the newest wine bar, taking random online classes, binge-watching Netflix or searching for her next adventure. Readers can find out more about Chloe and her books from her website at www.chloeblakebooks.com.

Books by Chloe Blake

Harlequin Kimani Romance

A Taste of Desire
A Taste of Pleasure
A Taste of Passion

Visit the Author Profile page
at Harlequin.com for more titles.

CHLOE BLAKE
and
NANA PRAH

*A Taste of Passion &
Ambitious Seduction*

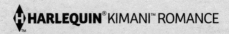

HARLEQUIN® KIMANI™ ROMANCE

ISBN-13: 978-1-335-43302-2

A Taste of Passion & Ambitious Seduction

Copyright © 2019 by Harlequin Books S.A.

The publisher acknowledges the copyright holders of the individual works as follows:

A Taste of Passion
Copyright © 2019 by Tamara Lynch

Ambitious Seduction
Copyright © 2019 by Nana Araba Prah

Recycling programs for this product may not exist in your area.

HARLEQUIN®
www.Harlequin.com

Printed in U.S.A.

CONTENTS

Acknowledgments

Many thanks to my agent Christine Witthohn,
the Kimani team, my writing group
and the friends and family who keep me sane.

A TASTE OF PASSION

Chloe Blake

Dear Reader,

Welcome to Paris—the city of love! Or in Nicolas Rayo and Maya North's case, loss. A sudden death has thrown these two for a loop. Not only are they reluctant business partners, their unrelenting attraction for each other runs deeper than they realize.

Maya thinks she doesn't want her father's vineyard, but she can't let it go. Or is it Nic that she can't let go? Nic's plans for the vineyard don't involve a partner, but he finds himself craving more of Maya, in and out of the bedroom.

But there is more than just passion bringing Nic and Maya together. Both have felt the loss of a parent and it's that hole in their hearts that drives them further and further into each other's arms.

Some say love heals all wounds. I agree. Have you found that to be true? Drop by chloeblakebooks.com and let me know.

Chloe Blake

Chapter 1

Maya North waved her key fob over the lock of her apartment door and heard the latch pop just as an arm snaked around her waist and twisted her into a hard kiss. She melted into him a little, liking the surprise display of affection, wondering if tonight should be the night that they finally made love.

"I had a really nice time tonight," he said, sliding his lips to the corners of her mouth and down her neck. Her gaze darted to both ends of the hallway, curious if her neighbors were at their peepholes. She and Rick had been seeing each other for several weeks, sometimes twice a week, prompting her married neighbors, Chris and Christopher, to show up at her door one night with a bottle of wine and their French bulldog Shania in hand, saying in unison, "Girl, you sent him away again? What are you waiting for?"

Honestly, she didn't know. A spark? Was there such a thing? She and Rick had a lot in common. They were both business consultants, both born and raised in California, both liked *Archer* and *Star Wars* and had an ongoing debate on whether Harrison Ford's character in *Blade Runner* was a replicant. Of course he was! Yes, Maya was a sci-fi nerd—a nerd with a thing for designer bags, but still—and she thought she'd found a kindred spirit in Rick.

They'd both had one too many when she literally bumped into him at a consulting conference in Florida, sending him stumbling into the indoor koi pond at the hotel. She'd given him her card, promising to pay for ruining his custom Italian shoes. Realizing they were both vice presidents at rival Los Angeles consulting firms, he'd reached out to have drinks instead.

But her gut told her it wouldn't last. Their chemistry was off, like now, when he could have held her hand at the restaurant or taken her in his arms during the car ride home. She understood an aversion to PDA, but he really only touched her when no one was around. And living in LA, people were always around.

"I did, too," she said, feeling the hardness of his bicep under his crisp suit. God, she loved a good suit. Gently, she pulled back, stopping him when he began to push open her door with their bodies. "But I have an early flight in the morning." It was true, but not really the reason she was ending the night.

He looked disappointed, almost angry. And the twist

in her stomach reminded her of the other reason she was hesitant. He might be a closet jerk. Pretty on the outside, rotten on the inside. It was the way he talked to waiters, dismissed his associate who had still been at the office when he called her during dinner, and sometimes made Maya feel like her lack of knowledge of certain subjects was inexcusable.

"It's a Dechamps. Can you taste the floral note in the finish?"

Maya had looked at the stately wine bottle with its gold lettering, then taken a sip. She'd tilted her head. "Mmm. Not really. But I like it." Rick had shoved his nose in the glass again and was swishing the liquid around and around dramatically when he jerked his head up. His brow had cocked, making Maya feel she had just given the teacher the wrong answer. She shrugged. "I'm more of a beer girl." Rick's eyes had widened. Thankfully, they had been interrupted by the appetizers.

"An early flight," he said on a sigh, pulling his hands from her body. He straightened and she took him in again, wondering if she was making a mistake. It had been a long time since she'd felt the weight of a man, and there were nights when her body seemed to be torturing her to just "go get some." She wished she could be that girl sometimes, like tonight, when Rick looked strong and very capable of giving her some. "Maybe it's best. I have a job interview in the morning."

"Leaving the firm?" she said neutrally on an inner sigh of relief.

"Maybe. A new opportunity popped up." He kissed her again, his hands on her face and in her hair. That

was another thing: she'd gotten highlights a week before, turning her dark hair into a dynamic display of
caramel-colored waves. He hadn't noticed.

Not completely immune to his kiss, the lower half
of her pulsed, and she imagined her inner self jumping
up and down and shooting flares into the air for some
much-needed attention. Should she just go for it? There
was a supplicant look in his eye, and on impulse, she
shoved open her door with her shoulder and raised her
hand to invite him in.

"Don't women like you do this all the time?"

Her head jerked. Which did she address first? *Women
like her* or *do this all the time*? She went with the latter. "Do what?"

"Random sex."

"Excuse me?"

"You're single, successful and obviously averse to
getting married—"

"What?" Maya's voice rang down the hall. "I'm not
averse to marriage. Why would you say that?"

"Look, I'm not judging. I'm a feminist, too." Maya's
head snapped back, but he continued. "You can't hold a
career like yours and have a husband and kids."

"Yes, I damn well can," she said. She thought of her
other neighbors, who were both doctors with two kids.
The bags under their eyes were permanent, but they
made it work. "Where is this coming from?"

"You're holding out because you think it will make
me come back for more or respect you or whatever, but
I'm telling you now that we aren't on track for marriage.

My wife isn't going to have a career. But we could be on track for casual sex, which fits into your lifestyle."

She was floored, and struggled to put thoughts and words together.

"Wow, Rick, you're more of an idiot than I thought you were."

"You're not getting my—"

"Oh, I get it." Her gaze flicked across the hall, where Chris and Christopher's door was almost imperceptibly ajar. "You think I'm following 'the rules' or some kind of mantrap etiquette. No, I just don't want to sleep with you. You're not good enough for this random sex chick, so lose my number and have a good night."

She slammed the door in his face, then listened for the elevator doors to close. Insistent banging followed. She opened the door, knowing exactly who it was.

There stood Chris and Christopher in fuzzy slippers with Shania and a bottle of rosé. Crying was not Maya's thing, but one tear did slide down her cheek.

Two months later, Maya whizzed her Range Rover off the 405 highway, turned up the music when Britney came on the station and swerved to a screeching halt in front of her office building.

She sang aloud, gyrating in her seat as she turned the car off and kept the radio on. She just wanted to savor the moment. First the phone call last night from the CEO to come in a little early for a meeting, then the zero traffic, and now Britney was on the radio? It was a sign that today was her day. She could tell by Dave's voice that he had good news, that he'd taken their meeting from over a month ago to heart.

As lead consultant for their largest client, Super-Foods, she saw potential for a combined consumer goods division, taking all of their applicable clients and assigning them specialized attention from a larger team under one chief—her.

She'd provided Dave with a PowerPoint presentation of her ten years of achievements, a ladder plan on how to grow the business and why he should promote her to executive vice president of consumer goods. Having such an amazing work distraction right now would be great, since her search for a significant other had stalled after her last online dating disaster, Rick, and she'd been gun-shy about tapping that app again.

Whatever. She couldn't think about it now. Now she was going to go into the office and become a boss. The trophy husband could come later. She readjusted the rearview mirror and relined her lips: Boss Red.

Oops, I did it again. I got that promotion. "Hi Chrissy!" She waved to her colleague's associate account exec as she strode by her car. *I'm gonna be your boss. Mhmm, mhmm.*

Maya got out of her car and brushed wrinkles from her pants, then she plopped her Jimmy Choos to the asphalt and slipped them on, noticing an obnoxious red Lamborghini a few spaces away. Maybe she should get a red Range Rover: Boss Red.

She was still humming when she plopped her things in her office and knocked on Dave's closed office door.

"Come in," Maya heard through the mahogany. With a smile, she turned the knob.

"Good morning, Dave." Her smile faltered. Dave was sitting at his desk, while a light-haired man sat across from him. "Oh, sorry. I thought you said come in." The man was staring at her and recognition flashed in Maya's mind. Rick? The jerk she'd dated just months ago. Rick the di—

"Don't be shy. Have a seat." Dave smiled. "I want you to meet someone. This is Richard Shade. Rick, this is Maya. She's the one who came up with the idea to consolidate the division. SuperFoods is our best client because of her. I want you two to really make this division soar."

"It's great to meet you, Maya." Rick kept it neutral as they shook hands, but his gaze held a sickening glint.

"And you, Rick." She tried to keep the sneer from her voice and focus on what the hell was going on. She turned to Dave. "I'm sorry. I don't understand. How are we working together?"

"Rick is going to head the division as executive vice president…" Her ears actually shut down. As did her facial functions. But she was blinking. A lot. "He'll be accompanying you on your trip to New York next week so you can introduce him to SuperFoods."

Several responses flickered in her mind. In the first, she let out a string of curse words with her middle fingers up in the air. In the next, she puked all over Rick and his shiny shoes. Another had her screaming at the top of her lungs, running down the hall and bashing Rick's car with a baseball bat.

"Oh. That sounds great," she managed, nodding like

an idiot. "Well, I should get back to work. Welcome aboard, Rick!" she said too loudly, with a plastic smile.

Somehow the hallway to her office stretched a million miles.

"Maya? You okay? He just told you, didn't he?" Dave's executive assistant, Carol, stood with a concerned look on her face. Carol was like the office mother. She knew everything and she took care of the employees, acting as confidante and guide. But, at the end of the day, she worked for Dave.

"You knew about this and didn't tell me?"

She looked stricken. "It happened quicker than you think. He considered you, Maya. He did."

"I know that guy, Carol. I dated him!" She frowned.

Carol's brows rose. "That's not Rick the d—"

"In the flesh."

"Oh, no. The one who—"

"Yep." Maya turned toward her office, wondering how her life had gone from Boss Red to shit brown in twenty minutes.

To make matters worse, Rick stood in her office thirty minutes later offering her a gourmet cup full of shit-brown coffee he'd ordered on his expense account. There for a minute, and he'd already been set up with an expense account? She wanted to throw it in his face. Instead, she smiled and reached for the cup.

"Thank you."

"No problem. They are still setting up my laptop, so I thought it would be a good time to talk. You look well."

"Thank you." Her record needle was stuck. When she stayed silent, he lowered his lids and leaned forward.

"Look, I know we didn't part well, but I want you to know it's water under the bridge. I really liked your presentation." God help her. "Great ideas. I mean, the ladder plan was aggressive and there is no way you can hit those numbers in a year—" She wished she had an electrocute button attached to his chair. "—but with some tweaks I made, Dave is totally on board. I'll email you a copy. We can do this. Together." Maya sipped her coffee, praying she was dreaming.

He looked at his watch. "Well, I have a breakfast with the chiefs. We'll touch base before New York."

"Thank you," Maya gritted out as he sauntered out of the office. She sipped her coffee, annoyed that he remembered how she took it. One sugar, no cream. She should hand in her two weeks' notice. She should get up and walk out. She should—

"Hey, Maya, this package was delivered to the legal department, but I think it's for you." Jen, the head of their legal team, slapped the package on Maya's desk with a thud. It looked like it weighed a hundred pounds, was stamped like it had been around the world twice and was torn open at the top. "I didn't mean to read it," she apologized.

"What is it?"

Jen hesitated, and Maya gave her friend a confused look. They had both started at the company around the same time, which had led to them being friends outside of work as well. "Some of it is in French, but from what I could make out, I think it's an inheritance." Maya's mouth turned down as she reached for the package and pulled out reams of paper with tiny writing. It definitely looked legal. "I—I think someone died," Jen stammered.

It was an unseasonably warm March day in Paris. Normally Nicolas Rayo would have taken a long lunch with a friend; instead, he sat on the other side of the desk of James T. Bauer, Esq., and tried to focus. Albert Belcourt was dead. It still didn't seem real, and yet there he was, listening to the last will and testament of the man who had been not only a business partner, but a second father.

The old lawyer adjusted his glasses and cleared his throat. "To Luca Nicolas Rayo Dechamps I leave my wine collection, valued at two million euro. Your father and I curated it together, and with him gone, I know of no one else who could take better care of it."

Nic smiled in spite of his sadness. The collection held several of the first wines Nic's father, Gabriel, and Albert had ever produced. Speaking of… "Can we get to the part about the business?"

James shifted uncomfortably. "In a minute, there is more I must read."

James droned on in legalese and Nic took a patient breath, wondering if his father and Albert were looking down on him from their vineyard in the sky, laughing.

In their twenties, Albert and Gabriel had built a successful vineyard, selling their grapes to France's most prominent winemakers. Eventually their vineyard grew into a wine brokerage, selling not just their own grapes, but selling and buying grapes for other wineries.

"This will be yours one day. Hard work will keep you

honest," his father had always said in response to Nic's refusal to go into the family business. Sure, wine was in Nic's blood. Gabe had been a vintner, Nic's uncle and cousins were vintners and his mother was a sommelier. But Nic had taken his own path into real estate, eventually investing in a hotel. He was successful, despite his father's refusal to consider buying and selling buildings as "hard work." Seven years ago, when Gabe had passed away and left his only son half the business, Nic assumed it was his father's last effort to "keep him honest."

Nic was pulled from his thoughts by a change in James's voice. "I also bequeath to Nic my art collection with the hopes he will cherish it." The lawyer looked up from the pages. "There is a notation that if you don't want the paintings, they can be given to a museum."

"I want the paintings," Nic murmured, wishing James kept a stocked minibar in his office.

Albert had welcomed Nic as an equal partner when Gabe passed, but Nic had given up his voting rights to act as a silent partner. His activity in the business had been minimal until a few yeas ago, when the landscape of the wine industry began to change and the brokerage took its first loss. Plus, Albert had been getting older, slowing down, so Nic had taken on a little more each day. Gabe would have been proud—running two businesses *was* hard work. But, without Albert, that model was no longer sustainable, which meant something had to give. Unfortunately, his numbers told him that liability was the vineyard, and if he could put that in someone else's hands, then he could hire someone to manage the brokerage. He just needed to take over Albert's shares.

So there Nic was, waiting to hear that sole owner-ship of the business Albert and Gabriel had built from nothing would be dropped into his lap like a hot potato.

"And last but not least, to Nic, who was like a sec-ond son to me, I leave my Oscar Wilde first editions."

James pulled his glasses from his nose, closed his folder and then smiled under his thick moustache. "There you are, my boy."

Nic frowned. "There I am what?"

"Your inheritance. That's all for you."

"That's all? You haven't even mentioned the busi-ness. *My* shares of the business." Nic tried to keep a handle on his rising voice.

"Oh, right…right." James opened his folder and flipped back through the pages. Nic leaned forward, ready to jump up and leave when the shares were declared his.

The lawyer cleared his throat. "Yes, now it seems that Albert had bequeathed his shares of the business to his only daughter, her identity to be revealed only if she decides to accept the offer. If she refuses, the shares are to go to the next living partner, which is you."

Nic's mouth dropped as he processed what he'd just heard. "Daughter?" He leaned forward. "A daughter? Albert doesn't have a daughter," he murmured as he ran a hand through his black hair. Nic whirled on James, who was tidying his mustache in the reflection of his business card case. "Does he?"

"He does. I have initiated contact with her and will be in touch about her decision. But it seems unlikely that a young woman with no knowledge of her father would take on his business. Preposterous, really. If you're lucky she'll just say no. Which is what I expect. But if she has any business savvy at all—"

"She'll want payment for the shares," Nic interrupted.

"Exactly."

"Draw up the paperwork."

"Excuse me?" James blustered.

"Albert clearly wants his daughter to have something of his. It wouldn't be right to just take the shares. I'll offer to buy them."

"That might be quite expensive."

"I'll make it back, and then some. I have a plan, and it doesn't involve a partner. Call me when you know something."

The busy streets of Paris were like a blur as he marched past the cafés and boutiques of the Marais. Not even the smell of the street crepes could pull him from his thoughts. He wasn't sure if he was angry or sad, shocked or resigned. A daughter? It didn't make sense. That business should be his. He wasn't going to let some stranger get her hands on it. How could Albert do that to him? Nic stared into the distance, focusing on nothing. How could Albert just up and die on him?

And there it was again, that tightening in his chest. He needed a drink.

Correction, several drinks.

Chapter 2

Someone died? Maya grabbed her cell phone and dialed her mother, whom she had just talked to the night
before. Her mother answered with a breathy hello.
"Mom," she said with relief. "Hi."

"Aren't you working? You never talk to me during
work hours."

"Yes, I just… Um, how's Steve?"

"Oh, he's watching the news." Never had Maya been
so happy to hear that her stepfather was on the couch.
"Is something wrong? Oh! You got the promotion!
Steve, she got the promotion!"

"No! Mom…" She sighed. "I didn't get it."

"Oh, honey, I'm sorry. Steve, she didn't get the promotion! What happened?"

Maya rolled her eyes. "It's a long story. Look, I need

to go, I'll call you later." Maya hung up on her mother's protests, once again staring at the packet.

She went through the motions of dialing the number of the law office, relieved when a British receptionist answered and said that Mr. Bauer had stepped out, would she like to leave a message? She explained about the packet and left her cell number. Seconds later it rang. Vaguely recognizing the number, she picked up.

"Hello?"

"Hello. May I speak with Maya Belcourt?"

"Oh. Uh, I think you have the wrong number."

"Erm." Maya heard papers rustling. "Maya Elizabeth North Belcourt? I believe you just called. My name is James T. Bauer. I'm so happy we've finally found you."

"Um… I'm just Maya Elizabeth North, I still think you have the wrong person."

"Your mother is Sandra North, yes?"

"Oh." She paused. "She is."

"Excellent! Well, not exactly. Miss Belcourt, I'm an attorney handling your father's estate. I'm afraid he passed away several weeks ago."

"No, see, Steve's not dead. This is definitely a mistake."

"Steve? I'm sorry, I don't know a Steve. I'm talking about Albert Belcourt."

"Well, I don't know an Albert Belcourt." Fragments of memories began to flash in her mind. Running through trees, kisses on her cheeks, someone teaching her French. Maya paused. Albert. It had been so long since she'd heard that name or even thought about her biological father. But why would she? He'd left her and her mother when she was a toddler, and they never saw or heard from him again. Steve wasn't perfect, but at least he'd been there. "Um, I'm sorry, I do know who you're talking about. It's been a long time."

"Yes, well I'm sure this is very confusing, but Albert made it clear that his daughter, you, receive his estate upon his death."

"I'm inheriting his home?"

"Well, yes, but also a portion of his business."

"What business?"

"Your father owns half of a vineyard and wine brokerage outside of Paris."

She straightened. "Paris, France?" This was too much, and it wasn't even ten in the morning. "Look, this can't be right. He left me… Why would he leave me anything?"

"Albert was a very private person. Even his business partner knows nothing of this, but *mademoiselle*, I assure you, this is no mistake. He wanted you to have it."

Maya paused, struggling to keep her breathing even. "You knew him?"

"I've been his counsel for over twenty years."

"What was he like?"

"Everybody liked him. A good businessman. Reliable and trustworthy."

"Humph." Trustworthy? She didn't think so. "Did he have a family?"

"No. He never married."

She ignored the tightening in her throat and stared hard at her cold cup of coffee, which began to blur through her tears. What was she crying for? She had a good life; what did it matter that he hadn't wanted her? She inhaled in a flurry of sniffles. James must have heard. "Oh, my, this must be upsetting. Unless you have any other questions now, I'll let you review the paperwork yourself. I'll call you in a few days to set up a time that we can discuss all of it in detail. You can have a lawyer look over them, as well, of course. And you know how to reach me if you have any questions at all before then. I'm so sorry to be the bearer of bad news, Miss Belcourt." Why did he keep calling her that? "I'll bid you good day."

She kept the phone to her ear, making it look like a client call, as Rick and the chiefs made their way past her office to breakfast. Suddenly her office felt like a prison. Maya grabbed her things and left, using the excuse that she didn't feel well. And it couldn't have been more true.

That position should have been yours. Days later, Maya pulled her tray table down and waited for the in-flight lunch service. She had been excited for her client meeting with SuperFoods, looking forward to plunging herself into work while Jen did her a personal favor and reviewed the inheritance paperwork, until Rick had decided to come along.

Maya shifted uncomfortably in her partially reclined economy-plus seat and stared ahead into the first-class cabin. Refreshments were being served, and she could partially see Rick in an aisle seat taking full advantage of his larger travel budget. His artisanal socks were elevated and stretched out in front of him, and a Tom

Cruise action movie played on the TV screen attached to his chair. He'd been watching movies since they boarded the six-hour flight from LA to New York. Was he ever going to read the detailed report of the company that she had prepared for him? His manicured hand reached for a glass of champagne, then a smiling stewardess closed the curtains.

After a smooth six-hour flight, they checked into their hotel, freshened up, then met the chief officers of SuperFoods for dinner at Cipriani. Rick was friendly and engaging with her clients, ordering the best bottles of wine and praising her several times in front of the team of powerful men, making Maya feel a little bad about secretly hating him for taking her position. She coaxed herself to give him a chance and even helped him out when he didn't know the answer to a business question.

The CEO of SuperFoods grabbed the neck of the wine bottle with his meaty hand. "A bottle of Dechamps?"

Maya held out her empty glass. "Wait until you try it. It's organic or biodynamic or something."

The CEO rolled his eyes. SuperFoods was famous for pumping out processed and packaged foods, including individual wines in a box. Nothing they produced was organic, but Maya helped boost their customer appeal by peppering their packaging with ambiguous words and phrases like "all natural" and "one hundred per-cent whole." It was one hundred percent whole—whole chemicals. They weren't breaking any FDA laws and customers thought they were getting healthy food. Their market share rose thirty percent in the first year.

"Not bad," he said, after taking a sip.

Maya nodded. "See, guys, it's good to bring the boss. His expense account is bigger than mine." The table chuckled. Rick sent her a secret nod of thanks and she smiled back. Maybe once her company saw what a good team player she could be, the next promotion would be hers.

"That went well," Rick said, as they walked down the hall to their rooms.

"They're a fun bunch after hours, but tomorrow they'll try to poke holes in our presentation. That's why I wrote it up in bullet points for you. Try to take a look before you go to bed." She stopped in front of her door and slipped the key in the lock. In a second, the door clicked and she stepped forward.

"Can we talk a minute? I think it would be good if we started fresh." She was halfway in the door and turned to see him with his hands in his pockets and a strange look in his eye.

"Oh…um." She looked over her shoulder at her room. Chocolates lay on her pillow, and the clothes she had left on the floor were neatly piled in the chair. "Sure."

He stepped inside and shut the door behind him. Before she knew what was up, she was pressed against the wall and his lips were on hers. Unable to believe what was happening, she jerked her head away and pushed at his shoulders. He didn't budge; in fact, her effort urged him closer. He grabbed her head and brought her face back to his.

"Wait…stop—" She struggled against his lips.

"Kiss me back." His whisper made her cringe, and she froze when his hand found her breast.

Her slap to his face was hard, the kick to his shin even harder, and this time her She-Hulk shove sent him backward a few feet. "Get the hell out of my room!"

"What the hell is your problem?"

"My problem?" Her voice hit the ceiling.

Rick sneered. "You were sending me signals all night."

"Signals? At our work dinner?" She couldn't form words, opting to just point to the door. "Please leave."

His jaw dropped and his gaze reduced her to a tease, even though she would never so much as touch the man, not to mention the fact that he was—oh, God—her boss. Slowly, he stood, rubbed his jaw and straightened his suit, all the while looking at her.

"So what now? You go to HR?"

She didn't know. Should she go to HR? They had a presentation the next morning with her most important client. Was it really worth ruining her career? His lips got thinner as she silently debated. "No." It came out in a rush. "We agree that it was a misunderstanding. We have work to do."

"Fine. I'm sorry for the misunderstanding. Good night," he spat.

He whipped out of the room before she could say anything. Then a feeling of dread came over her so strong that she had to sit on the edge of the bed and catch her breath.

"Her name is Maya Belcourt. Thirty-three years old. A business consultant in Los Angeles. Quite smart.

MBA from Stanford. Unmarried. No children. Travels frequently to New York—"

James's voice became an electronic hum as Nic pulled his phone from his ear and signed for the large delivery of party masks for their gods and goddesses lobby party that Friday.

Nic put the phone back to his ear while his staff opened the boxes and began to play. The plastic hand-held masks half covered their faces, making them look like marble renditions of Bacchus or his wife, Ariadne, from the nose up.

Those are for the guests. These are for you, Nic mouthed. He pinched his phone between his ear and his shoulder and reached into another box, pulling out a gold lamé loincloth and a low-cut sheath. "Try these on," he said to his dumbstruck staff.

Nic raised the phone back to his ear and walked across the lobby to his office. "Let me guess, she likes bubble baths and long walks on the beach. I don't care about her marital status, James. Does she want the shares or not?"

"She requested a full annual report for the last five years."

"Damn it."

"I think it would be a good idea for you both to meet."

"I'm not going to California. If she wants these shares she can come here."

"Precisely what I was thinking. You can show her the property and—"

"We can negotiate the share price and she can be on her way."

"My boy, I think you are forgetting something."

"What would that be?"

"She's just found out the father she never knew has passed. It might be nice of you to tell her about him."

He couldn't think of anything more excruciating. Would she cry? She'd probably cry.

"I'm not sure that's a good idea. Maybe Nathan can do that. He's good with the clients." Albert's young associate broker had taken on more responsibility and become somewhat of a right hand to Nic, as well.

"This isn't a client, Nic—this is Albert's daughter."

Nic ran a hand through his hair. "I'm sorry. You're right. I don't know what's wrong with me."

"You lost someone you cared about. And not long after your own father passed. It's understandable if you are…not yourself. You could always talk to someone, Nic."

"I'm talking to you."

"You know what I mean."

"A therapist? I don't need therapy."

"I'm not saying you do, per se. But we all need a little help sometimes."

"I'm fine, James. There is only one thing I need right now."

"A drink?"

"Okay, two things. A drink. And those shares."

"May I ask what you want those shares for so badly?"

"I have an idea to recoup some of the money the business has lost over the past few years, and I need full license to do it. Without those shares, I still don't have voting rights. All decisions must pass through this mystery woman."

"About that. There are several contingencies built into the contract that I need you to be aware of."

James continued. "First, Mademoiselle Belcourt has two weeks from the day I present the transfer papers to claim her shares, sign the documents, etc."

James cleared his throat. "My boy, are you listening?"

Nic was temporarily distracted when a few of his female staff members hovered outside his office door in their gold party costumes. He waved them in. "*Un moment*, James," Nic looked to the ladies. "*Mademoiselles*, what do you think? I want you to be comfortable. These are more flattering and less revealing than last year."

His female staff gazed at one another and adjusted the costumes to their liking. Anyone would make the mistaken assumption that he had hired them for their beauty, but the group before him was professional, and he didn't want them uncomfortable.

The cap-sleeve midthigh-length dress was loose and flowing, except for a gold tie at the waist. The low-cut neckline could be worn with an undergarment or alone with some well-placed fashion tape.

The ladies chuckled, twirled and gave their approval before leaving the room. Nic put the phone back to his ear.

"*Désolé*. You were saying?"

"Ah, the life of a man about town. To be surrounded

by such beauty at all times. I say, your girlfriend must get very jealous."

"I'm not attached, James." He was not sure he wanted to discuss his love life with his lawyer. "Now can we—"

"Is that so? I saw you and Daphne Rhone at the wine festival together and thought you two might be…" He trailed off suggestively.

Nic sighed, remembering the kiss she'd laid on him in public. "She's a family friend and her father is one of our biggest clients at the brokerage. It was an obligation, no more."

"Friends with…oh, what do you call it? Ah! Benefits? Eh?"

"No, that's not—"

"Good for you. You're still a young man, get out there and—" His voice muffled as if he was cupping the mouthpiece. "Don't limit yourself to just one."

"Says the man who's been married for forty years."

"Forty-five, my boy. And when you find a woman like my Victoria, you don't let her go."

"Noted," Nic murmured, wondering what the secret to forty-five years was. His parents had made it only to ten before his mother had upped and gone back to Spain, and his previous relationships had fizzled after a year or two.

And now a woman he wasn't interested in at all was pursuing him. Daphne was smart and beautiful, but every time she came around, his instinct was to run like hell.

The superstitious part of him wondered if he'd been cursed that day on the train platform when his mother packed her bags and boarded a train to Barcelona, telling him, "Don't let love ruin you." He'd been eight.

"Nic, are you still there?"

"Yes, I just…yes. Where were we?"

"We were on to contingency number two."

Maya sat in Jen's office peering at the overworked lawyer whose desk had disappeared under sky-high piles of paperwork. Jen looked up from the documents and looked at Maya through black-rimmed glasses. "The second contingency is some sort of an employee performance review, but this particular clause states that if one partner has been bringing in eighty percent of the revenue for the past two years, then shares can be automatically transferred to the more active partner."

"Seriously?"

"Yeah. It's a little strange, but they were a private partnership and—whatever—it's France. Maybe that's how they do things. It's based on a review at the end of every quarter, which would be in a few weeks actually, so it seems like a formal performance review."

"Well, there will be no reviews this quarter." Maya sighed. "So, what should I do now?"

"You gotta get the profit and loss statements."

"I already asked for them. And I've booked a flight to Paris at the end of the week. The contract seems to be time sensitive."

Jen leaned in. "You know, I think you can get some money from this. Sell the shares to the silent partner." She ruffled through the papers. "Luca Dechamps? Then go buy a house off the coast of Italy and write a best-selling novel."

Maya laughed, the first time in two days. "It's definitely crossed my mind."

"Or you could move to Paris and actually become a wine broker."

"All options seem way better than being here right now."

That last comment made Jen's head snap up. "Why? Did something happen with Rick the—?"

"We have to stop calling him that." Maya chuckled. She didn't want to go into the details of the subtle shade he had been throwing her way. "It's nothing that can't be worked out." She didn't believe that, but it got Jen to stop asking questions.

Jen handed over the contract and looked at her cautiously. "What did your mom say?"

Maya looked pointedly at her friend. "I haven't told her yet."

Those words lingered as Maya went back to her office and debated calling her mother. Sandra North talked about everything, except *her father.* She also didn't want to tempt herself to divulge what had happened in New York. She hadn't slept a wink since that night, and although the presentation went smoothly and Rick seemed content to act like nothing had happened, she still felt that jolt of dread every time she saw him. She held her breath every time she heard his voice and imagined people were staring at her. She couldn't stop thinking about it, but she had to. She had to stop thinking—she'd get some coffee.

Maya walked to the kitchen and shoved a K-cup pod and a mug into one of the four Keurigs lined up on the counter top.

"Wow, that's your third cup of coffee today. That must be some conference call."

Maya blinked at Carol, who was filling her own cup, then gave the executive assistant a weak smile.

"I'm just trying to get back on a sleep schedule after that New York trip. Hey, what conference call?"

Carol stared, wide-eyed. "The SuperFoods call. Rick and Dave are in there right now. I thought…" She stopped herself. "Maybe you should have a talk with Rick. I know he scheduled it."

"Yeah, I will."

"Is everything all right?"

"Yeah, I'm sure it was an oversight. He's new."

Carol nodded, but there was a "handle it" look in her eye, the kind women gave to one another when gender politics reared its ugly head.

Maya did a drive-by of the conference room. She couldn't see through the frosted windows, but the shadowed figures were enough to make her face hot. *That prick.* She slowed and stopped, trying to hear what was being said, but it was useless.

She fumed at her desk for another thirty minutes, then heard the grating tenor of his voice as he and the CEO exchanged last remarks on their way back to their offices. She was staring daggers into the hall when they appeared and the CEO caught her gaze.

"Maya." He smiled. "You missed a great conference call. Sorry you were too busy. Next time, okay?" He left Rick standing there in her doorway, an evil look on his face.

"I was too busy, Rick?"

"I looked for you, but you weren't in your office."

"Funny, I don't see anything on my calendar."

"It was impromptu."

"You could have texted or had one of the assistants page me."

"I'll think of that next time."

"Please do. Those are my clients."

"Our clients. I'm your boss, remember?" He tossed the line into her office like a bomb and hurried away before it exploded.

Paris couldn't come soon enough.

Chapter 3

Nic closed his office door and pulled the phone from his ear to check the time, thinking he needed to wrap the call up. "When do you think Mademoiselle Belcourt will give you an answer?"

"My guess is soon. She'll be here this weekend. I'll forward you the details."

Nic hung up and laid his phone on the desk, feeling very alone suddenly. When his father had passed away, he'd called Albert. Now that Albert was gone, the emptiness around him began to close in.

He had no desire to run the brokerage alone, or with a stranger. And he wouldn't, not if he could help it.

He picked up his two-way radio from his desk. "Can someone get Chef Joc for me?"

The radio crackled. "*Oui*, boss."

Minutes later, Nic almost lost it when Chef Joc, a six-foot-five Australian, walked into his office wearing nothing but a gold loincloth.

Nic grimaced. "What the hell are you doing?"

"What? I'm trying on the costume for the party." Joc flexed his arms and his abs, striking a Roman statue pose. A former footballer with a muscular frame, Joc looked—Nic hated to admit—great.

Then Nic shook his head at the bulge in his friend's pants. "That's a banana in your pants."

Joc shook his head seriously. "That's all me, mate. And look at these buns. The girls are gonna go nuts." Joc turned his back to Nic, then gave him a saucy look over his shoulder.

Nic laughed at his friend, something, he realized, he hadn't done in a long while. It felt good.

"Joc, you know those aren't for the kitchen staff."

"But why? We have an open kitchen. We need to be part of the backdrop." Joc tried a look over the other shoulder.

Nic couldn't hold in another chuckle. "Stop it. Health codes, blah-blah-blah, you know this. Why are you half-naked in my office?"

Joc stopped posing and put his hands on his hips. "You called me in here."

Where was his brain? "Right. I have an important meeting on Saturday. I'll need breakfast served for three, maybe four, if she brings a lawyer."

"She?"

"Albert's daughter."

"I didn't know Albert had a daughter."

"No one did."

Joc raised a brow. "All right. Not going to touch that one. Where do you want it?"

"In Le Salon Rouge."

"Ah, trying to impress?"

"More like intimidate."

"Mate, consider just impressing. You need to get as much practice in as possible."

Nic cocked his head. "I'm afraid to ask what that means."

"It means, you've been pretty focused on work lately."

"Yes, I have a business to run. So what?"

"So when is the last time you got laid?"

Nic paused at his friend's concerned look. It had been… Well, there was that woman from Colombia… It had to be around… He was embarrassed to say he couldn't remember. "I'm not answering that while that banana is still in your pants."

"All me, mate. But I get what you're saying, none of my beeswax. It's cool." Joc turned to leave, then turned back around dramatically. "But it wouldn't be unheard-of if you had a little fun at the party. All work and no play makes Nic a crabby boss." He struck another pose. "Maybe you should wear this."

"Maybe you should put the fruit back where it belongs."

The men were midlaugh when Nic's phone went off. His face must have fallen.

"Daphne?" Joc asked.

"She's called five times already."

Joc shrugged. "Remember what I said. You could do worse."

Joc left the office and Nic let the call go to voice mail. Then he pulled his laptop forward and typed "Maya Belcourt Los Angeles" in his web browser. A few images and some random links popped up. He ruled out the few pictures of older women then scanned the maybes for any likeness of Albert.

His phone went off again, and his hand hovered over the blinking face. It's for the business, he told himself, and swiftly answered before he changed his mind.

"Good morning, Daphne."

"It's almost lunch. I'm at the bar. Come say *bonjour*?" Although they weren't a couple, her sense of entitlement always astounded him. He held in an exasperated sigh.

"I'm—" Nic checked his desk for anything that looked pressing "—very busy."

"You have to eat, too, Nic. And I told Father where I would be. He might be joining us."

Nic gritted his teeth, hating the way she used her father to subtly threaten him. "I'll be right there."

He smacked his phone to the desk, wincing when he heard the crack of his screen. He closed his eyes and let his head fall back. *Dieu*, he really was wound up. Maybe Joc was right—maybe a party and some female company was just what the doctor ordered.

Maya's taxi rounded the corner of the Rue du Bourg-l'Abbé and stopped in front of a large unassuming concrete building with a Roman archway and cherrywood doors. Les Bains, or The Baths, was carved along a second-floor balcony while the stone head of a man watched over the door.

According to her research, because as a consultant she couldn't help herself, the nineteenth-century bathhouse turned legendary nightclub—Paris's answer to Studio 54—was now a famous boutique hotel rumored to have a secret nightclub inside. One hundred and thirty years of decadence all in one building. She wondered at her business partner's choice of meeting place.

Intrigued as she was, her consultant brain noted a lack of welcoming service, like a doorman or maybe a porter to help with her bags. She wondered how the hotel got their five-star rating and wondered if it was too late to book the Ritz.

With no one in sight, Maya stepped out of the taxi and had gone to help the driver pull her bags from the trunk when a man in black wearing a small headset appeared and grabbed them first.

"Mademoiselle North?"

"Yes…erm, *oui*," Maya said with an uptick in her voice. Where had he come from and how did he know it was her? He smiled and bowed his head. Color her impressed.

"Welcome to Les Bains. I am Jacques. Let's get you checked in."

Maya tipped the driver and turned to follow Jacques, then slowed to eye the stone head once more.

"Zeus?" she said to Jacques. She had taken Greek and Roman mythology with the hope of an easy credit and found herself studying harder than for her tax accounting courses.

"*Non*, but *mademoiselle* is close. I'll give you a hint. He is known as the party god. And remember, we are styled after the *Roman* baths."

Maya smiled. She loved games. "And what do I get if I guess correctly?"

"How about a complimentary glass of wine at the bar? And by the way, wine is our god's favorite."

"Then my first instinct is to say Dionysus, the god of wine, fertility and agriculture, but you said Roman, so it has to be Bacchus."

"*Mademoiselle* is correct." Jacques held open the door with a wide smile and escorted her to the check-in desk. Before she was done handing over her information, Jacques returned with a glass of red wine and a plastic half mask in the visage of a marble face.

"What's this?" She held up the mask by its gold rod.

Jacque winked. "It's for later. Enjoy your stay."

An hour later, Maya adjusted her strappy black slip dress and stepped off the elevator onto the first floor. The lobby buzzed with people, all of whom were twirling their half masks, transforming themselves into Bacchus or his wife, Ariadne, with the flick of a wrist. Her gaze swept the room. Opulent. It was really the only word for the hotel. Velvet upholstery, marble pillars, gold accents and the light scent of fig and coriander in the air. Whoa. She held the half mask up to her face. Where did she just get transformed to? In a minute, she found out.

The music changed and a procession of women in gold dresses and men in gold loincloths, all of whom were wearing gold Nikes with the wings, were passing out champagne and hors d'oeuvres…which was how she found herself lounging on one of the velvet sofas double fisting the champagne and being verbally stroked by Lars, the Swiss artist, who had clearly had more than his share of free drinks and was explaining that he would like to paint her naked form on the ceiling of the lobby. She lifted her gaze and tried to picture her nude visage spread out above them, then broke into laughter.

Normally she'd call the guy a creep and move away, but there was something inviting about the scene around her. What was before just a lobby had transformed into a wine-flowing watering hole for the glamorous. Her eyes darted to long legs in delicate heels, button-down business shirts open at the neck, laughter from glossy lips and lipstick-stained wineglasses. It was the type of place where you could forget who you were and what you had left behind. And for the night, that was exactly what she wanted to do.

The lights had gotten lower and the music a little louder. She'd taken a sip of her champagne and turned back to Lars, who had gotten a little closer. He was looking at her with bedroom eyes, and she tried not to laugh again. She had nothing against a one-night stand, but she had standards. Lars was cute, eager and definitely too young. She guessed he was early twenties trying to act late twenties, which was a turnoff to her early thirties.

Even in school, she had gone for the older guy. Her psychology professor was six foot four with hair black as sin and skin so beautifully tan. Handsome? She had thought so. But sometimes it wasn't about looks, but a combination of strength, intelligence and…sex.

"You want some?" She was pulled out of her head to

see Lars gesturing toward a server with a tray of mini-cakes. She put her half mask over her face and shook her head, relieved when he left to get himself dessert, wondering if her business partner could be anywhere in the room. Luca Dechamps had no Facebook, no Twitter and a defunct LinkedIn, devoid of a picture. Except for some group photos that had no captions and were too small to enlarge, this guy was a ghost.

An older gentleman in dark sunglasses looked interesting. He wore his silver hair in a ponytail and...oh, my God. It was Karl Lagerfeld. Definitely *not* her business partner. She stopped staring like a tourist, reminding herself that she'd meet the man who would buy her father's shares of the business soon enough. Across the room, the bar was filled with people in their half masks, teasing, flirting, playing god and goddess. It was Caligula, but clothed.

She was nose deep in her left champagne flute when tall, dark and handsome walked by. He ran a hand through black hair and swiftly buttoned a tailored suit jacket that fit his broad shoulders perfectly. He was late for dinner, she bet, with his wife. Because guys that hot don't get left alone for long. She couldn't help but watch his lean, long frame make quick work of the marble floor. She didn't care what people said about slim cut trousers on a man; this guy wore them *well*.

Her eye candy disappeared around a corner, only to be replaced by Lars, who had crusted icing on his mouth and sat down almost in her lap. It was time to go back to her room. Alone.

Five minutes later, she was still waiting for the elevator. She should have gotten herself another glass of wine, because it was going on six minutes when the elevator alarm went off. Maya sighed when she heard muffled giggling and a few bumps against the wall. She supposed sex in the elevator went with the theme. If she was honest, she was a little jealous.

Maybe it was a sign she should go back to the party. She looked over her shoulder and saw Lars with another drink in his hand, coming right toward her. Instinctively, she put her mask up to her face and lunged around the corner toward an exit sign, hoping for stairs. *Voilà!* She burst through the heavy door and hurried up the stairs, intent on making it all the way to the eleventh floor in her heels.

By the sixth, her shoes were off and she was practically crawling when a barrage of heavy footsteps above her filled the stairwell. Male voices got louder and closer, and for a moment she felt nervous. She looked up the dark stairs and suddenly she didn't feel safe. She turned quickly to run back downstairs and dropped a shoe. She picked it up, then shot back down the stairs, smack-dab into a tall, hard body. Her scream echoed. She jumped back and balled her fists, ready to defend herself, but when she looked up, an explosive *wow* registered in her brain.

It was *him*, the hottie she'd seen earlier in the slim cut suit. His black hair was ruffled. He looked leaner and more broad shouldered this close, and his frame was well over six feet. His brows were raised in supplication, and his palms were up, a mask dangling from in between his thumb and finger.

"Mademoiselle, vous allez bien?"

"I don't speak—"

"Are you all right? Are you hurt?"

"No, thank you, just startled."

His dark gaze dropped to her mask, then her bare feet. "How can I help you?" Before she could answer, the group of men attacking the stairs had arrived. They were dressed in service uniforms, and spoke rapid French with the hottie before the group ran past. "We're having a problem with the elevator."

Ah, he worked here. "Someone's having sex in it." She mentally slapped herself for being so gauche, but he laughed. The deep sound was pleasant, as was his smile, which lit up his handsome face.

"*Oui*, probably. Is that why you are taking the stairs?"

"Yes." She held up her heels. "Slowly but surely."

"What floor?"

"Eleven."

He shook his head in disapproval. "I can help you. If you'll follow me?" he said, reaching around her to open the door to the fifth floor hallway. She slid past him, feeling juvenile for a woman of her independent status to be rescued like a damsel in distress, in her bare feet, no less. He dipped his head as he closed the door, and she fell in step as they started walking down the long hall.

"There is a private elevator just at the end of the hall. I'll escort you to your room."

"*Merci*," she murmured. Normally she would be chattier, but she was feeling awkward and still a bit shaken from their surprise meeting.

"You didn't enjoy yourself at our party?" he asked, so innocently that she admonished herself immediately for being paranoid.

"The party was really fun, but I'm a little tired, and it was becoming a crush to get to the bar." She shrugged. "I can have wine in my room."

He smiled. "I'll have a bottle sent up for you."

She smiled back. "I'd love that."

"How is Paris treating you so far?"

"Well, I just arrived, so I haven't been able to say hello to her yet."

"Are you with the group of Americans here for the art convention?"

"No, but that sounds like fun."

"May I ask where are you from?" Just as she was about to answer, a loud crackling sound came from his jacket. *"Un moment,"* he murmured. He pulled out a small two-way radio and spoke back and forth in strings of quick French before putting it back in his pocket. He glanced at her from the side of his eye with a smirk. "The couple seem to have finished."

The private elevator bank was one skinny gold door. Her hottie, as she began to mentally call him, punched in a code and they waited. She turned her head to ask about his position at the hotel and caught him looking away quickly. She smiled inside. He was checking her out.

Suddenly he held out his hand. "I'm Nicolas. Nic."

"Maya North," she said, shaking his warm hand, wondering if his lips would be warm, as well. The elevator opened swiftly, and he waited for her to enter before entering himself. He pressed another code and then eleven. Because of the small space, he was standing very close—his delicious cologne filled her nostrils.

She decided to slip on her heels. "Careful," he said,

and held out his hand for her to steady herself. "If I may be so bold, you look very beautiful." She smiled and almost fell into the wall. She took his hand and sucked in a breath of restraint. This wasn't like her. Her skin had goose bumps, and she wasn't even cold.

"You're shivering." He frowned.

"Oh, it's okay. We're almost at the room."

He whipped off his jacket and placed it on her shoulders, his warm breath briefly caressing her ear. Her nipples hardened and she pulled the jacket tighter around her. "This building is old, and the elevators have the worst drafts." He came back to stand next to her. "Better?"

"Much better. You're my savior tonight."

"My pleasure," he whispered. "Although you seemed ready to take me out in the stairwell," he teased.

She blushed. "Just scare tactics. I watch a lot of Marvel movies."

"X-Men," he said, nodding in reverence.

"X-Men." She smiled her agreement.

The door opened to the eleventh floor and they walked in silence to her room. "Ah, *le chambre de la lune.* One of my favorites. If you leave the curtains open at night, the moonlight cuts through the room like a laser. It's gorgeous."

His voice was doing naughty things to her body, even as she fished for her key card. She slid it in the slot and turned to him when the door popped open. "I'll have to leave them open, then."

The alabaster white shirt enhanced his tan skin and dark eyes. He was stunning, and her mind raced with dirty thoughts of inviting him in and taking full advantage of what the hotel had to offer. But, as much as she wanted to put on that mask and act like the goddess she was, she just wasn't that type.

"Nic, I don't know how to thank you. I'll be here for a little while. I suppose I'll see you around."

Nic licked his lips as if to say something, then his gaze dropped to the floor. "*Oui*, if you need anything, please do not hesitate."

She walked inside and turned to him with a nod before slowly closing the door. Then she leaned her back against it in total disappointment. What happened to the pep talk she'd given herself about taking risks and being someone else for a night? Slowly she walked to the bed and kicked off her shoes, then lay back in Nic's jacket, pulling it tighter over her shoulders, fantasizing about what she would have done differently.

Jesus, Nic thought as he took the elevator down to the basement. His powerful attraction to the American came as a surprise to him; the minute she'd taken his hand in the elevator he'd had an instant hard-on.

Sex with guests was not good PR for the hotel. He had a serious conversation with himself as he walked into the wine cellar—think of the Yelp reviews. But his next thought had to do with which wine she would enjoy and what her red lips would look like closing over the glass. Not exactly the voice of reason he was trying to sustain.

He moved to the reds and chose a fruity Loire Valley Pinot Noir that would look beautiful against her red mouth. He'd get one of the porters to take it up, not trusting himself to knock on her door again.

There had been a moment where he was hoping she would invite him in, offer him something to drink from the mini-bar, kiss him. He ran a hand over his mouth and made his way back to the first floor, intent on finding someone in the kitchen to take the wine to her room.

The music pumped louder as more and more people filed into the lobby, waving their masks and drinks in the air. A crush, she'd called it. That was how he felt as he pushed through to the back of the bar and skirted in between the bartenders to find the good crystal. One perfect sparkling glass for the goddess upstairs. He heard a glass break across the room—the cleanup was going to be ridiculous.

Nic moved from the bar, allowing the bartenders their much-needed space, and waved over a young porter. "Nic?" he thought he heard mixed into the music. Couldn't be—then again, his name, louder this time. A woman's voice, one he recognized. Nic brought the porter close so he could hear him. "Is there a redheaded woman behind me calling my name? Don't be obvious."

"Oui, patron."

Daphne. Merde. "Never mind," he said to the porter. "I'll take it myself."

Nic took the private elevator to eleven, thinking more about getting away from Daphne than what he would say to Mademoiselle North. What had she said her name was again? God, he was horrible with names. He got to her door and hesitated, wondering if he looked creepy or desperate, realizing the longer he talked to himself outside her door, the more creepy and desperate he looked. He knocked lightly, then more forcefully when no one answered.

"Mademoiselle?" he yelled out. The lock turned and there she was again in her bare feet, still wearing the strappy dress that accentuated her body. Her eyes widened and she smiled. Breathtaking. He held up the bottle of wine and a single glass. "As promised."

Her surprised gaze touched the bottle, then his eyes. She seemed to debate for a moment, then stepped back. "Come in. Maybe you can open it for me?"

"Of course." The moment he stepped inside, she closed the door and came toward him, so close he could smell the vanilla scent of her hair. Then she kissed him, sweetly at first, her lips testing his, then bolder, their mouths fusing perfectly. She pulled back slowly, his lips following before he let hers go. There was a wicked gleam in her eye.

"I told myself I would do that the next time I saw you," she whispered.

He licked his lips. "I'm happy you did."

"Will you stay and have a drink with me?"

"I would love to," he said, staring at her mouth. He gave her the glass and moved to her small kitchen for the bottle opener.

She inspected the crystal in the light. "You only brought one."

He popped the bottle with a graceful flick of his wrist, then came toward her with a grin. "We can share."

Chapter 4

"I should let this breathe a little, but—" he looked into her eyes "—I can't wait." He wasn't talking about the wine. The attraction between them was palpable, almost suffocating.

She held the glass steady as he poured, her gaze lightly taking him in, making his body respond in kind. Her eyes traveled over his hands. "Are you engaged or married?" she whispered. She bit her cheek in embarrassment, but it was a valid question. Several men he knew didn't wear their rings. He had always felt that if he was going to take a wife, then he wanted others to know.

He finished pouring. "No, I'm not." He grinned, hoping he put her at ease. "Neither."

"Good." She grinned back.

He was right; the ruby liquid would look beautiful against her mouth. He brushed a caramel-colored curl from her shoulder. "Please, try the wine. I want to make sure I chose the right one."

She looked at him for a moment. "This is... I don't usually do this."

"Neither do I. I've never done it actually...been with a guest like this."

Her eyes widened. "Are you going to get fired?"

"I—" He started, then stopped, unsure he wanted to say he was the owner. Women he knew chased him for his money; it might be a nice change to be chased for something as mundane as his personality. "No."

"This is weird," she whispered, her lashes lowering. Her gaze flashed. "But good weird."

"Definitely," he said, wanting to taste her more than he wanted to taste the wine. He gestured to her glass. "Did I do all right?"

"I'm sure it's fine. I'm not much of a connoisseur." Her eyes danced. "I mean, I like wine, I just don't know much about it."

"Then you've come to the right place. The French are raised with wine in their baby bottles." He loved her throaty chuckles. "May I?" Her tentative look turned into a smile as she handed him the glass. Her skin glistened in the dim lighting; he imagined his lips trailing over her shoulder. "Wine tasting should be fun. Hold on." He tuned the radio to soft music, then came back to stand very close. He angled the glass and held it up. "First we check the color. This one I chose because the garnet color is very close to the color of your lips. So we already know it's perfect." Her shy look became bolder, ending in a sexy grin. Every time she smiled, he got harder. "'Next the aroma." He primed his nose with a sniff, gave the liquid a swish around the crystal, then breathed in again. "I can smell the fruit and floral notes. You try."

She lowered her long lashes and took the glass, mimicking his every move. "I think I smell strawberry." She frowned.

"Yes." He smiled wide, his gaze moving to the fallen dress strap on her shoulder. "Now, taste." Her dark eyes held his as she sipped.

"It's good." Her tongue came out to lick her lips and he almost lost his control.

"What do you taste?" he half whispered, lust palpable in the room.

"Chocolate, maybe?" She lifted the glass toward him, but he refused.

"Try again. This time, drink deeper."

She closed her lips more fully around the glass, and he was lost. She swallowed and handed it to him. "Rose?"

"That's an excellent start," he said, putting down the glass. Her gaze followed his every move. "My turn to taste." He kissed her fully, his tongue plundering her mouth. She wound her arms around his neck. "I taste fire," he said against her lips. He kissed her again, pulling small sounds from her throat as his hands roamed over her body. "I taste beauty." She didn't wait for him to come back to her, her hand finding the back of his head and pulling him to her mouth. He leaned her back with the force of his kiss and her dress slid up as her leg bent up to his waist. He caught her knee and pulled her off the floor, hitching her legs on either side of his hips.

He pulled back, only to look into her eyes and make sure they were both on the same page. "I taste passion," she whispered, lowering herself back down to his lips.

They savored each other for a long moment, and when they could no longer get close enough, she wriggled herself down his body, stopping briefly to caress the bulge between his legs and, with her gaze on his, slowly began backing up toward the bedroom.

The minute she entered the adjacent room, the motion-activated lights burst on, then lowered to a soft glow around her. The luxury suite suited her, he thought, moving forward as if pulled by an invisible force. The room was awash in shades of gray with accents of white gold and dark pink quartz.

He'd called it the Luna Suite because the location of the room in the northwest corner of the building made it the best for viewing the moon as she ruled above the Paris rooftops, hence the floor-to-ceiling windows and wraparound terrace.

Maya stood by the bed, and Nic was struck by how the waxing moon hung above her head like a crown. Her gaze boldly moved over him and then softened when she met his eyes.

"Are you having any second thoughts?" He wanted to make sure she was feeling what he was feeling. Lust.

"I should be, but I'm not."

"What does that mean?"

"It means I haven't had sex in a long time. I shouldn't have invited you in, since I don't know you from a hole in the wall. But you're very sexy, and as good as you look in that suit, I'd like to see you out of it."

"Don't be shy," he said, his fingers starting on his cuff links.

"When it comes to things I want, I never am."

"You're very confident. You'll have to tell me how you do that."

"Later." Reaching up, she pulled his head down and kissed him––a full-throttle, confident kiss.

It shouldn't have triggered such an intense reaction. It was something about her, even earlier, when he'd seen her in the stairs. She had been ready to fight him. It had been intriguing.

Maybe it was the full moon—*merde* if he knew— but he was all for it.

His lips moved over her throat when he turned her gently, slipped the straps down her arms.

Maya couldn't breathe or stand, held up by the press of Nic's lips on her nape and the hard frame of his body. The slip dress she wore lay at her feet in about three seconds flat. Unabashed in her lingerie, glad she'd chosen the good undies, she kicked the silk pool aside and spun around to face him. "My turn," she said with a smile.

He grinned back. "I'm all yours." His gaze flickered down, taking in her dark red lace strapless bra and panties to match. "Garnet," he whispered, referencing the wine they had just tasted.

"I like red."

His gaze was appreciative. "So do I."

His arms came slightly up as she stripped the white

shirt from his shoulders, her gaze taking in the muscled chest and rippling torso with its smattering of dark hair. "Nice. You must work out."

His smile was humble. "Not really. I do some work on a vineyard sometimes."

"Hmm. That must be nice."

"Not as nice as this." He pulled her against him, breasts to chest, and let the backs of his fingers trail down her side. In one move, those same fingers came back up and unsnapped her bra. Carefully, he pulled it from between their bodies and tossed it onto the dresser, then turned back and gave her the hottest, sexiest look she'd ever seen. "I don't want your clothes to get ruined. I want you to think about me the next time you wear them."

"That's very considerate," she murmured, reaching for a button on his pants, not sure she was going to last for the entire undressing with the hard, steady throbbing between her legs. A soft moan escaped her throat as he kissed her shoulder and then the swell of her breast. Her hands went into his hair just as he nipped, teased and licked her hardened nipple into the heat of his mouth. Her head lolled back. God, it had been so long.

His mouth found her other breast while his fingers slipped into the top of her lace panties and then farther. She shivered at his slow strokes, feeling her body open for him. She had never wanted anyone this much. Never! He eased her panties down her soft curves and tossed them with the bra. His gaze flicked down and then up again and met hers—causing her to start unzipping his pants.

She fumbled for the zipper pull and he kissed her

lightly then brushed her hands away. He had his pants, boxer briefs, socks and shoes off in a blur.

"Now then." He grinned. "It's just us and the moon. Look." As he'd mentioned, the moonlight cut across the bed like a spotlight.

"Wow," she whispered, her gaze lifting from his erection.

He laughed deeply. "That's not what I was talking about. But you naked with this satin skin—*magnifique*," he said, husky and low. With a polite lift of his finger, he found his wallet in the pile of his trousers, pulled out a condom and moved to place it on the nightstand. "For *mademoiselle*," he said when he came back to stand in front of her. Cupping her face, her kissed her gently, stroking her back in a lazy motion. He pulled back, his hands coming to rest on one butt cheek—waiting for her cue.

"I can't wait," she whispered, her thigh sliding against his, her stomach pressing against his rigid erection.

"You're beautiful," he whispered back. He returned his mouth to hers, kissing her deeply before swinging her up into his arms and laying her under him on the bed. His muscles rippled as he shifted to protect her from his full weight.

She moaned when his hand slid down her body and he slid his fingers deep. His gaze was dominant and seductive as she lifted and pushed against his hand, her orgasm churning from his firm touch. She gasped when he slid lower, kissing his way down her body, and parted her with the hot slow lick of his tongue. His electric strokes had her body undulating involuntarily, and he pinned her down with one arm and tortured her with his mouth as he took what he wanted.

"Honey," he whispered under his breath. "Sweet wine and honey."

She writhed against his restraint as he brought her closer to the edge, fanning the flames of her tremors with his lips and fingers, keeping her there until she was sure she could take no more.

"Nic—"

He looked up and saw her naked form spread before him, the light of the moon illuminating her body with ethereal blue light. He eased back up her body, reached for the condom on the nightstand and rolled it in place. Steadying her with one hand, he bent his legs, deftly positioned himself and took a small breath of restraint. He sent up a small prayer of thanks to *la lune* and pushed into her welcoming body with a smooth upward thrust of his hips.

She shivered, trembled as his rigid length slowly filled her, driving him deep. He shut his eyes against the wild, fevered lust exploding in his brain, overwhelmed by the feel of her. His mind blanked and he stalled as wine-infused pleasure washed over him.

"Nic?" she whispered, her mouth nipping at his chin and jaw.

He answered by rocking hard and deep inside her, the sounds from her throat urging him further, making him hotter.

"More…more," she panted.

"I don't want to hurt you," he whispered over her mouth.

"No—no—it's good," she gasped. "Perfect…" She sank her nails into his shoulders and pushed her hips up to meet him. His brain lifted away and he followed her body's cue, sliding his hands under her bottom and lifting her up, her legs wrapping around his waist so he could thrust in deeper—like that…

"Harder," she whispered. He obliged. Sex had never felt like this before.

Her fierce gaze was locked on his as he surged into her, rapidly throwing them both into a sexual frenzy. She suddenly went still in his arms, and knowing what that meant, he kissed her hard, lifted her bottom up and plunged to meet her orgasm.

Her eyes were wide, her body tightening around him in a death grip. Her orgasm began rippling up his shaft and, breath held, his orgasm exploded in a furious strike of lightning that snaked up and down his spine.

The soft music in the background was accompanied by the low- and high-pitched tones of both their screams.

When their breathing stabilized, Nic rolled to his side, discarded the condom on the floor and pulled his beautiful companion into the crook of his arm. He racked his brain for her first name, afraid of asking this late in the game, but all of that was forgotten as she licked a warm path up his throat and hitched a silky thigh onto his leg. "Mmm…" she said in the sexiest of whispers.

He was instantly hard, and without a word, he pulled

her on top of him and slipped inside her velvety sweetness. She moved roughly over him, her hips testing and rolling, rocking and riding. She found her rhythm, and using his shoulders as leverage, her breasts bounced beautifully for him. Deep moans came from his throat as her honeyed friction tumbled through his body, the pure ecstasy torching his brain. He was close again, his penis rigid, his muscles clenching; no wonder they called it the little death.

He wasn't wearing a condom. *Merde.* In a herculean move he never thought he would be capable of, he lifted her from him, flipped her on her back and covered her pulsing sex with his mouth. His lips worked furiously until he felt her skin quiver and heard a succession of screams each deeper and lasting longer than the last.

She propped herself on her elbows, her eyes glassy. "Why?" she breathed.

He kissed her inner thigh, crawled up her body and lay on his back beside her. "We were unprotected."

"You're strong," she said, coming off her elbows to lie facing him on her pillow.

"And you're soft." He turned toward her and pulled her closer, his hands smoothing over her hip to her bottom. "Really soft," he whispered, unable to believe that his erection began to respond. Just a touch of her skin; that was all it took.

Her gaze ran down his body and she watched as his lower half did its best to reach toward her. "Wow. Do you do yoga or something?"

"I don't, not that I haven't thought about it, but I

promise you, his behavior is out of character. He must really like you."

"Well, I really like him." She shimmied closer to touch the tip. "And I'd love to show him, but we'll need provisions."

The hunter-gatherer in him rolled toward the nightstand and found the hotel phone. He punched room service. "It's Nic, can someone get me Joc?" He watched her as he waited, pushing back down the sheet she used to cover her body. He knew their time was limited, and he wanted her naked for all of it.

"Sup, boss? Are you calling from a room?"

Nic kept his voice low. "Yes, I am. Can you please send up a charcuterie and cheese plate, another crystal glass and a box of condoms."

"Ah, yeah! You finally—"

"Now." Nic hung up the phone before Joc's loud mouth came through the receiver.

She was lounging, watching him. "What do you do here?"

The knock on the door was loud and obnoxious. Joc. *Don't embarrass me.* He gathered a sheet around his hips and kissed her lightly. "I'll be right back."

Nic slowly opened the door and stuck his head into the crack. "Don't say a word."

Joc's smile touched both of his ears. "*Oui,* boss." He held the wood cutting board with meats and cheeses with one hand. "As requested, plus I added a few of the special cuts, some pickles and honey, and a few chocolates for effect. Oh, and this." Joc produced a giant box of Magnums from behind his back. Nic's eyes darted down the hall, then he grabbed them.

"Give me the board."

"I'll be happy to set it down for you, just let me in." Joc stretched himself to look over Nic's shoulder.

"Get out of here."

Joc sighed, carefully transferring the cutting board to Nic. "All right, but this isn't fair. At least tell me what celebrity she looks most like."

Nic rolled his eyes, then looked back over his shoulder before turning back to Joc. "Beyoncé. But better."

"Wha—" Nic slammed the door in Joc's face, then shuffled into the bedroom, placing the board and condoms on the dresser.

"How hungry are you?" he asked. When he got no answer, he stood and turned…and his breath caught in his throat. She was naked, stretched out on her stomach across the bed with her upper body propped on her elbows as the moonlight slashed over her back, butt and thighs. The half mask of Ariadne was placed over her face. She lifted her feet playfully, pulled down the mask and gave him a sexual look.

"I'm pretty hungry, but not for food."

Nic released his sheet, letting it drop so she could see what her body did to him. He grabbed the box of condoms and slowly walked toward the bed.

He was going make love to her until he couldn't move.

And that was what they did until the sun came up and the birds sang and the streak of light across their faces reminded them it was morning.

Rising from the bed, Nic punched a button on the nightstand and sighed when the drapes slid closed. She was still asleep, her arms over her head and her breasts bared. His lower body stuttered, then gave up. In other circumstances, he'd be concerned, but judging by the wrappers on the floor, they'd had enough sex in one night to last them a lifetime. He padded to the bathroom, slapped some water on his face, then stumbled toward his clothes. One leg at a time, he told himself.

He didn't want to leave like this.

Not a useful feeling, because he had to go.

He heard the sheets rustle.

"Morning and reality—right?"

"Right."

"Well, thank you." She stretched in a lazy way. "I'm glad I invited you in. It was worth it."

"*Oui*, it was," he murmured into her eyes.

He found his phone in his pocket, grimaced at the missed calls, many from Daphne, then balked at the time.

"I gotta go," he said. "I have an appointment this morning I can't miss."

"Okay. Sure."

"Everything was—you were…*incroyable*." He smiled. "*Merci beaucoup*." He began gathering up the rest of his clothes.

She rolled over and pulled the sheet up to her chin. He saw her breathing grow even. Nic let himself out, irritable and surly. He didn't want to go, preferring to at least provide a breakfast for his lovers, but she needed to sleep, and he had an important appointment.

The closer he got to his penthouse suite, the more he saw the night as a gift. She was a beautiful stranger with whom he had no foreseeable future, which was a blessing, because his life was too complicated right now for a passionate romance—no matter how unique the woman might be.

Chapter 5

By midmorning, Maya was showered and dressed… exhausted, but in that deliciously satisfied way when you were up all night counting orgasms. Three for him, four for her and one electric moment when her body entered an extended buzzed state as they clung to each other in a climactic aftermath. She'd never felt anything like it. Her skin hummed with the memory as she got ready for her meeting.

Coffee and small bites had been sent to the room anonymously—what a gentleman—and she'd found a hastily scribbled note on the bedside table that read:

Thank you for a beautiful night. I would love to spend more time with you. He listed his phone number. Beside the note lay her mask. She should frame it.

Maya held her phone and thought about putting in

the number, but then let the note fall back to the table. It had been a perfect night, and he had been the most flawless of lovers. She knew nothing about him, and she didn't want to. Reality would ruin that memory, so she decided to shift her focus to the day ahead of her, which included a necessary phone call to her mother.

"You're where?" Maya's mother asked when she told her she was staying in Paris for a few weeks.

"Paris, France."

"For work?" Maya could tell her mother knew something was up. She had never just flown out of the country without telling her beforehand.

"No, not really."

"Well, you should have told me you wanted to go on vacation, Maya. I have enough miles to take us all to Cabo and—"

Maya let her head drop into her hands. "Mother! When was the last time you spoke to my father?"

"Well, he's right here, Maya. Why wouldn't I be speaking to him?" Her mother chuckled.

"No, I mean my real dad." She heard her mother's inhale. "When was it?"

"I don't know. Fifteen, twenty years ago maybe? Why?" Her mother was using that cautious tone she always got when talking about her father. Maya had always interpreted it as protective, but just then, it felt secretive.

"That long? He never reached out? You never reached out?"

"Why would I reach out to him? He left us, remember?" It was an expression her mother used often, with the emphasis on *us*. Maya had been so young she didn't remember. There were only snippets of big hands tossing her in the air, a deep voice laughing, presents at Christmas.

"Where did he go?"

"I told you. He went back to Chicago."

"But he wasn't American."

"No, but… What are all these questions about?" Maya paused. "He's dead."

"What?" Her mom's voice sounded smaller.

"He died."

Her mother paused. "How would you know that?"

"He left me his business. In Paris."

"Paris." Her mother's voice quivered. "What kind of business?"

"A vineyard and wine brokerage or something like that."

"Right," her mother whispered.

"You sound upset."

A sniffle followed a long sigh. "We were in love once. What do you expect?"

"I don't know. You never gave me that impression. You don't talk about him. Why did he leave?"

"Your grandmother didn't approve and sent him packing. I was young and scared then." Her distressed inhale made Maya wince. "I love your stepfather very much, Maya. But I always wondered—" A sob came then.

"You always wondered if you should have gone with him."

"Yes," she said on a swallowed tear. There was more in the silence, but Maya wasn't ready to pry.

"I have to go there to see it. I have two weeks to take it on, or it goes to someone else."

Another giant sigh came from the receiver. "Was he married?"

"I don't think so."

"Well, you're not going to take it, are you. What about your job?"

"I'll figure it out," Maya said quickly, afraid to tell her mother what had happened in New York. She thought of more to ask about her father, then stopped. "Um, I should go, I have a meeting."

"All right. But Maya? You're not going to take it over, are you?"

"Doubtful, Mother. I already have a job. I know nothing about wine and I barely speak French. I just want to see it."

"When are you coming back?"

"A few weeks. I'll talk to you later, okay?"

"All right. I love—"

Maya hung up, her grip on her phone a little too tight. She wasn't sure if she was angry with her mother or herself, but emotions she hadn't known were there threatened to come out in a string of questions. She'd never known about this man. Why?

And now it was too late.

She had been a teen when she'd found a shoebox of old Polaroids in her mother's closet. There was her mother in awful eighties' clothing, smiling, posing and laughing.

In several, her mother wore a minidress and showed off a pregnant belly. Maya had always wondered who had taken that picture. Her mother's eyes held a glint, like she was looking at a lover.

Then one picture had popped out of the bunch. A four-year-old Maya in green elf pajamas sitting on Santa's lap. But on closer inspection, the smiling man wasn't old or fat, and he only wore a red shirt, jeans and the Santa hat. Dad.

She had never told her mother she had seen those photos, or asked why those photos never made it out of the closet. She'd assumed there was a good reason, and by the time she discovered boys, she didn't much care.

Maya took the elevator to the lobby and was shocked to find it looking clean and professional again, almost as if Caligula had never happened. Her eyes darted around as she found her way to Le Salon Rouge, wondering if she would run into Nic. There were only staff in sight, but she did find the entrance to the salon and its host standing outside.

"I'm here to meet Monsieur Dechamps."

"Mademoiselle Belcourt, you are the first to arrive. Would you like to be seated?" First, everyone needed to stop calling her that. Second, she really had to work on being fashionably late.

"Yes, *merci*." She gave up her intent to correct the host and looked over his shoulder into the empty den. Red walls with golden tapestry and large leather booths dominated the room. She was seated in a far corner with the entrance directly in her line of sight. The host exited the room and closed the double doors behind him.

She fluffed her hair and felt a flutter in her stomach at the thought of meeting Monsieur Dechamps. Would he be a stuffy jerk? He had been partners with her father, and the lawyer said the stipulations of her father's will were a surprise.

Male voices echoed outside the door, and then it burst open. She recognized the lawyer from his photo. He was still talking when he came toward her with a small wave, then stopped and turned as if he'd lost something.

"Did you hear anything I just said?" he yelled to the empty doorway. With a shake of his head, he turned back toward Maya. "Apologies, Maya. We are having an unusual morning. Not like him at all." He said the latter under his breath before coming to a dramatic halt at the table. "Please allow me to formally introduce myself. James T. Bauer, Esquire. At your service." Maya shook his outstretched hand and James settled into the seat across from her. "We have much to discuss. I hope you've had your coffee."

"I could use another." Just as she said it, servers came in to pour coffee and tea, pushing a cart full of mouthwatering dishes. "And by the way," she said, stirring sugar into her lifeblood. "My last name is North."

James looked at her over his spectacles. "Not according to your birth certificate."

Maya's head snapped up, but her attention turned to the man who had entered the room and was walking briskly toward them. He was dressed casually in a crew neck sweater, jeans and leather sneakers, all black to match his hair. She swallowed hard when he slowed, his eyes narrowing as he recognized her. At least she hoped that was recognition—he'd left her bed only hours ago.

What was he doing here? He'd said he had a…meeting…*oh no*.

The color must have drained from her face because James put down his tartine to twist around in his chair. "My boy, you disappeared. I was beginning to wonder if you were going to join us. Erm, *mademoiselle*, meet Luca Nicolas Rayo Dechamps, your business partner, if it suits you," he added with a wink. "You may change your mind after this meeting." He chuckled. "Nic, Maya Belcourt, I mean North."

"Um, hello." Maya extended her hand, her gaze roaming over him, remembering him towering naked over her. Her voice cracked. "So nice to finally meet you."

"*Enchanté.*" Nic's grin slid to a dull slant as he accepted her handshake and tried to keep his face neutral. "So glad to finally put a name to a face. I am so sorry about your father."

She couldn't speak. "That's very kind."

They stared, shaking hands slowly, the air between them sizzling. The lawyer fell silent.

"Have you two met before?"

"No," they said in unison, breaking from each other's grip.

Maya sat back down and focused on her coffee, trying to ignore the fact that she'd slept with her business partner.

That it was the best sex she'd ever had.

That she was hyperaware of his every movement as he sat next to her and fixed himself a plate of food.

That he smelled amazing.

"*Patron*, Chef wants to know if you need anything else?" a server asked Nic. Nic shook his head, then glanced at Maya. Her French was sparse, but she knew that word.

He was the owner of the hotel.

Chapter 6

James didn't waste any time. Papers began to fill the table. Deeds, share transfers, business contracts—the latter still in French. Translated versions were being prepared for her so she could read it thoroughly, and by the better part of an hour, she was the equal partner in a vineyard and wine brokerage that generated about one to two million in revenue per year.

"And I think that covers the basic transfers for today. I have another appointment, but you and Nic should get acquainted since you are partners. At least for now. *A bientôt.*"

"Wait," Maya burst out. "You mentioned my birth certificate."

"There is a copy in the transfer documents. Full name Maya Elizabeth North Belcourt."

She gritted her teeth, trying to remember the last time she had even seen her birth certificate. Her mother had some more explaining to do.

James's departure left no distraction from the elephant in the room.

Nic put down his coffee. "Maya, maybe we should—"

"Is this a weird, sick game to you? Bedding your new business partner?"

He looked stricken. "I promise I had no idea."

"No? You didn't google me or anything? You weren't curious who you were going to meet?"

"I asked my assistant to look for a Maya Belcourt. A name you don't use." His dark lashes narrowed a bit, giving her flashbacks to the night before. "Honestly, Albert never mentioned that he had a daughter. I didn't even know you existed until a month ago."

She looked away and poured herself more coffee. She never would have dreamed this a month ago.

"Then I'll say thank you," Maya murmured.

"For?" He pushed the cream and sugar her way.

"Last night. I needed it." His eyes followed the cup to her lips. "Partner." She took a sip. "I'd like to discuss this thirty percent drop in revenue you've had over the past three years." She almost laughed when his mouth turned down.

"The brokering of our clients' grapes has been strong, but we've struggled with selling our own grapes. The vineyard is productive, but no one is buying."

"Yes, but your expenses increased last year even as your revenue continued to drop. Not good for profit."

"I'm sorry. Where are you getting this information?"

Maya flipped through the mountain of papers to a page full of numbers. "You didn't give this to James?"

"Nathan must have."

"Who is Nathan?"

"He's my, I mean, *our* assistant."

"Do you usually allow Nathan to just give out information without you knowing about it?"

Nic met her glare with his own. "Nathan knows what he's doing. And he was devastated by your father's death."

Maya's temper eased and she slowly nodded. She had to remember that while she didn't know her father, others did, and they would be affected by not only his death, but her unexpected appearance.

"So are *you* devastated?"

Nic's gaze dropped to the table. "It's been hard on me. He was like a fath—um."

"No, it's okay. He was like a father to you. My stepfather has always been there for me. I'd be very upset if anything were to happen to him." She hesitated. "What did happen? Everyone keeps saying heart attack, but no one has details."

"He was working. Nathan found him lying on the ground in the vineyard." Emotions she didn't know were there welled in her throat, and tears sprang to her eyes. Nic took her hand. "He didn't suffer."

"Was he sick?" Feeling uneasy from the contact, she pulled her hand away and dabbed at her eyes with the cloth napkin.

"Not that I know of. He was as strong and healthy as

an ox. Just the day before, he had been lugging a box of books around in his den."

They sat in silence for a long minute, then Nic spoke softly. "My father went the same way. They were best friends and went into business together. I grew up around the vineyard. My father passed and left his shares to me seven years ago. I've been working with Albert ever since."

"I'm sure you thought his shares would go to you."

Nic hung his head, and she remembered how soft his hair was. She stifled an urge to run her hands over the back of his neck. "Yes, I thought he would have, but we didn't know about you then."

She finished her coffee and declined his offer of more food. "You didn't answer my question. About the expenses," she said to his quizzical look.

One corner of his mouth turned up. "What was it you do again?"

"I'm a business consultant for Lynch and Company in LA. You look startled."

He looked her up and down. "I didn't expect that."

"What did you think?"

"You mentioned something about Karl Lagerfeld last night. I assumed you worked in fashion."

She chuckled, from both his mention of the night before and the fact that he'd actually been listening. "I've consulted for YSL, a competitor of Karl's."

"Impressive."

"Yes. I am." Her nod was serious.

That got a full megawatt smile out of him, and damn if he wasn't fine. "Americans."

"Yep. It's called confidence."

"That's what you call it?" Still smiling.

"Oui, oui," she said with flair. "Not that far off from French arrogance." His laugh was a deep vibration in his chest. She continued to tease, wanting to hear more. "You're French and something else, though, am I right? You spoke Spanish last night."

"Last night…" he said in a low voice with a shake of his head. He studied her face before speaking. "My mother is from Spain."

"Mmm," she said, remembering how he had whispered to her in another language. The sound had been her kryptonite. "So about those expenses. Partner."

He straightened as if he were a student caught by the teacher. "We upgraded our production equipment to increase our grape supply, but the demand continued to slow."

"You've written off the amortization of the equipment against the loss on your taxes?"

"Every year."

"I don't see any investment in marketing."

"That's because we didn't do any."

"You increased production, saw a dip in sales and didn't increase marketing?"

"We aren't a retail store—"

"No, you're a wholesale store, but still a store."

His jaw clenched as he looked at her. "So are you planning on taking over where Albert left off then?"

No, she wasn't, but she didn't like being brushed off. "It's half my business. I suppose I have a right to, if that's what I want."

His eyes narrowed. "Is it what you want?"

"I don't know. I haven't seen the place yet."

"We'll remedy that right now. But if you decide to do this, you'll have to move here."

"Okay." She shrugged. His eyes went wide and she held in a sadistic smile.

"What about Lynch and Lynch?"

"Lynch and Company. And I can work remotely."

Nic shook his head. "Good, because you can't work a vineyard remotely."

"I can't work a vineyard, period. We'll hire someone."

He shook his head. "There's no budget for that."

"I'll rework that budget. No more upgrades in a down market."

"It was the right decision to make."

"Did you get more sales?"

He cleared his throat and signaled a server. "We're finished here. Have my car brought around."

He took a deep breath and leaned closer. Her gaze dropped to his lips, and her heart pounded for a kiss. "I'll take you to the vineyard. Pack an overnight bag. You can keep the rest of your things here if you wish. Once you've become acquainted with the business, I think we can come to an agreement."

"An agreement?" She swallowed as he reached out and touched a lock of hair on her shoulder. "What kind of agreement?"

"A mutually beneficial agreement."

"Meaning?" She tipped her lips forward.

"Meaning, I'll be buying your shares." Her jaw

dropped. She blinked, and he was already by the doorway before he turned back to her. "We're leaving in twenty minutes. I'll be out front."

They sped out of Paris in Nic's silver Karma Revero hybrid, an expensive, tech-heavy but environmentally conscious car that made the Batmobile look like a Chevy. Maya had never understood the term "panty dropper" in relation to cars, but when Nic had pressed a button and the doors lifted like wings, she was pretty certain her panties had disintegrated.

"Nice car," she murmured, relaxing in the bucket seat, itching to play with the computer screen on the dash. She caressed the leather, instead. *Butter.* This was impressive. "So, you're a tree hugger, huh? Me, too." Okay, she drove a Rover, but she recycled. "This car company was started in California. My colleague did some work with them."

He nodded, staring straight ahead with his hands leisurely on the wheel. "That's where I first drove it. They have a spiritual approach to cars, if that makes sense. As a vintner, I should do what I can to respect the earth."

Maya nodded, wondering how he had gotten sexier in the last two minutes. No, she wasn't going to go there. She refused to be attracted to the man who had basically told her he was going to buy her shares of the business and kick her out. They had shared one night…an amazing night…but big deal. The memory would fade.

If past experience with men held true, the more time she spent with him, the less she would want to take his clothes off. It was always the case with her love interests. They were all knights in shining armor until the fourth date when, at the stroke of midnight, they turned back into pumpkins.

"I think more people would respect the earth if they had the money to buy cars like this," Maya said.

"You like cars?"

"I like businesses that disrupt the norm. For instance, there's a solar panel in the roof that powers the car." He glanced at her with an impressed look. "Meanwhile, what were you doing in California?"

"Your father and I had traveled to Napa Valley. Albert had hoped to work with some wineries, and he also looked at some land. Come to think of it, he was adamant about making something work out there, but it never came together. I always wondered why it was so important to him." Nic frowned and looked at her. "Maybe now I know why."

Maya looked away quickly, afraid she was going to say something insulting about the man he knew as a second father. Albert had been in California and yet decided not to visit his daughter. Her deceased father could take his shares of the business and shove them.

The computer panel lit up with a phone call that Nic quickly ended with the press of a button, but not before Maya saw the name Daphne. Daphne called right back and Nic turned off his phone. Maya glanced at him, but he didn't turn her way.

They drove in silence for a few minutes. Maya stared out the window and absorbed her surroundings. They were passing through a small village where the homes were all honey-colored cottages. Shops and cafés lined the streets, and families were out walking in wool sweaters and cozy scarves. Farther in the distance was a denser population of buildings.

"This is beautiful." Maya stifled a yawn, embarrassed that he knew exactly why she was tired. "Where are we?"

"We are on the outskirts of Orléans, the official capital of the Loire Valley. Joan of Arc saved the city from the English in the fourteen hundreds."

Maya's eyes widened. "You're kidding, and we're passing by? I need to stop here and drink the water or kiss the stones—anything to take in such female empowerment."

Nic chuckled. "We aren't far from Par Le Bouquet. All the water is the same, so I'll make sure Nathan finds you a glass, but I don't think you need it."

Maya turned her head quickly, her eyes narrowed. "What does that mean?"

"It means you seem strong enough already." Maya studied his face to see if he was mocking her, but his genuine smile said otherwise. She turned back to the road, wondering how she was going to keep her head in business when all her body wanted to do was sin.

The car emerged from a tree-lined lane, and a two-story gray stone château rose from the hills where it had stood for centuries. Vines and budding flowers snaked from the ground, while tiny lights gave a soft glow to the windows. The surrounding landscape was manicured while the trees and greenery on either side of the house were bolder and wild. To the right, running from the back of the mansion into the horizon, were rows and rows of grapevines.

"Welcome to Par Le Bouquet. We're right on the edge of the Loire Valley—known as the Garden of France—and not too far from Sancerre. Centrally located to many vineyards, several of whom are our clients—my uncle Armand Dechamps included."

They parked in a graveled area off to the side. Nic retrieved her bag from the trunk, shaking his head when she offered to carry it. Maya slowed as she followed Nic toward the arched doorway. Dechamps. Dechamps… It hit her like a boulder. "Your family makes the Dechamps wine?"

"Oui," was all he said, as if famous winemakers were the norm.

"I've had the cab franc. Didn't it win an award or something?"

Nic held open the door for her, his smile touching one corner of his mouth. "I thought you didn't know wine."

Visions of their sexy wine tasting the night before flooded her thoughts. She shook them off and passed by his towering frame. "I don't. I just know how to impress business clients."

The floral scent of Maya's hair teased his nose as she sauntered past him into the foyer. She wore a light gray cardigan with an ivory silk camisole underneath, and slim jeans that hugged her legs. Nice legs, he remembered, not that he was playing favorites with her anatomy. His lips had paid respect to every inch of her beautiful body, and if he didn't stop watching the way she moved, the only tour she'd be getting was of his bedroom.

"Nathan?" he yelled out, hoping the young man could take Maya around. When he received no answer, Nic maneuvered himself slightly ahead of her—to avoid ogling—and led her through the old country home that their fathers had turned into a small empire of grapes.

Nic led Maya through the modest foyer into the large open-concept tasting room, where bottles of wine in open cubbyholes and glass lockers lined the walls. Colorful tapestries and landscape paintings decorated the walls; leather seating was arranged by a fireplace, and a long curving bar sat on a small platform with rows of glass stemware at the ready.

"Wow, this is a nice setup."

"We renovated not long ago. The tasting room used to be enclosed, but we knocked out some walls."

"Mmm-hmm." Maya nodded. "I saw it in the expenses."

Nic licked his lips, wondering if she was looking at everything and putting a price tag on it. "Your father's office is this way." They continued through a side doorway that led to a private corner of the house. Nic turned the old brass knob and held open the door for Maya, who tentatively walked past him into the office of Albert Belcourt.

He cautioned himself to be sensitive, watching her turn slowly in the middle of the room. "Other than a few items of paperwork, the room is how he left it. Albert preferred things minimal, but he loved books and art." She didn't say anything, just held herself as she cautiously inspected the room around her. Tentatively, she leaned over the medium-sized desk, took in the few small wooden chairs and walked to the leather couch in the corner. She tilted her head back to stare up at the wall-to-wall shelves filled with books, her gaze flicking over the spines.

Nic's gaze darted around the room as well, noting that he hadn't gone inside much since Albert's death. Too many memories. A heavy vibration in his pocket interrupted his thoughts. Nic had ignored his phone while giving Maya the tour, but when the tenth consecutive call vibrated against his right thigh, he excused himself and pulled out the offending device. Daphne. He put the call to voice mail. Then he saw her text.

Where are you?

His call log read Daphne, Daphne, Daphne, Daphne. The phone lit up again in his hand. Daphne. Under normal circumstances, he'd be concerned and call right back, but Daphne was not normal. She was the overindulged princess of a rosé empire. Beautiful but spoiled, Daphne was the right hand of her father, Claude, who was a genius winemaker. No one could cultivate a rosé like Claude, and because of Maya's father, Claude was working on a new rosé and wanted to use the tempranillo exclusive to Par Le Bouquet.

The deal would reinvigorate the vineyard, which had been struggling since more and more of the established vineyards were investing in technology. Better soil readings, better weather prediction and automated grape monitoring equaled better grape production and less need to buy grapes from other vineyards. But where the vineyard suffered, the brokering business grew. Now the wineries had too many grapes, and he was happy to negotiate and take a percentage of their sale. Maya's father had been working out the details with Claude when he passed, which was how it fell into Nic's lap. Along with Daphne.

His family, Albert and the Rhones had been close since Nic was a boy. Daphne was like an annoying little sister until she had graduated from university. They'd tried dating a few times, but he didn't feel anything more than friendship. She, however, had a different interpretation of their relationship. *Soul mates* was one descriptor she had used. *Perfect for each other* was another.

And she knew that Nic couldn't rebuke her advances, not if he wanted to be the sole provider of grapes for Claude's new wine. No matter how many times he told Daphne he loved her only like a sister, her response was to tell him she would let him "sow his oats," but when the time was right, she would come for him. Apparently, that time was now.

She had unexpectedly showed up at the hotel again last night, which had him running right into the arms of Maya.

God, making love to Maya had been beautiful. Nic saw her pick up Albert's expense ledger and inwardly groaned. And now she was in the den, about to rip apart his business practice.

His phone vibrated again. This time it was Nathan.

"Nathan, where are you? I'm giving Albert's daughter, Maya, the tour. We're in the den."

"I'll come straightaway, but you should know that Daphne and Monsieur Rhone are here."

Nic checked to make sure Maya was occupied and walked farther into the hallway. "So that's why I have ten messages from her."

"*Oui*. Also, she came here last night looking for you, but I told her you weren't here."

"She showed up at the hotel. Fortunately, I was busy." He glanced at Maya, who was now sitting at her father's desk.

"They're in the tasting room right now," Nathan said.

"Okay, I'll deal with them. You come keep Maya away from the tasting room. Daphne will not be pleased, and we can't have a scene right now."

Nic and the young man passed each other in the hall with a nod, and then Nic found Daphne and her father helping themselves to a bottle of Dechamps.

"Apologies, Claude." Nic hurried in and shook the stately man's hand. "Did we have a meeting today? *Bonjour*, Daphne, you look well." Nic kissed Daphne on both cheeks, pulling back when she tried to catch his lips on the last one. She looked sullen and disapproving in black cropped trousers and tall heels. Her thin red hair was pulled back into a ponytail, which showed off large diamond stud earrings.

She didn't say a word as Nic and Claude discussed the timing of their venture, pouring herself another glass of wine and scrolling through her phone. Her father slid a glance toward Daphne.

"Are you listening?"

"Of course, Father." She looked up for one minute, then went back to her phone. Claude returned to his estimates, and Nic was sure they could deliver quality grapes in six months. Hidden in the extra expenses that Maya questioned was a rare strain of tempranillo, a resilient grape from his mother's native Spain. Because it was unique to the region, he had brought the grape to generate more interest in the vineyard. Claude was definitely interested. The men smiled and shook hands while Daphne took a seated selfie.

"I'm excited about this, Nic. Dry and savory with a light ruby color."

"We are, too, Claude." Nic bit the inside of his cheek.

"I know it's hard to accept," Claude said. "Albert will be missed."

Nic nodded, thankful that Claude understood, then he glanced at the empty doorway toward the den. Nic almost felt bad hiding Maya in there, but Daphne was a wild card, and he meant what he'd said: he was going to have those shares. He had plans for the business, and they didn't include a partner.

Chapter 7

Nic walked the Rhones to their car and began to breathe a little easier. "Come, Daphne," Claude said to his daughter. "Your mother needs us to stop at the butcher's."

"Don't forget about the charity ball, Nic," Daphne murmured, holding on to his outstretched hand as he helped her into the car. Her blue eyes were sharp. "Pick me up at seven?"

Merde. Albert had tricked him into taking her months ago. For the business, he'd said. "Ah…"

"Daphne," her father hissed. "Nic is still dealing with Albert's death."

"All the more reason to go," she said. "Get your mind off things. And it's for a good cause. Albert would have wanted us to attend."

Claude's gaze flicked to Nic's. *For the business,* he said to himself. "I'll pick you up at seven."

"Did I mention you have the Children First ball tonight?" Nathan said, coming up behind him as the Rhones drove away.

Nic rolled his eyes. "Please tell me I have a suit here."

"You do. And the masks arrived last week."

Nic whipped around. "Masks?"

"It's a masquerade ball."

"Oh, God." Nic took a deep breath, wondering what to do about Maya.

"She's remarkable, isn't she?"

Nic jerked his neck back. "Daphne? She treats you like dirt."

"I was talking about Maya."

"Oh." Nic's voice lowered and he smiled a little. "Yes, she is." Nic whipped back around. "Why, what did you two talk about?" He didn't like the idea of Maya pumping him for information.

"Albert. California. Her job. She's very astute."

"I know," Nic murmured with exasperation.

"I can't believe he had a daughter this whole time and we never knew."

"I guess he had his reasons. Is she still in the den?"

"*Oui.* She's reorganizing his paperwork."

Nic grimaced. He didn't want her eagle eyes on his paperwork.

The men went back to the den, startled to find it empty.

Maya was looking for Nathan when she spotted Nic through a hallway window helping a woman into a car.

Then the afternoon sun took her breath away as it sat farther into the hills and sent a burst of colors over the horizon. She thought scenes like that were only in movies. She hadn't gotten the outside tour yet, but she planned to explore the rows of vines and the rolling greenery that her father had loved so much—so much, he'd chosen it over her.

"Nathan?" she called out into the tasting room. The place was quiet except for the crackle of the natural fireplace. She walked toward an open wine bottle and three used glasses that sat on a gleaming wood bar. Dechamps, the bottle read in gold letters. Seriously? Her partner's family made Rick's favorite? What were the odds?

Work was the last thing on her mind, but she had an itch to check in with Jen. First, she'd need a booster. She leaned over the bar and found a clean glass, then poured the ruby liquid halfway. Just watching the red waves made Maya think back to her night with Nic and the way he'd taken her through the motions of wine tasting.

When Rick had tried to show her, it had been pretentious; when Nic did it…foreplay. She stared at the glass, remembering how gentle his hands had been on the glass. She placed her fingers on the stem, and then *swish*. The legs drizzled slowly down the glass. *Nice legs, Dechamps.* She stuck her nose in the glass. Floral? Fruity? No clue, but her taste buds were singing. She let the liquid flow over her tongue, and a flashback of Nic's wine-filled kiss came to mind. Her nipples perked up, and she quickly pulled the glass from her lips.

"What do you taste?" Nic appeared through the doorway, and she noticed above the door the familiar stone-carved head of Bacchus. The god of wine. Fitting.

"I don't know. You startled me."

"So try again," he said softly, coming to stand in front of her. He poured himself a taste and downed it like he needed a boost himself. When he was done, he watched her expectantly. Maya took another sip, willing her body not to respond as he watched her lips close over the glass. She sipped, took a swish, then sipped again.

"I don't know," she said, blushing.

"Just guess," he coaxed, his gaze roaming over her face.

"Raspberry."

"And?"

"There's more?"

"Again." He grinned and leaned on the bar. She took another sip.

"Vanilla?"

His eyes popped. "You're better at this than you think you are."

"Lucky you, partner." She loved the way his eyes darkened when she said it. "I can see why people like this wine, but I'm surprised you have it. It's not French."

"It's from a Brazilian winery owned by my cousin, but the strain is French."

"The strain?"

"The grape itself."

"Oh. Interesting."

"My uncle Armand's winery is not too far from here, but his son opened his own winery in Brazil. They specialize in the reds."

"Hmm. And are they clients of ours?"

"Of course."

"And were those clients that were here earlier?" He swallowed and poured the rest of the bottle into his glass, then made a show of tasting. She wasn't sure he was going to answer.

"They were. The Rhones specialize in the pinks."

"Pinks?"

"Rosé, and some of the orange wines, too, but oranges can be tricky to master."

"Orange wine? I've never had an orange wine."

"That's because it's not very popular."

"So you didn't want to introduce your new partner to our clients?"

Nic's lips flattened. He threw an elbow on the bar and leaned toward her. "About that. I'm willing to make you a very rich woman."

She raised her brows. "How rich?"

He found a napkin and a pen behind the bar, then scribbled on the cloth and handed it to her. She kept her cool as she looked at the six figures. It was half of what her father had made last year. Nic didn't know she had no interest in keeping the business, but she wasn't going to go out like a chump. He was lowballing her, setting her up for negotiations. Well, little did he know, he was messing with the wrong woman. She tore the napkin in half.

"I don't need your money."

His gaze flicked to the napkin, then back to her. "Why would you want to keep this business? You know nothing about wine."

"No, but I know people and I know business. Did you think I would just hand you my shares without knowing all the facts? I'm still reading through the contract. That money you're offering is based on whose appraisal? If you upgraded like you said you did, then you have a plan to make more money in the future, money I would be giving up. I'll have to take that into consideration."

"Jesus," Nic said, his face splitting into a smile. If she didn't know better, she'd say he was impressed. "You're a shark."

She gave him a humble shrug. "I know."

They stared at each other as a sexual tension rose between them like the beginning of an electrical storm. His gaze sizzled while her blood began humming a slow methodical pulse.

"Erm, I've put your suit and mask in your room," Nathan said to Nic, his eyes darting back and forth between Nic and Maya. They both turned their heads as if startled. Maya took a step back and gathered herself just as Nathan stopped at her elbow. "And I've had our housekeeper set up our largest guest room for you. Your bag is already there. It's ready, if you'll follow me upstairs."

"*Merci*, Nathan," Nic said in a low voice. "Maya, I have to attend a party tonight, but feel free to make yourself at home. Nathan will stay and make sure you are comfortable."

"Oh, all right. Have fun." She snaked her hand around Nathan's elbow. "I'm all yours."

"This way," Nathan said as he led her toward the exit.

She looked over her shoulder at Nic, just in time to see him watching her ass as she walked away.

A long walk along the back of the house and one beautiful cherrywood staircase later, she was dropped off in a cozy guest room awash in tan leather, beige tapestries and gold accents. A fire was burning low in the fireplace, and the corner table was set with an arrangement of meats, cheeses and breads. And, of course, a bottle of unopened wine rounded out the selection.

"It's lovely, Nathan. Thank you."

Nathan walked to the window and spread the curtain wider. "It was your father's favorite view."

"He slept in here?"

"No, his room is just down the hall. We've kept it as is."

"This must be hard on you. I'm sorry."

"He was a wonderful teacher. I wish you could have known him."

Me, too. And there it was again, that anger curbed in a bubble of confusion. Everything she had been told suggested he was a deadbeat dad, but those who had known him were devastated by his death. People like Nathan, who clearly loved him.

Nathan left her alone to unpack her bag. She'd brought enough for a few days, which she hoped would be sufficient time to go through her father's records and learn...well...something about the man she'd never known. She couldn't help but stare out the window as she placed her things around the room. Her father's favorite view, huh? She opened the door of her room softly, shuffled down the hall in her socks and came across an unadorned wooden door. She put her ear to the wood, then slowly turned the knob when she heard nothing. The door clicked open, and she slipped inside.

The room setup was similar to her guest room, except the bed was an oversize canopy. Rich oak furniture dominated the room, with black leather seating in front of the fireplace. A pipe lay on the dresser, along with a watch and a few coins. Pictures of landscapes adorned the north walls, but the south wall held only the window overlooking the vineyard. Other than that, there was nothing. No pictures of friends or family, no messy paperwork, no television or plants. Not even a mirror. Her gaze settled on the massive armoire in the corner. She opened it and was taken aback by the smell of cologne.

A full-length mirror covered one door, while a smaller one was on the other door. Suits and shirts were lined up in blues and grays, with a perfect row of leather shoes and boots underneath. Everything was pristine and color coordinated, somewhat like her own closet. Well, at least now she knew where her obsession with order came from.

The other door held small wooden pockets filled with toiletries and aftershave, and one held a plastic baggie. She pulled the plastic from the pocket and recognized old worn pictures. Carefully she pulled them out. She recognized him as a young man with another man about his age. They both held shovels, and a single stake stood between them. She flipped the picture around, but there was no writing on the back. Maya walked to the window and held up the picture. The horizon matched. She looked closer and saw a thin vine on the stake. He had planted a vine. Her gaze held the face of the other man, and she knew it was Nic's father.

The next picture was again taken in the field. This time a small boy was carrying a stem of grapes. She flipped the picture around and saw smudged writing that read: Nicky 1987.

She turned to the next picture, and her heart stopped. Her four-year-old face was staring at the camera as if she didn't know who was taking the picture. She wore a little red jumper and held a half-eaten sandwich in her hand. A woman's hand was visible behind her: her mother's.

Her heart raced as thoughts flew through her mind. She gathered the pictures in the same order, and then pulled out the last picture one more time. Stone walls were in the background and there, cut off high in the corner, was part of Bacchus's face. Impossible.

Her phone buzzed, making her jump and scramble to get the pictures back into their plastic sleeve. Reaching for the doors, she glimpsed her face in the mirror and was surprised by the watery rims of her eyes. She looked like him around the mouth and cheeks. Swiping at her face, she grabbed the other door and stopped when she noticed a black garment bag hanging flush against the inside. She found the zipper and pulled it halfway down, revealing a sparkling silver dress adorned with crystals. She ran a hand over its satin front, closed the armoire, then pulled her phone from her pocket. The office number flashed. Quickly she tiptoed her way back to her room and walked to the window to get better reception.

She called the number back and was greeted by Jen's hushed voice.

"Something is going down here. When are you coming back?"

"I took two weeks off. Why?"

"Rick has scheduled a meeting. He's restructuring the account lists. You're no longer on SuperFoods."

"What!"

"He claims he spoke to you about it, and you were fine with it."

"I haven't heard from him at all!"

"There's something else. He's claiming you tried to kiss him while you were in New York."

"On my life, Jen. He followed me into my hotel room and tried to get it on with me. I slapped him in the face."

Maya heard Jen's defeated groan. "Why didn't you tell me? Human Resources reports to me."

Maya paced. "Because he's my boss and we dated and I know how it looks."

Jen sighed. "What are you going to do?"

"I'm going to call Dave."

"You can't tell him I called you."

"I won't tell him how I know. I promise. Thanks for the heads-up."

Maya hung up and stared out at the beautiful colors of dusk. Los Angeles seemed so far away. Not because of the distance, but because in a matter of days, her life had seemed to change. No longer did her whole world center around proving to everyone that she was worthy to have a seat at the table. Now she just wanted to find out who she really was.

She dialed Dave's office number, and Carol, who of course already knew why she was calling, whispered good luck before immediately transferring her to his phone. Dave was jovial when he answered, but Maya knew that under that grandfather-like exterior, Dave was a businessman, and that was all he cared about.

"Maya, you miss us already?"

"Actually, I believe it's the office who misses me, Dave. I hear I'm no longer running SuperFoods."

Dave cleared his throat. "Uh, good news must travel fast. Rick was going to wait until you got back to restructure, but he'll be in New York with them when you get back."

"And why would I think this was good news?"

"Because we need you on the consumer pet accounts. If anyone can build that division, it's you."

"Pets, Dave? You want to put your A team on pets?"

Dave sighed, his facade already cracking. "Look, Rick told me you tried to kiss him in New York. It's probably not a good idea for you two to work together."

That mother— "Rick is a lying, scheming snake. You know me better than that."

"I know you were upset that I passed you over for the promotion."

"I *was* upset. But now I'm glad I didn't get it. I don't want to work for you anymore."

Dave's voice got softer, his facade back on. "Maya, maybe we should talk when you get back in the office."

Maya watched the sun hide behind the hills. She

couldn't remember the last time she'd even watched a sunset. "I'm not coming back into the office. Have my associate pack my things."

"Maya, you're upset. Think about this. You need a job."

"I *have* a job."

"Where? One of our competitors?"

Maya almost laughed at the desperation in his voice. Dave couldn't handle the humiliation of losing an employee to another firm, something she could leverage if she wanted to, but sticking it to him felt too good. Going to a competitor? SuperFoods did boxed wines, so— "Yep."

She hung up. Then she laughed, her shoulders already feeling lighter, picturing the look on Dave's face.

Her laugh faltered a little as she realized what she had just done. She'd thrown away her career. Shit.

Luckily, Nic's offer to make her a rich woman was still on the table, but now Mama didn't just need a new bag, Mama needed a new life. If she was going to get the maximum price for her shares, the earning potential of the company was more important than ever.

Chapter 8

Maya was seated at the dining room table when Nic walked in wearing a slim-cut black tux. "Wow, don't you look special." He was carrying a black satin eye mask and wore an irritated look on his face. He tossed the mask on the counter too hard and found his engraved invitation lying under his car keys.

"Are you going to be all right here?" Nic said to Maya.

Her eyes darted around dramatically. "Is Nathan dangerous?"

"Of course not. I just meant that I could cancel if you felt uncomfortable. Nathan will be heading home in a bit, leaving you here alone."

"As if Daphne would go for that." Nathan chuckled. He entered the room carrying two dishes of herb-roasted chicken. "And I'm happy to stay over if needed." A look passed between the two men that Maya couldn't interpret.

"That smells like heaven," Nic said, picking up a fork to dig in. His dark brows slashed over his eyes when Nathan snatched the fork from his hand.

"You're having dinner at the ball."

Nic turned his scowl to Maya, who had put his mask on her face. "I'm Batman," she said to Nathan, then smiled up at Nic, who tried to stifle a grin. "What is it with the French and masks?"

"It makes the wealthy feel like seventeenth-century royalty. They'll spend more money," Nathan joked. Nic's phone went off, and everyone saw Daphne's name appear on the screen.

"You wouldn't want to keep Daphne waiting," Maya said.

Nic's jaw clenched. "Then may I have my mask back?"

She slipped it off her head and held it up. "Have fun." She felt those tiny fingers of jealousy tickling her brain. Did he make love to Daphne the same way he made love to her?

"She's just a friend," he murmured, taking the mask from her fingers.

"I didn't ask."

He looked away, then back to her. "I was just explaining why she wouldn't mind if I stayed and had dinner with you both, but Nathan is right, dinner will be served. *Bonsoir.*"

He looked really sexy, Maya thought as she watched him walk out of the room.

"Daphne is in love with him," Nathan said around a mouthful of mushrooms. "He isn't interested, but they are clients."

"So he plays nice to keep their business."

"Something like that. They were your father's clients, though, and now he's trying to pick up where Albert left off." Hmm. If she'd read the contract correctly, and she had, all of her father's clients went to her effective immediately. She tapped her fork on the chicken.

"Was that them in the house today?"

"It was." Nathan explained how Monsieur Rhone was looking to use the tempranillo they'd planted last year for a new rosé.

"Daphne is very pretty. Nic could do worse."

"She is, how do you say in English, a brat?"

Maya smiled at the thought of Daphne torturing Nic all evening. "Well, I'm sure they'll have a nice time. It sounds fun. Have you ever been?"

Nathan's gaze dropped to the floor, then he shrugged. "Yes, it's the same every year. I'd prefer to stay and keep you company."

"I hope you didn't cancel a date to stay with me. I'm a big girl."

"Actually, my date was going to be your father. He liked the auction." A sad smile appeared on Nathan's face, then he busied himself opening a bottle of wine. Maya watched him, feeling awkward that she wasn't the one grieving. But how could she when she didn't know him?

"What was he like?"

"He was personable. Funny. Everyone liked him. He was the one who solved the problems." Nathan poured her a glass of wine and held it out. "He preferred red wine over white. Was a bit of a foodie, although he was allergic to peaches."

"So am I," Maya murmured, taking the glass. "Actually, I take antihistamine pills every day. It's like I can't even breathe the air sometimes."

"He saved my life once," Nathan said around a mouthful of chicken.

"What happened?"

"After a particularly hard storm, your father and Nic did some reconstruction on the back deck. I walked outside and knocked over a beam holding up the floor. It almost came down on top of me, but your father pushed me out of the way and held it up while Nic put it back in place."

"Whoa, that's pretty heroic."

"He was fearless like that. You remind me of him a little."

Maya straightened. "I do?"

Nathan nodded shyly. "You're fearless, too."

Maya smiled. "And also allergic to peaches."

Nathan paused, then gave Maya a solemn look. "Are you really going to sell your shares to Nic?"

Maya blinked. "Probably. I mean, I haven't decided, but it doesn't make sense for me to keep the business. My life is in LA. At least…it was."

"What do you mean?"

"Nothing. I mean, this is a shock for me, you know?

This man that you were so fond of didn't want to have anything to do with me, but he left me his life's work. It's so strange. And because of that, I'm not ready to just sign everything over to Nic. I'd like to learn a little bit about what I'm giving up. And about the man I never knew."

Nathan stared at her a moment, then jumped from his seat and hurried from the kitchen.

"Are you okay?" Maya said to his back.

He was gone for less than a minute, reappearing with an envelope addressed to her father, along with a medium-sized box.

"What's this?" She opened the box to reveal two masks: a larger solid one and a smaller delicate one with sequins.

"*Mademoiselle*, maybe you'd like to get to know your father by accompanying me to one of his favorite events?" Then Nathan's face fell. "Although, you don't have a dress."

Maya clapped her hands together. "Oh, I think I can find something suitable."

Dinner had been tolerable. The man to Daphne's right had kept her occupied, talking about the thing she loved the most: herself. Claude and Daphne's mother were seated at the table directly behind them. Then the empty seats to his left, Albert's seats, allowed him to enjoy his meal in peace.

But with peace came thoughts—Maya smiling up at him, Maya's soft lips, Maya naked underneath him, Maya at the table with Nathan. Nic speared a green bean and shoved it in his mouth. The young man was already half in love with Maya. If he so much as touched her arm, Nic would—

"Nicky, you've been very quiet."

He hated that nickname. "I'm just thinking about what to bid on at the auction."

"Well, I know what I'm bidding on." Her hand had made its way to his thigh. He covered it, wishing he could crush it. Instead, he held it and placed it back on her lap.

"Your parents are right behind us," he admonished. Her pout was exasperating.

"I'm going to bid on the Dechamps bath for two."

Nic tried not to sigh. "If you wanted a spa day, I could have just asked my uncle for you."

"But this is for a good cause, and it's for two."

In an effort to save his business from debt, Nic's uncle had partnered with a wellness group offering wine tours, spa facilities and spiritual healing workshops. Armand Dechamps had donated a full day of wellness services, including the famed red wine spa bath. Soaking in a Roman bath filled with red wine, while drinking red wine.

"I'm sure you'll enjoy it."

"We'll enjoy it."

Servers refilled drinks and cleared the plates, then distributed auction markers for each guest.

"We'll take two, please. *Merci*," said the soft voice to his left. His head snapped up. It couldn't be. All he saw was silk: silver silk dress, silken skin, silky red lips. "Fancy meeting you here," she said with a teasing lilt, sitting next to him.

He realized his jaw was open and clenched it shut. Her pink eye mask was shaped to look like flowers around her dark eyes. Her smile was breathtaking. He pulled his gaze away to briefly scowl at Nathan, who was looking nervously at him through his mask. Nathan wore his tux well, making them a striking couple. Nic didn't like it.

The audience buzzed with their arrival, and Daphne had already begun whispering in his ear. "Is that Nathan? Who is that woman with him?"

He was saved by the start of the auction and the booming voice of their moderator, but his peripheral vision caught both Daphne and Maya sneaking glances at each other. This wasn't good.

Maya leaned in toward Nic. "Which one are we bidding on?"

"We?" he whispered.

"The company. Which one are *we* bidding on?" While most left their masks on, his mask was on the table in front of him. Maya noted it and put it in her mental Nic file: stubborn and possibly rebellious.

"We've bought a table. I think that should suffice."

"That's not very charitable. Plus, it's a tax write-off for the company."

"I'll remember that when you sell me your shares."

Maya shifted her gaze and smiled at Daphne. "Aren't you going to introduce me?"

Nic shifted, blocking her view. "After the auction."

"You should have told me you had a girlfriend."

He gave her his full attention. "I do not have a girlfriend." His gaze dropped to her dress. "You've been snooping."

"Guilty."

"You look beautiful." They looked at each other a little too long, then turned back to their dates as the bidding began.

"She doesn't like me, does she?" Maya said to Nathan, who had greeted Daphne with a bow of his head.

"Daphne doesn't like competition. She's usually the most beautiful woman in the room, but not tonight."

"Why, Nathan, I had no idea you were so romantic."

"I am French, *mademoiselle*, I was born romantic."

"Oh Nathan, if only I were ten years younger." She chuckled. "Now, which one should we bid on?"

"Your father liked to bid on the paintings. Several hang in the hallway."

"Hmm." The list was in French but she could make out a few of the words.

"What's the Le Bain Rouge?"

"It's a red wine bath at the Dechamps spa."

"Seriously?" She looked at the price. First suggested bid was five hundred euros. She glanced at Nic from the side of her eye and gripped her marker tighter.

"And now we'll move on to our next item. Le Bain Rouge. Donated by the Dechamps winery. The starting bid is five hundred euros."

Daphne's marker went up confidently.

"Do I hear six hundred? I'm told you'll be luxuriating

in the award-winning Cabernet Franc while receiving a shoulder massage. Wondering if I should bid on this myself. Oh, *merci* to the man in the back. Six hundred. Do I hear seven hundred?"

Daphne's marker went up again. Nic wondered how far she was willing to go on the bid, and how he was going to get out of it if she won. He prayed another outbid her. But seven hundred euros to soak in wine? Ridiculous.

"Do I hear eight hundred? Ah, hello, *mademoiselle*. Eight hundred to the lady in silver."

Nic whipped his head to the left. Maya was lowering her marker and smiling. "What are you doing?"

"Winning," Maya said without looking at him. Her amused gaze was focused over his shoulder.

"Do I hear nine hundred? Nine hundred to the lady in black."

Nic's head whipped to the right. Daphne's scowl was directed at Maya. Oh, Christ.

"Do I hear a thousand? A thousand going once. Twice? A thousand to the lady in silver." An excited buzz had begun in the room. *No, no, no,* Nic thought as the tennis match between the two continued. The bid had crept to fifteen hundred, for which Daphne raised her marker and punted to two thousand.

He could see it now, Daphne insisting he take her to the spa and him fending off her advances in the bath. He couldn't let that happen.

"Five thousand!" Nic shouted, causing the room to sigh in awe.

"Five thousand, oh my, an upset." The host clapped

vigorously. "*Mademoiselles*, would either of you like to counter?"

Daphne shook her head with a smile, clearly thinking he'd won it for her. The host turned to Maya and raised his brows.

Nic leveled his gaze on Maya, who glanced his way before shaking her head at the auctioneer.

"Sold to Monsieur Rayo. *Merci beaucoup, monsieur*, from me and Children First. Now, our next item is the new edition Vespa…"

The table was silent as the auction continued. "I was going to stop, you know," Maya murmured.

"*Oui*, but Daphne wasn't."

"Well, I hope you two enjoy it."

He rolled his eyes. "I've decided to take Nathan."

They both chuckled, causing Daphne to frown. As the auction came to an end, Maya sought the ladies' room, and seconds later Daphne followed, leaving him and Nathan alone.

"Spontaneity is not like you," Nic said to Nathan.

"She wants to know her father, and Albert loved this event."

Nic couldn't argue that point. Actually, there were no arguments, he just felt…possessive. And Nathan seemed to be feeling the same way.

"She's not staying, you know."

"I know. Has she signed over her shares yet?"

"She will."

Nathan shrugged, and Nic was glad he let the subject go. The business was becoming a drain on him and his finances. He'd been using his profits from the hotel to float money into the vineyard. If the rosé deal didn't work, he was ready to close it down and convert the property into a charming bed-and-breakfast.

But none of that would be possible without Maya's shares.

Minutes ticked by as the men waited for the women's return. A sense of dread gripped him. Daphne could be unpredictable.

He and Nathan exchanged concerned looks. Nic scrambled to stand and headed into the hallway. He stopped short when he found the two women just outside the ballroom doors, their heads swiveling in his direction.

"I see you've met."

"Not formally, we just bumped into each other," Maya said with a strange look.

"Daphne Rhone, Maya North. Albert's daughter."

"Impossible." Daphne gasped, looking down her nose at Maya.

"Possible," Maya said in return. "I also own—"

"Um, Maya, may I speak with you privately?" Nic interrupted and took Maya's elbow. He turned to Daphne. "Excuse us."

Daphne's eyes narrowed. "Of course, darling. I'll get us more champagne."

Nic pulled Maya a short distance down the hall, looking for a private corner. He found a secluded alcove by the kitchen and stopped just in time for Maya to rip herself from his grip.

"Was that necessary, *darling*?"

Nic grit his teeth. "She calls everybody *darling*."

"I doubt that. Now, why are we hiding by the kitchen?"

"Because you were about to tell her you were part owner of my business."

"Our business. And it's true."

"Only for a short time, Maya. Be sensible. You're simply holding on to these shares because it's the only part of your father you know, but you won't be doing any of the work. You won't be getting us clients or taking orders."

"You want clients? I can get us clients."

He threw his hands up. "When? In a few weeks? You'll be gone in ten days."

Her eyes hit the floor, and he could have smacked himself for being so harsh.

"You're right. I don't know what I'm doing," she said in a small voice, lifting her mask from her face. A tear jumped to her cheek, then another.

"Oh no, don't cry. Yell at me." He pulled his handkerchief from his pocket and offered it to her. She took it and dabbed at her eyes, still refusing to look at him. He moved closer and dipped his head, his gaze falling on the cherry red of her trembling lips and her damp cheeks. He couldn't help it. He placed a soft kiss on her cheek. When she didn't step away, he pulled her closer and placed one on her lips. She kissed him back, increasing the pressure until they were locked in a heated embrace.

She rose on her toes and gripped his arms. His hands spanned her back; their tongues danced as they tried to get closer and closer until they were sharing one breath.

She pulled back suddenly and broke free from his grasp, her eyes bright with tears.

"I'm sorry," she said. "Your girlfriend."

"She's *not* my girlfriend."

Maya sucked her teeth. "She clearly doesn't know that. Nathan told me you're just using her to keep her father as a client. That's gross."

"That's not…entirely true. I don't *have* to keep her happy—it's just a good idea to do so. She acts familiar because we've known each other since we were kids. That's all."

Maya handed him his handkerchief and shrugged. "Nathan's probably wondering where I am."

Nic scowled. "You're leading him on."

"How dare you? I am not! You're just jealous."

"I am." He was a grown man and could own up to his feelings. He'd made love to her, had just kissed her and she had kissed him back. As far as he was concerned, she was his. "I don't like the way he looks at you."

"Kind of like the way Daphne looks at you."

Nic smiled. "Jealous?"

Her eyes narrowed. "No!"

"Menteur." He decided to kiss that lie off her lips and took another step forward.

"Nic?" Daphne's voice was close.

Nic stopped and sighed.

Maya smirked. "You have lipstick on your face."

Daphne appeared with two champagne glasses and a scowl for Maya just as Nic finished wiping his mouth. He tucked the cloth into his pocket and put a neutral look on his face. "Ah, champagne. *Merci.*" Of course

Daphne had gotten drinks only for two. "Maya, you may have my champagne."

"No, thank you. Nathan is waiting for me." She said that last part looking directly into his eyes, and it stung.

Chapter 9

The end of the evening couldn't have arrived soon enough for Nic. Dancing with Daphne was torturous, not just because she insisted upon feeling him up while they danced, but because Maya and Nathan were across the room laughing and smiling at each other like newlyweds. Nathan was an excellent dancer, leading his partner with ease and holding Maya a little too close for Nic's tastes.

"She's strange, isn't she?" Daphne started. Nic tore his gaze away from the couple and saw her staring at them with a narrowed gaze.

"How so?"

"I don't know. Just so… American, I guess. So competitive. She really was trying to outbid us for the spa."

He didn't answer, refusing to be led down that path. But he inwardly bristled at the term *us*.

"Look, they're leaving."

"What?" He turned Daphne in his arms and focused his full attention on Nathan, trying to telepathically reach him. He didn't want the couple home together, alone.

"You don't think she and Nathan are—"

"No. I don't."

"Maybe we should leave, too—"

"Perfect, I'll get your coat—"

"And go back to my place?"

Suddenly he wanted to stay, but she was already gathering her clutch from the table. Nic pulled his phone from his pocket and called Nathan. He cursed when it went straight to voice mail. Maybe that was good, because he didn't know what he was going to say—don't make love to Maya? He wanted to call *her*, but didn't have her number. He looked at his watch, then calculated the amount of time it would take to drop Daphne off and go back to the vineyard.

He couldn't beat them, but he wouldn't be too far behind.

Twenty minutes and three calls to Nathan's phone later, Daphne was sitting in Nic's car, refusing to get out unless he agreed to come inside for a drink. He was out of excuses and out of patience with the whole rosé deal. They wouldn't even know if the deal could happen until the grapes matured in another six months. Which meant at least six months of Daphne trying to get him into bed.

He debated floating more cash into the business himself and telling Rhone that if he didn't want the grapes he could stuff it, but then he'd be putting his other business in jeopardy. And tourism in Paris was down. He wasn't struggling, but they hadn't made the gains they had hoped for in the last year and he'd had to cut back. If he took more money from the hotel, there would be no money for his staff's bonuses. He wasn't going to let that happen.

With fewer and fewer new clientele, the rosé deal had to work just so they could break even. Then there was Maya to deal with. Speaking of…

"Look. Why don't I take you for dinner next week? I really have so much work to get done."

"Have Nathan do it."

"Daphne, please, where would you like to go next week?"

"Chez Janou."

"Done."

"When next week?" Daphne was a bulldog when it came to negotiations, which was why her father brought her to meetings.

"Thursday."

"Nine p.m.?"

For Christ's sake. *"Oui."*

"Fine." She still hadn't moved. He looked to the stars and prayed hard.

"Where is that girl staying?"

"What girl?"

"Albert's daughter."

"She's staying at the vineyard."

"For how long?"

"Not long."

Nic felt like he was going to explode with pent-up rage. He wanted her to get out. He wanted to take that suit off. He wanted to know what Nathan and Maya were doing.

"Daphne, I really have to—"

"Do you remember when we were little and my brother Louis chased me through the vines? I twisted my ankle, and you picked me up and carried me to the house."

"You were crying pretty loud."

"I think I fell in love with you that day," she said, running her hand over the back of his neck. "And then you brought me those flowers."

He wanted to roll his eyes. His mother had sent him over to the Rhones with flowers for Daphne—they were from his mother, not him! He was ten and embarrassed that she'd made him do it. "Daphne, please. You know you and your family mean a lot to me, but we are friends. I'm not in love with anyone, and I don't want you to get the wrong impression."

Daphne shook her head and smiled seductively. "I know, I know, but you can't stop me from loving you. I told you that. And sometimes being a couple isn't about love, it's about family and commitment. We could have a good life together. I have enough love for the both of us."

Alarm bells rang in his head. "If we're going to be in business together, then keeping things platonic is the best course of action."

"I disagree. There is no stronger bond than family." The shock of the conversation must have reached his face, because she laughed playfully. "Don't worry, I'm not looking for a ring…yet." She laughed again, and his stomach began to turn. "I'm just happy to love you and—no, don't say anything…because I know that one day you'll see how good we are together."

"Okay," he whispered, as if afraid to wake the sleeping bear that sat inside Daphne. He stayed silent, knowing she was immune to his explanations. She'd heard nothing he said; instead, she'd weaved a story all her own. "I'll get your cloak from the back."

After gathering her items, he walked around to the passenger door, opened it and put out his hand to help her up.

"I adored the ball. And I can't wait to go to De-champs. *Merci.*"

He'd forgotten about that damn bath. "You're welcome," he mumbled, giving her the quickest kiss possible on her cheek and shoving her cloak and clutch into her arms. Reaching around her, he slammed the door shut, then practically ran to the driver's side.

"Till Thursday, darling." She waved.

He nodded, incapable of thinking of anything but escape, then roared the engine and shot off down the driveway. His focus shifted to Nathan and Maya, and he surged the car forward.

Maya had pulled her attention from her father's business ledgers and checked the window at least a million times before she'd actually gotten up and stared out into the darkness. Her father's den was in the back of the house with a partial view of the driveway from the window. The ball had ended thirty minutes ago, not that she was counting. She heard the roar of a car crescendo then fade.

Okay, she was counting. She poured herself a glass of wine and thought about having Nathan call Nic—she did actually have some news to share—but she admonished herself for being so childish and dropped back into her father's leather chair. Her finger ran over the business statements, temporarily pulling her attention away from Nic's absence.

Since Nic had taken over for his father, they had made some much-needed improvements that brought in a nice profit, but there were still areas of the business that had gone neglected. Their website was ancient and provided only a phone number for inquiries. She saw no incentives built into their plan for clients to keep coming back. She also noticed that they'd had losses three years in a row, and an infusion of money from Bacchus Inc. kept them solvent.

She didn't need to be a detective to know that was Nic's hotel company. He'd been robbing Peter to pay Paul, which meant that the company shares were probably worth much less than she'd thought at first glance. Her professional experience told her that unless the business had a trick up its sleeve, selling the vineyard and focusing on the brokerage would be the smart thing to do.

Her gaze slid to the window. Nic was probably having dirty sex with Daphne, while she had profit-and-loss statements and a half-empty bottle of wine. If anything, she was definitely developing her palate. She'd never drunk so much wine before, but somehow it felt normal to enjoy it before bed, like coffee in the morning.

Restless and still a bit jetlagged, she was drawn to the wall of books across the room. Dickens, Brontë, Proust, encyclopedias and wine books. She spied several unmarked leather books on a shelf just above her head and stood on her tiptoes, to no avail.

"Nathan?" she shouted, her fingers struggling to grasp the spine. "Hey, Nathan?"

"I sent him home. His mother worries."

She yelped and swung around at the familiar deep voice, wishing she was wearing something sexier than her long T-shirt and leggings. Nic was still in his tux, leaning against the doorjamb looking delicious as sin.

"Oh, hi."

"Do you need help?"

"I can't reach this book." She pointed above her head, then quickly pulled her arm down. Her breasts had been squeezed uncomfortably in the dress, and she had thrown on a sweatshirt to hide her unbound state. Said sweatshirt was balled up across the room where Nic was standing, making her feel a little self-conscious.

He walked into the room and shrugged off his jacket, then tossed it onto the desk. The cummerbund and bow tie followed, along with the clink of cuff links on the desk. He was still dressed. He glanced at the open ledgers. "You've been snooping again."

"Just making sure you weren't trying to lowball me in your offer."

"So you're considering it?"

"Of course, but I have some questions."

"Such as?"

"Have you decided to let the business fail?"

He blinked. "What did Nathan tell you?"

"So you have."

"What did he say?"

"Nathan didn't say anything. It's all over the books. Bacchus hasn't infused any money this year and it's been the lowest on record. You're gunning for my shares. I think you have plans."

"I have a contingency plan if the rosé doesn't pan out. That's all." He cocked his head, and his gaze traveled over her. Her body heated from the inside out. "What do you need?"

"Huh?"

"Which book?"

"Oh. That one."

He strode across the room, stopping inches from her to reach over her head. She took the opportunity to ogle his upper body as he easily stretched above her. The urge to touch him was overwhelming. She swallowed. "Did you have a nice rest of the evening?"

"No, I didn't," he said, pulling the book down from the shelf. He frowned at the leather object for a moment then laid it in her hands. "Did you and Nathan have fun rushing back here?"

"Are we going to go over this again?"

His lips formed a flat line and his gaze dipped to her shirt. "You're undressed under that thin T-shirt. Did he see you like this?"

Normally she'd move to cover herself, but instead

his accusatory tone made her want to stand her ground, even though she secretly prayed for his touch.

"The dress was a little tight around my…upper body. And I was wearing a sweatshirt."

She winced as she awkwardly bent to rub her side, then froze when she realized Nic had moved closer, his brows drawn, inspecting the area she was trying to touch.

"Tight here?" His warm palm covered the sore spot, and his thumb gently massaged circles through the T-shirt. She licked her lips and nodded, tightening her grip on the book for fear it would slip from her fingers.

"Is that better?" She looked up, expecting to see a sexual look in his eye; instead, his serious gaze was trained on her side, intent on easing her pain. Her pain had definitely lessened, but had been replaced by a fierce, demanding arousal.

Maya grabbed his wrist and moved his hand to her breast. He jerked and met her eyes, his mouth parting as she pushed herself further into his hand. With his gaze on hers, he cupped and squeezed her flesh, pulling the fabric taut, kneading with light circles that started a simultaneous pulsing between her legs.

She opened her mouth to speak, but closed it when his free hand filled with her other breast. Her eyes drifted shut, then reopened as he pulled his hands away, but only a heartbeat passed before she felt him under her shirt, skin to skin.

He continued the erotic massage, gently pushing her back against the bookshelf. Both thumbs ran boldly over her budding nipples, and she gripped his shoulders to steady herself. The book she was holding hit the floor, but neither cared.

He bent and shoved his body in between her legs, using the packed bookshelves to lift her feet from the floor. Then he kissed her roughly, like he was on the edge of losing control. Thoughts of Nathan, Daphne and her father were wiped way as she shoved her hands in his hair and ate at his mouth. It occurred to her that she should not wear a bra more often, and with the insistent erection nudging her inner thigh, she shouldn't ever wear pants again, either.

"Do you feel better?" he whispered, his mouth sliding over her lips and his thumbs slowly teasing the jutting tips of her breasts.

"No," she whispered.

"No?" His head jerked back to look at her, his face cute with concern.

"I'm aching in other places now. I want you inside me." His worry melted into a sexy grin.

"My pleasure, *mademoiselle*."

She mourned his hands leaving her, but reveled in their replacement on her hips as he lowered briefly to the floor and swiftly removed her leggings and panties. With an arm around her waist, he placed kisses in between her thighs, his tongue finding her warm and ready. She threw her head back and marveled at how swiftly he could make her build toward orgasm, but she gently pulled his head away and pulled him to stand. She wanted him inside her when she climaxed, which would be soon if he didn't hurry.

Her legs wrapped around his waist, and his forearms

held her thighs as he unzipped and lowered his pants. She was vaguely aware that his phone fell from his pocket, but his mouth on her wiped all thoughts away. His hands gripped her thighs as a faint buzzing sounded from the floor. She glanced at the phone and whispered against his lips, "It's your girlfriend."

"She is not my girlfriend. Look at me." His voice was rough with sex, and she did as he commanded. He nudged at her core, easing slowly, so deliciously hard and gentle, filling her just a bit. Her eyes fluttered. "Look. At. Me." His hands slid up to grip her bottom and her ears buzzed with anticipation.

No, her ears buzzed with another call from Daphne.

Nic's head turned and Maya went cold. "You should get that."

His eyes went wide. "No, don't let that distract you."

"It already has. Let me down."

His look was incredulous. "I'm inside you."

"Put me down, Nic."

Physical pain registered on his face as he pulled back and released her. Maya easily pulled on her leggings just as Nic pulled up his pants with difficulty. He walked to the desk, poured himself a glass of wine and downed it in one gulp.

"Are you mad?"

"Not at you," he said over his shoulder. "At myself, maybe."

"I don't want to feel like the other woman, that's all."

He turned and gave her a pointed look. "You're not the other woman. And I understand. Maybe it's best that we don't continue acting on our—" he took a deep breath "—attraction. You'll be gone soon and my heart will be broken."

"I'm sure your heart will be just fine."

"You like to judge my comments. Why is that so hard to believe?"

"In my experience, men are excellent liars."

"I have no reason to lie to you." They stared at each other for a moment, and her blush embarrassed her.

"Could you toss my sweatshirt over?"

"Sure. Could you toss my phone over?"

They made a game of exchanging items. She lobbed the offending technology and he caught it effortlessly. She fumbled her catch, and the fabric smothered her face. Their laughter eased what tension was left. She slipped on the sweatshirt.

"Stanford," he read. "That's Ivy League, no?"

"No, but it's as prestigious as one. Surprised?"

"No, I am not." He opened his mouth, then closed it. Then tried again. "I want to explain about Daphne."

That was the last thing she wanted to talk about. Maya rapidly shook her head, scooped up the book from the floor and hugged it to her chest.

"Um, maybe another time. It's getting late and we have to get up early tomorrow."

"We do?"

"Oh, yes. I met Remy Bernard and Benjamin Thomas. Both have wineries in the Loire Valley and might be interested in supplementing their production with a rosé line. Apparently, when the Hamptons ran out of rosé two years ago, no one saw the pinks as an opportunity.

Now everyone is looking to produce rosé, and we are one of the few brokerages ready to supply."

"Almost ready," Nic said offhandedly, then cocked his head as if he wasn't hearing correctly. "You offered them the tempranillo?"

"I offered them a tour and a look at the rosé. Obviously, we haven't talked numbers, but I envision a bidding war, which will be amazing for business."

Nic's eyes flared. "Those grapes are supposed to be exclusive for the Rhones."

"And who says they won't be? But we have no contract, and handshake deals can be iffy. This could bring Rhone to the table now. Not later. Did you realize the fiscal year ends in a few weeks? We'll—" she corrected herself "—*you* will have to start looking for funding, and with these numbers, no one would float you capital. And don't forget, my shares won't be for free. Unless Bacchus is prepared to help again?"

Nic was frozen in his tracks. "Where did you come from?" he murmured.

"Heaven?"

His eyes narrowed. "That's not what I was thinking."

Maya's head jerked back. "You challenged me to get us clients. They are coming tomorrow at ten a.m. See you in the morning."

Maya gathered the leather book and her contract papers in her arms and left Nic standing there, half-naked, holding his phone.

Chapter 10

After a near sleepless night, Maya rolled herself out of bed and shuffled barefoot to the bathroom for a much-needed shower. Remy and Benny were arriving for a tour in a few hours, and she wanted to be on top of her game, or at least awake. She inhaled, then groaned. She also wanted to get the smell of Nic's cologne off her skin. She sniffed her T-shirt. Damn him.

Why did he have to be so attractive? After trying and failing to read the French writing of the leather diary she had taken from her father's den, Maya tried to sleep knowing Nic was right next door. The fact that she refused to take off her T-shirt didn't help. She was in and out of sleep, dreaming of strong arms and a hard chest, surrounded by the smell of spice and pine.

But now she was ready to rid herself of the short-lived infatuation. Being attracted to someone was just a frame of mind. Beauty was in the eye of the beholder, right? So, as the beholder, she needed to change her perspective on "the beauty." As of this moment, "the beauty" was hideous. She nodded at her newfound plan and grabbed the delicate eighteenth-century knob on the door. It wouldn't budge.

Strange, but that old lock had seen better days. She probably just had to pull a little harder. She did, to no avail, then shook the knob hard with both hands. She smiled when she heard a loud click as if she had loosened something within the door, then she blinked and backed away as the door pushed itself open with smooth force.

"I'm almost finished," said the wet, half-naked, clean-shaven god that half stepped around the door. She let go of the knob as if it burned, and dropped her gaze to the towel that covered his hips and the chiseled abs that she had touched only a few nights ago.

"What are you doing in my bathroom?"

"You mean our bathroom. It's shared."

"What!" She stepped toward him—he smelled so good—and peered into his bedroom. The sheets were askew. "I thought that was a closet door."

"No. Now if you'll excuse me." His gaze raked over her before he closed the door. Then she ran to the wall mirror and almost cried at the state of her hair and the dried mascara on her face.

"You better have left me some hot water!" she yelled. She only hoped that along with his smell, his image could be washed from her brain.

An hour later she was suited and booted, sipping a cup of Nathan's artisanal coffee. Her father's protégé had gotten to the house early and whipped up breakfast bites and beverages for the meeting. Honestly, her own assistant could barely get to Starbucks. Former assistant, she reminded herself, tamping down the urge to call and check on her friends. No one had called her to find out what had happened, not even Carol. It reinforced her idea that quitting was the right thing to do.

Her boss liked to say that they weren't a company; they were family. But family didn't treat you like a liability. Maya grabbed the diary from the table and walked over to Nathan. Family helped you succeed.

"Nathan, I found this on my father's bookshelf. Would you mind helping me translate it later?"

Nathan took the book and flipped through the pages with interest. "Of course."

"Thank you." A timer went off and Nathan put the book at the end of the counter while he pulled out peach tarts.

"Nathan, *merci*. This will be wonderful for our guests." Nic appeared in a casual sweater, jeans and work boots, making Maya frown.

"This is what you're wearing to our business meeting?"

"They want a tour of the vineyard, right? You can't do that in those." He jerked his chin at her suede-heeled booties. "Unless you'd like to stay here while I show them around."

Maya narrowed her gaze and turned to Nathan. "I'll be right back." She hurried to her room and returned in the tall silver rain boots she'd learned to always pack after weeks of business in Seattle.

"*Très chic, ma chérie*. Very appropriate," Nathan said, loud enough for Nic to hear. Nic stared at the boots.

"*Oui*, at least we'll be able to spot you if you get lost." He smirked at her and strode away, as cars could be heard arriving.

While Nic took the men through the vineyard, Maya stayed in the back, trying to imagine her father standing between the vines, speaking passionately about his work. She was doing the right thing, she told herself. Being there, participating in the business, even if only a little, was better than just coming to France and claiming a payout and leaving. Her father had to have known that selling her shares was a possibility, right? Maybe that was even what he wanted. Like giving an American Express gift card instead of an actual gift.

She inhaled and let the cool air fill her lungs as her gaze settled on the green expanse and the yellow horizon. Her unsatisfied arousal had kept her up most of the night, but she felt serene and energized and—she hadn't taken her allergy pill. She put her hand on her chest and measured the beat of her heart. Steady and strong. She was puzzled but pleasantly surprised. Her mother always said that fresh air would do some good, but even her trip to Napa Valley several years ago had ended with her running to the drug store for her prescription.

She might need one after she talked to her mother, she mused. The text she had woken up to—how's it going?—rankled. There were holes in her mother's story, and Maya was afraid to go down that road. She had never once questioned her mother's explanation about her father's exit, happy to lay blame on the absentee. But now she wasn't so sure that was the right thing. But digging deeper might expose something that would make her angry at her mother, and maybe even at herself.

Nathan appeared next to her with another mini croissant. She'd had five already, but what the hell, she told herself, taking the flaky morsel. She was practically hiking.

Their clients touched the leaves and fingered the young grapes as Nic continued to talk pest control, harvest and expectation of taste and color. She remembered the pictures of her father. Then she imagined a little girl running down the rows in wellies and a muddy dress, giggling when her father caught her and tossed her in the air. *Maya*, her father said, kissing her on the cheek. *Maya...*

"Maya?"

The deep voice ripped her from the daydream. She blinked and spun around, facing the men's questioning looks as they lingered in the doorway of the house. "Coming?"

She fell into step, checking the time and calculating the time difference in California. Her mother wouldn't be awake for another few hours.

The group settled in the tasting room, where Remy and Benny regaled their audience with plans for their wines. The two were obviously friends who thrived on besting one another.

Nathan poured them all a sample of the reds the vineyard was still producing: a medium-bodied Pinot Noir and a light Gamay. She watched and followed Nic's lead, swishing and sniffing, checking the color then tasting.

Benny held up his glass. "Nic, my boy, you've kept things up well here. I'm glad you have decided to keep the business. I must say I was surprised when you mentioned selling last we spoke, but it looks like you've reconsidered. Your father would be proud."

Maya didn't miss Nic's glance at her, or the way he shifted uncomfortably in his chair. She knew it—he had plans for this place and it had nothing to do with grapes. But the question was, why did she care? She'd be back in LA next week—she sighed—looking for a job. Or maybe with the money from selling her shares, she could finally start her own business. Her business card could read North Consulting, CEO.

"Unfortunately, because I thought you were selling, I've contracted for some lovely Pinot strains from the Van Dames."

Maya was pulled from her thoughts again. Tannins, wine color, taste, she knew nothing about. But competition? Bring it on.

"Who are the Van Dames?" she asked softly.

Remy chimed in. "They're another brokerage we've done some work with in the past, but I must say, they didn't compare to the business both of your fathers built here."

Maya saw Nic's gaze hit the ground as Benny jumped in. "They are strictly brokerage, which is why Par Le

Bouquet had an edge. Not only did your father produce quality grapes, he knew where to find the best."

"We still do, as you've seen outside. And have tasted." Maya held up her glass.

Remy raised his in salute. "Touché."

"And since you both want the best grapes, I think it's time you came back home. I'd be willing to match your price with the Van Dames and give you a welcome-back discount."

All looked at her with raised brows, even Nic.

"That is generous. But the Van Dames have promised they will be getting me grapes from Dechamps." Benny sounded innocent, but there was a devious glint in his eye. He knew that information would be a blow. Maya chewed her lip as Nic's brows dropped into a frown. He straightened in his chair. "My uncle is doing business with the Van Dames?"

Benny shrugged. "Apparently. You know Armand. He'd sell his firstborn to make money. *Mon Dieu*, he almost did!"

The two men were laughing so hard Maya was afraid they'd have heart attacks. She turned to Nathan and made a face. Nathan leaned over her shoulder and spoke softly.

"Armand Dechamps almost sold his son Destin's vineyard in Brazil out from under him. It was a nasty fight that caused a bit of a rift between Nic and Destin because Armand threatened to take his business else-where if Nic helped Destin rebuild his winery. Nic had promised Destin capital, then he had to pull the money."

"Sounds ugly," she whispered.

"It was. All is well now though," he said before leaning away.

By the look on Nic's face, it didn't seem like all was well. And by the mirth in Benny's eyes, he had been dying to drop that knowledge all morning. Maya waved Nathan back over and whispered, "What is going on?"

Nathan shrugged. "Armand rarely overproduces, but when he does, he calls Nic."

"But not this time?"

Again, Nathan's shoulders touched his ears. Maya decided to do what she did best.

"Curious. When Nic spoke to Armand last night, he said he didn't have extra Pinot. But he did invite us to the vineyard to discuss the extra cab franc. Right, Nic?"

Maya's gaze bored into Nic's confused eyes until he figured out how to speak. "Erm, *oui*?"

Remy put his wine down and leaned forward, his expression grave. "Armand is selling the cab franc? The Van Dames said—"

"I'm not sure the Van Dames would know about this, Nic being family and all," Maya said nonchalantly. "Nic, that reminds me. We have another appointment." She turned from Nic's stare. "Sorry to cut this short, but you are welcome to stay and taste more of the wines. Nathan will get you whatever you need." She rose and turned to Nic. "Shall we?"

Nic rose awkwardly, looking between her and Nathan for a lifeline.

"Wait, wait." Remy pulled himself to the edge of his leather seat. "If Armand is selling, I want in."

"Oh," Maya said innocently. "But you said the Van Dames—"

Benny burst from his chair. "*Putain* the Van Dames! I want that cab franc."

"We can't make any promises," Nic said smoothly.

Remy stood. "I want in, too. And I want first look at the tempranillo when it's ready. I'll pay full price."

"Outrageous, Remy!" Benny's blustering face darted from Nic to Maya. "You tell Armand that I will pay double and I'll buy the tempranillo right now!"

It was going better than she'd hoped. Both men had turned on each other and started a bidding war fueled by their own pride. It was classic negotiations. Sales 101. Nic and Nathan were looking at her like she'd started World War III.

"Gentlemen, please!" Maya shouted. "Your offers are generous, but we can't make any promises until we speak with Armand."

"And when will that be?"

"We're driving up tomorrow," Nic said quickly, cutting Maya off with a look, then striding out of the room. "We'll be in touch."

"Call me first!" Remy yelled at Nic's back while Benny silently shook his head and mouthed to Maya to call *him* first.

Maya chuckled to herself. Her tease had gone better than expected. "Good day, gentlemen. Nathan will see to you."

Maya hurried out of the room after Nic, finding him waiting for her in her father's den. She closed the door behind her and then turned back to him with a bright smile. "That was crazy."

"Crazy is right," he half whispered, pacing the floor. He stopped and crossed his arms over his chest. "What did you think you were doing out there?"

"Creating demand. You have it in your head that you need to sell the business, but you don't. You just need to sell the grapes to the highest bidder." Nic was silent. "You told those men to go elsewhere. There was no contingency plan. Your plan was to take my shares and sell this place off all along? And I bet you pitched it to Rhone." God, she was good.

Nic uncrossed his arms and sat on the edge of the desk. "No," Nic said softly, "I was discussing a partnership with Rhone to create a Le Bains bed-and-breakfast. Rhone would keep the vineyard, I would handle the guests. It wasn't what our fathers wanted, but at least the vineyard would have been intact." The picture of her father standing by the vine flashed in Maya's mind. Her stomach began to hurt as he continued.

"Why?"

"I can no longer do this alone. I've been ignoring the hotel since you've been here, but soon I'll have to go back to Paris, and Nathan is not strong enough to run this place on his own."

"But you weren't alone. My father—"

"Was slowing down. It makes sense now because he was ill, but at the time I thought he was just getting older and thinking of retirement. He knew of my long-term plans. I know he didn't agree, but looking back, I think he knew he didn't have much time left. In any event, his leaving you his shares was a surprise to me. Maybe he had hopes that you would come and take over where he left off, but that isn't realistic. You can't do this job from California."

Maya looked away. After watching Nic in the vineyard that morning, she was pretty sure she couldn't do this job at all. "So your long-term goals have arrived."

"But my plans can't go forward without my partner's approval."

"Then, no, I don't like it."

"Or her shares."

They stared at each other for a long moment. Nic looked away first. "In any case, we are still a brokerage and will act like one. Pack your bags. We have a trip to take."

Maya frowned. "Where are we going?"

"Dechamps."

"But I was just baiting them. I didn't think we'd actually go there and—"

"Well, now we don't have a choice. In two days you've put a wrench in my plans, and now I have to deliver grapes to those two old fools some way, somehow, or they will ruin my, and your father's, reputation. Then there will be no business to sell at all. We'll leave after lunch."

Maya stared at Nic's back as he strolled out, wondering if she should hand him his shares on a silver platter or with a pink bow.

Chapter 11

"We're almost there," Nic murmured as the mani-cured roads wound higher and farther into acres and acres of land. Grapevines marched in perfect lines over the hills, then suddenly her sight was cut off by large trees. Maya raised her head and peered into the sky, where the top of a white mansion played peekaboo with the tree line. Nic slowed, then turned into a driveway, the iron gate so large a giant couldn't have scaled it.

Nic reach out of his window and punched a code into the keypad. Just watching the gate slowly open made Maya feel like she was in an episode of *Game of Thrones*. Once they were past the gate, a barrier of trees on both sides of the road guided them into a football field–sized flower garden blanketed with benches along flagstone walkways and marble statues of garden scenes. Unlit tiki torches appeared on the paths and led down the hill toward a giant lake with actual swans. But none of it compared to the three-story towering palace made of gray stone, flying the French, Brazilian and American flags along its long roof.

"You said a château, not a castle." Maya worried about her lack of formal attire. Nic had said to bring a bag, so she'd packed light. And only on the way up did he ask her if she had brought a bathing suit. No, she hadn't. Men!

"I believe it used to be the home of an old French monarch. No one history would remember, but someone who apparently lost their head during the Revolution. Uncle pulled it out of foreclosure."

"This is your father's younger brother?"

"Yes."

"And where is your mother?"

"Spain. She moved back there after their divorce."

"Oh, so that's where Rayo comes from? Why don't you use your father's last name?"

"Having the name Dechamps was more of a hindrance than a help when I started the hotel. People assumed we were affiliated with the winery. I wanted to start my own path, so I dropped it for business purposes."

"Why Nic and not Luca?"

He smiled a proud smile. "My mother calls me Nic."

"Is she stubborn like you?"

He pulled around to the front of the manor and put the car in Park. Then he turned to her. "No, she's headstrong, like you."

She blushed at the intimate moment, then realized they weren't alone as Nic's gaze shifted over her head. She turned and saw people hovering around the car. Then she saw a stern-looking white-haired gentleman standing just inside the massive oak doorway. His suit was ivory and his gold-tipped cane glinted.

"Is that Armand?"

Nic let out a breath. "That's him."

"He looks intimidating."

"You have no idea."

In contrast, a very animated gentleman in casual dress opened her door and helped her out. With a short bow, he kissed her hand. *"Bienvenue, mademoiselle. S'il vous plaît permettez-moi de prendre vos sacs."*

"She doesn't speak French, Pierre," Nic interrupted.

"Apologies, *mademoiselle*. We are so glad to have you at Dechamps. Your father was a good friend of the family. *Monseigneur* is very anxious to meet you. Nic, it's so good to see you as always. Please, come with me."

Maya was about to get their bags when she heard running footsteps and saw a young boy and girl racing down the stairs. *Monseigneur* struck his cane on the concrete, and the two giggled then stopped in front of Maya. *"Bonjour!"* they yelled out, grabbing the bags from the back of the car and racing back up the stairs into the house. She remembered what Benny had said earlier, that he'd sell his firstborn…yikes.

"Who were they?" Nic asked Pierre, handing him his car key chain.

"Jillian's grandchildren. They are twins—mischievous

little angels. Armand has been plying them with cookies all morning, and now we are paying for it."

Nic and Maya fell in line behind Pierre as they ascended the stairs.

"Who's that?" Maya whispered, her chin jutting to Pierre's back.

"The butler," Nic whispered.

Of course, she said to herself. The butler.

"*Bonjour*, Uncle. *Ça va*?" Nic said to Armand as they approached. Nic towered over the older man and gave him kisses on both cheeks.

"*Bien. Bien*, Nicolas, good to see you. This must be Albert's daughter. Mademoiselle Belcourt." He took Maya's hand and bowed, his face cracking into a smile that made her less nervous. "*Enchanté.*"

"Maya, may I introduce Armand Dechamps, the legend."

Armand scoffed while Maya smiled back. "It's a pleasure to meet you."

"I knew your father. The pleasure is mine. Please, come in. Tea is almost served." Armand offered Maya his arm and led them down a long arched hallway.

"I know you are only staying one night, but I want you to make yourself at home." They followed the long carpeted hallway past numerous rooms, all decorated in luxurious fabrics, large furniture, expensive-looking artwork and wall paintings that Maya assumed were originals.

"Those are lovely pianos," Maya said as they slowly strolled by a blue-walled room with black dueling grand pianos.

"Do you play?" Armand asked.

"Unfortunately, no."

He patted her hand. "Maybe we can get Nic to play for us later."

Maya looked at Nic over her shoulder. "You play?"

Nic frowned and shook his head.

"He's quite good, but shy," Armand whispered. Maya looked back just in time to catch Nic's smirk.

They passed the billiard room, the den—which was bigger than her apartment—an arched opening to a downward staircase that led to the kitchen, and the largest forked staircase she'd ever seen leading upstairs. Next to it was a small elevator.

They made themselves comfortable in a large family room with a fireplace, a giant U-shaped couch, plush chairs and several Persian rugs.

"Should we get right down to business?" Armand asked.

"Uncle—"

"Nicky, please. You never visit me unless it's about business. What's happened?" Nic shifted in his seat. "Or would you prefer to wait until after dinner?"

"No… Benny said you had overproduction and were letting the Van Dames broker it for you."

"You said you were phasing the brokerage out." Nic lowered his eyes, and Armand's shifted to Maya. "But that seems to have changed. Albert left you his part of the business, didn't he?"

"He did," Maya said confidently. "And we are here to tell you that we can handle any overproduction you have."

Armand cocked his head. "What do you know about wine?"

"Nothing," Maya said with a wide smile.

Armand laughed. "So honest. You remind me of my daughter-in-law. She's from New York City. Very tough."

"Uncle, you know I can handle any overproduction you have. But since when do you have overproduction?"

"Since Destin revamped my production line. Destin is my son, *chérie*. I get more juice from the squeeze, so to speak. It's remarkable."

"And did you promise the Van Dames your Pinot?"

"We haven't signed anything, but yes, we discussed it. They seem to have found someone who wants it."

"Yes. Benny."

"What? Out of the question. I won't allow that man to ruin my grapes. Turning them into that acidic hogwash he calls wine."

Maya and Nic looked at each other. Maybe they should have waited until after dinner.

"Uncle, Maya won the Vinothérapie bath at the Children First auction."

"Oh, it's pure heaven!" Maya turned at the lovely English female voice. An older woman in a day dress with blond hair streaked with gray set down a tray with a large teapot and mugs. "Nicky, you look so handsome, doesn't he, Armand?"

"You look lovely as usual, Madame Le Blanc." Nic rose and hugged the woman. "This is Maya, Albert's daughter."

"Oh, goodness, you are gorgeous, aren't you? Call

me Jillian, dear. I'm a shout away if you need anything. Your room has a little call button. Don't be afraid to use it. Oh, it's so nice to have you both here, isn't it, Armand?"

Armand was busy pouring his tea and loading it up with sugar cubes when Jillian took it from him just as he was about to drop in another cube.

"Armand, you know what the doctor said. One sugar and one glass of wine at dinner. Don't think I don't know how many cookies you had today."

Maya and Nic looked at each other.

Armand struck his cane on the floor. "Madame, give me back my tea."

Jillian ignored him and poured Maya and Nic's tea first, offering them the sugar cubes and milk, then poured Armand's tea, placing one sugar in its depths. "Here you go, you sneak," she said to a frowning Armand before turning back to Nic and Maya. "Now, don't be shy, dears, help yourselves to whatever you want. The twins have taken your bags to your room. Dinner will be at seven, very casual. How about I make arrangements for your spa baths around five?"

"That sounds lovely, Jillian. But we will need two rooms," Nic said.

"Oh my, I thought—" She waved it away. "Never mind. I'll make up the rosé room."

"*Merci*," Nic said.

"*Oui, merci*," Armand said from the side of his mouth.

Jillian winked at Armand and sipped the sweet tea as she walked out of the room.

"That woman is going be the end of me," Armand murmured. "It's hard to find good help these days."

Nic laughed. "Jillian has been running this house for over ten years."

"Don't remind me. Now, Maya, tell me about yourself."

Tea was relaxing, with Armand yawning after thirty minutes. "I'm sorry, I must retire for a nap before dinner. I'll see you in a few hours. Enjoy the bath."

"Shall we unpack?" Nic suggested.

They took the wide stairs to the second floor, and Nic dropped Maya off at her room, a large alcove space with a white canopy bed, pink walls, a fireplace and a reading nook that looked out over the back of the house. She could see vines for miles. Her bag lay on the corner stand, but as she got closer, she realized it wasn't her bag at all. It was Nic's. She grabbed the leather duffel and strode down the hall. Nic opened his door with a smile and her Louis Vuitton duffel on his arm.

"You better not have peeked in there," she said playfully.

"Ditto," he said, and they exchanged bags. Then he invited her in. His room was similar to hers, but the walls were cranberry and the king-size bed was massive.

"Your uncle hates Benny."

"He does, but it's an old friend type of hate. They've been rivals for so long that his reaction is second nature. I have faith you can turn him."

"Me? He's *your* uncle."

"Yeah, but you're the expert at creating demand."

"Is that another challenge? Was this your plan all along, to come here and watch me fail?"

"I don't think you are going to fail. The word isn't in your vocabulary." Her head jerked back. It was the nicest thing anyone had ever said to her.

She turned toward the door as he set out his toiletries. He looked like a schoolboy, his hair falling into his face, that giant bed waiting for him. "We'll get him at dinner. It might help to soften him up if you played the piano later."

"No."

"Why not?"

"I'm rusty."

"So go practice."

Nic jutted his chin out. "Go have your wine bath."

"You're not coming?" She heard the disappointment in her voice and fixed her pout into a flat line.

"I don't think so. I have some things to do here first."

She looked him up and down, and when he didn't meet her eyes she shrugged. "Okay. See you later."

She didn't want to mention it, but he'd seemed distant in the car, his gaze focused on the drive. And then in his room, he could barely look her in the eye. Maybe she was pushing too hard. Or he was angry that she was interfering with his plans. Whatever it was, she felt her foundation was shifting out from under her. She supposed that when she was back in LA, it would be gone altogether.

She made her way the short distance from the back of the mansion to the spa, stopping briefly to gaze in awe at the miles and miles of vines that covered the landscape. She continued on a stone path to a vine-covered building that looked more like a small palace. The double doors opened before she even got to the entrance.

"Welcome, Maya." A smiling woman in a flowing purple sari opened her arms and bowed. Maya entered and awkwardly reciprocated the bow, noticing the Asian music lilting in the background, an altar of Palo Santo scented wood next to white candles, a giant mural of Kali and the shoes in cubbyholes against the wall. "Please take off your shoes and follow me. Your journey begins now."

They made their way across soft carpets and heated floors to a cozy rest area with wall-length lockers. Each locker held a white fluffy robe to change into, and Maya was given the option to enjoy the table full of teas and small plates of dried fruits before starting on her "journey." Maya panicked when she remembered that she didn't have a bathing suit, but she was told not to worry, that they recommend going "sky clad as nature intended," but bathing suits were available at her request.

Nude under her robe, with hot tea in her palms, Maya went through the large door labeled Spa and was taken aback. She was teleported from a modern lounge into a midcentury Roman bath with glittering beige stone walls. In the center was a giant bubbling mineral pool and several smaller pools marked with temperatures ranging from warm to freezing cold. Glass doors to saunas lined the wall across the room. She knew it was a weekday, but she had expected to see at least a few loungers. Nic had described the spa as quite popular, but from what she could tell, she was alone.

"Maya?" a deep voice asked. A man in a black T-shirt and pants came forward from a darkened corner across the room. He bowed slightly and held a towel in his hand. "I'm Renard. I'll be your servant today. If you're ready, I've prepared your wine bath."

Ooh. Servant? Yes, please. "I'm ready." She smiled and followed Renard into a beautiful open room lined with candles and fresh roses in giant urns. A round tub large enough for six people sat in the middle of the space, with fresh rose petals floating on top of the water and an open bottle of wine on its rim. Renard left the room while she disrobed and sank inch by inch into the warmth, finding a stone seat that allowed her to relax shoulder deep in what she assumed was diluted wine. She bade him enter when he knocked.

"And how is the temperature?"

"Heaven." Maya sighed, leaning her head and back against the tub. The lights dimmed and her peripheral vision caught the wineglass next to her filling with ruby liquid. She wasn't sure she could even reach for the wine; her bones were melting.

"So am I sitting in actual wine?"

"No, *mademoiselle*, just the antioxidant extracts from the grape itself, which is why the water isn't colored but opaque, and also darkened by the color of the tub. Don't worry, I can't see anything you don't want me to see," he teased. Maya relaxed even more, and she didn't flinch when Renard began lightly massaging her shoulders. With Renard's soothing touch and the soft music surrounding her, Maya breathed deep and let her eyes drift closed. But the deep voice she heard next wasn't Renard's.

"May I join you?"

Her eyes snapped open at Nic's voice. He stood by the tub in knee-length bathing trunks, but the rest of him was all skin: muscled chest, bulging arms, cut torso. Had the water gotten warmer? Her gaze landed on his full lips, then finally to his curling hair and dark gaze, which was angrily locked on Renard.

Oh, boy.

Chapter 12

Maya was staring at him, while he was staring daggers at Renard. The man's hands were all over her shoulders, given full license by the way her caramel-colored hair was piled high on her head. Renard's long fingers caressed down her arm and grazed the water, which was just covering the buoyant flesh of her breasts.

He licked his lips in a mixture of anger and lust. She wasn't wearing a suit.

"Welcome," Renard said with a smile, the disarming kindness making Nic's jaw clench. She must have seen his reaction, because her eyes flashed and she stopped Renard's hands with a gentle touch of her own.

"I thought you were busy," she said to him as Renard moved away and poured a second glass of wine, placing it within his reach.

"I've finished," Nic said, stepping with his long legs into the tub and settling in across from her. The truth was, he'd been having a hard time getting images of her in the bath out of his mind, and his visions did her no justice. When he'd walked in, she could have been Aphrodite served by one of her many conquests. "But if you want to be alone, I'd be happy to—"

"No," she said lightly. "There's room for a whole family in here."

"Will you be needing anything else?" Renard asked from the corner.

"No." Nic's tone was gruff, and Maya tried to talk over him with a sweet "*Non, merci*, Renard."

Renard bowed and silently left.

"You're naked," Nic accused.

Maya pulled her arms out of the water and hitched them across the back of the tub. "They recommend it. Sky clad or whatever."

Her new position pushed her beasts from the water a bit more, and she seemed to know it.

He couldn't stop staring, the water waving and splashing over her skin. Maybe she *was* Aphrodite. Maybe that was why he couldn't resist her. Well, two could play at that game.

"Is that so?" He reached under the water and slipped off his trunks in one swift movement, pulling them from the water and tossing them on the floor with a loud squish. He mimicked her position, spreading his arms and leaning back comfortably. "This does seem more comfortable."

She looked at him from under her lids, then he

watched her gaze dip to the spot between his legs before she smoothly turned to reach for her wine.

"You can't see anything," he said.

She smirked. "Well, neither can you." Her lips touched the glass and he got hard. Thank God, the water was dark.

"Did Renard see anything?" He tried to keep the jealous tone from his voice. Failed.

"If he did, he didn't say anything. Because he's a professional. He's my servant," she threw at him.

His brows went up. "So you want to be served."

"Don't we all?" she said sweetly over the rim of her glass. He'd be happy to serve her all night.

"What else was Renard going to serve you?"

She shrugged, disturbing the water and his resolve. "I don't know. We were interrupted."

"So sorry."

"Don't be. I'm happy to sit here and soak up these antioxidants." She closed her eyes.

"You know we're just sitting in the leftover crap from the wine-making process, don't you?"

Her eyes opened to slits. "Don't ruin this for me. First you chase away my servant, and now you're knocking the bath."

"I'm not saying it's not full of antioxidants. I'm just saying it's repurposed trash. It's brilliant really."

"You should tell your uncle."

"He didn't think of it. I did."

She cocked her head. "I don't believe you."

He shrugged and took a sip of his wine. The cab franc. Paired with a bath and a beautiful woman. Perfect. "It's true. The skins, leaves, stems and seeds—

called the marc—are all still high in polyphenols, aka antioxidants. You can soak in the extracts here or do a wrap or scrub. It makes a good pumice."

"I didn't know you were such a beauty expert."

"I'm not, except I can recognize it when it's right in front of me."

She blushed, and he felt it in his groin. "If I didn't know better, I'd say you were flirting. Still after those shares, huh?"

One side of his mouth turned up. "Something like that."

"I'm going to ignore you." A tiny smile danced on her lips as she closed her eyes.

"Should I call Renard?"

"And have you stare daggers at him while I get a massage? No, *merci*."

"Is that what you want? A massage?"

She didn't move, but one eye opened. "You should stay right where you are." Her foot grazed him and he caught it, pulling a small gasp from her lips.

"Yes, *mademoiselle*," he said, running his thumb over the sole of her foot. She didn't fight as he began to knead the ball of her foot, her sigh music to his ears. Yes, they had decided that sex was off-limits, but maybe they could play a little.

Her head lolled back as he transferred her other foot into his hands. He moved upward to the delicate joint of her ankle, and bolder still to the smooth skin of her calf.

Her eyes remained closed and she made no movement to stop him. Like a shark, he moved forward, using long strokes over her calf and up to the back of her thigh, reveling in how perfectly her curves fit into his hands.

Inch by aching inch, his fingers moved up her inner thigh, and little by little, his upper body moved above hers. He ignored the insistent pulsing of his lower half, bent on offering her his massaging skills where she needed them most.

One finger poised, then two, he slid forward and grazed the plump flush of her opening. She turned her head, her lips inches from his.

"I think you're trying to serve me."

He held back the urge to drive his fingers home, waiting for her permission. A pulsing beat passed. "I am." His voice was thick with need. They stared at each other, breathless. Her hand ran up his arm and she clung to him, pulling him toward her.

He kissed her then, a hard brushing kiss of pent-up desire that she voraciously reciprocated. He trembled, his fingers about to finish their mission.

"Ahem." A throat cleared.

Nic shielded Maya and whipped his head furiously toward the sound. There was Renard with that stupid grin on his face. "Madame Jillian has sent a reminder that she is serving dinner in thirty minutes." The man bowed and backed his way out of the room.

"Oh no!" Nic spit.

Maya began to laugh, the sound only urging on his engorged lower half. "You should see your face."

He was in physical pain, but the sound of her pleasure was beautiful.

"Humph." He slowly moved away, knowing thirty minutes was not enough time. Not for what he wanted to do to her.

"For the record," she said, "you were an excellent servant."

Her glossy lips beckoned him, and he cursed their interruption. There was something about that kiss, a lover's kiss filled with intimacy. It was the briefest taste of passion, but it had left a stain on his lips. "We're not done. Just on hold."

"Is that why you're still crouched in the water? Things are 'on hold.'"

"Things are deflating."

"Poor thing." Maya rose suddenly and he jerked back, as if seeing Aphrodite reborn. Water streamed down her body, glistening over her breasts and dripping from the hardened tips. Rivulets chased over her flat stomach and converged in a waterfall over the hairless mound between her slick thighs. She touched herself briefly, her finger tracing her folds, waiting for him. He couldn't breathe, nor would he ever go soft again.

He imagined himself a thirsty beggar, and she the goddess who offered him a drink.

His breath returned when she turned and stepped from the tub, his eyes roaming over her perfectly round bottom and back up to where tendrils of damp hair teased her nape. In one fell swoop, a towel shielded him from what he wanted most.

Her gaze was heavy when she turned to him. "See you at dinner."

He rose from the tub when she left, hoping the cool air would do some good on his rigid erection. Never had a woman had such an effect on him. Every brush of the towel had him harder still. At this rate, he wasn't making it to dinner. He padded into the hall and ignored Renard's smile as he slowly lowered himself into the cold pool.

Nic and Armand were already at the table when she arrived in the dining room, the two men stopping what sounded like a heated debate. Nic's gaze softened when he saw her, then he smiled a secret smile as Jillian ushered her into a seat next him. Jillian moved quickly, pouring wine and placing plates of food on the table: roast chicken, potatoes and various steamed vegetables. The children were keeping themselves busy snacking on little bits of cheese, apples and crackers.

"How was your bath, my dear?" Armand asked, his smile still tinged with tension.

"It was wonderful," she said, ignoring the rush of heat that stole through her body. Beside her, Nic wore a white button-down and camel trousers, simple yet masculine. She held back a powerful urge to touch him.

"I'm glad you enjoyed it. You are welcome to anytime." Armand waited for Jillian, who slid into a chair next to the children, and he began the procession of serving himself, then passing the plate on. He addressed Maya. "I'm sure you have questions about your father. You can ask me anything. He and my brother were best friends and they let me hang around sometimes, as younger boys always want to do. How is your mother doing?"

"She's well and happy with my stepfather. They're still in California."

"Ah, California. Albert talked a lot about Napa Valley, but I've never made the trip. Nicky, you used to go, didn't you?"

Nic finished chewing his food. "A few times. We worked with one winery there for a short while. Albert was trying to establish a market for the business."

Armand cut himself another piece of chicken. "Your father had an excellent palate and a good eye for quality. My brother did, too, I suppose, but as vintners go, Albert was superior. He practically ran the business himself after your mother left Gabe and went back to Spain." Maya realized Armand had directed the latter to Nic, whose gaze had dropped to his plate. She touched his arm, the small gesture resulting in a bolstered grin.

"I never met your mother, Maya, but I believe Gabriel did. I remember Gabriel going to California for the wedding, then he called me a few days later saying the wedding had been called off and he and Albert were coming home."

"Whose wedding?" Nic asked.

"Albert's. Stop that at once," Armand interrupted himself, distracted by the children's napkin war.

Maya felt her breathing shorten. A wedding? That would explain her mother's tears, but why wouldn't she have mentioned that? What did he do? What makes a man leave his unborn child?

A strong hand found hers under the table and infused a level of strength she didn't realize she needed. Briefly, his concerned gaze flicked to her, then turned back to the table.

"What happened after that?" Nic cautiously asked.

"I don't know. Gabe never spoke of it, and when he and Albert started grooming the land, I barely saw them. I may have even gone back to university by then."

Armand jabbed a fork into his chicken and shoved a sizable amount in his mouth, aware that the children were mimicking his every move. Giggles erupted when they lost their food from their mouths, but Maya's focus was on her plate, her appetite waning.

"Now that I think of it, Albert did go back to California at the end of the year. Just before Christmas. I don't remember why exactly—"

"I was born in December." It came out too curt. Even the children stopped playing.

"I was born in 'cember," said one of the kids.

"Me too, I was born in 'cember."

"You were not, you little ruffians," Jillian chuckled, trying to get them to eat more of their food.

Armand softly placed his fork on his plate and gazed at Maya. "Yes, that would make sense." There was something sad in his eyes, as if he were remembering something else that he wasn't mentioning. "Would you like more chicken? Wine, maybe?"

Nic looked at her and squeezed her hand in her lap. "No, thank you."

"Nic and I were discussing my overproduction. I have no desire to sell my grapes to Benny, or anyone else for that matter. I may just keep them for the spa or ship them to my son in Brazil."

"Okay," Maya said, finishing off her potatoes and pushing away her plate.

Nic and Armand looked at each other, then stared at Maya. She leaned back in her chair. "What?"

"I thought you would put up more of a fight," Armand said.

"I thought you would be more concerned about your brother's business, but I understand. Nothing lasts forever, right? Not relationships and certainly not business."

"Erm, right." Armand frowned.

"It's a shame that we can't hold on to the things we love. Twenty years of blood, sweat and tears, gone in an instant. Or transferred in a few legal documents. Maybe it's best to just pull the plug, right, Nic?" He was looking at her like she'd gone crazy. "We'll sell the vineyard to Claude, and you can have your bed-and-breakfast," she said to Nic, "and—"

"Sell the vineyard to Claude? Claude Rhone?"

Maya looked up innocently. "I think that's his name. He does the rosé? For now, he was talking about moving into some cabernets." She'd gambled and had been right. Claude was a competitor of equal standing, but with more land, he could produce more wines. That last part about the reds she'd made up.

Nic cleared his throat. "Yes, Uncle. You know I've been taking about dissolving the—"

"What do you want?" He was looking directly at Maya, his gaze piercing. Finally, there he was, the man who would sell his firstborn.

"Just the grapes," Maya said softly.

"Not to Benny!"

"Of course not. We'll sell it to Benny's friend Remy. That will keep his panties in a bunch for months."

Armand blinked, and the table held its breath as he began a staccato snorting sound that turned into a full-blown wicked laugh. Even the children looked scared. "Oh, my word," he said on a sigh, wiping away a tear.

"I haven't laughed like that in a decade. *Mademoiselle*, you have a deal."

Jillian jumped up from her seat. "Sounds like we should celebrate. Who's ready for dessert?"

Maya barely noticed when Jillian left the room and came back with two pies. Nic was looking at her in awe, and her idea of a celebration didn't include an audience.

After dinner, Armand coaxed Nic into playing the piano, and since they were celebrating he grudgingly agreed. The family reclined on the plush couches as Nic's tall frame hunched over the keys, his long fingers trailing expertly as he pounded out Gershwin and softly played Chopin.

Maya couldn't help but wonder if this was what her life would have been like had she known her father—family gatherings on vineyards and piano recitals after dinner. It struck her then that it would be over soon. She was pulled from her thoughts when Nic played Elton John at Jillian's request. He looked over and smiled, making her realize that soon their attraction, or whatever it was, would be over, too.

She was somber when they headed to bed, her hand on the doorknob when Nic swiftly turned and kissed her fully, thoroughly. "You were incredible tonight. Watching you… It's exhilarating."

She lowered her gaze, but he put a finger under her chin and lifted her face to his. "What's wrong?"

"Reality is setting in. I have to go home soon."

He looked at her, his mouth a flat line. He knew she was right, but slowly he began to shake his head. "I told you, we're not finished."

Chapter 13

Maya was in Nic's arms and splayed on his bed in two heartbeats. Her lips were soft and supple. He opened her mouth with his, loving the way her tongue slid against his. They were both impatient, their foreplay in the bath having been prematurely interrupted by a long dinner, leaving their desire on simmer.

Until now.

Their kisses grew from sweet to carnal in a matter of seconds; their hands ripped at each other's clothes, and their mouths quickly devoured every inch of skin as it was revealed. There was no teasing banter, no sexy laughter, now replaced by the urgent need to give themselves fully to the other.

His brain was on primal mode, registering nothing but her arms tightening around his neck, the small whimpers coming from her throat, her fingers in his hair and her sweet legs spread around his waist.

He drove deep in one swift motion, barely pulling back before surging forward again, rolling his hips against her heavenly body, stretching himself to nip at her breasts.

"God, Nic," she groaned into his ear. She kissed him hard, pushing her pelvis against him, grinding and rolling. He gritted his teeth at the rough pleasure that was somewhat painful. Never leaving her mouth, he pumped harder, pressing her close, the heat of her driving him into a state of pure feeling.

"You're so clever," he whispered as he drove her harder. "So sexy. So damn beautiful." Her fingers dug hard into his shoulders and met each driving thrust.

There was nothing but her, but this.

He felt the first contractions of her body tear through his own. His mind told him to slow down, but his body met hers kiss for kiss and thrust for thrust. Her breathing changed and her knees fell open, allowing him to push her further, drive in deeper, and once he realized that he'd lost all manner of self-control, her body seized and jerked around him, her long wail registering only briefly before his orgasm took over and he pumped uncontrollably inside of her, his mouth on her throat and his arms locked around her body.

Once his brain stirred and his surroundings came back to him, he found Maya with her eyes closed, breathing erratically. He shifted his weight off her but kept her close, pushing her hair from her face. She turned him into a raving sex maniac with just a look. He wasn't sure how he felt about it, not liking to be out of control.

"Mmm, you are so good to me," she breathed. "I love the way we fit."

He smiled. Maybe out of control wasn't so bad.

They lay awake in Nic's bed, tangled in each other's arms with Nic telling her about his painful piano lessons his mother had made him take. And how when his mother left, he thought if he practiced more, she would come back.

Maya thought of the childhood pictures she'd found. "I wish I had at least known him for a bit before he left."

Nic shifted onto his elbow, his gaze a caress. "I have something for you."

He threw on his pants and padded barefoot from the room, returning in seconds with a book in his hand.

"Is that my father's journal? I thought I gave that to Nathan."

Nic looked at her under his lids. "I took it from him."

"He's a kid, Nic."

He took her lips in a long kiss. "I know, but I'm jealous anyway. And I was curious, too."

Maya settled into the crook of his shoulder. "What's it say?"

"Most of it is daily musings and some business stuff, but I'd like to read you some important parts."

Nic flipped through the pages he'd previously marked, his eyes sliding left and right over the page. He cleared his throat.

"'The cancer Gabe kept secret had spread and become untreatable. Stubborn fool. He worried over the vineyard more than he worried over himself. His dying wish was to leave his son his share of the business and I

promised to make it so even as I know Nic's heart lies in real estate. Nic seems unable to deal with his feelings. It makes me long to hug my daughter. Who doesn't know me, and yet I think about her every day.'"

They were both silent for a moment, her father's sadness rocking them both to the core. Maya took a deep breath against the unfamiliar feelings ballooning in her chest. Her father thought about her. Yet he never wanted to know her? The heartbreak and confusion was a strange mix.

Nic turned another page, still reading.

"'Maya has graduated summa cum laude from Stanford. Even as I stood in the back of the auditorium, a stranger in the shadows, I couldn't have been more proud. Sandra looked well and although she was alone, I didn't make my presence known. Donating to the university had allowed certain privileges, such as being able to provide money to my daughter through anonymous grants.'"

"Oh, my God," Maya whispered. "They said those grants were because of my academic standing."

"Albert and I had an argument once about the amount of money he was spending on charities. Now I know. Are you ready to hear a little more?" She nodded and felt his kiss on her head.

"'I wonder if she remembers me in fragments of her young memories. Before Sandra remarried, I had agreed to stay out of Maya's life, but only if Sandra brought her to France for a time. She was four or five, loud and precocious, throwing a tantrum one minute and laughing the next. She looked at me with such caution, not knowing I was her father. Sandra and I fought

almost daily, the weight of our agreement too great on me. I had lost everything. When Sandra left, if felt like she was leaving me for the second time and taking my only joy with her.'"

She couldn't move. What she had heard was a contradiction to everything her mother had told her. Everything.

Nic snapped the book shut. "Are you okay?" he whispered, curling his arm tighter around her.

Even as she nodded, she felt the tears form in her eyes. With a stricken look, he threw the book on the desk.

"I'm sorry. Maybe I shouldn't have read it."

"No, don't be sorry. I'm glad." Her voice trembled and caught. She couldn't finish her words. He pushed away their sheets and brought her into his body. She murmured an apology for getting tears on his chest.

"Nonsense," he whispered.

She closed her eyes at the kisses on her hair and the rub of his hands over her back. He felt so good. So strong. Then she quickly pulled away and cupped his face. "What about you? There were things in there about your father."

Nic nodded, moving his face to the side to kiss her palm. "There were some things I didn't know, like how he had hidden the cancer. My mother made it no secret that she wouldn't leave Spain, but I didn't know that Albert had spoken to her many times on my behalf and had paid for her home using my father's dividends. The business isn't failing because Albert was a bad businessman. He was taking care of his family."

"Those damn expenses," Maya whispered. Nic

chuckled. Maya got serious and looked into Nic's eyes. "If I give you my shares, I don't want you to sell. Nathan can run it. Or hire someone else. Don't give it away. Please don't give it away."

"I won't. I promise." Nic kissed her protests away, rolling on top of her and sliding into her in one fluid motion. She closed her eyes and arched her back toward him, running her hands down his back, then rolling their bodies over so she straddled him. He pulled himself up to sit and nuzzled her breasts. Her rhythm was purposely slow, wanting to feel—really feel—every stroke, every caress, every inch of pleasure that Nic gave her.

She smiled into his eyes and buried her fingers in his hair, letting them drift down over his shoulders in a light caress. Their hands roamed and played, gently pushing and pulling, their lips never far from each other's.

Maya didn't know how long they held each other like that, Nic seated with Maya straddled on top, but their heartbeats seemed to beat together, and she was sure they were sharing breaths. She felt like she was floating in a state of continuous pleasure, until her fingers curled and his forearms tightened, her body shook and his trembled, their tongues reached for each other at the same time, and her nipples registered the wire of his chest hair.

Then they came together in wave after wave of colorful, mind-blowing, passionate gratification that seemed to jump from her to him and him to her in a continuous motion until they were sated and exhausted, sleeping peacefully in each other's arms.

Chapter 14

"**M**erci for a lovely time." Maya hugged Armand tightly, then put her arms around Jillian and gave the kids kisses on both of their chubby cheeks.

"Come back soon, my dear. You're welcome any-time," Armand said, stepping back from the car. "Nic, we loved to see you as always. Maybe now that we have some business together, you'll visit more often?"

"Of course, Uncle." Nic smiled. "Nathan and I will be in touch."

The two finished their goodbyes and climbed into the car for their short drive back to the vineyard.

The doors closed and they buckled themselves in. He was watching her when she looked up, and her blood slowed. They'd made love well into the night, only fall-ing asleep a few hours before dawn. She'd woken to his body folded around hers, his breathing slow and soft on her neck. Willing herself to keep still, she had committed everything to memory: his skin, his smell, his weight against her. He promised to keep what their fathers had built, and with that agreement, she felt that her purpose in Paris had been fulfilled. Which was good, because she only had three more days until her return flight to LA.

Their time together was ending.

Suddenly she didn't want to leave. She wanted to stay and explore Paris—she hadn't even gotten to shop. She wanted to go for walks through the vines in the morning. She wanted to eat those little croissants that Nathan made in the mornings. She wanted to wake up in Nic's arms.

He glanced toward her. "Are you okay?"

His voice was husky with little sleep.

"Yeah, I'm just thinking about those breakfast bites that Nathan makes." She stared straight ahead, pulling herself together. She'd come to France and taken a nice break from reality, but soon she'd have to go back to LA. Back to her life.

What life?

"I meant what I said last night," he said quietly. "I've taken selling off the table."

"I know." She half smiled. "When we get back, I'll call Jen and let her know we're moving forward with the share transfer."

She heard him sigh. "What's that dramatic sigh for?"

His mouth turned down and he shrugged, staring

over the steering wheel as if trying to find words. "Have you thought about staying?"

"What?"

"Would this life be so bad? If you stayed?"

She felt her heart speed up. What was he saying?

"Well…no…but giving everything up and staying here wasn't exactly on my agenda." And yet this morning it was all she could think about.

He glanced at her, and she saw genuine concern before he shifted his gaze back to the road. "Besides, I think we've established that I know nothing of this business. I can't even speak French. My palate is weak—"

"Your palate isn't weak."

"Well, it's not like yours."

"We can remedy that. You'll just have to drink more wine."

"Sounds grueling," she teased. Between her wine bath, the few glasses she had at dinner and the bottle they shared the night before, she wasn't sure she could ever look at another bottle of wine without thinking about him. By the way he was biting his lip, she wondered if he was thinking the same.

They glanced at each other and tried to chuckle away the electricity that seemed to be jumping between them. *Leave me alone,* she said to her raging hormones. She was going to give this man up in a few days, and she'd never be able to do it when she felt like this…like her whole world came down to just being next to him.

Like she loved him.

Don't love him. Don't!

Nic reached into the compartment between their seats

and clutched his phone. After a few seconds it glowed and began buzzing nonstop, making Maya glance at it. She almost laughed at the dance it was doing, until she saw a string of missed calls from Daphne. She hadn't realized that his phone had been off most of the weekend. Just seeing her name was a gross reminder of what she had just vowed. *Do not fall in love with him!*

Nic took his phone and made a call through the dashboard. "Nathan! Guess who got my uncle to give us his overproduction?"

"Thank God. I've been calling you all morning."

"Apologies. But we have good news. Uncle caved."

"He was no match for Maya?"

"He didn't stand a chance," Nic said proudly, his hand clasping Maya's and bringing it to his lips. Her heart filled when he kept her hand in his and rested both in his lap. "I saw that you called. We'll be back in half an hour or so."

"Oh. I thought maybe you were going straight to the hotel. Joc called to say your casino tables have been delivered but no one knows where they go."

Nic's mouth dropped open. "Oh no. Nathan, I completely forgot. I'll, um…" Nic glanced at Maya. "I'll call Joc."

He thanked Nate and hung up, then he pulled off the road halfway into a field and yanked on the brake.

"What are you doing?" Maya asked. In answer, he put both palms on either side of her face and pulled her mouth to his. Instantly, she was lost, opening her mouth to his onslaught of lips and tongue. The electricity she had felt earlier bubbled over into a rush of sensations that left her mindless. His hands were everywhere and she reciprocated, running her palms over his biceps and down his torso. The kiss ended in a slow, leisurely release of lips, their breaths mingling as they tried to find air.

"What was that for?" Maya asked softly.

"I've been wanting to do that all morning," he whispered. "And now I have work to do in the city. Hotel work, but I don't want to take you back to the vineyard. Come to the event tonight?"

"Is it formal? I only have cocktail dresses at the hotel."

He shook his head, then smiled as he punched the Karma forward. "Looks like we're going shopping."

They arrived in Paris by midmorning and stopped for lunch at a cozy corner bistro, where Nic made a few business calls while Maya sipped her café au lait and people-watched out of the window. It gave her a chance to see him in his element, which she found strangely relaxing. He spoke French, so she could only guess whom he was speaking with, but she smiled when he interrupted himself and apologized for being so rude. She didn't think he was being rude; she was finding it very sexy. Like crawl-under-the-table-and-unzip-his-pants sexy.

She rolled her eyes at herself. This was what happened when you finally had incredible sex, then realized you would never have it again. That last part had her reaching for her coffee, spilling it, then running to the bathroom. She dabbed at her stained blouse, which did no good, then caught a glimpse of herself in the mirror. Her lip quivered, then she hung her head and let a few tears fall into the sink. She was leaving in two days, going back to, well, nothing, but the reasons for her trip had been fulfilled. She'd found her father in the rows of vines and the pages of his journal. He had loved her; that was why he left her the business.

There were still questions, of course, which her mother needed to answer, but overall she was ready to move forward with what she'd come there to do. And now that Nic saw viability in the brokerage again, she felt comfortable signing over the shares to him. He deserved them, she told herself. More than she did…right? She had planned to sign his share transfer papers that afternoon, but now it would have to wait until tomorrow. Which felt better.

Nic was off the phone when she came back to the table. He took her hand across the table. "What if I told you we may have met before?"

"You mean in our dreams?" she teased.

"I was thinking of when we were a bit younger." His voice became careful. "I think your mother brought you here once when you were a child. There's reference to it in the journal."

She contemplated what to say. "There's a picture in his armoire of me as a toddler. So I think you're right."

"How do you feel about that?"

"About us meeting? I don't remember it."

"Maybe our souls met that day," he said.

"You are very romantic today."

"I'm romantic every day when I'm around you. It's strange."

"Strange good?"

"Yes. But I meant how do you feel about your mother—"

"Lying to me," she finished.

His face scrunched. "I was going to say about her trying to protect you."

"Protect me from my father? Yeah, he seemed real dangerous. Trust me, she was lying to protect herself." Maya swallowed her anger. She didn't want to feel it, not then.

"I didn't mean to upset you."

"It's not you."

"Have you talked to her?"

"No," she said to his concerned expression. "But I will."

"When?"

"Later. Right now I want to enjoy our time."

"We don't have much left, do we?"

She shook her head.

"You could stay, you know."

She looked at him, his eyes lowered, then he caught hers again.

"No, I need to get back home. My life is waiting."

"About the shares. I was thinking—"

"Tomorrow. Let's do it tomorrow. We can go to James's office. He'll have copies of your paperwork. I'll have Jen call in, as well."

Nic bit the inside of his cheek and squeezed her hand tighter, as if he didn't want to let go. Then he nodded slowly. "As you wish."

They finished their coffee in silence, holding hands,

staring out the window. Words with feelings hung in the air but were never spoken. Nic's phone jumped and he quickly grabbed it, only to grimace and turn it over.

"She's still looking for you?" Maya asked softly.

"She's always looking for me."

"You've never slept with her? Not once?"

He sighed, like a man caught. "It was a sloppy drunken thing. It was nothing."

"She thinks it was something."

"It was five years ago, and I haven't touched her since. Had I known I would be paying for it for the rest of my life, I never would have even kissed her."

Maya twisted her lips, unconvinced a woman would be pining over a man for five years without encouragement. "Why don't you just sit her down and tell her you're taken."

His gaze locked on hers. "Am I taken?"

Alarm bells went off in Maya's head. God, why did she always say the wrong thing? That sounded clingy. "I mean not interested."

He stared at Maya for a moment. "Are you finished?" he asked in a low voice.

She nodded without looking at him.

"Then let's find you a dress."

Maya had been to Paris twice for business and had seen the inside of many a hotel bar with a nice dinner peppered in, but other than the occasional visit to the Louvre and the Eiffel Tower, Maya hadn't been super-impressed.

But seeing the city through Nic's eyes was like seeing a whole other world. With her hand in his, Nic took

Maya on an errand run that included his caterer, where they sampled the hors d'oeuvres to be delivered at the hotel, and his wine merchant. The champagne was already on its way, but they stayed and sampled a pink cava from Spain. Nic insisted it tasted better when sucked from her lips. Maya agreed.

Maya had two Nutella crepes and was finishing off a third when she and Nic rounded the corner onto Avenue Montaigne. White-and-gold mini-mansions of luxury lined both sides of the street while the surrounding trees were draped in white lights.

Louis Vuitton, Chanel, Balmain—the list of luxury was endless, beckoning Maya to unleash her credit cards from her purse like ninja throwing stars.

"Did you want to go inside?" Nic chuckled.

She had been staring at the gold-colored tulle gown in the window of the Dior Atelier. Honestly, that gown would look amazing on her, and who cared if she didn't actually have a royal ball to attend?

"Why not?" she said around a mouthful of crepe. She took the last bite and stashed her garbage, then set her sights on the double doors, which were opened by a stone-faced footman. Rows of satin, lace and silk hung on the walls, and mannequins looked more elegant than she'd ever dreamed. She vaguely heard a cheerful *bonjour* from the woman who made her way toward them when Maya peeked into an adjacent room and found the ready-to-wear items on display by several more mannequins.

She stopped. Stared.

A red pantsuit in a feminine cut with a simple black bustier underneath. Boss Red.

"It's perfect, no? Feminine and elegant but bold enough for the office."

"I'll take it." Maya blinked. The woman clapped her hands in delight and snapped her fingers at a sales associate.

"I love it," Nic said in her ear. "But this is a formal event."

She whirled around. "This is for me. Not your event."

"All right." He looked in her eyes, trying to gauge her mood. She wasn't sure what mood she was in, either. Nic glanced at the manager. "May we see some cocktail gowns? And I need to pick up my tuxedo." Then he pulled out his wallet and handed Maya his black card. "I have to stop at the jewelers, then get to the hotel for preparation. They have my account number here so they will charge that, but if you want to shop around at other stores, use this." He caressed her cheek. "Get whatever you want."

"You're crazy. I can afford a dress."

"I want to buy it for you."

"No—"

"Yes. And I'll be angry if you don't allow me to." He kissed her protests away, then took his suit from the attendant standing to the side. *"Merci."* He turned to Maya. "Have fun."

Maya watched him walk out into the street. Still frowning, she turned back around and was met with a single row of sales attendants, each holding a number of floor-length, sparkling gowns.

Chapter 15

"Well, don't you look spiffy," Joc said as he slid behind the bar and grabbed a bottle of bourbon.

"As do you in your black chef's coat. *Merci* for wearing a shirt this time. What are you doing with that?" Nic asked absently. He'd been waiting for Maya at the end of the bar for what seemed like hours.

"Cooking, mate. What you pay me for. And you're the one who ordered the loincloths last time, remember?"

Nic smirked and his gaze slid back to the ballroom entrance, which was becoming increasingly packed with guests. In the front of the room, young and old tried their luck at the rows of slot machines while poker and blackjack tables were packed with amateur gamblers. Roulette tables spun continuously across the room from the bar, and the roar of the craps tables pulled his gaze up the stairs to the second floor. Whatever entrance she decided to use, he had an eye on it.

"Which charity is this again?"

"Action Against Hunger."

"Where's your date?" Joc asked.

"Dressing." Nic downed his old-fashioned and had the bartender make him another. Maya had texted him hours ago that she had made it back to the hotel and was getting ready in the penthouse suite. He'd debated joining her, but thought maybe it was best to wait for an invitation. Their conversation at lunch had him questioning his every move. The minute "am I taken?" came out of his mouth, he'd regretted it. He must have looked—what did Nathan call it? Thirsty? And apparently that wasn't a good look.

"Someone's thirsty."

"What? I am not."

Joc cocked an eyebrow at the brand-new old-fashioned in his hand and the two empty glasses that were soon swept away by the barkeep. "I'm just waiting."

"Well, slow it down, eh? You don't want to scare off your date, unless it's her, and then I'll be happy to take over for you. My God, who is that, and is she staying here?"

Nic pulled his gaze from the front door and looked up the stairs. He ran his eyes over the throng of guests, and then suddenly it was like he and the vision before him were the only two people in the room. Maya was standing at the top of the stairs in a strapless nude-colored dress that was covered in silver crystals from the bodice to the small train that followed her across the floor. Her deep red lips parted in a smile, and she gave him a small wave before gracefully moving down the stairs. Nic was frozen, watching her body glisten as she moved closer toward him. Strappy silver heels peeked from below her dress with each step, and his heart literally flip-flopped.

He felt a hard shove on the back of his shoulder. "What is wrong with you? Go get her!"

Nic shook himself and straightened from the bar, hurrying toward the end of the stairs to where she was quickly approaching.

"Hey, stranger," she said first, because he still couldn't find his tongue.

Her hair was piled on top of her head in a smooth bun. Her eyelids sparkled. Diamonds dangled from her ears. Her throat, chest and bare shoulders shimmered, beckoning for a touch. He took her hand and brought her knuckles to his lips, but he didn't let her go.

"You look stunning." A floral scent surrounded him.

"Thank you. You, as well. Oh, before I forget." She held out his black card.

He looked at her disapprovingly. "You didn't use it."

"No, I figure you'll pay enough tomorrow when you get your shares." She smiled up at him, but he couldn't return it, not at the thought of her leaving.

"No business talk tonight."

She shrugged a small shoulder. "If you insist. But we can settle the shares tomorrow, right?"

"James will open for us tomorrow afternoon," he said, already feeling her slipping away. He held out his arm and welcomed her small hand in the crook of his arm. She tightened her grip, and his hand came over hers.

"Great." She sighed, her gaze surveying the carpet before floating back up to meet his. He could tell she felt it, too. "I see blackjack tables."

Nic produced a few shinny casino chips from his pockets. "For the lady."

Her smile lightened his mood. She surveyed the one-hundred-euro chips. "Thank you. But I warn you, I've been known to break the bank."

"I'm not worried. The house always wins."

They started at blackjack, where they both lost, but it didn't matter. Because she was still here, and he still had twenty-four hours to figure out if he could make her stay.

"You're still here?" said a familiar feminine voice. Maya turned with a smile that died on her lips. Daphne. She looked immaculate in a black beaded floor-length dress, like a vampire. Maya glanced across the room at the bar where Nic was dealing with a drunk guest.

"I am. And what business is it of yours?"

"Just that I thought you would have sold Nic your shares so we could take over the vineyard."

"We?"

"Nic and I. Oh, I see. He didn't tell you that part." Maya kept her cool. Daphne was just trying to rile her up. "I heard you had a lovely trip to Dechamps."

How the hell did she know that? "I'm surprised you heard about that at all. Nic seemed reluctant to answer his phone the millionth time you called."

"Nic is a very busy man, and business will always come first. I love that about him, and as his fiancée, I accept him as he is."

Maya cocked her head. "His what?"

She held out her hand. Maya was blinded by the sparkles. "He picked it up this afternoon while he was out trying to make you…presentable. Perfect, isn't it? We wanted to wait until after your meeting with James, but we couldn't. Tonight is kind of like an engagement party for us."

Maya's lip curled. Her intuition told her this woman was batshit crazy, but Nic had gone to the jeweler that afternoon. And how did she know about Dechamps? And those phone calls.

Maya checked the bar again, but she didn't see Nic. Her gaze came back to Daphne. Beautiful, worldly, smiling Daphne.

Maya remembered something her mother always said. There was his side, her side and the truth. But what was the truth? Was Daphne crazy? Was Nic a liar?

Was this all a ruse just to get her shares? Was that why Nic had gotten so angry when she began securing clients?

Would she care about this when she was back in LA?

Her mind kept settling on the vineyard. Her father's vineyard. Even if they weren't engaged, Maya didn't want anything to fall into the hands of that woman.

She looked up and saw Nic, wide-eyed and frozen in place across the room. He looked guilty.

She wanted to scream.

She wanted to talk to her mother.

"Congratulations, Daphne," Maya gritted out. She ran for the stairs, her heels making it hard to ascend in a hurry. She felt Nic behind her, then felt his hand, gentle but firm on her arm. She stopped, but didn't turn around.

"What did she say?"

"She said you're engaged. Congratulations." She tore her arm from his grasp and continued up the stairs, but he was hot on her heels.

"She's insane. I told you—"

He got to the top of the stairs and Maya whirled around, her voice low but direct.

"So you didn't go to a jewelry store today and pick up a ring?"

His jaw clenched, and he seemed to stall for a moment. The bastard.

"You honestly think I would buy her a ring?"

"How did she know about our trip to Dechamps?"

"I have no idea, Maya. It doesn't matter—"

"Oh, it matters. Especially if you are planning on sharing my father's vineyard with that bitch!" Maya's voice rose, making a few guests turn their heads.

"That's ridiculous. I made you a promise. Come, let's talk about this somewhere else."

"No. I'm done with your smooth talk and your kisses and your—" She ran out of air. "And your body. I'm done listening to other people. I'm going after what I want…whenever I figure that out. Excuse me."

She stomped down the hall toward the penthouse elevators. He wasn't behind her, which felt like both a win and a loss. She jumped inside when the doors opened and jammed her finger on the button several times. When she looked up, Nic was still standing where she'd left him, his eyes searching.

Maya woke with the feeling that she was alone, and not just because she had decided to give away the last thing she'd known of her father.

"Well, I was wondering when you were going to call me back?" Her mother's voice was upbeat but laced with a questioning tone.

"Hi, Mom," Maya gritted out, barely keeping a lid on her feelings. "How are you?"

"I'm fine. Glad my daughter finally returned my calls."

Here we go, Maya thought. "Sorry, Mother. I've been meaning to call you back, it's just been really busy."

"What have you been doing that you can't call your mother back?"

"I've been getting acquainted with my father's business."

"Oh?"

"Yeah. I've been…finding out a lot of things about him." Pause. "Getting to know him, so to speak." Maya paused again, giving her mother the opportunity to spill the beans.

"And what have you found?"

"I think you know what I found."

"I don't know what you mean." Maya saw her mother in her mind's eye with her brow raised and a hand on her hip. Maya had a temper, but she didn't get that from her father.

"Were you ever going to tell me the truth?"

"What truth?"

"That *you* left *him*."

"Hold on," her mother said in a low voice. When she spoke again, she sounded far away. "It's Maya, dear. I'll take it upstairs so you can watch the game." Maya rolled her eyes at her image of Steve on the couch. After some shuffling, her mother got back on the phone. "And just what is it that you think you know?"

"I know there was supposed to be a wedding. Did you leave him at the altar?"

"Yes. Yes, I did. I was pregnant with you then."

Maya's jaw dropped and she scrambled to get herself together. She hadn't expected the truth to come out so quickly. "Well… I mean…why? You didn't love him?"

"I loved him very much. But we wanted different things. He wanted to go back to France and I didn't. He thought I would go. He had all of these plans about a vineyard and a life with you, but I couldn't do it."

"Why?"

Her mother sighed. "Maya, I've told you. Things were different then. I was young, and living abroad was scary. Your grandmother had all these ideas that I'd never see her again… It just didn't feel right."

"Then why did you take me there?"

"How…how do you know that?"

"Just answer the question, Mother. Honestly, please, because I'm increasingly annoyed at the fact that you allowed me to think my father never wanted to have anything to do with me. Or should I say, with *us*."

"He visited three times a year up until you were about

four. That's when I met Steve. He wanted to marry me and take care of us and…" Her mother stopped.

"And?"

"He felt threatened by Albert. So I asked Albert to stop coming around."

Maya was furious. "You asked my father to stop being my father?"

"It wasn't that simple."

"Really? I think simple might be Steve's middle name."

"Watch your mouth. Steve has been wonderful to us. He's been a loving husband and a good father. He's put you through school—"

"No, Mother, he didn't. Grants did, remember? They were from Albert. Did you know that?"

Her mother's voice shook. "No, I didn't know that."

"So then why did you take me to France?"

"Albert agreed to stay away, but he wanted you to come for a little while."

"How long were we here?"

"A week. He…" Her mother sniffled. "He was good with you."

"How did that make you feel?"

"Like maybe I had made a mistake. Albert did his best to show me we could be a family. He took you everywhere. Worked outside with you running around the place. I was afraid you were going to kill yourself in those vines. We even attended a party together as a couple."

"Did you wear a silver dress?"

"Yes, why?"

"He kept it."

Her mother sniffled again.

"Did you make love to him?"

"That is none of your business!"

"You did. What did Steve say about that?"

"I never told him."

"So many secrets. How do you live with yourself?"

"I did it for my family. So don't you dare judge me."

"Oh, I'm judging you, Mother. All these years I thought he never wanted me. He wanted me. Why was that so threatening?"

"Because I knew you would leave."

"What?"

"I wanted my family here, not spread out across God knows where! Girl, your grandmother, God rest her soul, had been born on a planation in Virginia. She had siblings who were taken away that she never saw or heard from again. She wasn't going to let her daughter go, and I wasn't going to let *you* go."

Maya struggled to speak through a wellspring of tears. "Mom, when you put it like that I understand, but maybe you didn't realize that *I* would never let *you* go. Even if I had gone to Paris to visit my father, you would have always known where I was, and I would've always come back."

They talked for a long time after that, years of secrets peeling away, and Maya was convinced that selling the business to Nic was the right thing to do.

But still one question remained. What was she going to do about Nic?

Chapter 16

Maya was fresh from a shower and raiding her mini-bar when an insistent banging on her door filled the room.

"Who could that be?" she whispered to herself sarcastically. If she stayed quiet, would he go away?

Nic's voice boomed through the door. "Open the door, Maya. I know you're in there."

Rolling her eyes, she clutched her robe to her chest and opened the door, surprised to find Nic still in his tux and clutching a very angry looking Daphne by the elbow.

"Putain!" Daphne's string of French sounded blistering. She ripped her arm from Nic's grip, then looked Maya up and down.

Nic dipped his head. "I'm sorry for the interruption. But Daphne has something to say to you. Don't you?"

Daphne shrugged a pretty shoulder.

The elevator dinged, and a few drunken revelers stumbled past them. Realizing they'd gone the wrong way, they stumbled back the way they came.

"May we come in?" Nic asked.

"I don't think so." Maya was done accommodating these two. "Better make it quick."

Nic nodded to Daphne.

Daphne's mouth flattened. "This is *stupide*."

"Spit it out!" Nic snapped.

Daphne turned to Maya with a haughty sneer. *"Pardonnez-moi."*

Nic barked a string of French at Daphne, which had her turning white. "Try again," he said in English.

"I am very sorry for the things that I said." Daphne's voice was nowhere near apologetic.

"Which things?" Maya asked sweetly. The elevator dinged again, and a larger and louder crowd spilled into the hallway.

"Merde—" her gaze narrowed as she took in the rowdy crowd "—this is not the place for this!"

"Say your piece and you can leave!" Nic snapped.

"Bien," she said with a huff. "We're not engaged."

"And," Nic prompted.

"We've never been engaged."

"And?"

"Isn't that enough?" she hissed.

"And you'll have nothing to do with the vineyard because…?" he said.

"Because I lied."

"Just like you lied about…"

"Our engagement," she said, heat rays darting from her eyes.

He turned to Maya. "How was that?"

Maya cocked her head at Nic, then turned to Daphne. "When did you last sleep with him?"

Daphne gave Nic a sly look, but he lifted a brow at her. "The truth."

"I don't even know…" Daphne rolled her eyes. "Five years or something."

Maya slowly shook her head. "You've been pining after him for five years? Jeez."

"It's not pining when you love someone," Daphne spit.

"It is if they don't love you back. Oh wait, that's not *pining*, that's *pathetic*."

Daphne let out a high-pitched roar before she lunged at Maya, but Nic caught her flailing arms first and secured Daphne in a bear hug.

Nic gritted his teeth against her struggling body, but kept his voice calm when he turned to Maya. "Have you heard enough?"

Maya held Nic's gaze and thought for a moment of all the secrets and lies she'd heard over the past two weeks. Yeah, she'd heard enough.

"I think we're done here," Maya said.

"Get off me then," Daphne spit. Nic pulled his arms away quickly, leaving her to stumble a bit before getting her footing. She graced the two of them with an evil look, then marched down the hall toward the elevators.

Nic turned back to Maya. "I'm sorry, too."

Maya clutched her robe tighter. "For?"

"For letting it get this far."

"I just don't understand how she knew all of those things. And that ring—did she just happen to have an engagement ring lying around her apartment to torture me with?"

"I don't know," he said, anxiously slipping his hands in and out of his pockets. "I just don't want you upset."

He looked so earnest that Maya felt her anger lighten. How much could she really blame him for Daphne's maliciousness? If she was honest, her anger was a by-product of jealousy. Even after she knew it wasn't true, just the idea of Nic asking Daphne to marry him was enough to make her want to set something on fire.

"I'm not upset…anymore."

"Can I come in?" he murmured, moving farther into the doorway.

"Um," she said to get a handle on her overactive mind. A movie reel of possibilities flashed behind her eyes. Her stripping him of his tux. Him shoving off her robe. Her legs wrapped around him. His mouth on her—"No, Nic. I don't think that's a good idea."

He frowned. "You're still upset."

"No, I'm just being practical. We have business to discuss tomorrow. Things are changing…ending. I need some time to process everything. So good night. Thank you again and I'll see you tomorrow."

She tried to push the door shut, only to feel a hard resistance. Nic held the door in place with one hand, anguish in his gaze. Before she knew what he was about, he grabbed her face gently and brought his lips to hers. Her lips met his so easily that for a moment she forgot that she had been angry, forgot that she was signing away her father's business the next day, forgot that she was leaving Paris.

But it all rushed back when he pulled away, his gaze roaming over her face. She thought he was going to say something, but he didn't. With a weak grin, he gave her a slight nod and backed away from the door.

"Sweet dreams, *chérie*. I'll see you tomorrow," he said before disappearing down the hall. She didn't close the door until she heard the elevator ding.

"Nicolas?" the old jeweler questioned when Nic hurried through his shop door, reached into his jacket pocket and placed a velvet box down on the glass showcase. "Is there something wrong with the ring?"

Nic put his palms up. "The ring was perfect, until another woman got her hands on it." The jeweler was wide-eyed as Nic relayed the story: Daphne looking for him in his office while he dealt with a problem in the kitchen. He'd left his jacket on the desk, where she had picked it up and found the ring in the pocket. "I never should have left my jacket alone. And now I can't give it to the woman I wanted to, not that she'd take it at this point." He ran a hand through his hair, remembering the look she'd given him before closing her hotel room door. Her eyes had held a distance that made him uneasy.

The jeweler bent over the ring and held a small glass to his eye. "The diamonds are perfect. I'll take it back, of course, but how would you like to replace it?"

Nic gave a blank stare to the jewels in the showcase, then looked at the jeweler.

"Second thoughts?"

"You must see this all the time."

"Not as much as you think. Men who design their rings usually know what they want, or should I say who they want."

Nic gave a slow nod. "I do want her. I'm just not so sure she wants me."

"Ah, a risk." The old man turned around and opened a locked cabinet behind him. He pulled out a long velvet display of six engagement rings and carefully set them on the glass with a smile. Each unique, intricate design held a dazzling stone that sat in a bed of smaller diamonds. "But one worth taking, I expect. I haven't shown these to anyone. They were specially designed for the royal family as choices for the prince's fiancée. I only show them to my best customers. And you look like you need something special."

They were special, just like Maya. He picked up the one on the end.

"Fifteen-carat emerald cut, flawless of course," the jeweler whispered. "We call it the Grace Kelly, as it's similar to the one Prince Rainier III of Monaco commissioned for the actress."

"It's stunning."

"Indeed."

Nic stared hard at the ring, hoping it would tell him what to do. Instead, all he heard was his mother's voice. *Don't let love ruin you.*

Too late, Mother. Too late.

Maya checked the time as she walked into James's office. His team of associates welcomed her and led her to his office, where he was pacing, on the phone with another client. He waved her into a seat, which she gladly took since Nic hadn't yet arrived and she was a little nervous about seeing him. The disappointment on his face when she'd refused his company the night before had stayed with her most of the night and reappeared this morning. He was the last person she wanted to hurt, and today, as they settled her father's estate, she would make that clear.

Maya scrolled through her phone as she waited, triple checking her flight times for the next afternoon. Her thumb hovered over a new email that popped through, an interview confirmation for One Consulting Group. She sighed. Executive vice president of consumer goods—the title rang in her ears and her business card flashed in her mind, and yet her excitement fell short. It was a great opportunity, she told herself. Probably everything she wanted and deserved. So why wasn't she happy about it?

She turned at the sound of footsteps and saw Nic striding quickly toward the office. He caught her gaze and smiled a little. Her heart beat faster and almost burst when he walked straight toward her and kissed her on the lips.

"Bonjour," he whispered.

"Hi," she breathed, trying to steady her pounding heart.

When they both looked up, James was staring at them, his phone held away from his ear and a blank look on his face, like a mannequin. His eyes darted between the two until Nic took a seat next to Maya, then he cleared his throat and took his seat. "Good morning to you both. Now, Jennifer will FaceTime in at any moment. Ah, here she is." James touched the iPad, which was set on a stand at the edge of his desk, and Jennifer's yawn was caught on video. It was early morning in California, and Jen, it looked like, was still in her pajamas.

"Morning all," Jen said, just before taking a sip of coffee. "If you don't mind, I need a quick word with my client. Maya, I'm calling you now."

James directed Maya to an empty office.

"You aren't even dressed," Maya joked, after she'd left Nic and James.

"You do realize what time it is here. Look, I know you are planning on giving up your shares today so I had Nathan send me the new figures—"

"Jen, don't try to talk me out of this. I know it's the right thing. I wasn't sure before, but I have an interview with One Consulting on Tuesday and it's everything I've been working toward. I think it's a sign that I'm doing the right thing."

"That's not what I was going to say—"

Maya turned and Nic was in the doorway. "Sorry, I'm just checking on you."

"No, it's fine. We're ready."

"Maya—" Jen started.

"Jen, I know what you're going to say. I want to do this."

"You want to give away your father's business?"

Maya paused, unable to answer. "I want to do what I think is best for my father's business."

"Maybe you being at the helm *is* best."

"I'm not at the helm. I have a partner."

"Not according to this—"

"I know."

"You've seen these figures?"

"Of course. The Dechamps contract gave us a nice end-of-year boost. That's what I wanted for Nic."

Jen paused. "Are we talking about the same thing here?"

Maya waved her hand in the air. "Of course we are. Let's get started."

"Okay…see you in the other room."

After emailing some things to Jen, they proceeded with what felt like a divorce. Every piece of paperwork James presented and explained was a transfer or dissolution of some sort. Jen chimed in several times to demand amendments where needed, while Nic and Maya nodded and listened, then secretly smiled at each other when the two lawyers got into a debate.

"Did you sleep well?" Nic asked, his voice only for her.

"Not really. You?" She wanted to touch him.

"Not at all. I… There…there was something I wanted to ask you."

Maya turned her body toward him, sensing unease. "What?"

"Maybe we could take a break for a moment—"

James interrupted. "Now, Maya." He handed her several papers. "If you initial here and here, then sign here, here and here, then the shares will be transferred to Nic, and then Nic will wire the money into the account specified within three business days."

Maya looked up and saw James holding a pen out to her. She looked at Nic, who met her gaze. "You don't have to do this."

Maya sighed and looked around the room before bringing her gaze back to Nic. "I think I do."

Nic frowned. "Because you want to get back to LA?"

"I…my life is there."

"What if it was here?"

Her eyes flashed. "What?"

Nic wrung his hands. "Let's talk for a minute. I want to run something by you."

"What else is there to talk about? You promised to keep the company intact. I believe you. Your offer for my share is generous. I appreciate that."

"You mean offer for the whole company, don't you?" Jen chimed in. All three heads swiveled to the iPad and the hard-nosed lawyer in her pajamas. "Because according to this fiscal statement, this is the third year that Albert's accounts, now Maya's accounts, brought in ninety percent of the revenue of the company and therefore can claim automatic rights to one hundred percent of the shares, per the clause on page twenty-one, section D of the contract."

"What?" All three heads swiveled around.

"I don't understand," Maya said to Jen.

Jen adjusted her glasses. "I thought you did… That's what I was trying to tell you."

Nic stood and walked behind the chairs, his hand clutching something in his pocket. Maya twisted toward him. "Nic, I didn't—" He ignored her, looking instead at James. "Is this true?"

James flipped through papers and punched numbers on his calculator. He sighed and slowly nodded. "Yes, it is. It seems that the lapse of the Dechamps account, which had been under your name, has decreased your contribution. And the current contract with Dechamps is under Miss North's name."

Maya shook her head rapidly. "Well, that's a mistake. Just reassign the account to Nic."

"The contract is done. Here is the copy, with your name as broker."

Maya looked at the contract, then whirled around to Nic. "This is a mistake. We can fix this."

"There is no 'we.' Only you and your company."

He wasn't looking at her; his brow was furrowed over a restless gaze that seemed to dart from the contracts, to her and then to the floor. He was sort of frozen in a state of mild shock, like she was. One moment she was handing him her shares, the next she owned the entire company.

The company his father helped to build.

Maya heard Jen and James in discussion, then walked to Nic and touched him on the arm.

"Nic, I don't know what to say."

Nic turned to her, but his eyes had changed. He looked at her like he didn't know her. "There is nothing to say. The business is yours. I hope you'll keep me on as an employee." The sarcasm in his voice stung. He stood and stalked toward the door.

"Nic," she called out. He turned at the office door and looked at her for a long moment before he spoke.

"Congratulations," he said in a low voice, then walked out.

Maya whipped around to James, whose face was red. "Fix this!"

James held his hands up.

Maya stormed out into the street, unsure of where she was going. Back to the hotel? To the vineyard? To LA? She wanted to go home, but she was no longer sure where that was.

Chapter 17

The next morning, Maya lay in bed at the vineyard—her vineyard—trying to find the emotional strength to get out of bed and face the fact that in her effort to keep her father's business afloat, she'd somehow taken it away from the one person who actually knew how to run it.

She rolled over and grabbed her phone, hoping to see a voice mail or a text. She let the phone drop onto her comforter. All of her calls and texts went unanswered. After leaving James's office, she had hoped to find Nic in his office at the hotel, but no one had seen him. Like a fool, she had stayed in the lobby hoping to run into him, but he never showed.

Rolling over in bed, she clutched the covers to her chin, afraid to admit the truth to herself. He didn't want to talk to her. The thought of leaving for LA without speaking to him made her shudder. Muffled male voices wafted up the stairs. Throwing back the covers, she jumped from the bed and scrounged through her disaster of a suitcase for sweatpants and a sweater large enough to cover the fact that she wasn't wearing a bra.

She took the stairs two at a time and ran toward the kitchen, halting just before the entrance, then leisurely strolled toward the kitchen island where Nathan had set out pastries and coffee. *That boy is going to get a raise.* She followed the voices into the tasting room and rounded the corner, anticipating a cold welcome. Instead, she was warmly greeted by Nathan and James, who was hoping to find Nic, as well.

"It seems he has disappeared. His mobile just rings and rings."

Maya clutched her chest. "Do you think he's all right?"

"I'm sure he is fine, dear. He'll turn up. I just needed him to sign these papers acknowledging the share transfer into your hands. Your papers to sign are here, as well."

"May I see those?"

James handed Maya the papers, and she tore them up.

"Miss North!"

"I'm sorry, James. But I need Nic to keep his shares, and if he would talk to me, I would tell him that. I asked you to fix this, not make it worse."

"Nic doesn't want the shares."

"What?" Nathan whispered. Maya finally looked at the young man, really looked at him. His face was puffy as if he hadn't slept, or had been crying. He'd lost Albert, and now Nic? She'd really done a number on this place, hadn't she?

Maya's mouth turned down. "When did he say that?"

"He called me last night," said James.

"Well, he is keeping them! He's a better businessman than this. You don't put money into a venture and then walk away from it. James, you tell him I said no!"

"All right, if I hear from him…"

"Why not go to the hotel?"

"I'm not sure he's in Paris."

Maya blinked, feeling a twinge in her heart. "Where else would he be?"

"Spain," Nathan said, his gaze on the small face of Bacchus over the door.

Maya jammed her hand in her hair, trying to get rid of the anxious feeling that she would never see him again.

"Well, I'm sure he'll be back," James murmured.

"I'm leaving this afternoon." Maya looked at both men, feeling she was being torn from something. "If you talk to him—" She paused. "Tell him… I'm not letting him off the hook that easily. Not until he calls me."

She turned back toward her room, afraid she'd blurt out what she really wanted to say to Nic.

"What do you mean she's gone back? She has a business to run!"

Nathan only stared at Nic when he returned to the vineyard a day later. "She's a better businesswoman than this. You don't inherit a business then let it run itself!"

"She's left the day-to-day stuff to me until she gets back. Luckily, it's slow now."

"Humph." Nic paced, his gaze falling on the closed door of Albert's office. "When is she coming back?"

"Why don't you call and ask her?"

Nic heard the blame in Nathan's voice and decided to let the young man have his judgments. He'd asked himself that same question. If he was honest, it was all he could do to stop himself from calling her back, but every time he dialed, he felt like a fool. He was in love with a woman who had taken his business and then run back to her life in LA.

He'd listened to her messages again and again, each time not trusting himself to call and beg her to come back. He'd spent the weekend in Spain with his mother, trying to figure out if proposing to a woman he'd only known for a few weeks was a good idea. According to his mother, it was not. What did he expect?

But he'd found himself feeling bereft without Maya; he yearned to show her his favorite places in Barcelona. He listened to her voice mails over and over, as if she would appear through the receiver. Yeah, he loved her. But he wasn't so sure that she felt the same, especially since her voice mails were all about business.

She'd gone back to LA for however long…and she probably didn't miss him at all.

"Why don't you call her? She's *your* boss," Nic said to Nathan's narrowed gaze.

"Technically she's your boss, too…unless you've quit," Nathan said. "I left her a voice mail."

"I haven't quit. I was pushed out," he said through gritted teeth. "And what is your problem? I know you have a thing for her, but she's old enough to be your nanny."

"I don't have a *thing*. I like her. She reminds me of Albert. And I think she's good for you, but you're too invested in your stolen shares to see it."

"For your information, she knows how I feel about her."

"Does she?" Nathan's brows lifted. "You told her you're in love with her?"

Nic blinked. Hearing it out loud felt strange, but his heart said it rang true. "Not in so many words."

"Well, no wonder she left."

"I'm not the reason she's gone!"

"You did nothing to persuade her to stay. You disappeared."

Nic sighed. "My mother needed me."

"You needed your mother."

Nic's head snapped up, wondering if Nathan would be able to take a punch to the nose. "And when did you get so smart?"

"Since first Albert and now you have let the woman you love go. Let's just say I've learned what *not* to do in relationships."

"So experienced, are you?"

"I've had my share," Nathan spit back.

"Women are different from girls. It's more complicated."

"It's not *that* complicated. It's called communication."

"Then what do you suggest I do, smart-ass?"

Nathan gathered his things from the desk. "Call. Her."

Nic rolled his eyes. He was a kid. What did he know?

A minute later, he pulled his phone from his pocket.

Maya sat across from the CEO of One Consulting Group, wondering how long she had to listen to him talk about himself before she could leave and have lunch at In-N-Out Burger. Since landing the night before, she had been craving some good ol' American fast food, although nothing topped Nathan's breakfast spread.

The thought of never having it again made her frown. She supposed she'd have to try to make those little pastries herself from now on, because she had this job in the bag. Her potential boss was visibly impressed with her presentation on account management and the revenue she'd generated with SuperFoods, and he'd complimented her on her shoes. They talked about never missing an episode of *Archer*, Marvel comics and the last *Star Wars* movie.

She commented on the pictures of his family, how beautiful his daughters were and how his husband could have been mistaken for Anderson Cooper. They were comfortable together. She was a confident, competent woman, and he wasn't threatened by her power. It was obvious she was a good fit for the company, and she would finally get what she had always dreamed of. Executive vice president of domestic *and international* consumer goods. Now that would look good on a business card.

Maya continued to smile and nod, her thoughts drifting to the last time she and Nic had made love. He still hadn't called her back, which made her feel rejected in a way that no man ever had. She'd woken up in her own bed thinking about Nic, wishing he was there holding her, then rolling over and grabbing her phone, wishing he'd at least text her. Her refrigerator had been packed with expired food so she'd driven to the café a few blocks away. Even the coffee tasted different. *This is what alone tastes like,* she'd said to herself.

"So, what do you think?" the boss asked with a grin.

"I think your company is going to knock 'em out of the water—with me on your team, of course."

"My thoughts exactly."

He offered her the job on the spot. And she feigned surprise and excitement, promising to give him an answer in a couple of days. She smiled, even as she knew that the one person she wanted to call wouldn't answer the phone.

The CEO walked her out, buying her a coffee and joking that it was part of her benefits package. She laughed at the bad joke, seeing a future of those ahead of her. She sipped the coffee on her way out to her car. The dark roast tasted like loneliness with a shot of exasperation.

She threw her bag in the back seat and checked her phone. Nothing. Instead of turning on the car, she stopped and breathed, wondering why she didn't feel even the slightest bit happy. She'd done it again, gone after what she wanted and gotten it. It wasn't the way she had hoped, but the universe had provided. So what was the deal?

Then it had occurred to her that this feeling, wanting someone who was never going to be a part of her life, was the same type of hurt her father had gone through. She couldn't hold back the tears any longer. Sitting in her car, shaking, coffee spilling on her skirt, she ugly cried. Hard. Hiccups and sobs escaped her throat as the tears kept falling. People walked by her car staring in. All of LA could have watched; she didn't give a damn. All she'd ever wanted was to be appreciated, to be loved. Her father had loved her. It felt good to know, but it was too late. And Nic...well... If he wanted her, he'd call her back. Or do something even more dramatic, like show up and beg her to come back. She wiped her face, murmuring to herself that she watched too many movies.

The truth was that she understood why he was ignoring her. He'd been the silent savior of that business, and although it wasn't his on paper, it was his in every way that mattered. She rolled her eyes. What was she going to do?

She jumped when her phone vibrated, and she quickly held up the screen. She let out her breath when she saw it wasn't Nic, debated answering it, then pressed Accept.

"Hey, Jen."

"Do not take that job at One Consulting."

"How the hell...? Hold on..." Maya started her car and took the call through the dash as she drove home. "How did you know?"

"Girl please, you know how small this town is. And I swear Dave has a mole in every competitor in this city. He just called me and told me to whip up a contract and get you back. Meanwhile, why *are* you back?"

Maya's head jerked so hard she swerved and got beeped at. She waved at the Volvo. "Sorry! Jen, I don't understand."

"Executive vice president of consumer goods. Do you understand that?"

"Um, I understand that is Rick's title."

"Oh no, Rick is getting fired at the end of the week. I have his paperwork all ready to go."

Maya slammed on her horn in celebration. The Volvo sped off. "You're kidding. What happened?"

"Chrissy filed a sexual harassment suit against him. Seems he's been saying some inappropriate things to her."

"Oh, my God, this made my day. You have no idea."

"Well, Dave is prepared to offer you anything you want. He wants you to name your salary."

"This is insane. I don't know if I can even think about this right now."

"Why? And you haven't answered me—why are you back? Oh, my God, did you sell the company back to that hottie without consulting me?"

"No, the company is still mine. And the hottie hates me for it." Maya turned into her condo parking lot and left the car running. What are the odds that she'd have two job offers in one day? So this was it, huh, universe? This was where she was supposed to be? Jen kept talking.

"You sound upset about that last part. Wait, did you and the hottie—"

Maya sighed. "Jen, I'll talk to you about it later. I have to go."

"Does that mean you're going to take it? Because I told him it was a long shot, especially since you're the CEO of your own company now."

Record scratch. "Um, what?" Maya said. "What did you say?"

"I told him now that you're a CEO, why would you want to be an EVP? It's like demoting yourself or something…" Jen's voice faded and Maya felt very calm suddenly, her mind's eye focusing on a small, white rectangular card with her full name, Maya Elizabeth North Belcourt, and the title CEO underneath.

"Jen." Maya cut off the rambling. "I have to go."

"But what do I tell Dave?"

"Tell him I already have a job. I have to go… I'm heading back to Paris. Tonight."

Chapter 18

His calls kept going to voice mail. It was after midnight, which meant early evening in Los Angeles. Where the hell was she? Was she blocking his calls? Was she with someone else? Nic wanted to throw his phone across the room. Instead, he placed it faceup on the desk in Albert's den and checked several times that the volume was on high. His fingers trailed over the colored Post-it notes, and he picked up a pen with purple ink. Maya was all around him. He looked at the books that were pulled from the shelves and stacked neatly where she had left them. She was coming back eventually, right?

"I need these signed." Nathan entered the room with a stack of papers and an open bottle of wine. Nic took the bottle first and poured them each a glass, then opened the folder of checks.

"Your boss will have to sign these," Nic said, scrunching up his face.

"You're still my boss, too, and nothing has been transferred yet, so please stop sulking and sign these before our vendors begin to hate us. They are past due."

Nic raised a brow. The nerve of this young man. He was wiser than his years, but Nic would never admit that; nor would he ever tell the millennial that he was right. He should have told Maya how he felt. He didn't know if things would be different, but he knew that this feeling—that he hadn't done what he should have—would be gone. Nic grabbed the papers and signed his name with a sweeping scrawl. "You're lucky you're indispensable."

"You're indispensable, too, you know. She knows that."

"She does?" Nic straightened. "Have you talked to her?"

"Only through email." Nathan began restocking the books that Maya had left out.

Nic stared at Nathan's back. "Are you really going to make me ask what she said?"

"She said she was figuring things out." *Okay*, Nic thought, *that's valid*. Then Nathan turned. "And she said she got a job offer."

Nic's eyes narrowed. "A job offer?"

"That's what she said."

"In Los Angeles."

"Oui."

A full minute went by as the men stared at each other. Nic's breathing changed. The woman he loved, who had just stolen his business out from under him, was rebuilding her life across the ocean. "Call her right now."

"But you just tried…"

"Call her! She'll take it if it's you."

Nic held his breath as Nathan dialed, waited then pulled the phone from his ear.

"Straight to voice mail." Nathan sighed. Nic bit the inside of his cheek. He was relieved to find that she hadn't blocked him, but he didn't like this black hole of noncommunication. He needed to do something shocking. That would get her attention.

"Give me her email."

"Why?"

"Just do it!" Nic had a plan that Nathan wouldn't approve of. So he didn't tell him.

The next morning, with said plan in play, Nic was in a fantastic mood. James had been a little skeptical, but when Nic explained that it was the only way to make sure she'd come back, well, the old romantic couldn't resist. He had even added a few frightening legal details of his own for maximum effect. The letter had been sent in an email last night, and although he had no Read receipt, he knew she'd get it. He also knew she'd call. He checked his phone for the hundredth time, then popped a few more croissants in his mouth. It was going to be a good day; he could feel it.

And yet by late afternoon, he still hadn't heard from her. He called James, who hadn't heard from her, either. He'd gotten off the phone when a call came through. His heart skipped, then sank when he saw Claude Rhone's name pop up. He sighed, debated, then took the call, inviting the man over to explain that the vineyard was no longer for sale.

The meeting was short, and Claude said he wasn't disappointed as long as he got first dibs on the grapes.

Nic and Claude shook hands. "I'll make sure of it."

"Can you say that for sure? I've heard rumors that you may no longer have the business."

"Those are just rumors, Claude. Maya will be taking more responsibility, but I will never let go of this business." Nic glanced at his phone, then back to Claude, distracting himself by offering Claude a tasting of some of the older peaking vintages.

Claude cleared his throat. "I'm aware that you and Daphne no longer see each other."

"Claude, your daughter is smart and beautiful." Claude puffed up his chest. "But I've never reciprocated any feelings for Daphne, which I have told her several times."

"My daughter can be tenacious when she sees something she wants, but I understand if the spark wasn't there. I'm disappointed that you won't be my son-in-law, but I guess it wasn't meant to be."

"Thank you for your understanding."

"I've been there myself. Daphne's mother wasn't who my family chose for me. But you can't choose who you fall in love with. The heart wants what the heart wants."

Nic heard his phone chime and slid his gaze to the text that popped onto his screen. It was from Maya.

You Bastard.

Nic smiled. His heart was jumping for joy. "It certainly does."

* * *

Taking the red-eye from LAX, Maya touched down at Charles de Gaulle Airport in the morning, rented a car and checked into a hotel nowhere near Les Bains. She wanted to surprise Nic with a brilliant idea that would take this whole my company/your company thing off the table, but she needed to do some reconnaissance first. She'd seen the missed calls, but hadn't checked her email. There was no time. This plan needed a well-thought-out strategy and an element of surprise, and she couldn't do all of that looking like she'd just got off a plane. She checked into the hotel, showered and did her makeup in record time, then pulled out her battle suit of armor. Her Boss Red Dior pantsuit.

Black lace bustier and patent leather heels in place, soft waves of caramel-colored hair on fleek, Boss Red lips ready for anything, she followed her GPS to the jewelers where Nic had bought something mysterious. She knew it was usually store policy to keep customer information a secret, but she only needed a few small details, and by the looks of the old man, alone in the store with all of these lovely sparkling jewels, he needed someone to talk to.

"Bonjour, mademoiselle."

"Bonjour, monsieur. Um, I'm in a bit of a bind. I hope you can help me. My boss came in the other day, Nicolas Rayo. He picked up a very special item."

"Oh yes, the ring." The jeweler smiled.

Maya's heart almost beat out of her chest. "Yes… the ring."

"It's already been resold, lovely design. Unique, the couple said."

Her heart stopped. He'd returned it. "Yes, it was lovely." Even if it was on Daphne's claw-like finger. "I think I was supposed to pick up the replacement today, but I seem to have lost the receipt." Her dumb-assistant act wasn't all an act; she really had no idea how ordering engagement rings worked.

The jeweler's face reddened. "Replacement? I have no order for a replacement." The man pulled out a giant book and began leafing through the pages. Wide-eyed, he adjusted his glasses. "Nothing. *Oh, la vache*, something seems to be amiss. I showed him several fine replacements, but he passed. Changed his mind, he said."

The only thing amiss was her self-respect. "You know, I'm just going to bite the bullet and ask him about this receipt." She began to walk toward the door.

"I'll be happy to call him for you."

"No! No, don't do that. I'll get this sorted."

"Well, if he decides to go through with his proposal, tell him I'll give him a good price."

Maya gave the man a defeated smile. "Good to know."

She believed that ring had been for her, but hearing that he'd changed his mind kind of ruined her world, and put a giant hole in her strategy. She walked slowly back to her car, buying a crepe, then checking her emails on her phone.

Her mouth was full of Nutella when she spotted an email from James T. Bauer, Esq. She clicked on the screen:

Dear Miss North Belcourt,

This letter is to inform you that Luca Nicolas Rayo Dechamps has filed a lawsuit against you claiming full rights to the Par Le Bouquet vineyard and brokerage and charging you with the misappropriation of company funds for personal gain, such as spa appointments, personal clothing shopping and personal travel expenses. A more detailed document has been mailed to you. Please have your legal representation call our office once received.

Good Day,

James T. Bauer, Esq.

Maya almost choked on her crepe. It couldn't be real. She paced back and forth, disrupting the pedestrian flow of lunchtime traffic. He wouldn't! Although, he did change his mind about the proposal.

"That bastard!" she said aloud, scaring a couple on the street. She had a mind to barge into James's office, but he would just claim he was serving his client. It wouldn't have satisfied her anyway. She wanted Nic's head on a platter, and the only way to get that was to see him in person.

She hurried to her car and dialed his number, then cut it off. No, she didn't want to waste all of her screaming over the phone. Instead, she sent a simple, elegant text: You Bastard. Then she sped off toward the vineyard.

Chapter 19

Nic and Claude were finishing up their tasting when Nic heard a door slam shut with a loud *bang*.

"Nathan?" he called out, glancing at the doorway.

A woman's heels on the wood floors could be heard in the hallway, and he got nervous that Daphne had come to be with her father. The footsteps got closer, then Maya rounded the corner in a blur of red, black and caramel, her red lips square with anger. She stopped just inside the threshold of the room, and suddenly no one else existed but her.

"It's not Nathan," Claude said, wide eyed.

"You're suing me?" she shouted.

"What's happened?" Nathan appeared. "Maya!" he said, excited.

Maya's narrowed gaze darted back and forth. "Hello,

Nathan. Claude. Claude?" She hit Nic with an accusing look. "Claude, the vineyard isn't for sale."

"Yes, I'm aware." Claude grinned, then turned to Nic, a knowing look in his gaze. He turned back to Maya. "I hope the grapes are still available?"

"Oh, yes, you can have those," she said with an off-handed wave. "Nic, I'd like a word. In *my* office." She turned on a shiny heel, and Nic began to follow, pretty sure he'd follow her anywhere. He stalled when he realized that Claude was still there.

"You're smiling," Claude said.

Surprised, Nic fixed his face, then couldn't help but smile wider.

"Try to keep it under wraps until she's done yelling at you. Trust me," Claude said.

Nic nodded. "You can see your way out, yes?"

"Of course," his old friend said. "Good luck."

"Thanks. I'm gonna need it." Nic turned to Nathan. "We may need a mediator."

Nathan grimaced and crossed his arms.

Maya was standing still and beautiful across the room, in the same spot where he had almost made love to her. Her gaze was heated, her mouth slightly pursed. His plan had worked better than he'd hoped. She was ready to do battle, and it was turning him on. She licked her lips and his body reacted.

"I'm going to destroy you," she said, her anger like music. He was certain sparks flew from her eyes. Magical.

"How did you get here so fast?"

"I was already on my way back. This isn't funny!"

He was smiling again. "You were coming back? Nathan said—"

"I don't care what Nathan said! You and that lawyer are not going to get away with this. Jen might conduct business meetings in her pajamas, but that woman is a beast!"

Nic raised his voice to match hers, his tone neutral. "Nathan said you were on a job interview in Los Angeles."

"I was. Stop changing the subject."

"You have a job here."

"That you are trying to take from me!"

"I'm not suing you," he said in a low voice. He stepped forward slowly.

"Excuse me? Would you like to see the email I just received?"

"You weren't answering my calls."

Her eyes flashed. "Ditto," she spit, then her gaze hit the floor. She bit her lip, then met his eyes. "You disappeared. And then the only communication I got was this? Why would you do this to me? I thought…"

He hurried forward and pulled her into his arms, his face inches from hers. "You thought what?"

She blinked, her gaze searching his, then dropping to his lips. He felt her hand caress his arm. "I thought maybe…" Her gaze darted around the room, then came to focus on him. "I had every intention of signing over the shares, Nic. But honestly, the minute I took the pen, I had doubts. I know you deserve it more than I do, but it's all I have of him. You know what I mean?"

"I do," he said, wanting so badly to kiss her. He leaned closer, his head dipping toward her mouth.

"And then you do this!" She hit him and wriggled from his grasp to stand by the desk. "Listen to me right now. This is mine and I'm not giving it up."

"Good. Don't."

She paused. "You're not making sense."

"You're not letting me talk." She opened her mouth, then closed it. Gestured with a raised brow for him to continue. "I was upset at the outcome of the meeting, but not for the reasons that you think. I'd gone to Spain to get my thoughts together. I wasn't avoiding you— okay, maybe I was a little—but I wasn't angry with you. I've never been angry with you."

"Then why this?" She held up her phone, then tossed it on the desk.

"When I came back you were gone, and you weren't returning my calls, so I needed to get your attention." He walked to stand just in front of her. "I needed you here." He gently ran a finger down a tendril of her hair. "And here you are. You look beautiful, by the way."

Her gaze was wide. She swallowed and sat on the edge of the desk. "So this was a joke?"

"Call it a ruse."

She smirked. "You're not suing me."

"No, I'm not." He straightened and slid his hands in his pockets. "But if you're taking jobs in LA, then I might have to."

A smile peeked out from under her frown. "I'm not taking jobs in LA."

He bent forward and grasped the desktop, placing his arms on either side of her. "Still want to destroy me?"

She ran her hands up his arms. "Not at this particular moment."

"Then what are your plans, Mademoiselle North? You came back for something. What was it?"

Nic's playful gaze roamed over her face, and his lips were on the verge of a smirk. How was she supposed to think when he was this close, looking this good? No distractions! He was a man, and her idea could send him into a cold sweat. That was why she had to be methodical in the negotiations, make him think it was his idea. She'd been pretty sure he'd at least thought about it, but after this morning, she wasn't so certain.

"Remember when we had that business meeting and I took your shares?" She heard his inner sigh. He pulled back his arms and stood, his eyes narrow. "I'd like to give them back to you."

He crossed his arms over his chest. "You want me to buy my shares back?"

"No, I have a business proposal."

"What kind of proposal?"

"The kind that makes things really clear. No special clauses. No strange reviews. What's mine will be yours…and vice versa," she added quickly. His mouth turned down as he tried to follow along. "You were right—I can't run this business from LA. And I can't run it without you. I know nothing about wine or agriculture. And like you said, this was your father's, too. You deserve this business more than I do—"

"Maya, I don't want—"

"I know, you say you don't want the business. But I don't think that's really true, or else you would have let it crumble years ago. You want ownership, you want the right to make decisions, you want to turn this business around. I know you do. I saw it at Dechamps."

Nic dropped his arms and slid his hands into his pockets, his gaze intent on her. "What are you saying?"

"Nic, do you care about me?" Her heart was pounding. What if he said no, what if he laughed, what if…

"Of course I do. Very, very much."

She smiled into his softened gaze, trying to ignore the fact that he hadn't said the words she'd hoped for. "I care about you, too." She licked her lips. "I think I might even lo—"

The door whipped open and Nathan stood in the threshold. "I was just making sure you hadn't killed him."

"Not now!" Nic shouted.

"Out!" Maya screamed at the same time. Wide eyed, Nathan closed the door behind him and Nic grabbed the knob and locked it. Which was good, because when he heard what she was about to say, there would be nowhere for him to run.

"Please, continue," Nic said, his gaze expectant.

Maya paused, unable to get her mojo back. She switched gears. It was negotiation time. "Nic, do you want the shares or not?"

"I'd like to be your partner, if you'll have me."

"I'm glad you said that." She paced, then stopped. "Because I think the best way to solidify our partnership is marriage."

Nic stilled, his eyes fixed on her for a long moment. "Did you hear me?"

He swallowed, then blinked. It was worse than she thought.

"Nic?" she continued in measured tones. "I know this is unconventional, but if you think about it from a business perspective, it's a good deal."

"You just proposed to me," Nic stated as if in shock.

"Yeah. I did."

"Do you love me?" he asked.

Maya nodded slowly, afraid he was going to keel over. "Yeah. I do." He blinked some more. "I didn't just come back for the business. I missed you."

He was across the room, unlocking the door and rushing out into the hall before she knew what was happening.

"Where are you going!" Maya hurried after him, trying to catch his long stride to no avail. "Hey! I just proposed to you!"

At Maya's statement, Nathan whipped his head around and watched first Nic then Maya disappear up the stairs toward the bedrooms.

Maya's black heels struggled to keep up while Nic took the stairs two at a time. He took a sharp left into his bedroom, leaving the door open. "You know what," she called out in a labored breath as she reached the top of the stairs. "Never mind. Clearly it was a bad idea," she huffed, walking toward his bedroom. He still wasn't saying anything. "You could have just said no. I'm perfectly happy running this business by…my…self!"

Maya entered his room and stopped short. There was

Nic, on one knee, holding an open velvet box. A gold ring glittered on its black pillow.

Her hand flew to her throat and tears began to stream down her cheeks.

Nic took a deep breath. "I couldn't stop you from taking over the business, but I won't let you take this proposal away from me." He smiled, making her lips curve upward even as she continued to tear up. "I've had a ring in my pocket for you since the night of the casino. We know how that went. This ring is my grandmother's. That's why I went to Spain. When you left, I had to do something dramatic to get you back." Nic took a breath and swallowed hard. "Maya Elizabeth North Belcourt. Will you do me the honor of entering into a lifetime partnership with me?"

Maya wiped at her eyes and nose, her heart racing as she looked at her future husband. "Is this just to get my shares?" she mumbled through tears.

He stood and brought the ring closer to her. "You told me you didn't know wine, you knew people. What does your heart tell you?"

"My heart tells me that this proposal is way better than the one I just attempted."

They laughed as he took her hand and slid the princess-cut diamond onto her finger. "This ring is our life contract. I promise to love you forever. I hope you can do the same."

She played with the beautiful but unfamiliar object on her hand and felt a swell of emotion fill her soul. She met his gaze. "You really love me?"

His dark eyes were earnest. "I think I loved you the

day you started grilling me on expenses." He took her in his arms and stroked her hair away from her face. "There is nothing sexier than hearing you talk profit and loss."

She grinned and wrapped her arms around his neck. "Well then, wait until you hear about my ideas for *our* brokerage."

"Our brokerage," he repeated. "I told you those shares were going to be mine," he teased. "I just didn't think I'd get such a good deal." He kissed her gently, then pulled back to hover over her lips. "So that's a *oui*?"

"Hell yes, that's a *oui*," she whispered, taking his lips with hers again. "I knew I loved you the day you let me negotiate with Armand. When you put your trust in me, I feel like I can do anything."

"You *can* do anything. I've seen it."

"But only because you support me. I've always been ambitious, but I've never felt so confident as with you beside me. You're focused and steadfast when it comes to your work. You have a passion for the vineyard that you mask as an obligation. You are committed to running the best hotel in Paris and I've never seen anyone do it better. And not once, even when you questioned what I was doing, even when you weren't sure you liked me, did you try to stop me. You gave me a seat next to you at the table, even though I hadn't earned it. Thank you for that."

He inhaled deeply. "You think you didn't earn it? That seat was yours the minute you walked into my life. You are fire and energy, taking no prisoners on your quest to rule the world. You're an inspiration to me."

She tightened her grip. "Maybe just one prisoner."

"And that wicked sense of humor." He grinned.

Maya smiled through a few more happy tears. "We're going to be happy."

Nic ran his hands down her body and lifted her just off the floor. "We are happy." He walked them to the bed and gently laid her underneath him.

"Do you think Nathan will approve?" she asked against his mouth, then sighed as his lips found her throat.

"I think Nathan will be making mini croissants for our wedding."

"Which will be in the vineyard, by the way," Maya said as she rolled them both so she was on top. He pushed her jacket off to bare her strapless black bustier. "The pictures will be an amazing marketing tool."

He sat up and shrugged out of his own shirt, then kissed the swell of her breasts. "I love it when you talk dirty."

She put her mouth to his ear. "Then listen to this," she said, undulating her hips over him. "We're going to revamp that website and commission an app."

He laughed, putting his hands in her hair and bringing her mouth to his for a long, deep kiss. "*Je t'aime,* Maya," Nic whispered.

"I love you, too, Nicolas Rayo. And I promise to always be there for you."

* * * * *

Leaning the back of his head against the chair, he recalled that day as if it had happened an hour ago.

He'd wanted to touch her flawless medium brown skin. From what he could tell, her makeup consisted of dark liner to emphasize her angled dark brown eyes and a rich burgundy lipstick, which drew his attention to her full lips. He'd found it unacceptable to be attracted to the most viable competition for the next open partnership position.

In those few seconds, he'd realized alienating her would be the only way to keep himself from falling into the attraction that lured him closer to her. The zip of electricity that stung his palm when they'd shaken hands had been the deciding factor.

Shaking away the guilt of the past, he focused on the scenery.

He'd been avoiding her. Ever since they'd engaged in the best sex of his life two months ago. One minute they'd been arguing, as they tended to do while working together, and the next… He shoved away the memory of her legs wrapped around his waist as his body started to react.

It had been a good thing the partners hadn't paired them to work together again since then. Even seeing her in the hallways had him itching to pull her into his arms for a repeat of that night. They were on a collision course for the same position. Being anything but a hostile colleague to Kamilla would end badly. For both of them.

Nana Prah first discovered romance in a book from her eighth-grade summer reading list and has been obsessed with it ever since. Her fascination with love inspired her to write in her favorite genre where happily-ever-after is the rule.

She is a published author of contemporary multicultural romances. Her books are sweet with a touch of spice. When she's not writing, she's overindulging in chocolate, enjoying life with friends and family, and tormenting nursing students into being the best nurses the world has ever seen.

Books by Nana Prah

Harlequin Kimani Romance

A Perfect Caress
Path to Passion
Ambitious Seduction

Visit the Author Profile page
at Harlequin.com for more titles.

AMBITIOUS SEDUCTION

Nana Prah

To my best friend and sister, Matilda Ampofo.
You are the type of amazing that I look up to
and want to emulate.

Acknowledgments

A huge thanks to Zee Monodee,
who is the best at what she does. Your guidance
has helped to propel me to be a better writer.
Once again, I'm sorry that my memory is so bad.

To Glenda Howard, Melissa Senate and Katie Ortolan—
my amazing editors. It's been fabulous working with you.

Thank you, Lisa Whittle. Your legal research and
explanation about money laundering was invaluable.
Your TEDx talk truly inspired me and
I'm so glad we became friends.

My gratitude goes out to every single one of my fans
and supporters. You're the best!

Cathy, Kiru, Debbie and Empi—my appreciation
will never stop flowing in your direction.

Dear Reader,

I'm ecstatic that you've decided to read *Ambitious Seduction*. Kamilla and Leonardo have an "opposites attract" quality that I loved writing.

Kamilla grew up in foster care. With intelligence, determination and numerous jobs (which we learn about), she was able to reach her goal of becoming a successful lawyer. Her burning desire of making partner at her law firm stems from the need for economic stability.

Why does a man who is an heir to a dynasty need to make partner, you ask? It has to do with his heart. That's all I'm sharing.

Kamilla and Leonardo are amazing together. It takes some interesting circumstances for them to realize it, but they're stubborn, not stupid. I hope their story makes you laugh, shed a tear or two and release a long *awww* at the end.

I'd love to hear from you. Find me at www.nanaprah.com.

Happy reading,

Nana Prah

Chapter 1

"If I don't have the file on my desk in two minutes, I'll make sure you no longer have a job in five." Leonardo Astacio slammed the phone into its cradle.

A light knock sounded at the door. If his secretary couldn't be efficient, she could at least have a backbone. "Come in," he growled through the raw soreness of his throat.

The short Latina woman in her mid-fifties, who'd lasted longer than any of the previous secretaries, drew up the courage to look him in the eyes. "I'm sorry, Mr. Astacio." She wrung her empty hands. "The Singleton Financial documents are with another lawyer."

As a corporate attorney, he excelled at all aspects of the practice, but acquisitions and negotiating corporate contracts worth millions had become his forte.

Few others at Peterson, Benton, Monroe and Lanner could touch him. One of them being the woman who drove him insane in more ways than he should allow. He tuned out any thoughts of her.

The rumors going around had everyone on edge. He'd heard that Singleton Financial, one of the highest-ranking financial institutions in the country, representing over fifty subsidiary companies, was thinking of not renewing their contract next month. Leonardo didn't need to be included in a meeting to understand that if the information was true, it wouldn't bode well for the law firm. In the past he'd worked with the Singletons. Although the partners hadn't asked, he'd decided to get a head start on getting them to renew with the firm.

Initiative, intelligence and hard work would get him to partner status. Reaching the goal on his own terms, not with his family's influence. He'd paid his dues to the company and soon he'd earn his reward.

Not hiding his impatience, Leonardo tapped his pen against the desk. "Who has the file?"

His secretary's voice quivered when she answered. "Kamilla Gordon."

Rather than give in to his rage by punching the desk or throwing his custom-made leather chair against the wall, he leaned back and counted backward from ten.

By the time he reached five, he could unflex his fingers, but his favorite Cross pen had split at the joint. He nodded to the woman. "Thank you…"

"Rosario."

Leonardo's sniffle reminded him of why holding on

to his temper had been so draining, and he attempted not to glower. "Thank you, Rosario."

Was she waiting for an invitation to scurry out of his office? He pivoted and gazed out at the expansive twentieth-floor view of downtown Cleveland. The scene normally gave him a sense of calm. Not today.

The morning had started out rough. He'd woken up with a stuffy nose, a sore throat, a cough and a headache. Being sick annoyed him even more than losing. Over the years he'd ensured that weakness no longer made up part of his constitution. The muscles he'd developed over the skinny frame he'd sported in junior high school that helped to catapult him to star quarterback should attest to it. Sticking to a healthy organic diet and strict exercise regime, he never got sick. A sneeze escaped, mocking him all the more.

Kamilla had set him off from the first moment he'd encountered her. It had been his first day transferring in from the London office to the Cleveland branch. He'd requested the transfer because most of the partners preferred to work in the home office and he had to be seen in order to propel himself to partner at a faster rate.

Leaning the back of his head against the chair, he recalled that day as if it happened an hour ago. The staff had gathered for a short introduction. He'd become immobile at his first sight of the woman. Her get-the-job-done reputation had reached him all the way across the Atlantic, but they'd never worked together. He'd wanted to touch her flawless medium brown skin. From what he could tell, her makeup consisted of dark liner to emphasize her angled dark brown eyes and a rich burgundy lipstick, which drew his attention to her full lips. He'd found it unacceptable to be attracted to the most viable competition for the next open partnership position.

In those few seconds, he'd realized alienating her would be the only way to keep himself from falling into the attraction that lured him closer to her. The zip of electricity that stung his palm when they'd shaken hands had been the deciding factor.

Noticing she'd worn a pin boasting of Harvard, he pounced on the rivalry between Yale, his alma mater, and her school. With a snarl, he made a comment about how it was too bad she had graduated from the lesser of the two Ivy League schools. The remark alone could have been seen as a joke, but the condescending tone he'd used had set the stage for enmity between them. Just as he'd hoped, although, he'd felt uncomfortable with his snideness.

Shaking away the guilt of the past, he focused on the scenery.

He'd been avoiding her. Ever since they'd engaged in the best sex of his life two months ago. One minute they'd been arguing, as they tended to do while working together, and the next… He shoved away the memory of her legs wrapped around his waist as his body started to react.

It had been a good thing the partners hadn't paired them to work together again since then. Even seeing her in the hallways had him itching to pull her into his arms for a repeat of that night. They were on a collision course for the same position. Being anything but a hostile colleague to Kamilla would end badly. For both of them.

Why had becoming friends, or maybe even starting a relationship, seemed more of a possibility since they'd hooked up?

Rolling the chair from the desk, he stood and buttoned his suit jacket. He had a file to retrieve and a full-fledged attraction to resist.

The hair on the back of Kamilla's neck stood on end. It would only be a matter of moments before the bull charged into her tiny office, demanding the file. It wouldn't matter. The rather exceptional secretary she shared with three other associates had made a copy of it as soon as it hit her hands.

Once she'd heard the rumor about Singleton Financial wanting to find another firm to represent their conglomeration, she'd dived for their information. After being trusted to work with them within the past year, although with Leonardo, she felt obligated to encourage them to stay. What had happened to make them want to leave? It couldn't have been the work she and Leonardo had done for them; they'd been happy customers two months ago.

She wouldn't focus on what else had transpired during that time, but her skin heated at the memory that was trying to make its way to the forefront of her mind. Soon she'd be face-to-face with the man she'd been avoiding. They'd never been friends, so it hadn't been that hard to stay away. And yet her body still betrayed her on a daily basis and longed for the bear's touch.

Shaking off the biggest mistake of her life, she zoned in on her career. If she could maintain Singleton Financial as a client, she'd definitely be made partner. No way would she allow the muscle-bound Astacio to snatch the chance away from her.

Once again she wondered why he even worked for the firm. His family possessed more money than Oprah Winfrey and Bill Gates combined. He could've gone to work for his family, started his own law firm or even retired. Jealousy roared to life at how easy his life had been.

A buzz from her phone brought her out of her musings just in time to prepare her for the bear who banged her poor door against the wall before storming in. Their erotic encounter hadn't changed him a bit.

Canting her head, she presented a smile sweet enough for him to develop cavities. "How may I help you, Leonardo?" For a rather uptight law firm, they held an open policy about calling people by their first names, although most of the employees called him Mr. Astacio out of terror. She'd rather scrub toilets at an office building again, a job she'd had in high school.

He stopped in front of her desk and braced his hands on it. "You have something that belongs to me."

A thrill shimmied down her spine at being so close to him. Ignoring the way his baritone voice sounded even huskier than normal, she looked around her shared office, glad to find they were alone so they could fight toe-to-toe. "What's that?"

"Don't play games." He pointed to his chest, about to speak again, when an adorable sneeze slipped out. Followed by four more. So the big bad wolf had a cold.

From the gossip mill, she knew he never got sick. Detested doing so.

She got to her feet and walked around her desk to the door. She used it as a fan to air the room out. "Since I can't open the windows, I'd prefer if you didn't share your nasty germs with me."

His clenched broad jaw didn't scare her. Especially considering how his upturned nose now held a tinge of red after blowing it. The man had a monopoly on sexy with his large dark brown eyes and sharp cheekbones. His tailored suit hugged a muscular body she'd jump hurdles to get reacquainted with if he wasn't such an arrogant ass. *And my competition for financial freedom. Mustn't forget that.*

Lèonardo held out his hand. "Hand over the file. It's mine."

She'd worn her favorite suit to work, so she had an extra dose of power on her side. Although her outfit wasn't tailored like his, she'd spent more money on the form-flattering dark plum skirt suit than she had on three of her others combined. Kamilla perched a hand on her hip and hitched her upper body forward in a challenge. "Who says?"

"I do."

Tapping her finger against her chin, she shrugged. "Well, that's all the verification I need. I'll give it to you." She sashayed to her desk and sat on the edge. "Right after I'm finished analyzing it."

His growl didn't last long, as a rough cough ripped from his chest. Concerned, she went to her fridge, but thought better of it and then grabbed a room-temperature bottle of water and handed it to him. To her surprise he took it and chugged down half. She didn't wait for a word of gratitude, knowing she'd probably reach menopause before that happened.

His glare should've been vicious, but she found it alluring as sin. He set the bottle on the desk. "I take it you've heard the unofficial news about the Singletons?"

She nodded once in response, something she knew annoyed him. He preferred speech when communicating with him. *Yes, sir* were the words that made him the happiest. Not that she'd ever said them to him or ever would.

His cocky grin set off a spark of anger. Good to know having sex hadn't blinded her to his annoying haughtiness.

"You don't have the skills or knowledge it takes to get the job done," he goaded.

Rather than rise to the bait, she studied her clear polished nails. Manicures were the one thing she never skimped on. She tended to shovel her money toward paying back her colossal law school loans in order to gain financial freedom, but not at the cost of her hands. They gave her a singular feeling of being a feminine professional. Her wardrobe, home décor and social life had suffered, but never her nails.

"Very funny. I believe you said the same thing just before I—" she pretended to cast a fishing line and then roll the handle "—reeled in the Frasiers. And then handled the Moore account in the same month."

His almost-perfect eyebrows scrunched together as his eyes narrowed. Although her heart started bounding in a struggle to jump out of her chest, she met his gaze. "We've both worked with Singleton Financial, but they like me better."

He grunted. "How do you figure?"

She pointed back and forth between them. "Because I'm likable. To the firm's detriment, you lack the charm your younger brother possesses."

The comment seemed to hit home, as his lips formed a thin line. "Kissing people's asses has nothing to do with hard work."

"How have you gotten so far in corporate law with your brusque personality?" she mumbled. It wasn't the first time they'd had this argument. His confidence overshadowed so many negative aspects he possessed.

"Results are borne through planning and persistence. Friendliness is not on the list." He smiled at her then. Wolfish yet sexy enough to make her shiver. Was it in anticipation or fear?

"Now give me the file so I can get to work."

With a long-suffering sigh, she went around her desk and closed the thick folder she'd been reading. Holding it out to him, she pulled it back just as his hand was about to grasp it. "I *will* get the Singletons to sign the contract, Leo." The use of the nickname brought on the twitch in his jaw muscle she liked seeing. "You can bet on it."

He reached forward and snatched the dossier. "I don't make bets I don't consider a challenge." His words lost some of his impact when he rushed to cover his mouth as another cute sneeze escaped. "Dammit."

"Feel better," she teased with a finger wave. And

she'd actually meant it. Having worked part-time for a year in college at a hospital, assisting patients to perform their basic activities of living, she hated seeing people suffer from illness.

He whipped out of her office so fast, she expected to hear the door slam. The man hadn't bothered to close it.

She'd expected something different from their little meeting. He really hadn't been affected by their one night together. She frowned in disappointment because that's all she seemed to think about.

Slinking into her seat, Kamilla made a resolution. She didn't care what had to be done—she'd get the Singletons to stay with the firm. No spoiled, rich brat would stop her.

Chapter 2

Kamilla tucked the gold cookie tin tight to her chest while beaming at the only person she'd ever truly been close to. "You're the best friend I've ever had in my life." She needed the fortifying gift after dealing with Leonardo that morning.

Casey Mendez's snort distorted her features as they spoke on Skype. "More like the only one. You have a habit of keeping people at a distance."

Kamilla tilted her head and feigned indignation with a fierce narrowing of her eyes. "I do not. I'm sweet, likable—"

"And possess more than your share of arrogance, which can come off as standoffish," Cass said with a sharp nod of her head.

Kamilla's hand rushed to her chest as she took in a

sharp inhale of protest. "I do not. The people in the office love me."

Bunching her hair into a high ponytail for the run she was dressed for, Cass rolled her eyes. "First you scare them into submission when you meet them and then you spoil them with a gourmet cupcake on their birthday. You're a manipulator. And I say that with respect because you came from nowhere only to work for one of the most prestigious law firms in the state."

Kamilla cleared her throat in an exaggerated manner and smoothed down the short dark hair at the back of her pixie-style cut.

"Fine," Cass relented, "the country."

"Since Peterson, Benton, Monroe and Lanner has a firm in London, you may as well say the universe." Kamilla opened the tin and inhaled the scent of enticing cinnamon cookies.

Cass chuckled. "You could've just said the world. Western hemisphere would've been even more humble. Besides, we don't know about the law firms on alien planets."

She waggled her finger in front of the computer screen. "You're not going there, Cass. Not today. You and your Trekkie behind need to change the subject."

Once again laughter burst from her friend. "How about we discuss what's been making you act like Ms. Cranky Pants for the past few months."

Air got trapped in Kamilla's throat as anxiety tightened her windpipe. Reaching into the tin of homemade snickerdoodle cookies Cass had overnighted, she broke off a large piece of one and popped it in her mouth. The succulent treat would prevent her from having to speak, but wouldn't stop her friend from utilizing guerrilla tactics. Cass would've made a fantastic prosecutor; instead she ended up becoming an editor for a big-time publisher. Kamilla couldn't be prouder.

Her best friend stared at her through the screen. Ever since becoming a mother, Cass's gaze had become more powerful and Kamilla felt the cookie settle hard in her stomach. They'd already discussed her incredible night with Leonardo and she didn't want to rehash it again. Maybe she could get around this conversation. "Speaking of silly nicknames, how are my nieces doing?"

The thought of her two energetic and loving daughters relaxed Cass's threatening glare a fraction. "They keep requesting their Aunty Kam. If I have to hear them asking when you're coming for a visit one more time, I think I'll scream. When are you coming down?"

Three hours wasn't a long way to drive to see the only people she considered family, even though none of them were blood related. She and Cass had hit it off from the first foster home Kamilla had been tossed into at age seven. They'd lived in the same house for three years before Cass had gotten transferred to another foster home, where the family adopted her.

Fate had been more than kind to them by letting them attend the same schools up until their sophomore year of high school, when Cass's family had moved. By that time their bond had been cemented. Their friendship had been the only stable aspect of her tossed-about life.

Kamilla sighed, wishing she could take off from work and hang out with the two little girls who thought she walked on water. She gestured toward a stack of files that were just out of screenshot. "The workload is crazy. And you know I need to impress the bosses if I want to be considered for partner anytime soon."

"Girl, you've been working for them for five years as if you owned the company yourself. When was the last time you took a vacation?"

"I came to see you guys a few months ago."

Cass sucked her teeth. "You were here for two days, that's including the day you arrived and the day you left."

Kamilla scrunched her nose. She'd committed to making partner and nothing would stop her. Not even missing the people she loved. "It's not about the quantity, but the quality of time I spend with you all."

"That's a load of puppy poop and you know it. You've made yourself a slave to that law firm. And all for what? So you can be partner in a branch of law you don't even like."

Kamilla's eyes snapped up to the door of the office she shared with another associate as she reached for her headphones to plug them into the computer. "Oh my goodness, Cass, are you out of your mind? I'm at the office."

"So? The truth is the truth. Tell me that you enjoy your job and I'll take back everything I just said."

Her shoulders slumped. Without ever having to speak the words to her best friend, she'd already figured it out. "I'm excellent at corporate law and I make a lot of money." She brightened. "I'm almost finished paying off my student loans. Just six more months and I'll be free of the system."

Cass shook her head slowly as a frown disturbed her mixed-heritage light brown skin. "At what cost, Kam? Nothing in your life has been easy, but you've succeeded despite the hardships." Cass's eyes took on a glossiness. "I just want you to be happy. Out of all the people I know, you deserve it most. Working for that firm isn't making you happy."

Kamilla swallowed hard to get rid of the lump. She hated getting sentimental. Weakness hadn't been accepted in the foster care system, so she'd never had the luxury of delving into her feelings. "Who in this world enjoys their job?"

Cass raised her hand and began to speak when Kamilla cut her off. "Other than your lucky-assed self. Most people do what they have to do. Making partner at this firm is what I need to do to make sure I have a job forever. I'll pick up a hobby or something once I get the position."

"I just wish—"

"I live in the real world, where wishes don't come true, so I stopped believing a long time ago." Why hadn't things gone differently in her life? She sometimes wondered what type of person she'd be if she'd been adopted instead of tossed around the foster care system until she broke free. Then she'd remember it didn't matter. She'd defied every single one of the odds set against her and made something of herself.

With her lips pursed, Cass nodded. "I hear you, but I won't stop hoping you get the better that you deserve."

Kamilla smiled. "You'd better not. I'm relying on your positive thoughts to catapult me toward partner. Keep these homemade care packages coming, too." She broke off another piece of the cinnamon-and-sugar-topped treats and held it up to the screen. "I think these might be the best you've ever made."

"Thanks." Cass perked up. "The girls said they put an extra helping of love in for their aunty."

She placed a hand on her thudding chest. She loved those girls as if they were her own. She'd have to take at least a day to go see them. Then she glanced at the amount of work she had to do. One day. "Tell them it made the cookies extra-special and that I miss them loads. I'll talk to them on Saturday. Enjoy your run and burn some calories for me."

Cass gave her a pointed look. "Is that your way of getting off the phone before talking about what's been bothering you?"

Uh-oh. "I'm fine."

"My ass," Cass mumbled.

Kamilla's eyes widened. Her friend never cussed. Once she'd learned about the parroting nature of children, she'd refrained from saying anything she wouldn't be proud to have them say in public.

"I see you're still in denial about that one-night stand you had with him."

Her heart sped up as heat raced to her face. Her dark skin hid her flush well. "It happened two months ago and you promised to never speak of it again." Fifty-four days had passed since she'd made the biggest mistake of her life with Leonardo Astacio. She'd paid for it every time he walked into the room and he seemed unaffected. Sure the sizzle of attraction that had been building since the first day they'd met a little over two years ago still swirled between them, but that was it.

He may have gotten her out of his system that night when they'd torn each other's clothes off after bickering while working alone. Damn those partners for seeing how good they were together. Damn Leonardo for a sexual experience so exceptional, she still throbbed when he came near. Damn them all.

"It was one—" Kamilla cleared the huskiness from her throat "—time. It didn't mean anything. Besides I can't stand his arrogant ass." Why did it bother her that they'd avoided each other rather than discuss the incident like two responsible adults?

"I've been around you two and I think you'd make the perfect couple."

"No, Cass. You will not go down this road again. He's a flipping heir to the damn Astacio dynasty. That family is worth billions. I still for the life of me can't figure out why he works for this firm, but he's good. Almost as good as me, and that makes him a threat."

"Whatever. You can deny that you like him, but I know you. You might even be in love with him. That's why he bothers you so much."

"Pah," Kamilla spat. "Love, my behind. He's a fine specimen of a man and we had a great time together, but that's all it will ever be." She wouldn't focus on how her fingers had caressed his tightly corded muscles under his glorious brown skin that almost matched hers exactly. No, the thought of him looking into her eyes with passion blazing as he drove into her would not help her case at this point in time. She shifted in her seat to reduce the unexpected moisture to her core.

"It was a onetime…mistake after a dry spell of three and a half years. Any man would've gotten the job done. Plus we were both exhausted from those late-night hours." The excuses she'd used to comfort herself after doing the unthinkable still didn't feel right. "If you'd stop bringing it up, I would've forgotten it by now." She crossed her fingers under her desk at the bare-faced lie. "He's a gruff, spoiled, conceited bastard who wants to take my job. One-night stand or not. I won't let him. I've worked hard for that position and no one's going to steal it from me."

Cass raised and pushed out both palms in Kamilla's direction as she smirked. "Calm it down, girl. Obviously you aren't in love with him since you don't even seem to like him."

She chose to ignore the blatant tone of sarcasm and gave a sharp nod of agreement. "You're talking sense now."

"On that note I'll let you get back to work so you can catapult up the ranks. I love you."

"You, too." Without a formal goodbye, they clicked to discontinue the call at the same time.

Kamilla sat back in her seat now that she no longer had to defend herself against allegations she didn't want to deal with. She and Leonardo getting involved in a relationship would be a joke of massive proportions and she wouldn't be the one laughing.

Chapter 3

Leonardo glared at Kamilla when she waltzed into the room. Interacting with her shouldn't satisfy him as much as it did. As always she looked good. A more tailored outfit would fit her better, but the cut of the navy blue suit emphasized her small waist, which flared out into curvaceous hips. He hardened recalling how his hands had dug into her flesh as he'd driven into her. He snatched his gaze away and thought of poisonous spiders crawling up his arms in order to get his lower body under control.

"Good morning, gentlemen," she said with a full smile before sparing him the slightest glance. "Leonardo."

He didn't have time for her particular brand of fire. He'd let his temper cool over at least five cups of tea with lemon, honey and ginger last night. Even with the fluids and bowls of chicken noodle soup he'd ingested, he still felt like crap and would rather be home in bed, but nothing outside of being knocked over by a semitruck and landing in the hospital would make that happen.

Patrick Benton, one of the firm's founding partners, waved in the direction of the aged dark leather chair angled toward Leonardo and the main desk. "Please have a seat, Kamilla."

Henry Lanner sat on the couch, while Patrick occupied the seat behind his desk.

Henry made eye contact with each of them in turn. "We've heard that Singleton Financial, a major client, has sent out feelers to other law firms." He leaned forward and, resting his elbows on the desk, steepled his fingers. "You've both worked on their account. I don't need to tell you how horrifically it would affect the firm if they left. Not only financially, but our hard-earned reputation would be downgraded. We've been attempting to figure out what has dissatisfied them and have come up with nothing. Our work is exemplary."

Leonardo held back a grunt. Didn't he mean the associates' work?

Patrick shifted on the couch. "We can't lose this client. Having them sign their contract next month is our number one priority. That's why you two are here."

Henry nodded. "It's no secret you're the superstar associates of the firm. You have the most billable hours of any other associate."

Was the man talking to him or Kamilla? Leonardo would feel better if he knew. Kamilla spent as much time in the office as he did, but obviously it had to be him. A quick glance at the woman with her proud grin told him she might've come to a similar conclusion with her as the victor.

"Don't think we haven't noticed just how good you are apart, but together, your work is impeccable. You get the work done in record time," Patrick said.

Because we can't stand each other. At least that had been the case before they'd had sex on his desk. Now he didn't want to be around her for other reasons. The longing desire to delve his tongue inside her sarcastic mouth ranked number one. He had to keep reminding himself that her status as the sole impediment to his making partner should've ranked as first. Yet something had changed. At least it had for him.

Henry tagged in on the conversation. "You're a perfect combination. A dynamic duo. That's why we've decided to pair you. Your duty is to secure the Singletons and ensure that they sign their contract."

The hint of desperation in Henry's tone told Leonardo of a whole lot more going on than they'd explained. Was the firm in trouble? Even if they lost Singleton Financial as a client, they should be fine. It'd be a hard blow, but nothing that their other prestigious clientele couldn't cover. The mystery of why Singleton Financial wanted to leave pressed on his curiosity.

Kamilla scooted to the edge of her seat and opened her mouth to speak. She must've thought better of it and closed it. Leonardo never thought he'd see the day when she'd keep her trap shut.

Henry leaned back into his tan leather chair. "Teamwork is absolutely necessary if we're to win the Singletons over. Kamilla's more personable approach with a no-holds-barred demeanor will complement your harder, more driven method of getting what you want, Leonardo."

He ignored Kamilla's pointed glance in his direction. Why was everyone attacking his personality this week? He could be charming. Okay, so maybe he couldn't, but it didn't make him an ogre. He worked well with people. Especially those who didn't need to be babied.

They wanted them to work together. A hell no sat on the tip of his tongue. He could get Singleton Financial to sign on his own. Without being tortured by her damn lavender scent. Fighting the need to smooth his fingers through her short hair. Nibbling on the sweet spot he'd discovered on the side of her neck that had made her moan. Tasting her succulent lips like he'd done in his dreams. Something he'd neglected to do when they'd had sex. He'd been kicking himself over the lost opportunity ever since.

Hauling out the tiny bit of humility he possessed, Leonardo rubbed his chin and cleared out some unwanted phlegm from his throat before speaking. "I'm not sure about working with Ms. Gordon. Of course she's an intelligent and hard-working woman and has been an asset to the firm." He ignored the choked sound that came from her direction at his genuine compliment. "But I firmly assure you that I can and will be able to gain the Singletons' confidence enough to sign with us again if I work alone."

Kamilla pasted on her fake grin. The kind that didn't set her eyes twinkling as she touched her palm to her chest. "I beg to differ. I would appreciate the opportunity to collaborate with Mr. Astacio. He's been nothing but an exemplary inspiration over the years and I believe we'll work well together, as we have previously, to keep Singleton Financial with our firm."

Couldn't they see her teeth gritting as she lied through them?

"Thank you so much for considering me," she continued. "His reputation precedes him and it's always a learning experience working by his side."

A cough of surprise escaped Leonardo as he realized she'd gotten the drop. His eyes watered as one cough kept replacing the previous one. Damn, he hated being ill. Grateful for the room-temperature bottle of water pressed into his hand, he drank. A quick look at the woman's calculating eyes that were contrasted with a concerned smile had him seeing red. Two could play at her little game.

"Thank you for the water."

"My pleasure," she said with a smirk. "I couldn't have my partner suffering."

"Partner." He nodded. "It has a nice ring to it." Yeah, just like standing inside a bell tower when it chimes. "If you don't mind working with me on such an intensive case, then I could certainly give it a shot."

The true Kamilla came out for a second with an eye squint. Of course she wouldn't believe the lies he'd spouted. The senior partners were the ones he'd been attempting to convince.

Most likely sensing the bubble of tension that had exploded between them, Henry clapped his hands and stood. He rounded his desk and stood in front of them. "I'm glad we've settled this. If you need any help, please don't hesitate to ask." Why did his tone sound disapproving? Would they make them take the fall if he and

Kamilla didn't get the Singletons to sign? He wouldn't put it past them. "Shall I remind you of the substantial bonus? And a potential shot at partnership?"

Leonardo couldn't care less about the money. He possessed more than enough. The manipulative man hadn't mentioned which one of them would be up for partner when they succeeded. It didn't matter. He'd made up his mind when he'd applied to the firm a little over five years ago that he'd get the position. He never failed. Ever.

Kamilla's eyes glittered for a moment before a husky laugh broke free from her mouth. "No need to remind me. It will keep me working hard to get the job done. But the true satisfaction—" she paused and patted Leonardo's arm "—will come from once again working as a team to accomplish the firm's objective."

She'd upped him again. It would've never happened if he'd been healthy. Damn cold. With a grace he knew other men of his bulk didn't possess, he stood, towering over her. "We should get started on our plan of action. I heard the Singletons will be back from Tokyo next week."

The flash of surprise that crossed her features at his intel on the power couple pleased him.

"That reminds me. I'm redistributing your current clients." Henry held up his hands to ward off any protest. "Don't worry, you'll get them back *once* Singleton Financial has signed with us. Until then I want you both focused."

Leonardo responded with a downward jerk of his head. There was that subtle threat again. Would either of them have a job if they didn't acquire the Singleton Financial account? It didn't matter, because he'd win. No matter what he had to do.

Chapter 4

Kamilla closed the door to Leonardo's office. The man had the whole place to himself. Sometimes it paid to be so mean that no one wanted to share space with you. She swallowed hard as she tried not to stare at the desk where they'd had sex. It had been almost two months since she'd walked into this room. When they had to meet, she insisted on using the large glass-walled conference room.

Daily pep talks ensured that her defenses against their attraction would never lower to the point of throwing herself at him again, but she'd prefer not to risk it.

A quick flick of her tongue against her lips returned the moisture to them. "Is it me or was that meeting coded and peculiar?"

For once that crinkle between his brows indicating his agitation wasn't directed at her. "It wasn't just you."

"Did they just threaten us with our jobs?"

He sat behind his desk and sneezed. "The most subtle threat I've ever received."

She walked to the small bar, bent behind it and pulled out an electric kettle. "I'll be right back." After a quick return trip to the coffee room, she plugged the filled device into the socket and switched it on. "If it's so important to them, then why not just approach the Singletons themselves?"

"Do you know who you work for?"

Her back straightened at the question and she opened her mouth to say something sarcastic when he held up his hands to ward her off.

"Calm down. I didn't mean offense."

She relaxed, but kept her mental guard up. It's what made being around the man so exhausting. "Then what did you mean?"

The kettle clicked, indicating that the water had boiled, and she flipped two mugs over. In one she placed a tea bag and then poured out water into both mugs. She grabbed a lemon from the bowl sitting on a shelf in the bar and cut it. Using the manual juicer, she squeezed the juice and poured it into the hot water. Then she squirted two tablespoons of honey into both mugs and stirred.

Careful not to spill the scalding liquid, she made her way to his desk and placed the water, lemon and honey concoction in front of him.

She took the seat across from him and looked up to find an expression on Leonardo's face she'd never seen before. Could the tilted head and wiggly brows be confusion? He was always so overconfident and sure about everything. She hated it.

Realization dawned that she'd made him something she'd only seen him drink when he'd been sick. It had happened once since she'd known him. He'd first returned to Cleveland and had to face the treacherous winter. He'd recovered in record time and ever since, she'd drank the same brew when she got a cold. Way more often than he ever did.

"You could say thank you," she snapped in an attempt to cover her embarrassment at having served him. She wouldn't have done it if he'd asked, but he looked miserable and it tugged at her heart. The man should be in bed, not dealing with manipulative bosses.

He picked up the mug and held it out to her. "If I didn't see you make it myself, I'd think it was poisoned."

On more comfortable ground, she winked. "Have you never heard of sleight of hand? Drink at your own peril."

He blew on the hot liquid and then took a sip. "Thank you." A small grin came to his face. "For not killing me…today."

She laughed before taking a drink of her own tea. She wouldn't think about how at ease she was with him at the moment. She'd enjoy it knowing that, like a clearance sale, it wouldn't last. "Tell me what you meant by the comment about me knowing the firm."

He took another sip and placed the mug on the desk before wrapping his hands around it. With the slight bags under his eyes and reddened nose, she restrained herself from getting up and placing her hand against his forehead to see if he had a fever. The man needed to rest, but she wasn't about to tell him. He had enough sense to discern it for himself. But then again Leonardo had to be the most stubborn man she'd ever met.

"The partners didn't get to the top of the corporate food chain by being kind and generous to everyone they encountered. There are rumors about just how dirty they can get when it comes to acquiring what they want."

She squirmed at the unsettling discussion. "Of course I've heard some of the rumors." She hadn't wanted to believe any of them were true. Working for people who would use blackmail and other underhanded, not to mention illegal, actions in order to obtain and maintain their position had never sat right with her. She'd brushed the talk aside as nothing more than vicious gossip.

"I have no doubt they'd fire, or even sue, us if we didn't get the Singletons to sign."

She took a gulp of her tea and, forgetting it was hot, scalded her tongue. This day was not going as she'd envisioned. First she was forced to work with Leonardo again, and then she had it confirmed that her bosses were the boogeymen. Now her tongue throbbed in pain.

"But we'll get the job done." When had she started thinking of them as a team? Probably around the time she realized her ass had been set on fire and she could get terminated instead of promoted if she failed.

His lids drooped as if he were fighting to stay awake. "Only if what the partners did to the Singletons wasn't so grievous that they refuse to forgive them."

She sighed, having come to the same conclusion when she'd heard about their wanting to leave the firm.

"Is this errand a way to get rid of us? Their best associates? Their biggest moneymakers?"

He lifted a hefty shoulder before he drank. "I have no idea. I learned about business from my parents, and they're honest with their dealings. Being underhanded, despite what people may think, is not my way."

Was he fishing for reassurance? "I don't think there's a single soul in this building who thinks that. We all know you're mean and surly, even on your good days, but you're honest, direct and straight as an arrow."

What road had the conversation taken that she'd complimented him? Just yesterday she would've rather knocked out two of her front teeth than be kind to him. Why was he being nice? Almost normal. Could it be a result of the sex? Incredible as it had been, did it have the power to change his attitude toward her? She'd been too busy eluding him to notice it before.

It had to be the cold making him seem more human.

He merely grunted at her. Typical. "All I know is that it's always best to have a plan B."

A moment of terror struck. She had no other plans. She'd worked her tail off and sacrificed having a life in order to be seen as partner material. If she didn't make it and she got sacked instead, she had no idea what she'd do. Calming herself with deep breaths, she remembered her bar certification and remarkable reputation would get her another job. She'd always landed on her feet, even if sometimes it had been in marshy areas.

"I'm going to stay positive." Standing, she indicated the Singletons' file with a wave of her hand. "We'll come up with a plan. In the meantime you need to go home and get some rest. You look like crap."

He chuckled and the sound resonated in her chest, spreading warmth through her. She shook it off because she had no business feeling anything when he was around. "Is that why you took pity on me and served me the hot drink."

"Don't get used to it, Astacio."

"Not even in my sweetest dreams."

Grabbing her mug, she resigned herself to leave. "Get some sleep. I don't need a zombie helping me to lose my job. I'd rather get the promotion to partner."

"Over my dead body."

Kamilla laughed as she looked over her shoulder. "If you insist." She could get accustomed to a nicer Leonardo. Even like him. Maybe… No. She wouldn't let her mind go there. Nothing had changed. They were still chasing the same position, and only one of them would get the chance to succeed.

Now that she knew she had more to lose than she'd initially thought, she'd make sure she got the promotion. By any means necessary.

Chapter 5

Leonardo parked in front of his brother's home. For such a worldly man, Miguel had chosen a simple building which melded into its surrounding environment. Nice, but much too rural for Leonardo to be comfortable with. His condo in the heart of Cleveland suited him. The steady stream of activity calmed him more than the chirping of birds and crickets ever could.

He rolled his shoulders, tense after working and arguing with Kamilla the day after she'd sent him home to rest and let his body recover from the ravages of his illness. He had no idea who he'd been more irritated with as they'd worked, himself for having been weak enough to sleep it off or her for her cocky, know-it-all smile when she'd met him in the conference room. She'd been right. The extra sleep had done him wonders, and although he wasn't up to 100 percent, he felt more like himself.

At least things were back to normal between them, as evidenced by their constant bickering. This time he did it because it entertained him to do so, not because he wanted to keep her at a distance. The opposite was the case, and he had no idea how to rectify it. Or if he should. Things had become blurred when they'd slept together. A part of him wished it had never happened, but the majority rebuked the thought.

The door opened to Miguel's perpetually grinning face, and he pulled Leonardo into a hug. "Hey, bro."

Leonardo embraced him. His family was the most important thing to him. And just like he did life, he cherished them. "Hey."

"Good to see you." Miguel glanced down at his watch. "What's going on, it's seven in the evening. Why aren't you still at work?"

The words weren't meant in a sarcastic way. He could be known to work until eleven at night. He'd set his mind on reaching his objective and he'd sacrifice his time to get there. "My partner told me to knock off early."

His brother quirked a brow. "And you listened? Wait, did you say partner?"

They'd reached the living room and sat. "Mom would scold you big-time. Don't you offer your guests a drink when they enter your home?"

Miguel laughed, something that came readily to him. Because he was the youngest, they'd all spoiled him. It didn't help that Miguel had gotten Leonardo's share of the family charm. Kamilla had been right on point when she'd mentioned it the other day. It didn't normally bother him that he lacked people skills, but it had irked him when she'd remarked on it.

"You, Nardo, are not a guest. You know right where the kitchen is and are welcome to anything in there."

Leonardo struggled to keep from reacting to the nickname his brother had garnered him with as children. He could tolerate the nickname Leo from some people, but he found Nardo unacceptable. Only his brother knew how to get on his nerves with a single word.

Kamilla's face popped into his mind. She had the uncanny ability to do the same. If only she wasn't so damn beautiful, witty and good at her job, he wouldn't think about her so much. "Fine, be a bad host. Do you have lemon and honey?" His throat still felt a little scratchy.

Miguel got up and slapped him on the shoulder. "I thought you looked worn down. Not feeling well?"

Leonardo couldn't help smiling at the memory of Kamilla placing the mug in front of him. It had been an act of pure kindness, something neither of them ever showed each other, and it had softened something in him. "Better than yesterday."

"Good. I won't tell Mom. You know how she freaks out when you get sick."

Leonardo cut his brother a look as he reached for the kettle. "Which is never." Ever since he'd been young, his parents had worried about him. Two heart surgeries when he'd been six to correct a congenital defect could do that to parents. He rubbed the scar on his chest through his shirt. "Besides, I'm fine."

Miguel studied him for a moment. "When was the last time you had a checkup?"

This is why he rarely visited the family he loved so much. They were always on him about his health. "I'm a grown-ass man. I know how to take care of myself."

"I'd believe it if you didn't work so hard." Miguel pointed an accusing finger in his direction. "For nothing, I might add. Dad's ready for you to get over this independent kick and come start the law firm for him."

Every moment he spent slaving away for his firm brought him closer to his ultimate goal of leaving. Making partner would reveal his readiness to take on the most important job of his life. Opening a law firm under the Astacio name to represent the subsidiary companies his family owned. His grandparents and parents had dipped their hands into every aspect of business that had interested them, from pharmaceuticals to fashion, and they'd succeeded.

Over the years he'd worked hard in order to prove himself. Not to his formerly overprotective parents or to the world who thought he'd gotten everything handed to him, but to himself. He needed to know that, no matter what happened, he'd be able to handle whatever came his way.

Leonardo brought his attention to the singing kettle and went over to it. "I'll make it there eventually. I just need to do this first." When silence filled the room instead of one of Miguel's smart-mouthed comments, he looked up. His brother was staring at him with concern in his easy-to-read hazel eyes. Did he look that bad? "What?"

Miguel's expression cleared to its normal jovial grin. "I was wondering what Lanelle would say if I told her you were sick and haven't been to the doctor to get checked out."

Every muscle in his body flexed as he glared at his youngest sibling. "You wouldn't dare." Their middle sibling was even more protective than his parents. Her caring nature extended to all aspects of her life, from the people she aided as a philanthropist to her family. If Miguel said anything to her, he'd be swept off his feet by Hurricane Lanelle to the hospital for a forced examination.

"Fine," Leonardo mumbled as he poured the water into the mug. "I went to the cardiologist last month for my annual assessment. All the tests came back normal."

"Good," Miguel said. "I don't understand why you couldn't have said that before I put the fear of Lanelle into you." His laughter filled the large kitchen. "For such a sweet woman, our sister is a force to be reckoned with."

Leonardo chuckled. "Damn straight." He wouldn't want her to be any other way.

Stirring his drink, he walked behind Miguel to the living room, now ready to talk about why he'd dropped by unannounced. Loathe to come to Miguel for help, Leonardo had no other option.

Miguel sat forward. "You look a little stressed."

Leonardo knew every intricacy on how to set aims and get them met. Once he had a plan, he'd go to any length to implement it. What he had no clue about, as both Kamilla and one of the partners had mentioned yesterday, was charm.

Kamilla had been right. Although they both did stellar work on the Singleton accounts, they preferred meetings with her present. He needed to change this. He refused to contemplate how much of it involved impressing Kamilla.

Leonardo would never be called a ladies' man. He'd learned long ago that women had their own agenda when it came to dealing with him. Unlike his brother, he refused to cajole someone when he didn't have to. He didn't live the life of a monk, but his numbers didn't come anywhere close to Miguel's, who'd previously been called a man-whore in more than one of the less reputable tabloids.

He took a sip of the drink and let the heat roll down his throat. "I need to become charming."

Rather than laugh as he'd expected, his brother considered him before moving to sit closer to him on the couch. "Have you finally fallen in love with someone who doesn't run away from your ugly grill?"

Although he'd been in relationships, they'd tended to be brief and unilateral, with the woman caring way too much and him not enough. Once again a woman with a nineties Halle Barry short hairstyle and hips that had him staring when she left a room came to mind. "Don't be preposterous. This is for work. There's a client I have to deal with."

Miguel laughed. "First lesson, charmers don't *deal*

with anyone. We play, sweet-talk and flatter. Second, you might have to break your jaw."

Leonardo shifted his chin from side to side. "Why?"

"You're going to have to smile and I don't think your face will allow it without a rearrangement."

"Funny," Leonardo spat out. So what if he wasn't as happy-go-lucky as his younger brother? He just didn't possess that type of nature.

"Baby," a female voice said. "Which floral arrangement would be best for the rehearsal dinner?" Tanya Carrington looked up from the iPad she held and halted. "Hi, Leonardo. Um, I see you're busy, Miguel, I'll—" she pointed behind her and started backtracking "—talk to you about it later." She spun on her heel and jogged out of the room.

Miguel's howl of laughter as he jumped off the couch almost deafened Leonardo. "Sweetheart," he choked out through his laughter as he ran to catch his fiancée.

So he hadn't made the best first impression on Tanya at Miguel's thirtieth birthday party. That had been months ago, and she still found it difficult to be in his presence. Something that had never sat right with him. His future sister-in-law should be comfortable enough with him to at least have a conversation.

Miguel wiped tears from his eyes as he held what seemed to be an unhappy Tanya beside him. He sat in the armchair and settled the woman he'd loved since college onto his lap. "My brother has come for lessons in how to be charming."

Tanya looked dubiously at Leonardo, who could've body-slammed Miguel. Instead, he nodded his head, which made his soon-to-be second sister throw him a genuine smile.

"You came to the right man." She spoke the words directly to Miguel as they shared a moment so intense, he felt an unexpected pang of jealousy for never having felt so deeply about someone. But then, once again Kamilla came to mind and his unease increased. He wouldn't think about her.

Leonardo cleared his throat, drawing the couple out of their cocoon. They focused their attention on him.

"I thought you could help me," Miguel said to Tanya. This made the smile she'd given him a moment ago pale in comparison.

"Be nice," she said as she looked Leonardo straight in the eyes. "You being charming would seem fake. It's just not what you are, but you can do kind. The basics, like *please* and *thank you*, go a long way. Asking rather than demanding something would be a plus, too. And compliments. Sincere ones also make people happy and comfortable."

Her words had a backhanded quality to them, but at least she'd been honest. "Been thinking about this much?"

"Since the day I met you."

The men laughed. Leonardo knew they'd have a better relationship. "Thank you, Tanya." And he meant it. "Would you like to add anything, Miguel?"

"Nope. My ultimate blessing said it all." He kissed her on the cheek. "Isn't she wonderful?"

For the woman to have captured Miguel, he knew she definitely had to be. Would he ever find someone he wanted to be with? His mind flicked to Kamilla's determined expression and something tightened in his chest. He'd have to deal with the powerful attraction between them one day. Maybe even have a long-overdue talk about the incredible sex they'd had.

What did he want from her? For the first time in his life, he had no idea what objective to set in regard to her. Yes, they were in competition for partner, yet at the same time she drove him to be a better lawyer. A better person. And that he couldn't walk away from.

Chapter 6

No better time to make a change in his life than as soon as possible. Leonardo had asked his brother for help and had gotten it. Just not in the way he'd thought. Something easier would've been appreciated. He could be nice. Maybe not nice, but kinder than he used to be. Tanya had mentioned baby steps. He tended to leap when it came to reaching objectives, but he'd follow her advice.

He set the box of chocolates he'd picked up from the grocery store last night onto his secretary's desk. He'd been harsh when he'd been sick, even worse than usual. He had difficulty drawing forth a smile, but was able to speak without grumbling. "Good morning…" Damn, what was her name again? Miguel had mentioned the importance of calling people by their correct name, smiling and being interested in what they had to say without cutting them off. No matter how much nonsense they spouted.

The woman stood and stepped around the chair. He presumed for easier access to an exit. "Rosario."

"Right, Rosario." He tapped the flat cellophane-covered box. "These are for you." He gritted his teeth and then remembered he wasn't supposed to do that either. "I've been a little…difficult the past couple of days." As close as he'd get to an apology, he watched her eyes shift between him and the chocolate several times.

She took another step toward the exit and made an audible swallow. Keeping her gaze on Leonardo, she mumbled, "Thank you."

More uncomfortable than he'd been approaching Miguel and Tanya for help last night, he took off into his office. Slumping into his chair, he relieved his quivering legs. What the hell was wrong with him? He'd done nice things for people before.

The near apology he'd ripped off his tongue had been new. A fierce shake of his head brought him back to his normal work-driven state. At least his cold was almost gone. He'd woken up fully rested after not having hacked his lungs out with vicious coughing as he had the past few nights. And his throat held no pain.

Now he had to figure out ways to be nice to people without getting nauseous while doing it.

A glance at his Rolex told him Kamilla would be arriving soon. The woman would be too much of a challenge to practice his newfound not-quite-charm on just yet. Besides, she'd see right through him and laugh her cute behind off. Then they'd fight.

He squelched the anticipation.

Kamilla hauled Rosario down the hall and peeked into the break room. The tantalizing scent of the gourmet coffee Kamilla had savored only fifteen minutes earlier filled the empty area.

Two minutes ago she'd dragged herself from her office to Leonardo's for their meeting. Combing through the Singletons' file and brainstorming with him last week had been taxing. On a normal basis he tended to be difficult to deal with. Working with a sick Leonardo, she'd barely stopped herself from jumping over the conference table to put him in a sleeper hold to knock his ass out.

The presence of a box of chocolates on Rosario's desk had spurred the mini abduction of the administrative assistant. "Tell me again, word for word, what happened."

After Rosario's second telling of the tale, Kamilla leaned against the counter. "Has he ever apologized for his behavior before?"

"I've worked here for six months. Although he's never been as much of a bastard as he's been this week, he takes it as his right to treat people the way he wants. Usually brusque, impatient and selfish."

Kamilla grinned at Rosario's marked lack of apology for the slight against her boss. Kamilla had often called him worse by adding colorful expletives.

Rosario pointed a finger toward the ceiling. "Although I remember this one time."

"What?" Kamilla braced for the story, oddly excited by the prospect of Leonardo being a human with actual feelings and the ability to be kind. She'd bandied the term *android* about in her mind much too often regarding him.

The twinkle in Rosario's eyes indicated she had some juicy gossip to share. "He asked me to send a copy of a file to the city court on his personal letterhead. The case had nothing to do with the firm. As I made the duplicates, I noticed the invoice. He never charged the client for his services."

A double gasp of shock scraped down Kamilla's throat. "Was he working pro bono?"

Rosario nodded. "That's the exact same reaction I had. The address of the small company he represented was set in one of the rougher areas of the city."

Kamilla pulled out a chair and sank into it as the most unethical thought flew through her mind. She wouldn't believe it unless she saw those files for herself.

It must've escaped her lips, because once again Rosario's head bobbed. "I know it was none of my business, and could probably get me fired, but I was so shocked that the dragon would do something nice for another that I couldn't help myself."

Kamilla yearned to run and gain access to Leonardo's files so she could rummage through them. "What did you do?"

The woman stepped closer and whispered. "I looked up his client information on the database."

She really shouldn't be supporting the woman's intrusive behavior at the workplace, but Rosario was one of the sweetest and most industrious workers in the firm. Kamilla had heard that she'd bawled after hearing about her assignment to work with Leonardo.

"And?" Kamilla prompted.

Rosario smoothed her already perfect bun. "He takes on one pro bono case a month. Sometimes two. He's done this for the whole time he's worked here in Cleveland. I couldn't find out about his work in London."

A rush of air left Kamilla's lungs as the information registered. Did he have a heart under that tough-as-nails exterior? Having too much to process at the moment, she stood. "We'd better get going. I wouldn't want him to bellow down the hallway, looking for you. And if I'm late for our meeting, all hell will break loose. Thanks for the information, Rosario."

"You won't tell anyone what I did?"

"Of course not. But I'd stay out of the system files if I were you. I'm sure there are things in there not everyone is meant to know."

"Thank you." Rosario's brows knit together. "Do you think it's safe to eat the chocolate he gave me?"

Kamilla laughed as they left. "I'm pretty sure. Check carefully for tiny holes and rips around the box, indicating tampering."

"You're very funny."

Her jar of gossip had been filled to overflowing. The fact that the man who irritated her the most out of anyone she'd ever met did good things for other people had shaken her foundation. *If he's capable of this, what else is he capable of?*

* * *

Leonardo glanced up at Kamilla sitting across the way from him in the smallest of their conference rooms. When she'd walked into his office, looking bright and cheerful, his body had responded with a thudding heart and a tightening in his groin. Damn if he didn't still want her. She'd been so passionate and giving that night as they'd made love.

He couldn't focus. Not with her enticing fragrance of lavender calling out to him to get closer. Her full lips pursed to the side as she concentrated, inviting him to kiss her. They still had to talk about what had happened between them. But what did he want from her? To make love again and again until he was finally satisfied. He hardened at the thought of sinking into her heat and hearing her moan of pleasure as she raised her hips off the desk to take in all of him. They'd been so good together. No fighting, just loving.

"Leonardo, are you okay?"

He blinked repeatedly to find Kamilla staring at him. "Yes."

Her continued look of concern didn't do anything to help dispel the tightening in the crotch of his pants. He shifted to make himself a little more comfortable. "I'm fine. What were you saying?"

"I have a friend from law school at Remington and Associates. He told me he heard Singleton Financial is discreetly shopping around for new counsel."

His ears had perked up at only one word, *he*. Her voice had softened. Was he an ex? Were they dating?

What the hell was wrong with him? Her personal

life shouldn't concern him. So what if she'd been the last person he'd had sex with and he was plagued with thoughts of doing it again? They were colleagues, that's it. *Are you sure?* his mind taunted.

He brought himself back to reality. "We already knew that."

She smirked. "We didn't know they were looking at upstart firms like Andrews, Green and Bartel."

He'd heard of them. In the past three years, they'd become one of the fastest-growing law firms to watch. "Andrews was a couple of years ahead of me at Yale. He asked me last year to join them as partner."

Kamilla's lack of reaction surprised him, considering he'd intended to shock her with the news. "Makes sense."

Was she being sarcastic? "What do you mean?"

"Calm down, Astacio. You're good and you know it. I'm surprised more headhunters aren't trying to knock down the door in an attempt to get to you."

If he'd been a peacock, his feathers would've been in full plume. Kind words from Kamilla made him feel way too good, simply because he knew she meant it. "Andrews topped the class and, from what I hear, ended up becoming an extraordinary lawyer."

Kamilla tapped her pen against the table. "Why would the Singletons go to such a small, fresh firm?"

"Maybe they want a more personal touch. Compared to the hundreds of clients we represent, Andrew's is probably in the tens. They can shower Singleton Financial with all the attention they desire."

Her chair shifted with the sudden straightening of her back. "We work hard for them."

He held back a smile. He loved when she became indignant. She cared so much. What would it be like to have her affection aimed in his direction? His skin went hot and tingly at the thought, and right then he wanted nothing more. He had to get his head back into the game. These thoughts about Kamilla weren't helping.

"It turns out someone or something in our firm has pissed the Singletons off. Did the intel from your boyfriend give any indication as to why they want to leave us?"

She cocked her head. "Boyfriend?"

What had he gotten himself into? He was supposed to suggest that they keep digging into the paperwork; instead, his jealousy gave him a shove into a situation he hadn't intended to broach, but had desperately wanted to.

He looked her in the eyes. "I meant your friend at Remington and Associates."

At the flare of her nostrils, he realized he'd blundered.

"Every word that comes out of your mouth is intentional." She narrowed her eyes, pinning him with a concentrated glare. "If you wanted to know if I had a man, you should've just asked me."

His gaze flicked to her breasts as he became enticed with every harsh breath she took. Perfect handfuls with dark, almost black, nipples, which had brushed against his chest with each thrust. When he forced his gaze to meet hers, the raw heat in her eyes had him standing to circle around the table with the aim of grabbing her hand to haul her to his office, where he'd lock the door and—

His unwise intentions were brought to an abrupt halt when James, one of the other associates, poked his head through the door. "Monroe wants to see you two in his office."

For once Leonardo wasn't as annoyed at being summoned by a senior partner. At least it was the one he liked. Monroe had been the reason he'd come to work for Peterson, Benton, Monroe and Lanner in the first place. He'd needed to get ahead through his work, not his name. He'd known by Monroe's unyielding reputation that the industrious, unpretentious man would provide him with what he needed.

Leonardo sucked in a huge breath to try to clear the ever-present need for Kamilla from his system, mentally thanking his mentor for his timing. It had saved him from making yet another mistake.

Chapter 7

A heads-up on the peculiar interaction between them would've been nice. As it stood, confusion ruled Kamilla's world where Leonardo was concerned. One moment Kamilla was telling him off for being indirect about digging into her personal life and the next she was ready to jump into his arms and kiss the handsome off his face. They'd never kissed. At least not on the lips. The memory of his mouth on her neck and breasts set her on fire.

At that moment his firm lips, usually set in a scowl, had appealed to her more than anything else in the world. The bells dinged and alarmed. Doing something once and then never again made it a mistake. Doing something twice, well, that would mean something. Wouldn't it?

She calmed her racing heart while gathering her things. "Why would only Monroe call us to see him?" The sole African American partner at the firm was known for his direct manner. Leonardo reminded her of him. He wasn't one to deal in nonsense and would say what had to be said despite whoever's feelings it may hurt. Respected, but tough.

He shrugged. "Maybe for once we'll get the truth without veiled threats attached."

They took the same route and dropped their things in Leonardo's office. When she handed him her papers, their hands brushed and a tantalizing tingle swept through her. What would've happened if they hadn't been interrupted a few minutes ago?

Her thrumming body had voted for being kissed, stripped and sexed. Her mind, on the other hand, had problems with having anything to do with Leonardo. The competition for partnership put aside, they were opposites in almost every sense of the word. Except their political views. They also liked to have blues music playing in the background when they worked. She'd noticed a copy of a book she'd read and enjoyed back in college on his bookshelf. So maybe they had a few things in common. But they were still too different to work as a functional couple.

His tall muscular physique, as he sauntered toward her to leave for Monroe's office, left her mouth parched and her fingers flexing to replace his suit jacket with her touch. With his stern clean-shaven face, closely cropped hair and radiation of power and control, an outsider may have believed he'd once been in the military. They'd be wrong, but he was just as disciplined. Another commonality between them.

They needed to clear the air about what had happened. Their still-lingering sexual attraction. It would be the healthiest thing to do for her mental health. Maybe.

After they gave a brief greeting to Monroe's administrative assistant, he gave them permission to enter their boss's open door. Kamilla knocked and, when Monroe nodded, they walked in together. For once looking like a team with their uniform stride rather than rivals. She had to keep in mind their rivalry. They weren't friends, lovers or even amicable colleagues. At least not until recently.

Monroe waved toward the two seats in front of his massive dark cherrywood desk. "Have a seat." The African American man didn't appear a day over fifty, even though they'd celebrated his sixtieth birthday two months ago. Many had called him a handsome man and Kamilla could see the appeal, with his distinguished pepper-gray hair and matching goatee. He epitomized wealth with his tailored suit, gold cuff links, designer eyeglasses and subtly patterned tie that she wanted to stroke because of its fine silk.

"How are you two doing?" The man had held on to his Southern manners even after moving North.

"We're well, sir," Kamilla answered for both of them.

His smile drew out the wrinkles at the corners of his eyes. "Good to hear. How far have you gotten on Singleton Financial?"

Instead of answering with a vague response like

she'd been about to, Leonardo jumped in. "Do you know why the Singletons want to take their business elsewhere?"

He'd get them fired before they had the chance to prove they could complete the task. She jumped in to soften the question. "It's just that it would help us to encourage them to stay."

Monroe rocked back in his seat, placing his clasped hands against his flat stomach. "I understand. Their decision to leave came as a surprise to all of us. They'd been happy with our work." He raised his palms upward. "I was on the green with Alfred last month and he was very pleased with how you handled their latest subsidiary."

They had needed the jewelry company assessed and then integrated into their system by contract. Something hadn't sat right within her about the company, but all of their financials looked good. She'd have to remember to go over them again with Leonardo to see if he got the same feeling.

Monroe leaned forward, resting his elbows on the desk. Unlike Leonardo, the man was always in motion. "Since they haven't come to us with a complaint, and their possible separation is merely circumspect, *we* will not directly approach them." He leveled each of them with a look. "But that doesn't mean two of the associates who have worked with them and heard rumors about their possible departure from the firm cannot inquire and intercede."

The disconcerting politics of the situation made Kamilla dizzy. So the partners couldn't deal with Singleton Financial directly even though they'd be the ones most affected by the loss. She stole a glance at Leonardo. The slight twitch of his jaw muscle was the only thing that gave his annoyed reaction away.

They waited for Monroe to tell them why they'd been summoned.

"The Singletons will be in Aspen, on vacation for one week. That will be the best chance you'll have to approach them, because they'll be leaving the country soon after."

Just when she was about to ask him how they'd infiltrate the couple's most likely much-needed vacation time, Monroe spoke again.

"The firm is sending you two on an all-expense paid trip to the same resort where Alfred and Sophia will be staying. They own the hotel. You will pretend to be on vacation." He slid a piece of paper to each of them. "Here are your itineraries. They've undertaken the same activities every time they've visited for the past five years. Alfred once told me it was his only opportunity to have consistency in his ever-changing world."

He stared directly into Kamilla's eyes and then at Leonardo, who still resembled a stone carving with his lack of movement or reaction. "Do what you need to in order to get them to sign the contract next month."

Their boss rotated his seat slightly to the left and started reading from his computer. They'd been dismissed, so they stood and left the room. She could feel heat radiating off Leonardo as she passed him to walk through the door.

Although she had no desire to be around when he exploded, they had to discuss their plan for the impromptu trip. If her job weren't on the line, she'd be happy about the impending journey to Colorado.

When they entered Leonardo's office, she jumped when he slammed the door. Unaccustomed to such overt anger from him, she remained standing while he paced the length of the room. When he didn't speak for a full two minutes, she cleared her throat. "We may be pimped out, but at least we get a holiday out of it."

His inferno of anger blazed in her direction. "It's not funny. They're treating us as if we're puppets. Easily controlled by the pull of a string. I have half a mind to cut them all."

Her stomach tightened with dread at the thought of him leaving. She needed him. She was a better lawyer when they worked together. Even if she could convince the Singletons to stay with the firm, if he left they may drop them as soon as they found out Leonardo was no longer part of the team.

She'd never seen him so livid and she didn't blame him. Not knowing if what she'd say would tip him toward packing his things and leaving or letting out a roar, she took a seat, watched and waited.

After a few minutes of observing him struggle to control his rage with stiff strides back and forth as he massaged the back of his neck, his fear-inducing scowl relaxed into a more neutral expression. He sat behind his desk, still resonating with anger, yet more controlled. "When are we supposed to leave?"

She blinked at him as her jaw dropped. He still wanted to go?

He grinned. "Close your mouth. As much as I like seeing you speechless, I'd hate for you to lose your job. Which would definitely happen if I'm not around to help you."

"In your dreams, Astacio," she bantered, happy to return to solid footing with him. She picked up the paper Monroe had given her. Leonardo's lay torn and crumpled in the trash bin, where he'd slammed it. "On Sunday. They're scheduled to arrive at the resort on Tuesday and we need to be there ahead of them to make it seem more natural."

He snorted. "I'd smell the setup a mile away."

She nodded at his astute point. "Me, too. That's why we need to spend the next three days figuring out a way to make our running into them seem accidental. And how to approach them."

The indent in the middle of his forehead appeared when his brows creased together. "I have an idea, but I don't think you're going to like it."

Kamilla narrowed her eyes. "And how is this different from any other idea you've ever had?"

"Because if this is going to work, things might have to get a little…personal."

Chapter 8

Kamilla tossed a pair of light blue long johns into her suitcase. "The man has lost his ever-loving mind."

Cass didn't even ask whom she was referring to. Whom else did she complain about with such vehemence? "What happened?"

She might as well tell her the whole story. It wasn't as if she'd taken an oath of confidentiality or anything. And maybe Cass could help her find a way out of the mess. "This afternoon we were told by Monroe that we've been scheduled to head out to Aspen to meet up with the Singletons. Our mission is to convince them to stay with the firm, since the partners can't do it themselves."

"Okay. I don't understand why, but I figure, like everything else at your firm, some kind of convoluted politics is involved."

"You've got that right. Leonardo and I are caught smack in the middle." She grunted as she debated which pair of black trousers to include. "Not a fun place to be in. A couple days ago, two of the other partners basically threatened us. If we don't get the Singletons to sign, then we'll be out of a job. If we do, then one of us will make partner."

She could swear Cass sucked some of the enamel off her teeth. "Those people are bastards, pure and simple. Did it convince you to give in your resignation like I've been advising since you started working for them? You can do so much better doing something you actually like."

Kamilla sat at the end of her bed, in the midst of the hurricane of clothes, and sighed. No matter what she'd been through with the firm, she'd never considered leaving. Making partner had always been foremost on her mind. Financial security. Job stability. Two things she'd never had in her life. She needed them. Would do anything to attain them. Even unwittingly work with unscrupulous leaders in order to become one of them.

"Their behavior isn't surprising." At least not to her. She still hadn't gotten over how pissed Leonardo had become after the meeting with Monroe earlier today. "That's not what's got me upset."

"Oh?" Cass asked, hinting at her doubt.

"Well, it does, but not as much as Leonardo's plan." This time her "oh" held a more interested pitch.

"The Singletons own the resort we're going to. They seem to have a routine they follow every year. He thinks we should leave tomorrow in order to get there a couple of days before they're due."

"Doesn't sound bad. At least you won't be hanging around in the den of vipers that employs you."

Kamilla smiled. God save the world from a best friend who thought she'd been wronged. Cass wouldn't be happy until she found a new job. "Do you want to hear his plan or not?"

"Fine."

"He proposes we stay there as a couple. I'm talking sleeping in the same hotel room and hanging out together so everyone in the hotel sees we're there on vacation rather than to lay a trap to meet with the Singletons."

She waited for her friend's shrieked response of repulsed incredulity. Seconds of silence passed. "Well?"

"What?"

Had Cass been listening? "Isn't it a horrible idea?"

"Not at all. You'll get to encounter your target accidentally. The only issue is how to bring up their wanting to leave the firm once you get to them. You're a magician when it comes to convincing people to do things they don't want to." Cass giggled. "Remember in high school when your crazy ass talked me into ditching school to go buy concert tickets to the Mary J. Blige concert?"

"We would've gotten away with it if you hadn't ripped your pants trying to get through the gate." Kamilla let out a hoot of laughter. "Hilarious."

"Not from where I stood. My point is that pretending to be a couple is a good idea. You could even try to have a good time and relax while you're there."

"With Leonardo? I might end up in jail for doing bodily damage. We'll kill each other."

"Hmm."

Kamilla rolled her eyes. "Just say it."

"You two slept together." She mentioned the event as if stating that her children had curly hair. "I'm sure something has changed between you. At least it would if you sat down and talked to him. Attraction doesn't hover for two years, preventing you from dating other guys, and then explode in one night of working together if you didn't at least like each other."

"Not true. I've been on a few dates. It's not my fault things didn't work with any of them. Plus I've been extremely busy at work and—"

"Cut it out, Kam." Cass cut her off without compunction. "Just admit you like him and are excited about pretending to be his woman because it's what you've wanted since you first met him. This partnership competition crap was just a front and you know it. Everyone likes you. Even in your foster homes and at school, people would bend over backward to make you happy. Your personality is like potent champagne and folks like being around your sparkling ass." Kamilla could imagine Cass's arms flailing. "His meanness when he first met you hurt. Unlike everyone else, he didn't fall all over himself to get to know you."

Kamilla pouted remembering the put-down he'd given her about being so proud of graduating from Harvard that she sported her pin. Other Yalees she'd met over the years had added a smile to their ribbing, and she'd made fun of them in return. "He started it."

"That's what I just said. He was a jerk. Did you try to befriend him after that?"

She slammed her back down on the pile of clothes. "No."

"And why not, again?"

Kamilla hated when her best friend played psychologist. She had half a mind to not answer. "Because I thought he was a spoiled brat who'd gotten everything he'd ever wanted in his life and I was jealous. Are you happy?"

Cass heaved a sigh. "Not at all. Your background of living in the system and having to work for everything you have is your single greatest strength and weakness rolled into one. It's made you who you are and yet you're super sensitive about it."

Kamilla rubbed at the tightness that had formed in her chest and cleared her throat. "What's your point?"

"If he hadn't come from a famous, hyper-rich, close-knit family, would you have reacted the same way? Especially considering you were attracted to him?"

Was it fair he had so much and also wanted to snatch away the job she'd worked so hard for? "We'll never know, will we?" Time to change the subject. "Help me come up with a different plan to help us win over the Singletons while I pack."

Thirty minutes later Kamilla was speaking to her energetic nieces with her bag packed and no alternative to Leonardo's scheme. Was Cass right? Did she want to be with him? It would've seemed so when she'd lain on his desk, enjoying every amazing inch of him.

She couldn't afford to desire him. She didn't need to analyze it; she just had to keep herself guarded and reach for her goal.

Chapter 9

About to board the plane the next day, Kamilla still hadn't formulated a plan that wouldn't involve being close to her enemy in order to get a job done. Her face contorted into an involuntary grimace. Maybe he'd slid into a more amicable position this past week, but she still considered him competition.

Cass was right about one thing: she and Leonardo had to have a talk about that scorching night. Had it meant anything to him? Did she want it to?

An important question she hadn't been able to answer was, did she want it to happen again? Her body screamed yes as a repetition of what she'd told him that night over and over again. Her mind knew better. What would come from hooking up again? A satisfying pleasure she'd never experienced with any other man she'd been with. Would it be a bad thing to have a sexual encounter in Aspen? Far away from work and closer to Vegas, where everything stays secret.

Knowing that even on his good days, he tended to be a bastard couldn't keep her in camp have-sex-with-Leonardo-again. She didn't need a man with a penchant for cruelty in her life. She'd had enough of it when she was younger from a couple of her foster parents and other kids in the system who'd been jealous for no reason. She'd had the same amount of nothing, sometimes less, than they did. As a grown woman, she deserved and would have nothing but respect when it came to her personal life, because that's how she treated others.

More bubbled under the surface than Leonardo showed everyone. The man who did pro bono work for those who couldn't afford his services hid somewhere beneath the nastiness she'd experienced from him over the years. She just wished he didn't hide it so well.

Leonardo looked over at her as they walked. "Are you still not speaking to me?"

She ignored the thrill tripping down her spine at the sound of his voice. After picking up her speed, she paused to hand the airline worker her boarding pass.

"Have a wonderful flight."

Kamilla flashed a smile. "Thanks. You too." Then she recalled the woman wasn't going anywhere. "I mean...thanks." She hated hearing Leonardo laugh at her, so she rushed onto the walkway, which would keep her safe from the cold November Cleveland air. On the plane she headed for business class and hoped they'd plopped Leonardo in coach. An aisle seat right in front of the toilet, where people passing would hit him every time they went to use the bathroom. A crying baby next to him would do nicely.

She found her seat and placed her carry-on into the overhead compartment. Heat burned into her back as a hard body leaned into her. "You can't stay angry with me for the whole trip." He whispered into her ear. "You know the plan is good. Is the fact that I came up with it what's eating you?"

An elbow to the gut had him stepping back with a grunt.

Comfortable in her seat, she broke her vow of not speaking to him. "I'm sure you're accustomed to flying first class instead of slumming it in business. Feel free to ask the airline hostess to upgrade you." Then she made sure to look him in his dark eyes. She knew she'd made a mistake when her belly decided to flutter. Not something new when she got this close to him, but it still disturbed her because she wasn't supposed to feel anything where he was concerned.

He'd gotten a fresh haircut. She longed to smooth her hand against his close-cropped hair. Then down his neck, around to his chest and lower to— She cleared her throat before delivering the now ineffective line, "I wouldn't mind."

Dammit. She'd intended to sound mean.

"I'm fine where I am. Besides, now that you're talking to me again, the chill in the air has lifted."

Kamilla patted her head to maintain the slick style she'd had her hair dresser style the short strands into instead of curling them. She figured a hat would be in order at some point during the trip, so it would be fruit-less to waste time doing it.

Flipping through a magazine didn't distract her from the creeping fear settling into her stomach when the plane rolled along the tarmac. Having flown a few times for business trips to meet clients, she should've been more comfortable with the flight process.

She wiped sweat from her brow. Had they turned up the heat?

Leonardo leaned toward her. "Are you okay?"

"I'm fine." She wished she could slam down the win-dow shade. Once they got into the sky, this phase of her fear would pass. She wouldn't think of the possibility of turbulence.

Just as she'd done during her work-study jobs in the biology lab during her sophomore year of college, she breathed deeply to maintain her calm. Unlike the poor defenseless mice she'd been tasked to feed to the snakes, she'd get through this flight. One moment at a time.

"Are you sure? You look a little green." Then in an unexpected manner, he reached for his barf bag and handed it to her. "Just in case, okay?"

Touched by his kindness, she nodded as she accepted the bag.

"Just remember to do it in the opposite direction from me."

She should've expected it. "I'm not going to throw up. I get a little nervous during takeoff." *Turbulence, landing and anytime the captain puts on the fasten seat belt sign.*

His stare unsettled her even more. "What are you

looking at?" she asked with annoyance she didn't try to hide.

"You're afraid." He shook his head as if disappointed. "I never would've thought it possible."

She thrust her shoulders back. "What do you mean?" She had many fears. Returning to a state of poverty and government dependence completely overshadowed her discomfort of flying.

Leonardo shrugged. Would he be able to fit in coach with those massive shoulders? With his wealth, he never had to find out. "Nothing."

"Don't you dare let it go, Astacio."

He darted his eyes to the opposite aisle before whispering. "Keep your voice down."

"What? You don't want people snapping pictures of you and posting them all over social media?"

"You sure are a smart woman," he drawled out and then paused. "On rare occasions."

Gritting her teeth, Kamilla knew better than to respond, but she was wound so tightly, she couldn't help it. Before she could speak, she noticed two things. The glint in his eyes and the fact that they were ascending. They'd survived the takeoff. Had he distracted her on purpose?

He rested his head against the backrest and proceeded to ignore her.

Nope. He didn't have it in him to do such a nice thing. Those pro bono cases came to mind once again. Rather than relinquish the idea of him being nothing but a bully, she put on her earphones. Then she turned to the window and smiled.

* * *

Leonardo clenched and then extended his fingers several times to recover the circulation. If he could drag Kamilla into his lap and comfort her, he wouldn't be suffering. He couldn't act on his instincts. Due to the turbulence two hours into the flight, they had to stay belted in. The official reason for keeping her in her own seat was minor compared to the fact that she'd probably claw his eyes out if he tried to hold her.

He'd never seen this vulnerable side of her. Always on top of her game, no matter what went down, she never let her weaknesses show. Not even when he harassed her. Sure she'd get angry and retaliate with her sharp tongue, but she handled her business.

This sweaty, shaky, gripping-his-hand-during-the-major-dips female intrigued him. How much about her didn't he know? His family tended to be in the newspapers for the world to witness. Leonardo had done more than his fair share of magazine interviews to keep from appearing too mysterious to the press.

He'd never once asked her a personal question. Before he'd slept with her, he hadn't really wanted to. Getting to know her would've been an impediment toward his objective of making partner, so he'd wanted to keep everything professional. And now things had changed, at least for him.

Something in his heart tugged at her defenselessness. Distracting her had worked during takeoff, so maybe it would for this obnoxious turbulence. Although he might regret it once she returned to her normal vivacious, challenging determined self. "Where do you come from?"

The brown of her eye obscured the white part in an officially freaky side-eyed look. "What the hell kind of question is that?"

Or he could regret it right then and there. "I take it you want me to guess."

"I'd rather you stop being weird and bring back the man I've had difficulty with for the past few—" Kamilla snatched the hand that hadn't had the chance to recover when a deep dip had his own stomach lurching. Scrunching her eyes, she mumbled words he couldn't understand.

"What are you saying?"

"Shhh. I'm praying."

"What are you praying for?" As if he didn't know, but he hated seeing her so afraid. He preferred her feisty and argumentative. He'd do anything to get that aspect of her personality back.

When the turbulence eased, she released his hand and he shook it. "If you won't tell me where you come from, then I'll guess," he taunted.

She opened her eyes. "We're about to plummet to the ground in a fiery death and you want to harass me with a guessing game?"

"We're not going to die." Adding *unless we do* wouldn't have been reassuring to either of them, so he kept it contained. "The plane's just going through a few air pockets. How come you didn't take anything for the flight?"

"You mean like a sedative?"

"Yes. It would've relaxed you."

Kamilla rotated her fingers in a circle at the sides of her temples. "I tried it once and it made me loopy. By the time I got to my destination, I was dancing at the baggage claim." Then she giggled. "With no music to be heard by anyone but me."

Picturing the situation, Leonardo laughed.

He braced himself at her inhaled gasp, but the plane remained steady.

"How come you don't smile more often?" she asked. "It completely changes your face. Makes you seem more human."

That's why. By appearing friendly, people tried to get close in order to manipulate. Leonardo had learned the painful lesson in his younger years. He'd found the combination of scowling, sarcastic comments and being brutally honest to be the best deterrent for people trying to enter his world uninvited.

The only people he could trust were his family and a few guys he'd bonded with over the years. Everyone else could stay the hell out of his circle.

Women came and went. None had held his interest for as long as Kamilla. Although he behaved as if he couldn't stand her, he'd go out of his way to make sure he saw her at least once a day. And if he was lucky, he'd spark her temper and they'd get into some kind of debate.

He continued with the game. "Since you don't have a Southern drawl, I'll rule out those states."

Kamilla rubbed her hands down her lap, smoothing the material of her pants. "Are you back on this?"

"I'll officially stake you as from New York, but I won't name a city."

She scoffed. "Of all the states, why New York?"

A wave of turbulence overtook them. The only hint

that Kamilla had felt it was the scrunch of her nose, but otherwise she remained calm. Leonard held his pride of her in check. "You seem like a New Yorker. Tough."

"Are they the only people who have grit in the country?"

He shook his head. "You have a street-smart edge to you."

She didn't blink as she stared at him. "I'm from Cleveland, born and bred."

"Hmm. I'm never wrong."

She waggled a sexy French-manicured finger at him. "You stand corrected, counsellor. You're wrong more than you like to admit."

"I will neither deny nor confirm your claim. Do you have any siblings? I can't see you being an only child. Your confrontational personality came from somewhere." They hit another air pocket and this time she looped her arm through his and hung on tight.

He disengaged her, raised the armrest and wrapped his arm around her shoulders, drawing her as close as the seat belts would allow. Her lavender scent teased his nostrils as she held herself board-straight. "It's okay," he crooned as his other hand smoothed her short hair, encouraging her to rest against him.

After a moment she relaxed. Not wanting to disturb this tenuous balance of pleasure and peace, he kept his mouth shut. She felt so good. No need to remind her how annoying she tended to find him and have her scoot away.

Once the turbulence passed and Kamilla still sat in the same position, he increased the depth of his breathing to normal, or as close as possible with the beauty listening to how rapidly his heart was beating.

"I'm an only child. At least as far as I know," she mumbled without moving.

Where had that come from? Oh yes, his question. He'd rather give up his Audi A5 than have this moment ruined. "How was the experience?"

Feeling her stiffened shoulders, he knew he'd lose contact with her in a few seconds, but then she calmed. "I grew up in foster homes."

Not the answer he'd expected.

"My mother died when I was young and my father couldn't take care of me, so he left me at a church and took off."

His nostrils flared at the emotion raging through him on behalf of this woman. Grief for her loss rivaled anger over her father's inability or unwillingness to take care of his own.

Her hand rested on his chest and his heart stopped for a moment.

"It's okay. I made my peace with it a long time ago." She cleared her throat. "I more than survived."

At what cost? He'd never taken for granted the closeness of his family, even though his parents had traveled for most of his life and his younger sister and brother had attended different boarding schools. No matter what happened, he knew they'd support him.

Who had been there for her?

Chapter 10

Kamilla would rather have all her immunization shots redone than tell people her story. Just because she'd grown up in the system didn't mean her life had been bad. Granted, she'd had her share of struggles, but she'd be a completely different person if she hadn't gone through those hard times. She liked the strength her experiences had infused into her.

Of course if she'd been offered the opportunity to grow up in a loving, supportive family, she wouldn't have turned it down. It had been what she'd prayed for as a child. A chance to be adopted like Cass had been, but no one had chosen her. By the time she'd reached twelve, she'd made her peace with growing up in the foster care system.

As she rested with her head on her nemesis's strong

and wonderfully supportive chest, listening to the reassuring beat of his heart, she waited for the barrage of questions that tended to come when people learned how she'd grown up.

Blessed silence met her. "It wasn't horrible," she volunteered. "I only had a couple of foster parents who were in it for the money rather than the care."

His arm stiffened around her.

"In all, I lived in seven foster homes."

"Why so many?" Asked by a man who knew nothing about the system.

Now that the turbulence had stopped and the captain had turned off the seat belt sign, she should at least think about peeling herself off him. He was better than any pillow she'd ever rested on, so she snuggled closer and held back a sigh of bliss as he glided his hand down her arm and back to her shoulder, tucking her in.

"It's the foster care system," she answered. "Very few people get adopted, and that's how people tend to stay permanent in a house. I realized it early. As a ward of the state, belonging to no one, I made sure I was always packed and ready to go."

Her breath caught in her throat and her stomach did something weird as his lips brushed her hair. Had he, Leonardo Astacio, bane of her existence, just kissed her in comfort? Looking up at him would only break whatever alternate universe bubble they'd found themselves in, so she stayed still, inhaling what had to be the most intoxicating cologne to ever pass into her nose. She let the scent transport her to what she could only imagine to be the forest after a cleansing rain. Fresh and calming.

The next thing she knew, her upper body was being jiggled.

"Wake up."

She snuggled into the comfy embrace. "Just five more minutes." The noise of people chattering hit her at the same time she realized she wasn't in bed. Sitting straight up, Leonardo didn't relinquish his touch as her vision cleared and she stared at him. "I can't believe I fell asleep."

"And snored like a boxer who's had his nose broken a few times."

She slapped his chest and, for a second, thought of leaving her hand on the hard pecs. Then her common sense returned and she raised it to slick back her hair. "I don't snore."

"If you say so."

Had she really told this difficult man about her past? Had he actually listened? "Thanks for distracting me from the turbulence."

He looked into her eyes for the longest moment, nodded and then stood without replying. What was going on in his mind? Removing his carry-on, he left hers in the overhead compartment. No surprise there. She'd formulated no delusions that a few moments of compassion would change anything between them, but it would've been nice.

The business class remained with only them as a few stragglers from coach filed past. Getting to her feet, she reached up for her bag. She paused when he trapped her with his body. The rumble of his voice erupted goose bumps on her skin under her turtleneck and thick sweater. "Will you let me get it down for you without a feminist fight?"

Unlike the first time they'd been in this position, for the slightest moment, she leaned back against him, savoring the hardness of his body. What would it be like to have the freedom to turn around and press her chest to his? Stand on her toes and slide her lips against the firm warmth of his. Would he kiss her back or push her to the side? She didn't have the courage to try.

With his offer, she knew something monumental had shifted between them during the flight. If she told him no, he'd return to his brash ways. A yes could open a door she wasn't ready to walk through. "Okay. But if you ask to carry it, I'll give you all of my luggage."

His chuckle once again unsettled her peace of mind with its richness. "You're safe."

When he'd brought down her bag, she turned and held out her arms. Raising her eyes to his, she remembered their main reason for being on this trip. She had a job to secure. No one would stop her. Not even her unwarranted attraction to Leonardo the Great.

"Um…" She cleared her throat. "Thanks again for helping me out during the flight."

For the tiniest moment, sympathy and something unfamiliar flashed in his dark eyes. Then the familiar scowl made its appearance. "Next time don't be such a baby about flying."

Out of a debt owed, she held back her retort.

Waiting for their car to take them from the airport to the hotel, Leonardo pondered the fact that Kamilla still hadn't accepted his scheme of pretending to be a couple. The idea was sound, but he couldn't blame her for rejecting it. He'd planned to convince her on the plane, but that idea fell to the wayside when he'd found he preferred being the one to bring her comfort in her time of distress.

He couldn't imagine how someone who'd had such a difficult life could end up as amazing and ambitious as she'd turned out. He hadn't made life any easier by pestering her over the years. The more he thought about it, the more he reminded himself of a kid who pulled on a girl's pigtails to get her attention. Only this time he utilized the art of sarcasm and subtle digs.

Would he stop? Not a chance. He enjoyed the mental sparring too much. What he wished would go away was the deeper awareness of her as a woman. How her firm breast had pressed into his side as she rested against him. His desire for her had jacked up even more. The plan for them to act as a couple wasn't only for the Singletons' benefit. He wanted her. To hear her moans of ecstasy as they made love again. The next encounter would be nice and slow. He'd take his time getting to know every curve of her body by sight, taste and touch.

When their Uber pulled up to the curb, he assisted in placing her massive suitcase in the trunk, along with his more moderate one. Once they'd settled in the back seat, he turned to her. She had her profile to him and sat as if she were a stately Nubian queen. Stunning. Yet he knew how dangerous she could be when it came to anyone trying to get in the way of what she wanted.

"Have you come up with a different strategy to make our being here appear accidental?"

She tucked a corner of her bottom lip between her teeth as she thought. "I was thinking we could be here for a meeting with another client and happen to be staying at their resort."

He gave her a gimlet stare.

She huffed out a breath. "Fine, so they might think it's suspicious, considering we know it's their hotel, but no more so than you and I being a couple. No one would buy it. Not the way we fight."

"Well, then we'll have to make them believe."

"Pah," she said with the flick of her hand. "Only an idiot would think we're together."

Truly confused, he drew his brows together. "Why?"

"Well… It's just… Um…"

She never stumbled over her words or avoided eye contact, especially with him. He knew for certain that whatever she'd say would upset him, but he had to hear it. "I don't understand why you're stalling. It's not as if you've ever thought I possessed feelings for you to hurt."

She snapped her gaze up at him. "You want the truth. Here it is." She pointed between them. "We're not a realistic couple." She held out her arms wide, hitting one hand against the rear windshield. "Our personalities are as different as a tornado—that's you, by the way—and a gentle breeze. We've been at each other's throats for the past two years and I'm not the kind of woman you'd date."

He angled his body more toward her. "For a moment there, I thought you were going to lie and say we weren't attracted to each other."

"Of course we are." She slammed her hand over her mouth.

The air hung heavy as their driver pretended not to be listening to their conversation. Time to discuss their erotic experience together. Not the best environment, but would they ever get the opportunity if he didn't grab it now? "About—"

"Don't you dare talk about that *here*."

He smirked. "So there will be a time to discuss it."

"It's not like you've ever brought it up before. It happened and then it was as if it didn't. I took it to be—" her gaze flittered to the driver and then back to him "—a tension reliever."

How could one person be so entertaining? "Is that how you normally get rid of your stress."

Crossing her arms over her chest, she pouted. "No."

Leonardo hadn't thought so, but her answer still pleased him. Like him, she spent way too much time in the office and not enough of it living or having a productive social life. "Good."

They rode in silence as the vehicle sped them along the highway to their destination "So, have we agreed to going through with my plan?"

"No."

Of course she'd fight. It's what Kamilla did best. He'd always wondered why she'd never gone into a branch of law where it would be her duty to defend others in court. She'd be damn good at it. "Why not?"

"Because it's stupid."

He relaxed his head against the backrest, sure that

within the next five minutes he'd have worn her down. "Can you expound on the eloquent words you just used?"

"I know you can't help it most of the time, but don't be an ass."

He raised his brows. "Asking you to clarify what you said offended you?"

"It's the way you said it."

He grit his teeth. Before the week ended, one of them may end up off the side of a mountain. "Fine, how about if I told you to stop being so damn stubborn and just agree. You have no reason not to, so just fall in line so we can get the job done."

She pointed a finger in his face. "You see, that's it right there. You're so overbearingly arrogant. Expecting everyone to do what you want when you want it. Not me, buddy. I'm not the one."

By this time they'd squared off. He should've known better than to push her. It had never worked in the past. He took a deep breath and backed down by breaking eye contact. He lowered his voice and leaned closer so only she'd hear. "I thought we'd sleep in the same suite with two different rooms, to make it seem more likely that we were together. I also booked the room on my credit card rather than the firm's. The only thing we'd have to do to perpetrate the illusion is pretend to have fun while following the roster they gave us at the office."

Kamilla's body seemed to sink into the seat as she uncrossed her arms. "Okay. I can live with that."

Had he heard correctly? Agreeing without further argument? He wouldn't push his luck. At least not yet.

Chapter 11

The dramatic splendor of the resort's lobby had Kamilla captivated. She wiped the corner of her mouth just in case she'd been drooling. Two large fireplaces with actual crackling fires sat across the room. The space boasted of the most comfortable-looking cushiony seats set in warm brown tones and accented with orange, yellow and red cushions. If she weren't staying at the resort to save her job, she'd spend all day tucked into a chair in front of the fireplace with a novel in one hand and a cup of spiked hot chocolate in the other.

The glass at the top of the door they'd entered let in both light and the splendiferous view of the snow- and tree-covered mountains. Growing up in Cleveland, she was no stranger to snow, but she'd never recognized it as glorious until this moment.

While she'd been unable to tear her gaze away from her new home for the next week, Leonardo took care of the room. Where the hell had life taken such a detour for her to now have to pretend to be involved with him? She must've been a really bad person in a previous life. She gazed at his broad back, recalling the slide of her fingers along the plane of muscles as they'd made love. She swallowed hard. *Or a really good person.*

She snapped out of her musings long enough to see Leonardo take the key card from the smiling receptionist. "You're in chalet number five, Mr. Astacio." Had she said his name with a breathless awe or was it her imagination? They'd worked together for so long, she'd almost forgotten he held a pseudo-celebrity status. Heirs of multi-billion-dollar companies tended to.

The woman's smile was too damn bright as she did something with her eyelashes that would make Kamilla look as if she were starting to have a seizure. "A porter will be with you in just a moment to help you with your things."

Anger at the receptionist rose up from her chest into her throat. How dare she flirt with him while Kamilla stood at his side? Never mind she didn't even like Leonardo as a person, much less a man; it all boiled down to the principle of the situation.

Kamilla sidled up to him and rested her breast against his arm. She ignored the hardening of her nipples as she smiled up at him before looking at the receptionist. "Thank you. It's been a long journey and we'd like to…" She tilted her head to glance up into Leonardo's eyes and lowered the timbre of her voice so no one in hearing range could mistake her intent. "Settle in."

At Leonardo's hard swallow, she slid her hand into his and pulled him from the desk. That ought to teach the woman. Unfortunately she'd learned a lesson, too, as an electrical current made its way up her arm from his touch. She didn't want to release the strong hand surrounding hers. Fortunately she didn't have to. Not until they were alone.

"Did the green-eyed monster bite you in the ass?"

Ducking her head, she smoothed down her hair to hide the truth in his words. "Don't be ridiculous. This was your crazy idea. No woman should take me for a sucker who'd let her man out to play."

A grin spread across his face, creating a flutter in her belly. "I see." And then he raised their joint hands and brushed his lips against her fingers.

Where had all the air gone? There had been plenty of it a minute ago and now she couldn't get any into her body.

"If you'll follow me, I'll show you to your chalet." The stranger's voice magically returned the atmosphere to normal and she inhaled deeply. Tearing her attention from Leonardo, she tugged his hand to follow the porter. Fear and pleasure battled for control. This once, she'd let pleasure win. She couldn't have him in real life, but they'd left reality when they stepped into the fairy-tale setting of the resort.

Why couldn't she relax and freely enjoy the attraction between them for the week? She'd been fighting it for two years, and had proved her failure by sleeping with him. Although it had been the most gratifying experience of her life, it had set her more off-balance than a drunk tightrope performer.

Making partner took precedence over everything. This week she'd be able to do her job while enjoying Leonardo's tingle-inducing touch. She didn't have to fight her attraction while still setting herself on the road toward achieving her goal. Win-win situation.

A short walk took them out the back of the building, into the cold and down a pathway lined with fir trees. Taking a right, they were led to a lone building with a gold number five above the threshold. The porter opened the red door and escorted them in.

Amazed, she stood in the doorway as she took in the living room. Hadn't she seen this fabulous decor in a home magazine? Like a zombie she walked through the space past the cream-and-light-gray furniture, large oil paintings, silk flowers in exquisite vases, a fireplace and a huge flat-screen television. The crystalline lake and towering mountains beyond captured her attention. The resort would be even more majestic in the spring and summer.

The coolness of the glass door when she touched it added to the reality. She wasn't dreaming. "This is the most beautiful place I've ever been." She couldn't hide the reverence as she spoke to the reflection behind her.

"It reminds me of the Swiss Alps."

Her amazement flashed to annoyance as she swung around, planting her hands on her hips. "You couldn't let me have this and just agree?" How could she have ever thought they'd be able to get along for the week when she wanted to throw his arrogant ass out now?

"I never said it wasn't a nice resort."

"Nice?" She shook her head and walked around him, barely taking in the kitchen or the fact that the porter had left. "It must be good to have grown up rich and traveled the world."

He rushed to her and stopped her progress. "Look, Kamilla. I can't pretend to be who I'm not. I've seen sights that have brought tears to my eyes because they were so spectacular. It's hard to get excited about things that don't reach that level."

The passion in his voice melted away her anger. "I may have overreacted a little."

At his raised brows, she added, "Okay, a lot. I'm overwhelmed at everything that's happened this week and exhausted from the wretched flight." Would he make fun of her? She'd always hated appearing vulnerable in front of anyone, but he'd seen her at her worst and had even helped her through it by distracting and holding her.

Leonardo nodded. "I understand. Why don't you choose a room and rest?"

Her knees nearly buckled at his response. Who was this sweet man and why hadn't she been introduced to him before? She nodded and stepped around him. "Good idea."

The rooms were nearly identical in decor. It didn't stop her from jumping up and down when she saw the Jacuzzi tub in the smaller bedroom. She could do without a couch in her sleeping space if she could soak with jets massaging her on a daily basis. The mountain view from the window next to the bed helped to make up her mind.

She lay on the mattress and sighed. As soon as she gained control over her reactions to Leonardo, she'd be fine. One minute she wanted to slather herself all over him and the next to shove him out the door. It wasn't like her to be so extreme with her emotions. But he brought it out in her. From the first time she'd met him, until now.

Kamilla hauled herself up and returned to the living room. Her whole body heated when she found him sprawled on the couch with a glass of amber liquid in his hand. His eyes were closed as jazz music played from the small speakers surrounding the space. With his suit jacket off, tie loosened and shirt rolled up to expose his muscular forearms, she'd never seen a more sexy version of him. Other than when he'd been naked. She pushed the memory away.

"I've chosen the room on the right." Not knowing what else to say once he nodded, she escaped to the safety of her new domicile. She'd put those Jacuzzi jets to good use before taking a nap. Ridding herself of extreme exhaustion would surely help her hormones to settle. Maybe she'd gain control of the need to observe his handsome features, to touch him, nibble on those luscious lips and oh so many other places on his perfect body. Fanning her face with her hand, she amended the plan. A cool shower would probably be better.

Chapter 12

Leonardo debated whether to wake Kamilla from her three-hour rest. She deserved it after the stress she'd experienced on the plane, but she also needed to eat. When had he become so concerned with her welfare? Even worse, why had he started missing her when she was just in the next room?

Did it matter? The woman had latched on to him, even without trying, and he liked having her close. Sure they were competing for the same position. It didn't matter anymore, considering how alive he became when he was with her. She respected him, even though she hadn't liked him. Impressed by her honesty and genuine lack of trepidation in regard to his social and financial status, he found her resolute passion to be the most amazing aspect of her.

He'd become aware of her incredibleness long before they'd slept together. It had probably been the driving force to get them together. Fear had kept him away from her for so long. Months of debating if she were worth the risk, all the while every time he'd seen her, which he'd tried to avoid doing, he'd wanted her. Yet he had no desire to forgo his goal for her, because he'd worked too hard to reach it. He'd hate to think he'd wasted five years of his life because he knew he couldn't have both her and the partnership.

His ears perked up as the door to her room opened. "It's about time you woke up," he said as she stumbled into the living room. Even with her short hair spiked in every direction, no makeup and wearing sweatpants with a loose T-shirt, his skin heated.

She flopped onto the couch. "Couldn't find anybody to torture while I slept?"

"You know you're my favorite."

"I'm hungry."

He figured she would be. For such a small woman, she always had an appetite. "How about we go down to the dining room for dinner?"

She groaned and plucked at her shirt. His eyes diverted to her chest. Her perfect breasts with dark berries for nipples, which he'd rolled his tongue around. He snapped his gaze back to her eyes and shifted in his seat.

"That means I have to get dressed." She wrinkled her nose. "And eat with you. Can't we just order room service?"

Was she really trying to extricate from him? He had to get over this insecurity he'd developed when it came to her. She tended to wear *independent* as a name tag and he knew she could take or leave any relationship that didn't add value to her life. In order to ingratiate himself into her world, he had to play his cards right, which meant treating her as he always had, but also making her aware that the attraction between them wasn't going anywhere.

He shrugged. "We need to show our faces. Besides, would it hurt to look a little presentable around me?"

Her laughter hit him straight in the chest. He loved making her laugh. "Why?"

"Because I'm supposedly your man." He touched her knee and received the shock he'd expected. "You're supposed to want to look good for me."

"Hmm." She angled her head as if considering. "You have a point." She nodded once with her head dipped to the side and her lips bunched. "How about if we consider ourselves in the middle of a relationship. The point when you don't fear losing each other because you're already so in love and vested it would hurt too much to let each other go. You know, the comfortable part where you wear what you want and fart in front of each other." She pointed a finger at him. "Don't be dropping any bombs anywhere near me, though."

He couldn't help laughing. "I'll try. Is that what you want? The middle?"

"It's the best part." Her eyes glazed over. "There's still passion, but it's not as fierce as the beginning. The middle is the knowledge that you'll be together for the long haul because you really know each other."

His skin became taut enough to rip as trepidation sent a chill up his spine. Was she in love with another man? "Have you ever been there?"

She sighed and closed her eyes while leaning her head against the back of the couch. "No, but I've seen my best friend go through it."

His muscles relaxed. "Have you ever gotten close?"

Lolling her head to the side, she looked at him. Would she tell him the truth? "Once, back in college. I thought we'd be together forever. I was wrong."

"What happened?"

"He found what he thought to be his true love"

Leonardo shook his head. "He was a fool." The words slipped out before he could stop them.

"You won't get an argument about that from me. He married the woman he cheated on me with and I learned they got divorced two years later. But you know what?"

Every word she spoke intrigued him. When was the last time they'd ever had a personal conversation that didn't involve work? Aside from the plane ride over, never. "What?"

She scooted forward, placed an elbow on her knee and rested her cheek on her palm. "Learning about their breakup made me sad. I believe in a forever kind of love. Once those vows are said, there's no shaking me. We would've had to be in the middle for a long time before I agreed to marry a guy."

Fascinating. "What if he hits you or cheats on you?"

"Please. I'd just have to invoke the part of 'until death do us part.'" She laughed at her own joke. "For real, though. Let's just say he'd know what he was getting involved with before he tried some nonsense. I like showing my true self." She scrunched her face. "It's not always pretty, but at least you know what you're getting."

Leonardo no longer wanted to leave the chalet. Maybe they should order in, because he suddenly became selfish about sharing this amazing woman with anyone else. Not tonight, or ever. For the first time, he could see himself settling down with a woman and it felt right. The fact that he'd found it with Kamilla shook him to the core.

"A smart-assed, hardheaded woman," he said.

The chuckle came from her throat as she stood. "Exactly. I'll be right out."

He'd heard those words before. Women tended to take forever to get dressed. "So it'll be an hour before we head down to eat?"

"Fifteen minutes."

"Huh." He reached for the television remote and changed the channel. "I'll believe it when I see it."

"Funny. Those are the exact same words I said about you acting like a human being who belongs in polite society. I'm still waiting, Astacio," she sang the last part while sauntering to her room.

The smile spread across his face. Yes, she'd be good for him. She'd pushed him professionally over the past two years. The more he learned about her, the more he liked. If he could convince her that they had a strong potential for being right for each other, his life would never be boring, and he had a feeling he'd smile a whole lot more.

Kamilla held back a gasp of surprise as Leonardo pulled out her chair at the table. "Where have these manners been over the past two years? I don't recall you ever holding the door for me."

He picked up the menu. "They've been there—you just didn't deserve them."

Why did he have to start? Hadn't they had a peaceful walk from their chalet all the way to the resort's restaurant without bickering? "May I remind you of who laid down the gauntlet when we first met?"

The waiter came over. "Good evening. May I take your drink order while you peruse the menu?"

She smiled up at the young man dressed in the same black bow tie and white shirt as the others. "Diet cola."

"Whiskey. Neat," Leonardo said while still looking at his menu.

The waiter nodded. "I'll be right back."

Kamilla tapped a nail against the food list. "Why were you rude to him? Waiting tables is a difficult job."

"I wasn't rude. Or do you want me to gush all over him?"

She rolled her eyes. "You could've at least looked up at him when you gave your drink order."

"Why?" he challenged. "Would it have changed how he'd heard it?"

"No, but it would've made him know you acknowledged his presence. That's the worst part about the job. The snotty, arrogant, rude people."

He pierced her with an assessing stare. "How would you know?"

She straightened her shoulders, proud of the work she'd done to put herself through school. "I worked a summer as a waitress back in in college."

"I see."

"What? No condescending comment? I've worked a lot of jobs to pay for my education. I wouldn't have made it through otherwise." Why did she feel the need to explain?

His sweet smile and cocked head indicated his thoughts had tumbled him back in time. "I worked in the mailroom one summer. My parents thought it would help me get to know all the offices in their main building and become accustomed to the system."

Which shocked her more? Him having to work during his school break or the fact that he'd shared personal information? She gave a self-righteous sniff. "I worked out of necessity."

His head jerked back. "Me, too. My parents wouldn't have it any other way. They've never been about spoiling us. Working at the Astacio headquarters helped us learn the business from the inside out."

One-upping him now became a necessity. "I'm sure you still would've been able to afford personal items for the semester if you hadn't worked."

"You're right. Working for my parents was never about the money, but the experience."

Ha! She'd won. And yet she would've given away everything she'd accomplished in life to have been able to trade places with him. She picked up her menu and sought the fish section.

The waiter returned with their drinks and placed them on the table. "Are you ready to order?"

She was about to speak when Leonardo looked up at him and said, "Please give us a few minutes."

When the man was out of earshot, Kamilla smiled. "Are you breaking out in a cold sweat because you were polite?"

His laughter pleased her. "If you don't choose what you're going to eat, I'll do it for you when he returns."

She grimaced and looked down at the menu. "Knowing you, you'll probably order frog legs or snails."

"I was thinking tripe."

The thought of eating the lining of a cow's stomach had her focusing on the words rather than the man.

By the time the waiter returned, she'd made up her mind. "Shrimp scampi."

Leonardo handed over his menu. "Chicken alfredo. For an appetizer, we'll have the Italian sampler platter, but please make sure there are absolutely no nuts in any of the food."

Kamilla omitted the reprimand about him ordering their appetizer plate. "You don't eat nuts?"

"I eat everything. But I know you have an allergy."

Her mouth opened and closed several times as she tried to get her muscles under control. "How do you know?"

"Contrary to what people around the office think about me, I pay attention. Especially when an ambulance has to be called because someone gave you a gourmet cookie with nuts in it. You played a dangerous game by not making the time to buy a new EpiPen after your previous episode."

She agreed, but she'd never admit it to him. "Glad to see you using your keen observational skills," she said in the driest tone she could manage in order to hide her pleasure at him having remembered and caring enough to protect her from it happening again.

The more she learned about him, the more she liked. Not good.

Chapter 13

Leonardo had never enjoyed a meal more. The food wasn't as spectacular as the company. Why had he been so pigheaded when it came to Kamilla? They could've been friends, or maybe even more, this whole time. And now that he'd come to his senses, winning her over may not be a possibility.

He'd made her life difficult, or had at least tried. He grinned to himself. Unlike others, she'd been too resilient to break.

Kamilla looked at him with narrowed eyes. "Why are you smiling?"

Resting against his seat, he enjoyed the intrigue of her dark eyes. "Is it a crime?"

"It means you're plotting."

He laughed. "Or like most other people in the world, I could be happy."

She swiped her gaze up and down what she could see of him. "You're not typical, but you already knew that." She finished off the last of the salted-caramel-and-dark-chocolate mousse on her plate and sighed. "What will we be doing tomorrow?"

Knowing her, she already had their day mapped out. She had to be the most thorough planner he'd ever met. A trait he didn't find adorable, because she could take things overboard. Or maybe she'd done it to annoy him. He wouldn't put it past her. "How about you tell me."

Her eyes glimmered. He'd only seen the look directed at him just before she gave him a piece of her mind. "I have to do a little more research, but I'll let you know at breakfast tomorrow."

Of course she had to be exhaustive. "How about we play it by ear."

She gasped with her hand on her chest as if offended and then laughed. "We may not get along, but I know you know me better than that."

He finished the last of his coffee to help settle his nerves. The time had come to start off on a new footing. One that would help get her to trust him. "You mentioned earlier that the harsh dynamic between us is my fault. I'm sorry."

When she sat with her eyes wide and her palm over her mouth for an uncomfortably long time, he continued. "When I first came to the Cleveland office, of all the associates, I knew you'd be the biggest threat to me becoming partner. I'd heard about your reputation as one of the most ambitious workers at the firm."

She reached for her water glass and brought it to her lips, only to find it empty. Leaning forward, she grabbed his and drank it down while glaring at him. Then slammed it onto the table. "What the hell are you playing at, Astacio?"

Of course it wouldn't be easy to get into her good graces. How could he explain he wanted to at least see if they could explore their reactive chemistry without scaring her onto a plane? "I haven't done well by you and I wanted to apologize."

"You never apologize, so I'm not buying it. Tell me the truth. Where is this coming from?" She leaned forward and lowered her voice. "Is it because we had sex? Do you think I'm going to charge you with sexual harassment or something?"

Her reaction snatched him off-balance and he mirrored her position. "First of all, that was consensual. All I heard was yes in various pitches from you. So no, I don't fear you going to HR. Remember, I could do the same. I just want to start over."

"Why?"

He scrubbed his hands over his face. *Because you're amazing and I've finally opened my eyes to see that we might belong together.* He'd never met a woman like her and knew without a doubt he never would. "Because I like you." *I'm in love with you and I need you in my life.* When the realization had initially hit him a few hours ago, he'd raged against it. Of all the people he could've fallen for, his formerly perceived enemy had to be the worst. He still hadn't fully accepted it, but the more time he spent with her, the more real it became.

She studied him for a moment and then her shoulders started to shake. With laughter. It went on for a while. Not seeing the humor in the situation, he waved his hand and got the waiter's attention. He raised their glasses to order and the observant young man nodded.

The laughter finally abated. "Stop playing, Astacio. If you want to get into my bed, just ask. No need to be all dramatic."

He'd expected as much. If she'd admitted something similar to him a few months ago, he would've called her a liar and walked out of the room. He'd made sure their relationship hadn't been a cordial one over the years, so he didn't blame her.

The waiter set their drinks in front of them. "Is there anything else you'd like?"

A reversal of time to change my behavior toward her from the first moment we met. He made sure to look at the waiter. "No, thank you."

The whiskey burned on the way down. He'd have to take a different tactic. Prove his legitimacy with actions rather than words. In the meantime they could have some fun. "Would you be amicable to having me in your bed?"

"No." She chewed on her bottom lip. "Maybe."

He stopped breathing at the unexpected answer and waited for her to explain.

Playing with the condensation on her glass, she avoided looking at him. "I mean, if we weren't fighting for the same promotion, then…"

Excitement like he'd never known before rushed through his body. "Right now we're fighting for our jobs, and we have to do it together, not as rivals."

She looked into his eyes. "True."

As he held her gaze, his mind raced with the possibilities of the week ahead. "And you have to admit we're sexually compatible."

Her perfect dark brown irises glazed over as if recalling their one night together. "We were."

"So why not go for it?" Was that all he had to convince her with?

She picked up her glass and took a drink. "I'll think about it."

The woman didn't have an impulsive bone in her body. She analyzed everything ad nauseam. "Of course." His offer of friendship had been shot down, but the possibility of making love again sat on the table. He could live with that. For now.

Kamilla looked at her phone screen. Midnight in Colorado, but two in the morning Cleveland time, and she was still tossing and turning on her queen-size bed. Had she really told Leonardo that sleeping together might be a possibility?

Of course sex had been his aim in telling her he liked her. She punched her pillow. He'd been manipulating her. She'd rather have had him ask straight out.

Having sex again would definitely stop the memory of them entwined together from lurking in her thoughts. She'd make new ones to salivate over once they reached Cleveland and their affair ended. After all, they were still up for the same position. No matter who got it, things would change.

Even if they weren't both vying for partner, she couldn't have a relationship with him. He was too arrogant and overbearing. She couldn't forget spoiled, in a way that bordered on royalty. Recently she'd experienced a different side of him. One she liked way too much, even though she behaved as if she still didn't care for him.

Who was she kidding? Her heart had tripped over to team Leonardo once she'd learned about his pro bono work. The man helped others when he didn't have to. That said a lot.

Stretching out her arm to the side table, she attempted to grab the Singletons' file, but the television remote jumped into her palm. She switched on the flat-screen television and scrolled through the stations, something she rarely made time to do, so she lived with the basic channels at home.

At least she'd come up with a fun itinerary for the next few days. Leonardo would hate it, but she couldn't be bothered. She'd get to do all the winter-wonderland things she'd never experienced and that alone would be worth this trip.

Sex with Leonardo would merely be the sumptuous icing on the cake. She just had to be careful not to want more from him.

Chapter 14

Kamilla's snow pants spoke with every step as she grabbed the matching jacket and went into the living room. Leonardo hadn't liked the itinerary she'd given him at breakfast and had told her. Surprisingly, his brutal honesty had eased the tension that had wedged itself between them last night.

No one had ever proposed a sexual relationship to her before. She just wasn't the type. Even in her few relationships, it'd taken a lot of getting to know the guy before she'd slept with him. How was she supposed to act? She had no idea, so she'd been quieter than normal. Until he attempted to cross things from her list. She'd snatched it away and responded to each of his protests as she ate.

The swooshing of the waterproof polyester stopped

when she saw him. Dressed in a hunter-green ski jacket with white-and-yellow trimming, along with matching snow pants, she couldn't help staring. This luscious man wanted to sleep with her? Again? She went to the kitchen for some water to wet her now parched mouth.

He dragged his gaze from her black-capped head to her sturdy dark boots and then back up again as she rustled past him. She didn't miss his snarl.

"What the hell are you wearing?"

Ignoring his harsh tone, she filled her glass with tap water and drank before placing the empty glass in the sink. She looked down at her padded black snow pants with the matching black coat draped across her arm, seeing nothing wrong. It wasn't fashionable, but it would keep her warm. "It's my snow gear. Let's go."

She couldn't get past the new door he'd made of himself. "I'm not going anywhere with you dressed like that. You look like the grim reaper of snowboarders."

Taking offense, she plunked a hand on her hip, but it slid off. "It kept me warm enough in Alaska."

He blinked a few times. As he tilted his head a groove appeared between his brows. "What were you doing in Alaska?"

"During one of the summer breaks in college, I went deep-sea fishing. All that's missing is the yellow waterproof slicker to wear over this and I'd be set." An icy chill slid down her back, making her shoulders shimmy. It was a wonder she hadn't moved to Florida when she'd returned from the work experience in the tundra.

"Are you telling me you worked as a fisherman in college?"

She gave him a crisp nod and once again attempted to bypass him. "The best money I ever made in two months. I would've done it again, but the minor case of frostbite on my toes and never feeling warm the whole time deterred me. When I returned to school, I slept under three comforters."

Kamilla watched his eyes glaze over. Not an unusual reaction for most people after hearing about this particular job.

"The salmon run was crazy," she explained. "We'd be up for forty-eight hours at a time on the boat. And those suckers were heavy. Only my previous gym time with free weights saved me from crying every night. Can we go now? Time is ticking and I'd like to get the fun started."

Recovering, Leonardo held her by the shoulders. "You are not going anywhere with me dressed like that. You need a new suit."

Stepping out of his grip, she glared up at him. "Then I'll go alone. Why would I spend all that money for a new one when this is fine? How many times in my life will I play in the snow again?"

"I bet you said the same thing when you bought that ugly monstrosity."

She pointed a finger his way. "For your information, my employers were very concerned about things like hypothermia and losing body parts to extreme temperatures, so they provided us with this. Boots and all."

Leonardo pinched the bridge of his nose. The low baritone of his voice counted backward from five. "You're going out there as my girlfriend, not as a fisherman." Each of his words came out distinctly. "You're buying a new one."

Once the thrill of the word *girlfriend* wore off, anger settled in. How dare he give her orders? "No, I'm not. I don't need to waste the money." Not that she wouldn't like to look sporty and a lot less bulky, but it wasn't in her budget. They were in Aspen for goodness sake. She couldn't even imagine how much a snowsuit would cost. Paying off her student loans came first. If she found she liked winter sports, then she'd buy a new suit during the summer sales.

"Take off those hideous pants and put down the jacket." He held his hand palm-up and flexed his fingers. "Never mind. Give them to me. I'll have the concierge incinerate them."

At the way his nostrils flared, she would've thought she'd insulted his mother. "No."

"Kamilla."

Did he think his overwhelming demeanor would work with her? She wasn't one of the multitudes of people at the firm who feared him. She'd seen people drop their coffee when he used that tone. "Leonardo," she returned in the same manner, adding her own intimidating glare.

The battle of wills could've lasted for the rest of their stay. Even with the five feet between them, his minty breath came out with such force that it brushed her cheek.

"Damn, stubborn woman," came out low and distinct. The rest of his words were a jumble as he raked a hand over his brush cut.

"Fine. Since I know you have a birthday sometime this year, and you refuse, for some illogical reason to purchase a better snowsuit. I'll buy you one." He turned away as if he'd resolved the situation.

Her anger flared, making her see a red so vibrant, she swore she'd burst a blood vessel in her eye. She chased him into the living room. "Who the hell do you think you are? What makes you presume I'll let you buy me anything? I'll do with what I have or nothing at all." She stepped up to him and poked his chest. Ignoring the pain in her finger, she stood on her toes so they'd be a little closer to being eye-to-eye. "I've been taking care of myself for years and will continue to do so until I die." She swished a hand in the small space between them. "I don't need your charity, Astacio, so you can take it and stick it up your—" She cut herself off as she whipped away from him toward the glass doors of the veranda.

His reflection stood beside her as the tension throbbed. His voice came out hushed. "I didn't mean to offend you, Kamilla." He blew out a breath. "Your life must've been tougher than you let on."

Shoving down any trace of emotion, she looked him in the eyes through the glass. "The only thing that matters is that I survived."

"For you to come as far as the woman standing before me, you thrived when others with more money, support and guidance may have failed."

Her heart warmed and she bit her lip to stave off the burn behind her eyes.

"Since this is a company trip," he said, "how about if we let the partners pay for your new snowsuit? And a pair of boots. Let's not forget a hat that's not used in burglary heists either."

The corners of her lips tugged upward without her intention.

The gentleness of his voice made him unrecognizable from the gruff man she knew. "What do you say?"

Unsure now of how to answer, she remained silent.

"If you're worried about never wearing it again, it's not a problem. I have a feeling once you learn how to ski, you'll be on the slopes every chance you get. Besides, I saw this suit with matching boots in the gift shop I know you'll want on sight. If you don't like it, we can go to the shopping center."

She turned to face him. The hat flopped in Kamilla's hands as she waved it. "How do you know I'll like it?"

"Because it's your favorite color. Turquoise."

All of a sudden she had difficulty inhaling. He'd been paying attention to her. She rarely wore anything with a turquoise hue, except for the one silk blouse on occasion beneath her black suit. Yet she surrounded herself with the color. From her sea-green phone cover to her keychain. She still couldn't believe he'd noticed.

Kamilla cleared her throat. "Fine. The company can buy me a new snowsuit."

His smile set off a chain reaction of flips in her stomach. "Good. Now get out of those excessive noisemaker pants and let's go."

Leonardo's heart had ached when he witnessed the pain in Kamilla's eyes as she went off on him. What had she gone through in life to never be able to depend on anyone?

Holding him in her arms as they zoomed down the hill in a sleigh, he relished the way she squealed as they sped over a bump, flew for a second and then landed. At the base of the hill, she was all giggles as she tried to stand, stumbled and then landed on her back.

How come he hadn't noticed before just how perfect she was? A little short-tempered, especially with him, yet just as quick to laugh, but not so much with him. He'd finally gotten to experience her free spirit and it made him feel as if he could soar.

Still smiling she stood and dusted snow from her new snowsuit. He'd been right about her loving the color turquoise and it looked great on her.

She started trudging up the hill.

"Aren't you forgetting something?" he asked.

She looked back and pouted. "Are you sure you don't want to drag it up this time? It would be the gentlemanly thing to do."

He chuckled. "Since when do you expect that from me? We had a deal and it's your turn."

She scrunched her nose before returning, grabbing the rope of the sleigh and ascending the hill.

When had he last had so much fun? He couldn't recall. Such a simple activity had elicited more laughter from him within a couple of hours than he'd done most of last year. *It's not just the activity, it's the woman.*

He snuck up behind her and swooped her up off her feet. Off guard, she dropped the rope and he swung her around until he became dizzy. She hung on tight and hooted. When he settled her onto the snow, she fell to the ground and rolled down the short distance they'd ascended. All the while her laughter touched something deep within him.

He needed more of this in his life. Fun. Spontaneity. Kamilla. He went to her, held his hand out and hauled her up.

Perhaps she was drunk on joy when she said, "I love this side of you."

Before he could process the words, she placed her gloved hands on his shoulders and leaned into him. The brief touch of her lips against his didn't satisfy. Before she could pull away and regret her impetuous maneuver, he tugged her in close and captured her mouth. The chill air disappeared as he warmed from the tips of his toes to the top of his head at her sensual response. Her moan exhilarated him as the initial coolness of her lips transitioned to warm and yielding. Lavender mingled with fresh air as he breathed her in, unable to get enough.

As he was about to deepen the kiss at her invitation of parted lips, the sound of people in various states of sledding enjoyment registered. With one last nibble on her bottom lip, he pulled away, mentally promising to return to them soon.

If either of them spoke, the moment would be ruined, and he wouldn't allow that to happen. He grabbed the rope of the sleigh with one hand, took her hand with the other and then headed up.

Chapter 15

Kamilla tried in vain to settle the butterflies in her stomach as she knocked on Leonardo's door. They'd only be going for lunch. She smoothed her moist palms down her pleated ankle-length black suede skirt. She'd paired it with an olive-green cable-knit sweater. It hadn't escaped her that Leonardo liked green.

What had she been thinking when she'd instigated the most romantic kiss of all time? Happiness had over-ridden good sense as she'd risen on her toes to play with him a little more after getting up from the snow. She'd meant to give him a lighthearted peck to end a couple of hours of fun. He'd turned it into something much more passionate. Her face flushed as she recalled how the heat of his touch had boiled her blood when he'd captured her lips and did the most amazing things to them.

Their first kiss had been almost as perfect as the first time they'd made love. What did it mean? She wouldn't delve too deeply into it other than acknowledging their bone-rattling attraction.

She'd seen a different side of him today. One she couldn't resist. He'd laughed and had fun, ensuring that they'd enjoyed every moment together.

He'd been born into a wealthy family, so what in the world did he have to worry about that made him such a hard man? She, like everyone else who gossiped about him, had always wondered what made him work as if his welfare depended on it. Or at all. No one had the courage to ask, nor the knowledge to speculate, so it remained one of those great mysteries.

Once again she found herself in unfamiliar territory with him and she didn't know how to behave.

The door opened, releasing a waft of Leonardo's unique scent. With nothing left to do, she held out her arms to the side. "I'm ready."

How come she'd never seen the fine lines at the corners of his eyes before when he grinned? Because meteor showers happened more often. "So I see. I'll be ready in a minute. I just have to put on my shoes."

She pointed to the living room. "I'll wait for you in there." Why hadn't she done that instead of knocking? Had she been so eager to see him?

He came out wearing dark gray pants and a pale orange sweater, which molded to his muscular torso.

She cleared her throat. "Thanks for carrying the sled up that last time. And for going sledding with me."

And for the kiss that had us melting the snow. "I had a good time."

His wink pleased her. "You looked good doing it."

Kamilla couldn't deny how confident she'd felt wearing the turquoise and white-accented snowsuit. The price tag had sent her looking for another one, but he'd insisted. "Thanks." She'd let him determine if the gratitude was for the suit or the compliment.

He held the door open for her with a look of concern. "Do you need your coat? We'll have to walk outside to reach the dining room."

Feeling bold and desiring his touch, she grabbed his heavy arm, draped it over her shoulder and then wrapped her arm around his waist. "You'll keep me warm until we get there." When had her voice ever sounded so sexy?

He closed the door and tucked her in close. "And it adds to the illusion of us being a couple."

She was about to be disappointed at his response when he stopped and whispered in her ear. "You're beautiful." He traced his lips along her jaw until he met her lips. The kiss electrified her as she gripped the muscles of his back. When their tongues touched, she fell into him as her knees weakened. They explored each other for what seemed like forever, and just as she was about to suggest they return to the room so their bodies could get reacquainted, he pulled back.

He looked her in the eyes and she lost all sense of herself. He bent forward and kissed her on the forehead. She sighed at his sweetness before he draped his arm over her shoulders and led her to the dining room.

She had little doubt that before the week was through, she'd end up in his bed.

For the second time in a row, Leonardo must've unconsciously doubled his repetitions, because his biceps burned more than usual for being on the fourth count. Distracted by Kamilla slicing through the water as if she were an Olympic swimmer, he put down the weights. He admired her through the glass of the indoor pool. She must've done at least fifty laps.

When she lifted herself out, using only her upper body strength, he was glad he'd put the weights away. A broken foot may have resulted if he'd dropped one in his shock. Her body had no business being so amazing, especially not in a functional navy blue one-piece. He flexed his hands at the memory of squeezing her full hips as he drove—

He found himself inhaling chlorine fumes from the pool. How had he gotten to the other side of the glass?

Last night had been rough. After spending the afternoon together going through the files and discussing ways to impress the Singletons with no solid plan set, they'd gone for dinner and then ended up relaxing in front of the fireplace, talking for hours. By the time they'd decided to call it a night, when he'd reached his room and she'd left him for her own, he'd felt empty.

He brought himself back to the present. She wrapped the large towel around her chest, obscuring his view of her luscious curves. He stepped back so he wouldn't rip the piece of terry cloth off her.

"Where did you learn to swim?"

"One thing about being poor is being able to attend the free summer camp at the Boys and Girls Club. At least back in my day, it was free." Her face broke out into a smile as if pleasant memories had entered her mind. "They taught us everything from swimming to arts and crafts. Knowing how to swim came in handy my junior and senior years of high school, when I worked as a lifeguard as one of my jobs during the summer."

He recalled how he'd been touring Europe and South America with his parents on his summer breaks once he'd finished his obligatory work at the Astacio head office. "What other work did you do?"

For a moment he thought she wouldn't answer as she slipped on her flip-flops. "At this point I knew I wanted to go to college, but had no idea how much the government would pay, so I worked like a dog those summers. Lifeguarding during the day and working at Walmart as a cashier in the evenings."

"When did you have fun?"

She scoffed as she tugged a long T-shirt over her head. The shirt hit mid-thigh when she removed the towel, and her sleek legs remained exposed. He tried to bring moisture to his mouth and blink like a normal person as she put on a pair of socks, boots and then her coat.

"There was no rest for the driven," she answered. "I knew what I wanted and refused to let anything stand in my way."

"To be a lawyer?"

Something in her dimmed smile saddened him. She

turned and opened the heavy glass door leading outside the pool area to the hallway. "Freedom from the system."

Captivated, he followed her out, leaving his uncompleted workout behind. He'd skip the five-mile jog for the day and pick up his coat later or have the concierge drop it off. He refused to miss the opportunity to learn more about Kamilla.

Pride filled him at everything she'd accomplished. "So now you're a lawyer with a top firm and are out of the system."

She'd forgotten to smooth down her hair after rubbing it dry and it stuck up in all directions, giving her a sexy mussed look. At the door leading outside, he smoothed it down for her, letting his fingers linger at the shorter hairs near the nape of her neck as he stared into her eyes. *One more taste.*

His hand hovered when Kamilla stepped beyond the range of his greed. He let his arm drop to his side with regret at the loss of her touch. Being underdressed for the weather, they jogged to their chalet.

Once inside she turned to him. "Did you pay for your Yale education?"

"My parents did."

Resting against the wall, she crossed her arms over her chest. "The government paid for my undergraduate degree, including housing, at Cleveland State University. I provided for my living expenses with the money I'd earned with my jobs. Law had always been my passion. No one could tell me I wasn't going to be a lawyer. I made sure I got excellent grades in college and applied for every single scholarship in existence and received a couple."

Kamilla held him enthralled with her story. "I was no longer a minor in the system, so the government didn't owe me anything. But they did assist me with some financial aid to Harvard, which included a work-study program during the semester. By the time I left law school, I owed seventy-five thousand dollars in student loans."

He'd heard even more horrific stories about paying back accrued student loans, so the amount didn't shock him. A couple of the pro bono cases he'd handled over the years had dealt with bankruptcy stemming from student loans that had snowballed.

What would she say if she knew about the free law advice he provided? If she ended up believing him, she'd most likely snicker and tell him it was his moral obligation to help those less fortunate. He'd agree with her 100 percent.

She sighed. "I don't have to tell you that money is power. I never had either growing up."

Did she really see herself as powerless? Afraid she'd stop speaking, he kept his mouth shut.

Kamilla crossed her never-ending legs at the ankles. "During my junior year in high school, a friend of my foster father offered me a deal. He said he'd give me anything I wanted. With the expensive cars he drove and the flashy jewelry dripping from his neck, hands and ears, I believed him. The catch being that I had to work for him."

Leonardo's jaw clenched as anger inflamed the back of his neck in anticipation of her next words.

"All I had to do was sleep with him. And anyone he set me up with."

Putting a hole through the wall wouldn't obliterate her past. Finding the bastard and kicking the life out of him sounded like a better idea. Kamilla's hand on his chest brought him back to her. Her eyes, usually bright and so full of life, had darkened in their dullness.

"What happened?"

"I told my social worker. She pulled me out of the house, and then had both my foster parents and the man investigated. The couple turned out to be innocent, but the guy went to jail after being discovered as a pimp to minors."

He pulled her into a tight hug. Her arms wrapped around his waist and clung. The scent of chlorine seeped into him. "I'm sorry you had to go through such a rough childhood."

"It made me stronger." She pushed away and slapped his arm. "Better able to deal with bullies like you."

He rested his hands on her shoulders and massaged. "I'm not a bully."

She moaned and lowered her head, allowing his ministrations. "If you say so. How the hell did I get to telling you my life story?"

He slid his fingers up along her neck. "Money and power."

She nodded. "That's right. From that moment I knew I had to be financially independent—otherwise I'd always be in the system and prey for slimeballs."

"Is that why you went corporate instead of into family, civil or immigration law?"

Her eyebrow rose. "Why'd you mention those three?"

"If anyone's a poster child for a bleeding-heart case, it's you." He held up both hands. "Don't get me wrong, you're brilliant at your job, but corporate doesn't fit you."

Kamilla raised her shoulders, reminding him to continue with his massage and grinned. "So you've noticed how good I am."

"My point," he stressed, "is that I'm pretty sure you'd be happier as a public defendant than you are working for our law firm."

"Corporate is where the money is. I'm almost done paying off my student loans and once I make partner, I'll always have a job."

He shook his head. "Unless they toss you out."

"Which they won't because, as you just mentioned, I'm fantastic at what I do." She reached up and touched her cheeks. "I must be an ashy mess leaving the chlorine on my skin for this long."

She'd never believe him if he told her how beautiful she looked, dry skin and all. "Lotion wouldn't run away from you."

Her tinkle of laughter made him smile. Before she could walk away and disappear into her room, he lowered his head and gave her a slow, lingering kiss on the lips. With a herculean strength of will, he pulled back from her sweetness rather than giving in to the lust driving him. Leonard gazed into her eyes. "You are one of the most powerful women I've ever met, Kamilla Gordon. Never believe otherwise."

He watched her disappear into her room. With each encounter, the woman proved more spectacular and he wanted to give her the world. Even the partnership? Would he be willing to give it up for Kamilla when he'd worked equally as hard? He was starting to believe he could.

The man held magic in his kisses. Kamilla touched her lips and sighed as she recalled the light touch of his mouth and his inspiring words. Recovering from the encounter, she slipped off the T-shirt she'd used as a cover-up. What had possessed her to share so much about her life with the last person on earth who'd care?

He'd seemed interested enough.

A perverse sense of joy had infused her when he'd vibrated with anger on her behalf as she told him about her encounter with the pimp. She'd left out the part where the twice-cursed pathetic excuse of a man had cornered her and tried to entice her into giving him what he wanted. A knee to the groin kept him away for a long time afterward.

What would it be like to have Leonardo on her side?

She adjusted the water in the shower so it flowed the perfect temperature of warm before shimmying out of her damp suit. Letting the water sluice over her, she lathered the luffa.

She'd always been able to take care of herself and didn't need anyone fighting her battles. Not even the man whose simple smoothing of her hair had set her skin on fire, making her forget she never shared her stories with others. What was the point? It wouldn't allow her to change her life.

Living in the present and heading toward the future was the only way to exist. Then why did she feel light and bubbly after sharing such a disturbing aspect of her life with Leonardo? She wanted him to know more, and hear all of his experiences. She craved him more with every conversation and touch.

Was that his plan? To keep her off her guard so he could swoop in and take the partnership away from her? She wouldn't put it past him.

She didn't need the complications he brought, and yet found it difficult to stay away. Sex had complicated things between them and if they did it again, would they be able to go back? Be colleagues and professional with each other?

She could already feel her emotions getting involved. Better to stay away. Then she sagged as an ache filled her chest at losing whatever had sparked between them. *If only I can.*

Chapter 16

Last night at dinner Leonardo had sensed that Kamilla was pulling away. As much as he'd attempted to engage her, her responses were less than enthusiastic. They'd parted in the living room without even a chaste good-night kiss.

At breakfast she'd seemed to take delight in telling him they'd have to separate for the day because of the ski lessons for beginners she'd be taking.

He seized the opportunity to be with her. "I've been skiing for years. I'll teach you."

She snorted. "You're more likely to push me down the hill and watch me turn into a huge snowball than to instruct me."

"Sometimes trial by fire is the best method. Besides,

we'll be on the bunny slope. It's basically flat. You'd gain more speed snowshoeing."

At the mention of the new activity, her eyes lit up. "Can we?"

Leonardo laughed, finding her willingness to try all things new refreshing. "I see your agenda is flexible and dependent on any snow activities you learn about. Let's start with the ski lesson. Maybe tomorrow we can go snowshoeing. That's if ice-skating doesn't catch your fancy."

The quick scrunch of her nose gave him the answer.

"I've been ice-skating once. I fell so many times, my ass got bruised."

A guffaw exploded from his chest. "Let's finish eating and then go skiing. You're a fast learner. Maybe you'll end up on a slope where your velocity increases to about five miles an hour as opposed to the two you'll get on the beginner hill."

"You don't need to stick with me. I won't mind if you go do something more exciting."

He leaned across the table and crooked his finger. After a quick glance around the crowded dining room, she rose, meeting him half way. Bracing his hands on the table, he closed the last few inches separating them. His lips met hers. Sweet strawberry jam assaulted his tongue as he teased her mouth. He ended the kiss long before he wanted to and settled into his seat.

"I want to be with you," he said honestly. "And besides, I'm at the mercy of your agenda, remember? I can't back out now."

Her smile brightened his morning. "Don't say I didn't offer when you're bored out of your mind."

"Somehow I doubt I could ever be bored when I'm around you."

"Okay." Kamilla's breaths came out in white puffs as they reached the bottom of the hill without her falling. She'd even kept herself in a straight line. No veering. "I've mastered the second kiddie hill. What's next?" She gestured to the massive mountain to the left. "How about we take the ski lift and whoosh down that one?" Not in the least bit serious about her request, she held back a giggle at Leonardo's wide-eyed expression of horror. "I'm kidding. Although I wouldn't mind taking a ride up and back."

"It can be arranged."

She'd expected a huge fight from the beginning to the end of the ski lessons, but he'd been a patient teacher. Not once did he rush her to do something she wasn't ready for. She hated liking this side of him. Detested it even more that he possessed it. Even the fact that he laughed each time she fell didn't annoy her. Too much.

He headed them toward the ski-rental area. "We won't need our skis if we're only riding the lift."

"What's the matter?" she teased. "Afraid I'll jump off and head down, leaving you in the dust?"

"More like breaking your pretty little neck as you plummet."

She tried not to let her pleased reaction to his compliment show. She really did, but the smile wouldn't be repressed. He'd been praising her all morning and damn if she didn't like it.

"How come you don't have your own skis?" Kamilla asked as they stood in line, waiting for a chair after returning their equipment.

"I'm not much into it. I know how to do it—I excel at it. But it's not something I love doing."

"I keep forgetting how humble you can be." His comment had sparked the need to learn about what, or maybe whom, he loved. "Other than working, what do you enjoy doing?"

He looked at her for a long moment, making her wonder if he'd give an honest answer, or if a sarcastic retort would slide off his tongue. "I can spend hours building a model airplane and never miss the time."

Was he for real? This man who exuded authority and confidence in spades enjoyed such a simple hobby? He took off his glove and lifted her chin. His touch aroused the need for more, like the way he'd shaken up her world at breakfast with his kiss, but he released her with a soft brush of his finger once she stared him in the eyes. "What did you expect me to say?"

Catching her breath, she prattled off the first thing that came to mind. "Yachting."

He shook his head. "I'm not a fan of the water."

"Traveling all over the world."

"I like it, but it's not something I'm—" he pinned her with a direct gaze "—passionate about."

The cold air dissipated as heat rushed to her face. *Sexy, flirtatious* and *delicious* were new words she'd use to describe him. She had trouble recalling the more negative ones he'd earned over the years. Attempting to distance herself last night and this morning had been an abysmal failure. His admission of wanting to be with her had made her feel too good to deny herself what she also desired.

The line moved forward and she went through the files of her mind to figure out something wealthy people tended to do that her poverty-stricken life had never brought to her door. "What about galas and fancy balls?"

He chuckled. "I attend because I have to. Especially when my sister holds them for her charities."

Kamilla grinned at the single encounter she'd had with his sister, Lanelle, at a benefit the firm had thrown last year. The woman had been sweeter than cotton candy. She'd had difficulty believing Lanelle and Leonardo shared blood.

She snapped her fingers. "Eat at fancy restaurants with your girlfriend?"

"I definitely appreciate good food, but I'm just as content eating at home. Fewer people to recognize me." Once again all of his potency focused on her as he stared into her eyes. "And I don't have a girlfriend to go out with."

He'd passed the test. If he hadn't, he would've found himself rolling around in the snow, clutching his groin for leading her on. She swallowed hard and then tried to lighten the mood again. "Play golf at a country club? Heck, just hang out at one?"

He pretended to wield a club and swung. "I've got game, but I play more for business reasons than pleasure."

The same reason she'd taken up the sport. Only, she

couldn't claim to be even marginally good at it. She did enjoy riding around in the carts, though.

His parents owned a billion-dollar enterprise. Was he as simple as he was making himself out to be? Why would he lie? Don't all women want an unassuming rich guy to chill out at home with, creating model planes? She wouldn't mind. "How about dating gorgeous, leggy, stick-thin women who work as models?" She'd never heard about any of the women he dated in the tabloids, but she sent up a silent prayer that he'd say no.

"Far from it. I think you're confusing me with my brother, Miguel. At least before he got involved with his college sweetheart. I like an unpretentious woman. One who's not in the limelight. Someone who can spend hours with me conversing, watching movies or just being together without doing much of anything except enjoying each other's company."

Her heart strummed hard enough to bruise her ribs. Not caring if she sounded a little desperate, she asked, "Are you sure you don't have a girlfriend to do those things with?"

"I've been too busy to get into a serious relationship over the past couple of years."

Boy, could she relate. Just as she was about to ask another question, their turn came to hop onto the lift. Not having skis on would make things easier to keep from falling and embarrassing herself. Especially in front of this amazing man she was discovering.

Focusing on letting the chair carry her away rather than jumping onto it, she clung to the side as it lifted off.

"You can relax now. You did well."

She exhaled as she released her tight grip. "Thanks."

"I would've fallen off my seat laughing if you'd missed."

Leonardo had returned. She did have to admit to the hilarity of such a situation.

"Now that you've interrogated the hell out of me," he said in a voice that held amusement, "tell me what you like to do for fun."

Did he really want to know? "I don't live the life of the rich and famous. Basic things like hanging out with my best friend and her children when I can get the chance makes me more than happy."

"No man to whisk you away to special places?"

"I've been working so hard for the firm that the only thing I have time for is the occasional drive to visit my friend. Everything else is extraneous."

"So you've given up your life for the partners."

She shook her head. Would he understand? "Not for them. For my own security and stability." Could he see her shrug in the jacket? "It's been a goal I've had all my life."

His dark brown eyes captivated her more than the picturesque snowcapped-mountain scene surrounding them and she couldn't break free. "It's difficult to explain." Especially to someone who has always had parents to take care of them and money at their disposal.

"I can imagine."

She doubted it. "Can you really?" And then she remembered his volunteer work. Wanting to ask him about it, she held her tongue. How could she explain discovering the information? Her gut told her he didn't want anyone to know he was a big softie underneath his tough guy image. "Why are you so…" How to phrase it so he wouldn't throw her off the chairlift. "Hard?"

At her choice of word, her face went up in flames and she wanted to take back the question. Instead she dug herself in deeper in a different direction. "I mean you act like a bastard most of the time." *Do not cover your face in utter embarrassment. Stand by what you said and he'll respect you for it.*

Or laugh his ass off as they reached the turn and headed downhill toward the flatland.

She grabbed his arm as the chair wiggled. "Be careful you don't fall off. I have no idea how I'd explain it to the partners. They'd never believe you'd laughed yourself off the lift."

"Yeah, they'd be more likely to believe you pushed me."

The seat shook at her enthusiastic nod. "I know, right. And no one in the office would blame me."

A smile of amusement lingered on his face. "I know what people say about me, and it doesn't matter."

"Why not?"

"Because they deserve their treatment. I give people what they need, not what they want."

She sat up straight and attempted to slide her arm from the crook of his. His flexed biceps kept her in place. "Excuse me, but I don't deserve it."

A few moments passed before he looked down at her. "You didn't believe me when I apologized for my past behavior toward you. Maybe you'll believe me now. I'm sorry about how I treated you. I was wrong." He shrugged. "To be honest I found you to be a threat, and it unnerved me. A new feeling for me, which I didn't handle well."

The tightness of her lips pursed to the side must've been response enough.

"I don't lie, Kamilla. I may be…harsh at times, but I'm always honest. About everything."

"So you really hate people from Harvard?"

He laughed. "I may have exaggerated a little when I first met you. The rivalry is strong between the schools, but it's not personal for me."

"You could've fooled me. Do you know that I wore something from my alma mater every day for a month straight just to piss you off?"

"I noticed, and I deserved it. Although I did enjoy finding and doling out anti-Harvard cracks."

She smiled. "I never knew so many existed about Yale. Some were really funny."

"I had to bite my tongue to stop from laughing when you let a few of them rip."

They'd come to the bottom of the slope and she braced herself to get off the lift without falling flat on her face. "I'll take my arm back now."

"How about if I hold on to you and we get off together?"

They'd always made an effective team. The partners recognized it, and begrudgingly so had she. Would they make a good couple, too? Something to think about. "If I fall, I'm taking you with me."

The softness in his eyes sent her stomach quivering. "I'd have it no other way."

Chapter 17

"Cass, you would love this place," Kamilla gushed when her friend's face showed up on her phone.

"Girl, what have you been drinking? Snow and I don't go together. Hell, I would've never come back to Ohio if Michael hadn't bribed me with having three children instead of two."

Every year, Cass complained about winter from the first fall of snow. "And where is my third niece or nephew?"

"Two is more than enough. So, tell me what makes Aspen so fabulous."

"Leonardo taught me how to ski."

Her friend sitting frozen made Kamilla wonder if the line had been dropped. "Casey? Are you still there?"

"Did you say the monster taught you how to ski?"

"And that's not all. We had a real conversation and he apologized for treating me badly over the years." She paused for dramatic effect. "Twice."

The news got a triple gasp. "Do you believe him? What did you say?"

"I laughed at him the first time because I thought he was joking. I've never heard him apologize for anything." She paused, now a little embarrassed at her behavior. "He kind of seemed sincere, but still…"

"Yeah, you never know with tormentors. What happened the second time?"

Kamilla sighed, recalling the earnest look in his eyes. "I believed him. I didn't want to, because it's so much easier fighting with him than liking him, you know. After all he's my competition." What would she do if she didn't become partner? The next opportunity probably wouldn't be for years.

"Or—" she held up a finger as she elongated the word "—you could get a new job. One you actually like."

Not this again. "I've put in too many hours and given up too much of my life to start over somewhere else."

"Okay. I hear you. I don't agree, but I hear. What do you think brought on this change in him?"

"I know you have your ideas, so just say it."

Cass laughed. "I want you to admit it."

"I've got no clue. You'd say it was the sex, but I think he might be playing some kind of game. Trying to get into my head so he can knock me out of the running for partner."

"Okay, Miss Conspiracy Theory. To be honest, I think he likes you. Just as you do him."

What good would it do to deny it? Especially now that she'd gotten to know him better. "I'm not ruling out manipulation."

"Fair enough." Cass leaned close to the phone. "Now tell me about the sex."

Confusion slammed her brows together. "What?"

Cass huffed out a breath. "You heard me. How's the sex? Is it as good as the first time? When we spoke the next day, you were glowing as if you'd eaten a star."

"Am I glowing now, observant one?"

She traced a finger in a circle. "Why do you think I asked? You have joy and dare I say peace about you."

"Maybe you need to turn down the brightness of your screen. We've kept our clothes on the whole time." She held back news of the toe-curling kisses they'd shared, along with his very tempting offer of sleeping together. It would merely fuel Casey's perception that she liked Leonardo.

"He may not be doing you, but he's doing something good for you." Cass grinned. "I like that. I'll let it go for now if it makes you uncomfortable."

Her friend knew how to push her buttons, but she wouldn't fall for it this time. "Tell me what the girls are up to for the weekend."

"But—" of course she'd add one "—you've already mentioned he's more than he appears to be."

Kamilla raced through the recent conversations she'd had with her friend. When had she mentioned something she'd only recently discovered? "When?"

"Didn't you tell me last time that he did free law work for the community or something?"

It seemed so long ago. Had it only been last week? "Yeah."

"You were shocked at the revelation," Cass said as if it should be enough of an argument to convince her. "Plus I can hear it in your tone that you like him."

"You need to cut it out. And besides, we have nothing in common." Other than enjoying staying at home, chilling rather than going out. Having sharp minds that enjoy engaging in witty repartee. And an attraction she feared would singe her hair off.

"You may come from completely different financial backgrounds and social standings," Cass insisted, "but I'm sure you have a whole lot in common. Like some burning-hot chemistry."

Time to get Cass off her back. "Let me talk to my babies since you won't tell me anything about them."

For the next ten minutes, Kamilla listened to every minute detail of what the girls had planned for the weekend. By the time she hung up the phone, she was confused about how she'd been reacting to Leonardo. What did it mean that she wanted to kiss him so badly, she had to step away in order to not grapple him?

She scrubbed her hands down her face. Not only were they in competition for the same position, but he was an Astacio. Hooking up with him would be equivalent to sleeping with an American royal. He couldn't really be interested in her. Other than her sharp tongue and unwillingness to treat him as no one special, she had nothing to offer him.

She must merely be a way for him to pass the time.

Did he only want her body? A better question might be, did it matter?

What was it about Kamilla that had him aroused every time he saw her? Knowing what was under her maroon wrap-around dress didn't help. Did the dress unzip somewhere, or could he pull it up over her head, exposing inch after inch of soft, beautiful skin until—

"Did you hear me?"

Leonardo shook his head hard and shifted forward in the couch to strategically angle his hands over his groin. "What did you say?"

"You'll need your coat. We aren't eating in the dining room today."

Must be why she looked extra good this evening. She'd even worn color on her eyelids. "Where are we going?"

Her grin was mischievous. "I'm not telling you."

Scowling never worked on her, but he tried it anyway. "Because you know I won't like it?"

"Eh," she said with a shrug. "I'm hungry, let's go."

"Am I underdressed?"

Her gaze raked over his button-down shirt and slacks. Had her breathing increased as she licked her already glossy lips? He wished she hadn't.

She shook her head. "No. I'm overdressed. I never get to go out, so I'm taking this opportunity to look good."

He stood and walked toward her. He'd promised himself he wouldn't push her, but he couldn't help bracing his hands on her hips, leaning in and swiping his lips against hers once. It wasn't enough, so he repeated the motion again and again until she wrapped her arms around his neck. She kissed him with so much passion, he almost forgot about his resolution.

Forcing himself to drop his hands from her body, he stepped away, pleased when she whimpered her protest. He left the next move up to her. If she wanted to make love, she'd be the one to initiate. "You're stunning."

Lowering her lids, she smiled. "Thank you."

The sweet shyness made her even hotter. "I'll be right back." Walking away took effort, but he rushed to his room, grabbed his coat and ran back out to her. Not even a minute had passed, but it had been too damn long to be away from her.

He was definitely whipped. He just wished she were, too. "Let's roll."

Twenty minutes later he couldn't believe where the Uber had delivered them. "Are you sure this is the right place?"

"Yes." She grabbed his hand and tugged. "I spoke to the concierge and told him we were in the mood for simple yet delicious food, which would allow us to experience the local life."

"You lied when you said *we*." He didn't resist when she led him toward the door with genuine laughter.

"I took liberties. We're supposed to present as a couple, remember?" She batted her lashes up at him in what he could only assume to be mockery. "He directed me here."

"Why would you do this to me? Have I pissed you off that much over the years?"

"Yes, but that's not why. I just thought my man should be exposed to the finer things in life."

"You have a warped definition of the term."

She grinned and nodded. Her eyes sparkling with joy caused his heart to tighten. "I know. Isn't it great? Drinks, food and dancing all under one roof."

Inside, the clean interior held a definitive country-and-western vibe with the US flag front and center, an elevated ancient truck behind the bar, and a scuffed-up wooden floor. The mechanical bull in the corner of the room didn't drive him out, but the men and women in cowboy hats and boots—and some with chaps—did concern him a little. If it made Kamilla happy, he could hang out here for a few hours without dying.

"You know we'll be the only two black people in the building, right?" Just as he finished the sentence, a brother walked by and nodded in his direction. Leonardo returned the salute.

"You were saying? Loosen up a little. This'll be fun." The smile was probably a permanent feature tonight. "Wait until they open up the dance floor."

A hostess—at least they had one—welcomed them. "Welcome to the Boot N' Scoot. Will y'all be eatin'?" Her accent was much too heavy to be real.

"I made a reservation. Two for Gordon."

The woman checked her computer, grabbed menus and said, "Follow me." She showed them to an empty table in the crowded dining area. "Just so y'all know, there'll be free line dancing lessons at seven. They're for beginners, but the regulars like to show off. Don't mind 'em."

"Thanks, we'll be sure to take advantage," Kamilla said with a wide grin to the hostess before she stepped away.

Had he ever seen her so happy? Yes, sliding down the mountain in a toboggan. Reaching the bottom of the kiddie hill without falling had brought out the brightness in her eyes, too. He liked this relaxed side of her, especially since she was with him.

"Get it out of your head. You won't be seeing me doing the Achy Breaky or whatever on that dance floor."

"Why not? It'll be fun." Then she winked. "I'll take pictures to use as blackmail."

He laughed. He'd been doing a lot of it this weekend. "No one would believe you."

She snapped her fingers, angled her head. "Aw shucks, you're right. I'll just have to keep them as a memento. I'll label them, the time Astacio bust a move. I'll laugh and laugh every time I look at them."

"I'll definitely be going onto the dance floor then." Nobody would be able to miss the sarcasm in his tone.

"Fine. Then I'll just do the Tush Push by myself." She stuck out her tongue and giggled before studying her menu.

Air refused to make its way into his lungs as realization dawned that he really had fallen in love with her. Needed her as if she were the only thing on earth that would make him feel truly alive. And happy.

Chapter 18

Kamilla had brought him to the country-and-western restaurant to irritate him. Maybe snap him back into the more brutish man he'd been until recently. Who'd have anticipated they'd have such a great time? Getting him to do a line dance would've taken a hypnotist's power of persuasion, so she'd given up and had a blast learning the Cowboy Charleston and the Country Slide.

Each time she'd searched for Leonardo, he'd been watching her, and her body hummed with excitement. His gaze followed her as if he couldn't get enough. She'd lost step a few times as her skin heated with more than just the dancing.

The dance floor opened to the regulars and the place filled up. Not knowing the steps didn't stop her from moving to the back and participating without tripping someone else up.

When they switched to a slow song, the people paired up for a two-step. She was just about to join Leonardo when the prettiest man she'd ever seen came up to her. Slightly effeminate, but he gave off a manly vibe. Were his eyes really that green? He flipped his blond hair from his forehead with a flick of his head and smiled down at her with perfectly even white teeth.

"Would you like to dance?"

Before she could say a word, a hand landed on her hip, sending her jumping. A quick look to her left revealed a glaring Leonardo. The difficult man she'd gotten to know over the years had finally made an appearance.

When Leonardo didn't say anything, she hitched a thumb in his direction. "Thanks for the offer, but I'm going to dance this one with my boyfriend." She didn't stutter over the word, and it actually sounded natural. Appealing.

The beautiful man took a step back with a nod of his head and a hasty retreat after glancing at Leonardo.

Kamilla rounded on him with her own glare. "Do you know how to two-step?"

He pulled her into his arms so their bodies were flush and he moved his feet from side to side in place. The others gracefully glided across the floor, doing fancy twirls, dips and spins. She and Leonardo danced, with their arms wrapped around each other as if they were in a decorated high school gym.

She laid her head against his shoulder, not minding that they weren't even attempting to do an actual country two-step. Her body hummed with awareness as they swayed to a song she'd never heard before. She was unlikely to forget it. The lyrics were about time, love and having to run because someone was waiting for the male singer with the deep, twangy voice.

Right where she wanted to be, Kamilla hoped the song never ended. God, she loved being with Leonardo. For once she accepted it without a fight. She liked him. Hell, she may have taken the tumble toward love. She clutched him a little closer and allowed her mind to stop thinking so she could spend these precious minutes feeling.

When the song ended, they peeled themselves apart. She could barely restrain herself from grabbing on to him again as he led them to the bar. He glanced down at her with raised brows.

"Draft beer," she answered to his unspoken question.

The brows stayed up, and a grin was added before placing their orders. He carried their drinks to an empty table and they sat.

A minute later he tipped his head at her drink. "I didn't know you drank beer."

"There's a lot you don't know about me."

"Obviously." He gave her an intense hooded stare, which had her center pulsing. "I'd like to find out everything."

Beer in hand, she gulped the cold liquid. Was he for real? Her instincts told her he was as serious as a person could get. "You may not like what you learn."

He shrugged. "You aren't perfect. No one is."

To lighten the mood, she slapped a hand to her chest and drew in a shrieking breath. "Are you admitting you have flaws?"

He chuckled. "I don't have to tell you, of all people, that I'm not a faultless individual."

They sat, watching the people dance, as they sipped their drinks.

"Can I ask you a question?" She didn't wait for an answer. "Why are you so driven?"

"You say it as if it's a bad thing."

"It's not, but you're an Astacio." She didn't miss the stiffening of his shoulders. "You were born into money. You don't need to work."

Regret churned in her belly as his eyes turned glacial. "I take it you're the official expert on the Astacio family."

What had she done? Needing the more relaxed Leonardo back, she tried to rectify the situation. "Forgive me for being presumptuous."

"And wrong."

She held his gaze. "Yes."

He downed the rest of his whiskey and stood. "If you've had enough dancing for the night, let's head off."

As if she had a choice in the matter. The man was ready to ditch her. She hadn't even drank half of her beer. She wanted to reverse the hands of time and retract her words. But had what she'd said been so wrong? She'd pointed out the facts. Just because he didn't like them being voiced didn't mean he had to get all pissy about it.

Great. He'd somehow ended up ruining a great

night. Another reminder that no matter how much the air crackled when they touched, they'd never make a good couple. They were too different.

Why had she gotten into his private business? Just because he claimed he wanted to know everything about her didn't mean he was willing or able to share anything about his life. A friendship, maybe something more, had bloomed between them. She was sure of it. And now whatever rode him about being rich, famous and powerful had shoved them back to their previous roles. Colleagues and competitors.

He'd been an Astacio all his life. He knew nothing different. Privilege, wealth and unearned respect had been showered onto him because of the family he'd been born into. He'd had no right to go cold on Kamilla when she'd asked him why he worked so hard.

Telling her the truth would've been fair. After all, he'd told her that he wanted to know all about her. Why couldn't he have reciprocated?

Habit. Fear. Self-preservation. During that moment it hadn't kicked into his mind that Kamilla wasn't asking so she could use him like others had. No, she was different. She'd asked out of pure curiosity. And he'd reacted in the same way as always, by shutting her down.

He had to apologize if he wanted to salvage the friendliness that had been developing from her end. When they'd danced, everything had been perfect. He wanted it back.

"Can I talk to you for a minute?" he asked before

she headed to her room once they had stepped into the chalet.

She paused and turned. "If it's about tomorrow, I've canceled our plans." Her tone lacked any of the joviality of the night. "We can go over the Singletons' files. I have a niggling feeling there's something wrong with one of the subsidiaries. I can't remember which one, but something came to me—"

"I'm sorry."

"Me, too. We should've been working the whole time."

He reached for her hand. Before he could touch her, she'd pulled away. He'd really messed up. "This is a sit-down type of conversation." He indicated to the living room with a sweep of his hand. Her few seconds of hesitation caused sweat to break out on his palms. Had he lost her before she'd even been his? Over something so small that could've been avoided with open communication on his part rather than a knee-jerk reaction.

He released the long-held breath when she went in, removed her coat and sat, perched on the edge of an armchair. If she were willing to listen, then maybe he still had a chance.

"There are two things that drive me. Push me to work hard."

She held up a hand. "You don't have to explain. I shouldn't have asked. It's really none of my business."

He shrugged off his jacket in the now sweltering room. "You had every right. I want to explore what's raging between us. I like you, Kamilla."

The lack of reaction didn't give him hope. "I'm sorry I reacted so harshly. It's habit. One I need to break."

Unbuttoning his shirt exposed the gift the surgeons had left him when he'd been six. He looked up to see her watching him, at least her face held an expression of interest. "I was born with a congenital heart defect where the aorta narrows and the blood can't get pumped to the rest of the body as well as it should.

"Since I was pretty much okay, they wanted to wait until I got older to see if they needed to do something about it. They weren't looking to do surgery on a toddler, and some people can live their whole life without it bothering them."

"You weren't one of them."

He shook his head. "I didn't eat or play like I should've, because I suffered from fatigue. I was the smallest in my kindergarten class, too."

Her upper lip curled. "I'm having a hard time believing that."

"It's true. The cardiologist took me to surgery. The first time, he did it without cutting me, but something went wrong and he had do an emergency open-heart surgery later that evening." He rubbed the scar and looked back in his mind. "I don't remember much, but I do recall waking up in pain and crying. I'm sure recovery for a kid is easier than for an adult, but it's still a rough process."

The sympathy in her eyes was clear. "I'm sorry you had to go through that."

"Thank you." He extended his arms out wide. "As you can see, I'm now physically exceptional."

She laughed. "And humble."

"My parents spent years trying to control my environment. Attempting to make my life easier at school and home. I got mercilessly teased by my schoolmates because the teachers babied me."

"I can see how that could get a kid made fun of."

"By the time I reached junior high school, the tables had turned. I was the same size as the others and even bigger than some. I had no difficulty showing those kids just how strong I'd become."

Pleased by her laughter, he continued. "My parents laid off, too, especially once they noticed how determined I'd became to do things on my own and excelled."

She pointed a finger at him. "Now that sounds like you."

"I work hard for everything I have because I can." He assessed her. "Does that make sense?"

"Why did you get so upset when I asked you about it?"

He sat back in the couch. "People can be jerks when it comes to thinking they know who I am."

The muscle in her jaw jumped as she sprang up. "Excuse me for being a jerk. Thanks for explaining. I'll see you tomorrow."

Before she could take a step, he inserted himself in front of her. "I didn't mean you. As much as I love being my parents' son, it can be hard when people try to use me to get to them. I sort of get defensive when my name or the fact that I have money comes into the conversation. Do you understand?"

She glared up into his eyes. "Sort of."

"Anyway, it's become habit to put people in their place. I shouldn't have done it to you, because you have every right to know."

"Why?"

"I mentioned earlier that I like you."

"Why?"

He rolled his eyes. "Because you ask questions as if you're four years old."

She smacked him on the shoulder. "I'm serious. You could be trying to make a play for the partnership by softening me up or something. Or you could be manipulating me to get back into my pants. Or—"

"I could've realized just what an amazing woman you are. How incredibly intelligent, beautiful and kind. Need I mention this attraction? It's not an everyday occurrence between two people and I'd like to explore it. And besides, tell me you think anyone can soften you up enough to make a play for the partnership without you knocking them off at the knees."

Her eyes glittered when she smiled. "You're right about that. One more question while you're being open."

He braced himself for the worst. "Shoot."

"You could've worked anywhere. Why did you choose Peterson, Benton, Monroe and Lanner?"

Not a difficult question after all. "Because of Monroe."

"Not the nicest man in the world, but he's one of the best in corporate law."

Leonardo nodded. "Like you, he worked his way up from the ground. As a black man, it wasn't an easy accomplishment, especially when he had no one to support him. He's friends with a few people on my mother's side of the family, so he's seen me grow up. He knows I work hard, not living off the laurels of my name. Other law firms would've promoted me just to have the Astacio name as an attachment. Not Monroe. If I were to ever become a partner in his firm, I'd have to be worthy."

"The only way to prove yourself. I get it."

Of course she would. "Are we okay?"

"Only if you promise me one thing."

I should make love to you and take you to the heights of pleasure? Gladly. He took a step backward to prevent himself from grabbing her. "What?"

"You'll talk to me instead of shutting me out."

"I can try."

With a brisk nod, she pivoted toward her room. "Have a good night."

Disappointment speared him once he realized that the conversation was over and he wouldn't be seeing her again until the morning. "You, too." *My love.*

Chapter 19

A thirty-minute warm soak in the Jacuzzi tub and Kamilla still couldn't relax. A roller-coaster ride with an eighty-degree drop was less dramatic than what had happened tonight. Transitioning from a state of possibly loving Leonardo to not being able to stand him, and then back to caring for him again. This was why she preferred being in the middle of a relationship. At least it tended to lack turmoil. Mostly.

He'd been so open with his story and his declaration of how he felt.

She'd stopped counting the number of times in the past hour she'd gone to her door to storm over to his room so she could throw herself at him. What would be the harm? They'd already had sex once. So why couldn't she just go out there, knock on his door and invite herself in?

What if he'd changed his mind and didn't want her anymore? Or what if she got addicted to his loving and he left her for someone else?

The phrase *he's not your ex* kept looping in her mind. By staying in her room, she remained emotionally safe, yet sexually frustrated. She opened the first of the wooden panels separating her from Leonardo and marched out. Backing down as she saw the single barrier to getting to him, she turned and headed for the kitchen. Maybe a mug of hot chocolate might help calm her.

She screamed when she tripped over something as she passed the couch.

Strong arms holding on to her didn't shut down the fear as she struck her captor.

"Kamilla, it's me." Leonardo's voice penetrated and soothed.

She backed away and turned on the side lamp so she could lambaste him properly. "You scared the crap out of me. What are you doing here, sitting in the dark?"

"Couldn't sleep."

His voice came through a little muffled as her focus caught attention to his shirtless body. Her mouth watered at the wide expanse of muscular chest, shoulders and abs she could grate cheese on. Coming back to her senses, she flung her gaze from the small disk of his nipples to his eyes. "Um…uh…me neither."

The lout didn't even pretend to ignore the effect he

had on her. He stalked toward her. Kamilla tried to hustle away, but her feet refused to move.

Close enough for her to feel the enticing masculinity he emitted. Raw need possessed her. She couldn't resist anymore. In a rush she leaned forward and covered his lips with a hard kiss. Without hesitation his arms banded around her and pulled her to him as his tongue delved into her mouth.

Her tongue found itself dueling with his in a battle that mimicked the verbal slayings they tended to engage in. And yet it wasn't enough. She stroked her hands up the hard planes of his body until she clung to his neck, bringing herself flush against him with a moan of satisfaction.

He gripped her ass and lifted her off the ground. She needed no more prodding to wrap her legs around his waist. Their movement to his room barely registered as he tore his lips away from her mouth to suck a spot on her neck that had her legs flexing to ensure he didn't leave her.

Ignited by his exclusive scent, she grabbed the sides of his head with both hands, bringing his mouth back to hers to dive into his heat. Relishing the taste of whiskey and the sultry feel of him, she brushed her hand against his head. Her feet slid to the floor when he released his hold.

He separated them long enough to undo the tie of her robe. "I wanted to strip that dress off you all night."

She'd wanted the same. "Do you want me to go put it back on?" She teased in what she hoped was a sultry tone.

His eyes blazed as he slipped off the robe to reveal a simple navy blue satin nightie, which reached past her knees. "What you have on is better."

She looked down to find her nipples beckoning him. He zeroed in, rolling the peaks between his fingers. The throbbing heat at her center was almost too much to endure. He slid his fingers beneath the straps of her gown and lowered them until her breasts were free.

Her world went dark for a moment when he caressed her breasts in his large hands.

She had no doubt they were doing the right thing. The only thing that could happen at this point in time. She went for the elastic waist of his pajama bottoms and circled her fingers against the rim. The heat in his eyes goaded her. Her vision got a little blurry when he kneaded one breast while sucking on the other.

She slid his pants down only to find he wore no underwear beneath. She licked her lips as she remembered the mind-shattering orgasm his hard length had once induced from her.

He smoothed the nightgown over her hips and thighs, leaving her wearing absolutely nothing. He looked into her eyes and gave a lopsided, wolfish smile. "Were you expecting me, or do you always sleep without panties?"

She reached for him and wrapped her hand around his length. His eyes fluttered closed. "I'm sure that's not the most important thing on your mind right now."

His lips worked their magic on her mouth as she stroked him. "I have to get a condom," he whispered. She nodded and let him go, scoping him from broad back to a narrow waist, a tight behind to thick, muscular thighs. Perfect. The unzipping of a bag drew her attention. He removed a box from the side pocket and opened it.

She blinked at what she saw. Stepping in his direction, she plucked the individual packet from his hand and reached for the box. Removing the other two condoms, she held up the one she liked best. "Blue is pretty, but I'd like a red one. You have a way of setting my body on fire."

His answer was to slam against her and kiss her as if it were the only thing they had to do. She couldn't focus while he touched her, so she backed away, tore open the packet with shaky fingers and slid the condom onto him as he watched. The moment she finished, he lifted her. She wound her legs around him and pressed her chest against his, finding his strength to be an aphrodisiac.

She kissed her way along the side of his neck, up to his ear, where she rimmed the shell with her tongue as he backed her up against the wall. Ready and wet for him, she loosened her legs, looked down and reached between them to guide him into her. She screamed at the exquisite invasion of his hard thrust. Better than she'd remembered. When he paused, buried deep inside her, she looked into his eyes. The concern in them brought her mouth onto his as she clenched her inner walls around him to let him know he hadn't hurt her.

Withdrawing, he slammed into her. His moan of pleasure turned her on as much as being filled by him. He became her world. She absorbed the full length of him over and over as she held onto his sleek, sweaty shoulders. Still inside of her, he moved backward until he sat on a chair. Stabilizing her legs on either side of his strong thighs, she slid up his length and then back down. Slow at first, and then she sped up their rhythm. Lifting his hips he drove himself deep into her with every thrust. All it took was the hard suckling of her nipple and she exploded all over him as she called out, "Leo." Not able to clear the other syllables as she came. Kamilla clamped onto his shoulders, digging her nails in as he thrust up into her hard and fast. He set off another out-of-body orgasm as he came with her name on his lips.

Collapsing against him, she panted as she kissed his salty shoulder. Licked his neck and ended up at his lips. The kiss was so sweet, she started rotating her hips on him again.

He chuckled. His large hands held her hips still. "You're going to get us into trouble if you keep moving."

She whimpered in disappointment when he slid out. She hung on as he held her close.

Leonardo pulled away first, lifting her onto her gelatinous legs as he gazed into her eyes. He hooked an arm beneath her legs and lifted her, movie-style. He walked to the bed and laid her down. After a lingering kiss, he covered her with the sheet and comforter. With a brush of his lips to her forehead, he headed to the bathroom, leaving her with one thought: *Why didn't my stubborn ass do that sooner?*

Chapter 20

Leonardo startled awake when something kicked him.

"Get the elephant." Kamilla said in a forceful tone as she flailed on the bed. "He's not himself and he'll feel bad if he hurts anyone."

He watched her for a moment, expecting her to open her eyes and start laughing. Deep, even breathing met him. What was that all about? Should he wake her up?

"Kamilla," he whispered. No response on her now peaceful countenance. He stroked the side of her smooth cheek, feeling overwhelmed by her beauty. They'd made love last night. His body stirred as he recalled just how he'd felt plunging into her.

Just like the first time, she'd been volcanic. Smiling, he recalled her choice of the red condom over the blue one. He'd have to thank his brother for the gag gift. It had made the chore of protecting them sexier and added a bit of fun to their lovemaking.

He studied her. So peaceful. Would it be a bad thing to wake her up so they could do it again? As he contemplated the question, he stroked his hand down the satiny-smooth skin of her arm.

A smile spread across her full lips before her eyes opened. Her scream may have pierced his eardrums.

With her hand on her chest, she breathed hard as she glared at him from a seated position. "What the hell?"

"You're the one who kicked me out of a sound sleep. Literally."

She blinked down at him and giggled. "Oh. I'm sorry. I talk and move in my sleep."

"Would've been nice to know before we slept together."

The strap of the nightgown she'd put back on slid down her shoulder. He had difficulty tearing his gaze away from her covered breasts. He reached out for one when they puckered.

He looked up into her eyes as he rubbed her nipple with his thumb. Her groan replaced any comment she'd been about to make. Lying next to each other, they kissed. Nothing sweet like their last one. It was meant to tell him how much she wanted him. Maybe almost as much as he did her.

He slid his hand lower, over the satin of her gown. He reached the hem and pulled it up, making sure to skim his hand along her thigh. "Why didn't you just sleep naked?"

"I'm not comfortable sleeping without clothes. I grew up in foster care, remember. Never any privacy."

Wishing he could make it up to her, he slid his hand over her hip until he cupped her mound. "I may have to break you of that habit. It's just you and me."

Her coy smile made him harder. "I made a concession with the panties."

"It's a start."

Her side of the conversation ended when she moaned as he slipped a finger through her folds and circled her sensitive bud. "You're so wet." He slid a finger into her, drew it out and then sent a second in with the first. "So slick. Do you like that?" He watched as her eyes closed, her neck arched back and she simpered. "You like it."

She wound her hips against his hands. "When the hell did you become so talkative?" She tugged the gown up to expose her breasts. "I think your mouth has something better to do."

He laughed as he lowered his head and obliged. It didn't take long before she squeezed her thighs together as she quivered with her orgasm. Nothing could be as gorgeous as her coming apart. The opposite of the controlled woman he knew.

He reached for the box of condoms on the nightstand. "What color?"

"Huh?"

"Or I have glow in the dark, flavored and pleasure shaped, whatever that means."

She levered herself up onto her elbows. "Where did you get these condoms? And how much sex were you expecting to have?" Her eyes went wide as she reached for the sheet to cover herself. He held her hand still, keeping her exposed. "Did you think I was a sure thing?"

"No. My brother put them in as a gag gift of sorts. He has a warped sense of humor."

She resembled a statue as she studied him.

Naked physically, he may as well expose himself emotionally. "You're the one person in my life I can't predict, Kamilla. When I think you'll go left, you shoot straight up. If it hadn't been for my brother, we would've used the condom I keep in my wallet." He held up a finger. "One wouldn't have been enough."

That got him a small grin before she got on her knees, dragged her gown over her head and kissed him. When she pulled back, she looked down at his erection and licked her lips. "You'd have to leave the bed to get the flavored ones. Let's use the yellow one. For now."

In record time he'd sheathed himself and had her lying flat on her back with her legs spread wide. He held himself at her entrance. "This is our first time in a bed."

"You obviously need assignments when it comes to keeping your mouth occupied." Their lips collided as he slid into her. Their lovemaking was unhurried as he savored her. Her tight warm heat engulfing him. The way she met him with every thrust. The tenderness in her eyes as she gazed up at him.

He could've stayed inside her forever.

"Please." She whispered and he knew just what she needed as she raked her nails down his back. Together they set a faster rhythm, bringing them both closer to the edge.

"Oh my…" she breathed out when she came. He

grabbed her hips and thrust hard into her until he followed her into the heavens.

Kamilla placed the now empty tray room service had delivered onto the table in Leonardo's room. The server didn't bat an eye when he dropped off the meal at three in the morning. Neither of them had thought to buy food to keep in the refrigerator or cabinets of the designer kitchen.

"I changed my mind about scrapping the agenda for tomorrow."

Leonardo groaned in misery even as he tracked her movements. She put a little extra swing into her hips as she made her way back to the bed.

As soon as she bounced onto the mattress, he pulled her onto her back and rested his leg over hers. Who knew he'd be such a cuddly man?

He kissed her temple and rested his head on her chest. "We could just stay in and make love for the rest of the day. And night. Until we have to leave."

The offer held appeal. If the real world didn't intrude on them, maybe they could enjoy this fantasy for a little longer. She had to be real. "Remember we have work to do?"

He lifted his head and looked into her eyes. "I could give a damn about the firm and the need to keep the Singletons as clients. I care about you and building what we've started."

Unable to decipher if he wanted to continue having sex or start a relationship, she focused on the part about the firm. "If we don't reacquire the Singletons, then we lose our jobs."

"Would it be such a bad thing?"

Jaw dropping to her chest, she pushed his leg off her and sat up. "Weren't you listening when I told you about my past?"

He sat to face her. "I heard every word, but there's more than this firm. More than making partner."

"Puh. This coming from my main competitor. Are you telling me you've given up on becoming partner?"

"All I'm saying is that law consists of more than Peterson, Benton, Monroe and Lanner."

Was this the same man? "Where is this coming from? I've worked my ass off for them. I deserve to be partner. You know if I made a lateral move to another firm, it could be years before I'm considered. Years of having no life and never seeing the only people in the world I consider family. All the work I've done proving myself would have been for nothing."

He touched a hand to her knee, creating tingles that both distracted and calmed. Did he know the effect he had on her?

"You graduated top of your law school class. I heard about your reputation all the way in London. What makes you think others haven't heard about you, too, and would do anything to have you on their team?" He placed the fingers of his other hand over her mouth before she could argue. "Trust me, you'll always have a job. You found the stability you've been seeking all your life the moment you graduated college and law school, and passed the bar exam. No one can take that away from you."

She sighed in defeat. Of course he was right, but making partner would be irrevocable. Mostly. The partners could let go of a junior partner, but if they ever decided to make that mistake, she'd go down fighting. She set her lips in a deep pout. "You never answered my question. What's going on with you?"

Sighing, he lay back on the bed. His scar caught her eye. Without thinking, she reached out and traced her finger down the center of his chest, along the raised area. As a boy he'd had his chest cut wide open. His heart exposed so it could be fixed. He could've died. She leaned over, kissed the scar and rested her head on it. His heart beat strong and sure.

After minutes of lying there, he changed their positions so they faced each other. "Would you believe me if I told you I've fallen in love with you?"

The honesty shone in his eyes for her to see. He never said what he didn't mean, so she had no reason not to believe him. She nodded and placed her hand back on his chest, not knowing what else to say. If she told him she loved him, would it mean giving up her dream?

He fell onto his back and wrapped an arm around her. "My sister got married and had a baby last year. The most adorable creature I've ever seen in my life. I'm not the biggest fan of children, but when she smiles, my heart squeezes. Her husband has a niece. Vanessa fought cancer when she was younger and won. She's the second liveliest nonrelative I've ever met. Full of life and willing to learn. Because of our shared histories, we clicked right away."

Kamilla didn't understand where he was headed,

but enjoyed learning more about the people in his life. "Who's the first?"

"I'll give you a hint. She's gorgeous, intelligent, never backs down from a fight, is not easily intimidated, has worked more jobs than my friends in high school combined and is lying in my arms, asking me questions when I haven't answered the one she initially asked."

She laughed and settled against his firm chest. "It better have been me."

"Miguel got engaged. It shocked the hell out of everyone in the family. She's good for him. My parents are still young, but they're getting older. We have get-togethers and dinners but I only attend half of them, if that. When I did show up, I was never fully present. Making partner had become my obsession."

She still failed to see the direction of his story.

"About four months ago, I felt a burning in my chest, so I rushed to my cardiologist."

She snapped her head up. She hadn't seen anything wrong with him. But then again other than when they'd worked together on a project, they hadn't spent a lot of time in each other's presence. "What was it?"

"After a slew of tests, they diagnosed me with indigestion."

She let out the air she'd been holding and tapped his chest. "So it wasn't your heart?"

"No, but it could've been. Or I could get run over by a car. Be shot by a stray bullet or caught in a terrorist attack. This might sound corny, but life isn't guaranteed."

He'd just preached to the choir. "It's realistic," she contributed. "Most people don't live their lives understanding that." Over the past five years, she'd been one of them. Yes her goal was important, but so was, well, everything else. Now she understood the path of his thoughts.

"It was like lightning hit me with the realization that at any moment I could die and I had yet to start living. I just didn't know how. Until that night in my office when we set the furniture on fire."

She giggled. "I do vaguely recall."

He rolled over, sprawling her out beneath him. "Funny. I took a risk that night and felt free." He nipped the side of her neck. "Definitely satisfying, but also confusing because my life had been all about setting and meeting objectives, forsaking everything else to make it happen."

Were they really in bed together, talking about his life? She reached up and stroked his cheek. The bristly hair abraded her palm. The conversation as real as the solidness of his body pressing her into the mattress. "I haven't noticed a change in the past two months. You're still driven."

"Change takes time. I'm working on it bit by bit. With you, my family and even my concept of the partnership."

She nodded in understanding. "It's important, but not the be-all and end-all of life."

The brightness of his smile seeped into her. She pulled him down and kissed, loved and cherished him until they fell asleep in a tangle of limbs.

Chapter 21

Kamilla stretched the kinks out of her muscles as she woke up. Reaching across the bed, she found Leonardo gone. She recalled his quick kiss and an invitation to go to the gym earlier in the morning. She'd waved him off and curled up under the covers, considering their night as enough of a workout to last her the rest of the week.

She still couldn't believe the talk they'd had. *He loves me.* Although she hadn't admitted it out loud, she'd fallen in love with him. How long had this feeling been lingering inside of her? She'd fought and cloaked it as antagonism, but even her best friend had realized it. Could they really be together as a couple? She had her doubts. And hopes.

Leonardo's door opened and he strode in sweaty, hot and sexy. "You're still in bed?"

"Great to see you haven't lost your powers of observation."

When he leaned over to kiss her, she turned her head. "I haven't brushed my teeth."

He placed his hand on her chin and turned her in his direction. Staring into her eyes, he touched his lips to hers before rubbing their noses together and standing up. "Sweetheart, if the crust in the corners of your eyes didn't turn me off, your breath won't either."

She reached up to wipe her eyes and found nothing. She grabbed a pillow and tossed it at his retreating back as he headed toward the bathroom. She loved this playful aspect of him. *Life is to be lived.* She reminded herself of his resolve.

After hopping out of bed, she ran to her room. He wouldn't catch her unprepared for one of his heart-melting kisses again.

Forty-five minutes later they sat in the dining room, eating breakfast.

"Let's go ice-skating instead of using the skimo-biles." He wiggled his brows. "I want a chance to hold you for everyone to see that you're mine."

She paused mid-chew at the shock his words brought. Did he really want her? He did profess his love. What would it be like dating him? Never dull.

His hand waving in front of her face brought her back. "Did you hear me or did your fear of skating paralyze you."

Anxiety formed a tight knot in her belly. "I'm not afraid of skating. I just don't like it."

He shook his head. "I'm an attorney, remember. I

heard the distress when you said you fell a lot. I expected you to slide down the hill more on your behind than on your skis the other day, but you were steady for most of the runs. I figure you lied about being bad at skating."

Kamilla cut her sausage as she tried to play it cool with a shrug. Why didn't she just tell him what had happened? A previous experience had tranquilized her with terror when it came to ice-skating. Because she was screwed either way. Whether she told him or not, he'd made up his mind. For Leonardo, fear needed to be overcome, not entertained.

Normally she would've agreed with him, but this time she wished he'd just back off. Which of course he wouldn't.

"Good." He pointed the prongs of his fork in her direction when she didn't reply. "We're going to the rink after breakfast."

She tilted her head and smiled at him, hoping she looked at least a little sexy. "Wouldn't you rather stay in and…" she finished the sentence with a lick of her lips.

His eyes widened for a moment and she thought he'd nix the new plans he'd come up with. "Nice try, vixen, but we're still going skating."

"Great," she said with the same amount of enthusiasm she'd placed on the word when she'd first learned she'd be paired up with Leonardo for a project.

"The trick to ice-skating is balance." Leonardo attempted to coax Kamilla onto the rink after displaying his own skill by skating once around the rink. The boarding school he'd attended had taught him how to do almost everything he'd need to enjoy a full life. They'd had lessons from cooking to mechanics to dancing. He and his buddies had always joked that the school's main aim was to train them to be some sort of male Geishas. The institution excelled at creating well-rounded young men.

He stepped off the rink and sat beside her on the bench. Her gloved hands twisting together didn't bode well. Had he ever seen her so nervous?

He grabbed her hands to steady them. "What are you so afraid of?"

"Falling."

The non-snide remark caught him off guard. "But you fell on the ski slopes."

"Yeah, but no one can cut off your fingers with skis."

Confused, he backtracked. "Tell me what happened when you went ice-skating the first—"

"And only."

"—time."

He wrapped her in his arms when she trembled. "You're safe, sweetheart." He planted a kiss on her exposed temple and she leaned into him. He sank into the role he'd wanted to play in her life for so long. Her staunchest supporter. The strength she could tap from. He'd more than willingly give her anything she needed.

"It was horrible." She gripped his jacket. "In the sixth grade, we went on a class trip to a skating rink. It looked so beautiful on television and we were all excited, ready to do spins and fly through the air. When we got there, we were given a little lesson, but I hardly paid attention. Rather than cling to the side rail like the other kids, I glided onto the ice as if I owned it."

She looked up at him. "I was really good, too. I didn't wobble or fall once."

He smiled at her gloating. If she could be paid for excelling at the things she tried, she'd have been able to buy their law firm five times over. "I can imagine."

"My foster brother at the time, Tim, was a mean bastard. A bully in the house and at school."

He squeezed her. "What did he do?"

"The punk shoved me and I fell. When I got up, he looped around and pushed me again."

"That doesn't sound too bad."

"It wouldn't have been, but that's not the awful part. He left me alone for a little while and I got up, determined not to let Tim land me on my ass again." Still tucked into Leonardo's side, she angled her head up. She'd never looked more endearing. Almost innocent. Until she opened her mouth. "If you haven't noticed, I'm fantastic at everything I try."

He chuckled. "And modest about it, too." He prodded her with a jiggle. "What happened?"

She rested her head back on his shoulder and growled. "Andre Burton."

He waited for her to expound.

"I was minding my own business, gliding around with my best friend Casey, when he came up from behind and tripped me. I caught my balance before I plowed into the ice with my face, but unfortunately I overcompensated and went backward. I hit the ground so hard, I got the wind knocked out of me and had difficulty breathing." She balled her gloved hands. "One of the rules they taught us was to curl our hands into fists if we fell. I was too busy struggling to inhale to remember it. And then Casey screamed at me to watch out. I looked up and saw Tim barreling in my direction. I tried to pull my hand closer, but it was too late."

With the drama of a master storyteller, Kamilla paused, pulled off her glove and presented her hand as she swiped the air with her opposite arm. "There was blood everywhere."

He analyzed the appendage. "What am I supposed to be seeing?"

She pointed to the tip of her middle finger, not as rounded as the others. She gazed at it with regret. "He sliced the skin-tip clean off. My glove was ruined. Which I didn't mind so much because they were gigantic men's hand-me-downs."

He stifled his laughter at her lament for something he barely noticed. The situation must've been traumatic at the time, but she'd gotten off with little more than a scratch. "It could've been worse. At least he didn't cut through bone."

"It's bad enough. That boy ruined any chances I had of being a hand model."

Leonardo pulled away and studied her guileless eyes. "Is this a true story?"

"Of course it is. I didn't say I wanted to be a hand model, but the opportunity was ripped from me."

This time he laughed loud enough to draw attention from the few people enjoying the ice.

She swatted her glove at him and shimmied her rear

across the bench. "It's not funny. I had to go to the emergency room because I was bleeding so much."

He gave her a poignant look. The kind he gave to clients to determine if they were lying.

"Okay, so it was their first-aid room, but still I had to get medical treatment."

He tried to sober up from the laughter—he really did—but failed. After a full minute of being doubled over, his stomach hurt. Kamilla sat pouting with her arms crossed.

"I'm sorry. It's just that you were so theatrical about it." A chuckle escaped. "How about if I look up Andre Burton and this Tim guy and sue the hell out of them?"

That brought a slow, contemplative smile to her lips. "I already got my revenge."

Of course she did. Who would be fool enough to cross her without suffering the consequences? "What did you do?"

"Since the statute of limitations is over, I can tell you. I mentioned Tim was a bully."

Leonardo nodded, wanting her back in his arms. He kept himself still, knowing the moment had passed and she might fight it. Besides, a niggling fear careened down his spine about her next story. He'd seen her come up with some ingenious ways on how to phrase a clause in a contract so that it became ironclad. He'd never been prouder of her, but he'd had to convey it through sarcasm or perhaps an insult. If she hadn't been such a strong woman and took no offence at his mean-ass ways, he wouldn't have respected her as much. Even though he'd been completely in the wrong the whole time.

"I gathered everyone Tim and Andre had tormented the most." She bunched her lips to the side as if lost in the memory. "You have no idea how hard it is to get people who are afraid of someone to band together. Anyway, after a whole week of persuasion, then another one of planning, we got him." Kamilla tapped her chest. "*I* wanted to cut off his finger."

At least she hadn't thought of cutting something lower. "Tell me you didn't."

Her lip raised in a snarl. "Casey talked me out of it. Just before recess ended, we lured the two into a corner of the playground. We were twelve in all. Two people held each of them. One kept a lookout, while the others surrounded us so nobody could see. Then I took a water bottle and…"

Leonardo leaned closer to her. "What did you do?"

"For laughing at my poor finger, I'm not going to tell you, but it was good."

The glint in her eyes teased him. "Is that so?" Before she could protest, he scooped her up and sped to the rink. He glided with her on the ice, liking how she clung to him with her laughter ringing in his ears. "I'll set you down in the middle of the rink to crawl off if you don't tell me."

Her laughter halted. "Fine, put me down outside the rink first."

"No. Your fear is irrational, and just like you do with everything else, you have to conquer it."

She stared at him as if seeing him for the first time. Only, this time she seemed to like what she saw as her gaze dropped to his lips. It was the most inopportune time for his knees to weaken. He skated them to the side of the rink and set her down. Instead of hanging on to the rail, she clung to him.

Then she came to her senses and looked down at the ice. For an instant she wobbled and held on tighter. After a deep breath she pushed away, sliding on the ice like a newbie but keeping her balance. They made their way around the rink once. And then he clasped her hand and squeezed it, hoping to convey his pride at her strength.

"By the way," she said. "I wet their pants with water so they looked like they'd peed themselves. They never bothered anyone again."

If he'd had any doubt before, he no longer did. His spirit had chosen the right woman.

Chapter 22

Growling stomachs had roused them from Leonardo's bed after they'd made love. It turned out ice-skating had made Kamilla so greedy for sex that she'd attacked him as soon as they'd stepped into the villa.

She wiped the grin from her face. It hadn't been the skating, but the man. He'd helped her to overcome her long-time fear of the activity. What woman wouldn't get turned on? It had certainly done it for her. Never mind his dark sexy eyes, sensuous skin and tingle-inducing lips.

How in the world had she been able to stay away from him for two years when sitting across from him at the restaurant now tempted her to pull him out of his seat, find the closest private area and rip the sweater off him to expose his glorious body.

Gaining control, she looked down at the table, where his hand rested. Those elegant fingers had stroked her until she'd had an orgasm so intense, she'd forgotten everything but him. Her gaze glided upward to take her mind from the pleasure those digits had induced. When would the food arrive so they could get back to being naked?

Is that all she could think about? What about her future with the company? The partnership? The Singletons? She sighed, knowing they'd have to forego the fun she'd become hooked on over the past few days. "The Singletons will be here tomorrow. We really need to get some work done. We still don't have a plan for how we're going to interject ourselves into their vacation."

He shrugged. "It'll all work itself out."

What the hell? She definitely didn't like every aspect of this new Leonardo. "Nonetheless a plan A, B and C would be a good idea."

The server arrived with their orders, placing them on the table.

Famished, she plowed through her food. When her stomach protested with major discomfort at receiving any more, she slumped into her seat.

Leonardo sat staring with an adorable half-quirked smile. "Were you a little hungry?"

Her cheeks heated with embarrassment. She hadn't eaten that quickly since she'd lived in foster care. People stealing food from your plate had occurred more often than she'd liked. "I see you're almost finished, too." The three quarters of food left mocked her.

He chuckled. "I'm glad I could make you so—" he placed a piece of roasted lamb in his mouth "—ravenous."

The sexy drawl of the word brought moisture to her core. He knew precisely how he'd affected her when she groaned.

She had to take her mind off the delicious things his body could and had done to hers. She took a sip of passion-fruit juice and then set the glass down carefully. "What kind of watch are you wearing?" The timepiece's gold-and-silver face dazzled with gizmos she couldn't even think to comprehend how to work if she wore it. How come she'd never noticed it before?

Leonardo looked down at his wrist and jiggled it. "It's an Asombra."

Why did the name sound familiar? And then it hit her. "Isn't that the watch the huge star Lowell Evans is a spokesman for?"

He nodded once as he chewed a forkful of roasted vegetables.

Why did she sometimes forget how rich and powerful his family was? "Your family created the jewelry line, right?" Before he could speak, a memory did a touchdown. "There's an issue with one of the Singletons' subsidiaries. Something seemed off about their third quarter financial report."

His brows twitched together. Obviously he hadn't noticed anything wrong. "What was the problem?"

"I'm not sure. Something went off in my head, but the partners wanted the work done in such a rush that it completely slipped my mind. I had meant to mention it to you before, but got so busy that it completely slipped my mind." She pushed her chair back, ready to run to the room to figure out what she'd missed. "I'd like to take a look at their quarterly reports and compare them."

Instead of hopping up to join her, he remained seated. "How about we finish our lunch first? The files aren't going anywhere. Besides, there's really nothing in there that will help us keep the Singletons."

All she could do was stare, disbelieving. Who was this man? Business used to be his first, middle and last name. And now he'd actually eased back into his seat. "But if we find out what's wrong, why they decided to leave, then we could talk to them about it. Let them know we're on the ball, hell, that we're carrying the ball, when it comes to handling them as clients."

She wasn't telling him anything he didn't know. What was going on? Did he already have the partnership? Not likely. He'd been as upset with the partners as she had when they'd threatened them.

He placed his fork onto his plate as he stared at her. "I can see the convoluted wheels in your mind turning, Kamilla. What are you thinking?"

For once she didn't have the courage to speak. She had a feeling whatever he told her would break her heart. "I'm just ready to find out what's going on with the Singletons' jewelry company." She stood and forced a smile. "Finish your food. I'll meet you in the room."

He'd never understand women, especially the one he'd fallen in love with. Leonardo left his food and chased after her. What kind of asinine conclusion had she come up with when she'd been studying him? A frown had drawn down the corners of her lips. His gut had screamed that trouble was headed his way.

Maybe he should've told her about his desire to leave and finally start the law firm for his parents. It just didn't seem to be the right time. Especially since he wanted her to come with him and be a partner. Not just in the firm.

Marriage. Something he'd never considered, but now longed for. Kamilla had him desiring to have her by his side forever. Once he'd accepted that he loved her, nothing less than being hers and everything it entailed would do. He'd lived his life in an all-or-nothing manner and thrived at every turn. Joining forces with Kamilla would lead them to the ultimate success. He just had to make sure she agreed. Convincing her would take time.

Revealing his plan wouldn't have been wise, considering the newness of what he'd discovered regarding her fear about the future. So he'd kept his mouth shut. And now she'd discerned he'd been hiding something. She definitely knew how to listen to her instincts.

She stuck a file under his nose after twenty minutes of flipping sheets back and forth. "Look at this."

He dropped his gaze from her excited face to the papers. Dated from the first quarter of the year, he didn't see anything out of place. "What am I looking for?"

Shifting so she sat closer, she distracted him with her lavender scent.

"Look, there are seven times within January where the same amount of money is transferred in and out of several of his customers' accounts. At the end of the month, that same amount is placed into one last account. The same thing happens in March. The money was dropped into the same account in the end." She flipped the pages of the file to the second quarter's reports. The same thing happens here, only with a different amount. But it happens more often than the first quarter and with varying higher amounts."

Once again the papers flew at a rapid speed until she reached the last quarter on record. "In the third quarter it happens a lot more often and with bigger sums." She gazed at him. "It looks like money laundering."

From the numbers in front of them, he had to agree. Before doing so he went through the file again only to come to the same conclusion. "The Singletons acquired major shares of this company last year, in December. I remember working on the contract with Benton. Everything checked out with the financials."

Kamilla stood and paced the room. "Maybe they weren't doing it then. Or they could've fudged their numbers and nobody caught them."

His pride prickled at her words. If there had been a problem with the company, he would've tracked it down. He unclenched his jaw. One of the partners had worked on the Singletons' file for the first and second quarter of the year. And then he and Kamilla had been forced to work together under rushed working conditions during the third quarter.

His heart scare hadn't helped and his head had been a mess. Still no reason to have missed something so important.

The whole damn firm had neglected to see the disparities for the greater part of a year. Money launderers were slick and difficult to catch. They had a way of layering cash until it all seemed normal. Clean. Unless they got sloppy, greedy or had a tracker like Kamilla on their asses.

"Money laundering," he stated.

She flopped into the armchair, which was perpendicular to him. "I wonder where the funds come from. Blood diamonds? Drugs? Prostitution?" The muscles in her face drooped. "Human trafficking?"

The need to comfort her engulfed him. "For all we know, it could be a matter of good old-fashioned blackmail or extortion. That's for the feds to figure out. Not us."

She rushed to his side and grabbed his arm. "What if they support terrorists with the money?"

"You need to calm down. We have no idea what they did with it. They could be padding their pockets with smuggled or stolen diamonds, trying to avoid taxes. It's for the Treasury Department to decipher."

To her credit she hauled in a deep breath, releasing the tourniquet-like grip on his arm. She stood and tugged the hem of her top down. "You're right."

Hearing these words he'd never heard from her before, took him aback. "Do you think the Singletons are involved?"

Wrong question to ask, he berated himself as the blood drained from her face, creating a sallow complexion.

Chapter 23

Hyperventilating would only get Kamilla knocked onto her rear.

Missing the edge of the couch when her knees gave out, she slid to the floor with a sense of dread. Were the Singletons involved? Burning acid forced its way up her throat. She swallowed it and took deep breaths only to look up to find Leonardo offering her a glass of water.

Holding it with trembling hands, she took a few sips. "Thank you." Realizing her graceless sprawl on the floor, she lifted herself up until her backside met the soft cushions of the couch. She drank again.

Leonardo sat beside her. The warm hand he placed on her knee provided confidence and calm. "We'll call Monroe and see what he wants us to do. I'm sure they'll handle reporting the situation to the authorities."

The scenarios her high-powered imagination had dredged up about where the ill-gotten money had come from and what it had obtained had sent her mind spinning. Now she felt a bit calmer. Ready to deal with the situation head-on. More like herself. "Monroe, it is."

Before he could stand, she grabbed his arm. "This isn't exactly the kind of thing you talk about over the phone."

He grinned down at her—something she was rapidly getting used to. "We'll just have to do some creative communication. He's a smart man—he'll figure it out."

She released him and he reached for his tablet. A few swipes and taps later, they came face-to-face with Monroe. With the greetings out of the way, Leonardo took control. "We've discovered some extraordinary information while on vacation."

The older man's brow lifted. "What is it?"

Over the past couple of minutes, Kamilla had been racking her brain to figure out how to tell their boss the horrific news. Her mind had come up with zilch. Hopefully Leonardo had something brilliant.

"We saw a brief documentary of a malicious terrorist attack that occurred in France a few months ago."

Monroe nodded his pepper-gray head, with a slight downward curve of his lips, while still keeping eye contact. "I heard the same. Ten people died with thirty-five injured. Terrorists are everywhere these days. Virtually unstoppable and growing by the minute. If only every country had the same diligent intel as the US, they'd be able to stop the horrors."

She stole a glance at Leonardo. His strong jawline had become even more rigid by his clenched jaw. What had upset him? "It's more than knowing about the attacks. If terrorists weren't funded, they wouldn't be able to cause destruction. The sponsor got sloppy and left a traceable trail, which led back to their money laundering and eventually their terrorist support. The evidence was undeniable."

Monroe nodded in what appeared to be understanding. Whether he comprehended or not, she had no clue.

Time to get a little more direct with the information. "When the officials went in, they not only took down the company that had laundered the money to supply the terrorists, but the parent company of the subsidiary. It has yet to be determined if they had anything to do with the funding or if they were even aware."

The older man didn't even take a moment to think about what he'd been told. "I see. It would appear their law firm will have a lot to contend with. It's unlikely they knew what representing them involved. It's a good thing our firm vets the companies under us more carefully."

As she was opening her mouth to ask what the hell that meant, Leonardo touched the side of her leg to stop her from speaking.

He leaned his face closer to the screen. "So if the law firm of the corporate business had known that the subsidiary was into such shady and detrimental dealings, the firm would've dropped the parent company?"

Monroe's eyes flitted to the left before returning to look between them. Not catching either of their gazes. Her heart sank, landing in her stomach. "As a wizened lawyer, I have learned that anything can be dealt with for the right price. If things aren't going well for my client, I can and will do everything in my power to protect them. But they must be mine."

He nodded, looked at Kamilla and then Leonardo. "We miss you both here at the firm. It's been a long time since you've taken a vacation. I hope things are running smoothly." His fake laugh had Kamilla ready to fight. "Kamilla, I hope your penchant for planning isn't keeping you on too tight of an agenda. You have to make time for some enjoyment, too."

He wanted them to continue to get the Singletons to sign with the firm, even though he knew they possessed a company that was most likely involved in money laundering. He hadn't told them that he would discuss it with the partners. *He already knew. They all did.*

Unable to speak, Leonardo answered on her behalf. "She's kept us on a short leash, as always. Things will go on as planned, sir."

"Good to hear. Everyone here will be happy to have you back once you've had a chance to relax." Monroe raised a palm. "I don't need to remind you about how seriously we take confidentiality here." How come she'd never noticed before how nasty his smirk could be? "Keep everything you know to yourselves, get enough rest and we'll be considering a new partner as soon as you return."

Without another word, the screen went dark as Monroe cut the call.

She sank back into the couch. "They already knew. Those mother fu—" She stopped herself when Leonardo's rant registered, making her ears burn.

"We need to go," he proclaimed when he'd finished dragging the partners for their unethical, self-serving business practices. "They don't care about anyone but themselves. Hell, it wouldn't be beyond them to throw the Singletons to the FBI once they renewed their contract. They'd definitely get more money with the extra legal counsel."

Kamilla's chest burned. "They wouldn't!"

"The firm we work for is evil. They'd do anything to stay on top of the game. Including blame us once shit hits the roof. Everyone, including us and the Singletons, are expendable as long as they get their money."

She had to give the partners the benefit of the doubt. After all, she'd worked for them for five years and was ready to join their ranks as a junior partner. There had to be a reasonable explanation. Her job security depended on it. "Maybe they have information they aren't sharing. Categorical proof that the Singletons aren't involved with the subsidiary's activities."

His frosty glare pushed her back a step. "Are you going to tell me after listening to Monroe speak, after what you've learned over the years, that you really believe that?"

Her sock-covered feet on the light beige carpet came into view when her neck could no longer support her head. Denial hadn't lasted long. "No."

"I'll book us a flight back for tomorrow. You should prepare your letter of resignation. The bastards don't deserve it, but you don't want to burn any bridges."

She hadn't heard correctly. "What? Why would we leave tomorrow? The Singletons are coming."

Large hands braced narrow hips. "What does it matter? We no longer have a job to do for the firm."

Would he really leave the couple in the lurch? "We have an obligation to the Singletons. To let them know about what's going on right in front of them."

"Don't be ridiculous, Kamilla. Warning them will mean you'll be headed to jail *when* they go."

Her nostrils flared. "I don't appreciate you taking that condescending tone with me. And besides, the Singletons are innocent."

"You're not getting involved."

She narrowed her eyes. "I don't know who the hell you're talking to as if she were a five-year-old, but I know it's not me. You need to calm your ass down and think for a minute. The Singletons are not involved in this scam. You've met them. You know their reputation." She threw her hands up and let them fall onto her lap. "There's no one who loves America more than they do. They sent us a damn flag cake on the Fourth of July. And didn't Mr. Singleton lose a nephew on 9/11?" She shook her head. "There's no way I can believe they'd help terrorists in any way. Not at all."

She'd leave out the part where her instincts told her they weren't involved. He'd only laugh at her when she needed his support.

"We have no idea if the money is for terrorist activities." Leonardo sighed. "But you're right, they're good people. At least from what I know about them. It still doesn't mean we have to get involved or that we won't report it."

She swayed to the left with a sudden onset of dizziness. Leonardo caught her before she hit the ground, made her lie down and then encouraged her to take a drink of the water he'd brought earlier.

Scowling brows over concerned eyes met her gaze as a gentle hand stroked down the side of her face, leaving a trail of heat and awareness. If they'd left well enough alone, they could've been making love.

Instead they had to turn in the nicest people she'd ever worked with, she'd lost her job and there was a chance she'd have to go to court to testify. Wishing she could turn off her brain, Kamilla rested her head against the back of the couch and closed her eyes.

She shot straight up when an idea hit her. She ignored the spinning of the room. "We're still their lawyers. Can't we present the information we've found and let them figure it out? I'm sure they'd report their subsidiary that same day, if only to protect their own asses. Then we'd be out of the loop."

Leonardo shook his head. "What you're suggesting is too risky. I like being a lawyer. I'm damn good at it and no one is going to take my license away for collusion. I say we be the ones to report them."

"Even though they're most likely innocent? Their business reputation will be ruined."

He shrugged. "Not my problem. Let the feds sort it out."

She tapped her chest. "I can't live with that. I need to help when I can."

"And get yourself banned from the bar association in the process? It makes no sense."

Had she really thought Leonardo had a heart? That he'd changed from the hard man she'd gotten to know over the years? She'd been a fool to believe it. No matter how much pro bono work he'd ever done, he was and always would be out for himself. She would've been better off staying away from him.

Wobbly when she got to her feet, she headed for her room.

He followed her into the short hallway. "I'll arrange a flight for tomorrow."

With her back to him, she tried to make sure her voice didn't tremble but failed. "Make it for one, because I won't be on it. I'll be meeting with the Singletons. If not tomorrow then on Wednesday. They need to be made aware." Then she turned to him. "I know you don't care about anyone but yourself, but can you please give me two days before you turn them in?"

Pain flashed in his eyes as his head jerked back. Had she been wrong? *Please let me have underestimated him.*

"I love you, Kamilla, but you're being unreasonable. Think about your future."

A childlike temper tantrum took over as she stomped her foot in an effort to release the pain that had built up behind her chest. "Don't you ever say those words to me again!" she said through gritted teeth. "You don't love me, Astacio. You're too self-absorbed to love." She combed her fingers through her short strands. "For a moment I was fool enough to believe you." *To realize I'd fallen in love with you.*

She backed away when he reached for her shoulder. He fisted his hand before dropping it to his side. "Because it's the truth, Kamilla. But love isn't blind. I can't sit around and watch you ruin the career you've worked so hard for."

God help her, she believed him and it tore her apart. What she wouldn't give to fall into his arms and put everything behind them. No matter how badly she wanted to be with him, she couldn't betray her conscience. "I can't let them take the fall. I wouldn't be able to live with myself if I didn't do something to help."

She'd been reaching for the stars when she'd thought they'd had a chance of ever being together. They were much too different. Where she cared about other people, he only sought to protect his own.

"I can't believe you're willing to do this!" Had his voice cracked? Did he realize they'd reached the end of their short relationship, too? "You have so much to offer the world, Kamilla. Don't give it up. Don't give up on us."

She'd have a panic attack and cry her eyes out about losing the man she loved and her job on the same day. Later. "Nothing you say can change my mind, Leonardo. I know what I have to do. My gut tells me it's the right thing, so I'll follow it." She studied the tightness around his eyes and mouth, which revealed his frustration. She swallowed down the tears threatening to choke her. "Have a safe flight home tomorrow. And take care of yourself."

Hand shaking as she opened her door, she let herself in before he could say another word. Crumbling to the floor as a sob tore through her, one question roared in her mind. *What have I done?*

Chapter 24

Kamilla stiffened at the soft knock on her door in the morning. Did she need to hear him say goodbye or to tell her how stupid she'd be if she went through with meeting the Singletons. A second louder rap followed. "Open up, Kamilla. We need to talk."

On principle of hating being told what to do, she took delight in not opening the door. Then she remembered she detested passive aggressive behavior even more. Slinking to the threshold, she refused to look into the mirror, knowing just what she'd see. A zombie-like shell of a woman with red puffy eyes. She didn't doubt her nose held a pinkish tint to it.

Crying all night over something she should've known would've never worked out proved fruitless. On a normal day she'd run to the bathroom, splash water on her face and smooth down her hair. Maybe grab a sweater and swing it over her head to cover her face.

What did it matter if she looked awful since he'd be leaving her?

At the flick of her wrist, the doorknob unlocked and she opened the rich dark wood panel. Her gritty eyes went wide. He looked as bad as she felt, with a dark tinge under his eyes and unusually ashen skin. Her heart hurt for him. The decisions they'd made hadn't been easy for either of them.

A tight frown appeared as his gaze roamed her face "Can we talk?"

Body too heavy to hold up on her own, she slumped against the threshold. "I think we've said everything we're going to. Neither of us will change our mind. Have a safe journey." And a wonderful life.

As if he hadn't heard a word she'd torn out of her raw throat, he reached for her hand and pulled her into the living room. Fatigue, not his energizing touch, made her follow his lead rather than resist.

When they'd settled onto the couch, he held her hand between both of his. She waited for a long-winded speech, but nothing came for a few moments.

"I can't support your decision to inform the Singletons. Lord knows I wish I could, but I can't. It's not a good career move. Hell, it's illegal in the sight of the law. If you go through with it, not only could they take away your license, but you could be fined and go to jail." His eyes pleaded with her. "Please don't take the risk."

Sorrow stabbed her in the chest as she slid her hand

out of his. He still didn't understand and doubted she could make him, but she'd try. One last time with the absolute truth. "You are such an arrogant ass sometimes. You think everything is black and white. Stacked in neat little piles. Life is either a yes or no." She shook her head. "I'm sorry to have to school you, Leonardo, but there are more grays and maybes out there than your judgmental mind can comprehend. And to be honest, I don't blame you. I'd love to have grown up in such a straight and narrow type of world. It would definitely make a lot of things easier."

She raised her hand to stop him from speaking when he opened his mouth. "At the age of twelve, on my way home from school, I got a strange feeling as if someone was following me. When I turned around, nothing looked suspicious. A few minutes later, this man pulled up beside me and parked his car."

The memory glimmered in her mind as if it had happened yesterday. "The guy behind the wheel got out and without a word walked with me. My father had turned up for the first time since he'd left me."

Leonardo's mouth gaped. At any other time she may have been entertained by the surprised expression. Now she fought for his acceptance. "For four blocks neither of us spoke. When I reached the steps of my foster home, I turned, looked him in his eyes and said, 'It's okay, Daddy. I loved Mama, too.' He sank to his knees and bowed his head low as if before a priest, seeking absolution."

She swallowed hard and reached forward, just as she'd done that day and touched Leonardo's shoulder.

"I told him, 'I'm happy. Better than when I was with you. I eat every day and there's always someone around to help me. I'm not scared of noises on the street anymore because I'm never alone like I was with you.'" She swiped a tear from her face. "It hadn't taken me long as a child to realize the gift he'd bestowed on me by leaving. He'd been too self-absorbed in his grief to know how to care for a young child. He dealt with it by drinking, which led to my neglect and near starvation. Leaving me had been the best thing he could've done as an ill-equipped parent. It told me how much he truly loved me."

Leonardo ducked his head and rubbed a hand under his nose with a sniffle. "You came to this realization at the age of twelve?"

"Earlier, when I started hearing about the wretched things some of the other foster kids had gone through while they'd still lived with their parents or family members, I considered myself blessed that he'd come to the realization that he couldn't take care of me."

"It still sounds selfish."

Kamilla shrugged. "Or selfless. Depends on how you look at it. I understand why you don't want me to tell the Singletons. I do." She inhaled a deep breath. "But I have to."

He blinked at her. They'd come to an impasse. He'd never see her side of the chasm as anything good to cross over to. "Okay."

"Okay," she said past the recurring tightening of her throat she stood, knowing he'd still leave her. "Have a safe flight home." She ticked her lips up into a brief smile. "At least it'll be peaceful without me trying to break your hand."

With a wave she walked to her room with her head high and tears held at bay. She'd learned a long time ago that being the leaver hurt a lot less than being left. Not much of a victory, because in the end she'd be alone in the big gray world.

The sliced cucumbers she'd ordered and placed over her eyes had felt good until she'd started crying again and had to remove them. Damn him. Damn him for loving her, yet not being able to support her. Didn't that reveal the depth of his love? As shallow as a few drops in a sink and worth nothing.

Then why couldn't she make the pain in her chest go away or stop allowing thoughts of him to depress her. She'd never see him again. One day she'd look back and send up a prayer of gratitude for his decision. Today she'd let the agony rage through her and try to survive. Ragged after shedding tears all morning and afternoon, she'd gotten out of bed to get ready for the encounter with the Singletons.

No man was worth giving up what she believed in, even if she had to forgo his love. If things could've gone differently, she—

Stopping the thought, she outlined her lips with a red lip liner, which she filled in with a similar color matte lipstick to draw attention away from her eyes. Ha. Maybe she'd meant to match them.

The smile she displayed in the mirror wobbled as she blinked back tears. "No regrets."

She glanced at her watch. Six o'clock. According to the agenda Monroe had given them, the Singletons always had dinner at their special table at this time. Had they even arrived? She'd been wallowing in so much self-pity that she'd neglected to sit in the lobby to catch their appearance.

Now she wished she could've gotten it over with in the afternoon, but she hadn't been in her right mind. Still wasn't.

She grabbed her attaché case, with their file tucked inside, and left her room. At the sight of Leonardo's closed door, she stopped and fought the tears threatening. Damn him.

Principles. She'd do the right thing even if it killed her. A lifetime of relying on her instincts had never steered her wrong.

A short trip along the picturesque snow-cleared path and she stood in the dining room. Scanning the area, she searched for the older African American couple, who appeared to be more in their early fifties than their sixties. After a couple of minutes, she located them, but they weren't alone. When she recognized the third party, every muscle in her body went limp and the attaché case tumbled to the floor. If she hadn't caught herself by leaning against a railing, she would've, too.

Chapter 25

Leonardo had never understood the word *empathy*. How could someone share the feelings of another without being that person? After hearing Kamilla's story about her father, the meaning had slithered into his heart and clawed.

Rather than taking his packed bags and leaving immediately to allow her to deal with the situation she insisted on placing herself in, he'd put on his coat, rented a pair of snowshoes and trekked the woods. The peace and solitude of the quiet environment relaxed him as he thought. And felt.

Throughout his life he would set goals and maintain a singular course to obtain them. Deviations had been unnecessary because of impeccable planning and timing. And then Kamilla slammed into his life and shook up his world. Now he noticed what he'd never dared to look at before. Could he have been wrong? A rarity, but possible.

If he were to testify on a Bible, he'd state what he knew to be the apparent truth. He didn't think the Singletons had anything to do with the money laundering. So why hadn't he been willing to side with Kamilla?

Self-preservation. Where she'd made her decision with her mind and heart, he'd done it with fear as the catalyst.

He'd always thought of himself as strong. Yet where he'd be classified as steel, she possessed the qualities of titanium mixed with diamonds, and yet still possessed enough flexibility for change. Kamilla Gordon was a more powerful individual than he'd ever known himself to be.

After acknowledging how right she'd been, he'd hiked his way back to the resort and waited in the lobby for the Singletons to arrive. The time had seemed to drag on for days rather than sixty minutes. The whole time, he hoped Kamilla's plan didn't involve intercepting the couple before they settled into their room.

Once they arrived he had explained the extreme importance of meeting them and they'd escorted him to their room. If anything were to happen with this case, he, not Kamilla, would take the fall.

He knew he loved her, but being willing to give up his career for her proved to him, and hopefully it would her, just how deep it went.

Taking a sip of whiskey, Leonardo felt Kamilla's presence before he saw her. When he turned toward the entrance, his stomach plunged to his feet. She appeared ready to fall, looking worse than in the morning, when she'd left him sitting in the living room. Had she taken their disagreement that hard?

After excusing himself from the couple at the table, he rushed to her side and grasped her elbow.

In typical Kamilla fashion, she snatched her arm away and bent to retrieve her bag. "What are you doing here?" She turned her back to the Singletons and scowled. "You were supposed to be on a plane to Cleveland."

For the first time since making the dramatic gesture of self-sacrifice, he had doubts. Had he done the right thing by leaving her uninformed? Yes. She wasn't the only one who could do right. "I didn't go. Instead I caught up with the Singletons and told them what was going on with their jewelry company. Either they're damn good actors or they really didn't know anything about it."

"Just like I said." How had she gotten the words out through gritted teeth, and how come her smile of gratitude hadn't appeared?

"True. After explaining what we'd discovered, they called the Treasury Department and reported it."

She did a military-precision turn on her chunky-heeled pump and headed toward the lobby. He chased after her. "Where are you going?"

"To my room."

"Why? Didn't everything go as you planned?"

Her reddened eyes glared when she made an abrupt stop. She grabbed the sleeve of his sweater and led him into a secluded alcove. She released him and flexed her fingers at the height of his neck. "You are such a control freak. Did it ever cross your mind to come talk to me? I've been in the room all day."

What the hell had he done wrong? Saving her behind shouldn't have made her angry. "I didn't want you involved. There was no need for both of us to hang our licenses on the line."

The blaze of anger transitioned to what he recognized as disappointment. "You don't get it." She shook her head. "We can't leave the Singletons waiting."

He rested his hands on her shoulders. "After saving their asses, they can wait. Tell me what has you so upset? Did you want to take the credit? I told them how you first discovered the problem. I only wanted to spare you any of the risk involved with informing them rather than taking it straight to the authorities like the law dictates."

When she stepped out of his reach, his hands fell to his sides. "Why didn't you come to me?"

He shrugged. "I didn't think it was necessary."

The shriek of laughter she emitted actually scared him. What had he done that was so wrong? "Let's go. I'm hungry," she said.

Craning his neck forward, he raised both brows. "We'll talk about it later?"

"No need. You did the hero thing and swooped in to save me." Her tone couldn't have been any drier. "We're set."

Then why did his insides coil as if they were anything but?

* * *

Heart sore, Leonardo had turned to the only person he thought might have the answer to his problem. "Miguel, can you please explain women?"

His little brother made a raspberry sound with his lips, adding a lamentable shake of his head. "Nope."

Leonardo held his arms out wide, exposing himself like he'd done for Kamilla. "I put my law career on the line for her. At dinner with our client, she was all smiles and charm, but when we got to the room she barely looked at me while giving one-word answers to my direct questions." Why had she left in the early morning, the day after their dinner meeting with the Singletons? Why hadn't she returned his calls for the past three days?

He'd delivered his notice to Monroe at the firm as soon as he'd arrived in Cleveland. Monroe had called Benton and Peterson into the office. They proceeded to attempt to express their disappointment in words that no one, not even his father, had the right to throw in his direction.

Without responding, he'd left the room, gone to human resources and put in for two-weeks worth of accrued sick leave, never to step foot in the building again. To hell with not burning bridges. They deserved it.

Foreboding for Kamilla's welfare burned a hole in his stomach. Temper be damned, he shouldn't have left her alone at the office to fend for herself. Distress came from not knowing if she'd have the courage to quit. She held on to the objective of making partner, and even with the Singletons not signing with the firm, they'd keep her. Especially after losing him.

If only she'd answer her phone, he'd know she was okay. Then he'd talk some sense into her.

He'd called her secretary and with more than a little bit of anxiousness in her voice, she'd told him Kamilla had requested vacation time. When he'd probed further to find out where she'd gone, the woman had clammed up.

A low growl rumbled in his throat at the frustration one woman had put him through. "She's avoiding me."

Miguel rolled his eyes and filled the air with an over-the-top theatrical sigh. "Of course she is, Nardo. You acted like a Neanderthal."

"By protecting her? Makes no sense."

"Have you learned nothing from Mom and Dad's relationship? Hell, you've known them longer than me. You should've caught on by now."

Angry heat erupted in Leonardo's face. The younger man would get pummeled in a moment if he didn't stop pushing his damn buttons.

Miguel chuckled. "You are the most uptight, entertaining big bro a person could have." Then he sobered. "How many times have you seen Dad do something for Mom she could've done herself?"

The embarrassment of how little he really knew his own family hit him square in the gut. "I've been busy." Did he have to say it with such petulance? It would give Miguel more ammunition.

His brother held up a hand and connected his thumb with the other fingers in a zero symbol. "None. Once,

Mom got so angry, she started yelling at Dad. It went on for a good thirty minutes. I'd never seen her so pissed in my life."

Intrigued, Leonardo pushed himself to the edge of his seat. His mother epitomized calm and grace. It had to have been something big to upset her. "What set her off?"

"You." The beard of Miguel's goatee made a scratchy sound when he rubbed an index finger along his chin. "Actually, it was your football coach. He'd announced the starting lineup in your sophomore year and you were on it."

He remembered that year. His parents had supported him by being at every game when they hadn't been out of the country. He'd never heard that his mother had been upset.

"She'd gone to see the man about taking you off the team because of your heart, but the coach had stood firm with his decision."

His parents had still tried to control his life? "How come I never knew about this?"

"Who knows?" The grin Miguel was known for brought out his dimple. "Wait, I remember. When Mom calmed down, she walked to the door and saw me lying on the floor, eavesdropping." He crinkled his brows. "For some reason she didn't get mad at me. She bribed me with a toy I'd been pestering them for in order to forget everything I'd heard."

"What's the point?"

"Before she discovered me, I kept wondering when Dad was going to offer to go beat the coach up for Mom.

During her tirade, Dad had listened. When she'd ask him a question, he'd answer, but that was it. He didn't offer to do anything."

"Again, little brother. What the hell is the point?"

"I'm getting to it. When Mom left the study, I went to Dad and asked him what he was going to do? He placed his hand on my shoulder and said, 'My most beloved and favorite son—"

"Miguel," Leonardo growled.

"You know I am." His light chuckle didn't deter him from the story. "He told me he'd learned a long time ago that women, especially strong ones like Mom, don't need someone to do anything for her, because she's just as capable of taking care of a problem as any man. What she needs is a sounding board. Someone to listen to her."

Leonardo narrowed his gaze. "Are you telling me Kamilla didn't want me to do anything?"

"I don't know about that, but you should've communicated with her before you jumped in to save her. I'm sure she had it under control. Consequences and all."

The sportscaster highlighting the basketball game was the only sound in the living room. Of course telling her what he'd decided to do had come to his mind, but he knew she'd want to go through with her plan and he couldn't allow it. As a man—her man—he needed to protect her. Only, it had backfired and now she couldn't stand him.

"You know what?" Miguel didn't wait for an answer. "Dad is the wisest man on the planet. His strategy works. Every single time. Listen and support."

Sinking into the couch's cushions, Leonardo sighed. He'd messed up. Badly. "This information comes too late. What am I supposed to do now?"

"I have the answer to that, too. Follow my example with getting Tanya when I mucked up."

His world clouded over, but he knew he'd do whatever it took to get Kamilla back. "Grovel, plead and propose?"

Miguel's laughter brought a momentary smile to Leonardo's grim face. "You can hold off on the proposal." He raised both brows, exposing more of his hazel irises. "Unless…"

Once again he smiled through the pits of his despair. "Yes. She's the one, but unlike Tanya, she'd throw the ring in my face. We need more time to get to know each other."

"So she can find out you're not always a heartless bastard?"

"Exactly." *And to fall in love with me.* Something he desperately desired from her.

Chapter 26

The rapid footfall of slipperless feet against the wood floor preceded the presence of two beautiful girls plowing into Kamilla.

Lea, in all her six-year-old glory, plopped onto her lap. "Aunty Kam, you're still here?"

"Five days is the longest you've ever stayed and today makes one week." Belinda turned to her mother. "Is it a cold day in hell, Mom?"

Kamilla's eyes went wide as she caught her best friend's gaze. "Is this what you're teaching my babies about me?"

Cass raised her shoulders in a shrug as if the comment her eight-year-old had made was normal. "The last time you came to visit, they bugged me about how long you'd stay the next time. I told them if it was longer than five days… Well, you heard the rest."

"You're not right, sometimes," Kamilla said.

"Come on, girls. Go get ready for school and then eat your breakfast." Cass pointed a warning finger at her mini doppelgangers. "You missed the bus yesterday and I won't be driving you to school again."

"Yes, Mom." The girls chorused in unison and trudged up the stairs.

Kamilla watched them go. "You trust them to dress themselves."

"Not at all. You forget I have a very capable husband who adores his children and doesn't mind getting them ready for school in the morning."

Would Leonardo have been a good father? She'd only recently learned about his playful side, but she could envisage him wanting to spend time with his children. She winced at the sharp pain in her chest. Too bad she'd never get to see it happen.

Cass sat next to her on the couch. "You need to get over yourself. So what if the man you love did a good deed on your behalf without consulting you. He could've done worse."

She rested her head on her friend's shoulder. "You know it's not that simple. He's an alpha. I'm talking rule-the-whole-damn-pack-and-the-surrounding-territories type of man. He'll always want to take control, even when I can handle the situation." She expelled the air from her lungs on a sigh. "I can't have that. I've worked too hard for my independence."

"And where has it gotten you? No life, no man, no job."

She sat upright. "Is it my fault the company I invested

my time and energy into ended up being a dud? Besides, I already have an interview with a family practice law firm tomorrow afternoon. They seemed eager to have me, too. The money isn't great, but like you keep telling me, I'll be doing something I love by helping people."

Cass raised both hands, threw her head back and sang, "Alleluia." They giggled.

"Why don't you move closer to us?"

Kamilla scoffed. "What in the world would I do in this podunk town? You said you wanted me to have a life, right? This place won't do. Just because your veterinarian husband got you stuck here doesn't mean I have to join you with all the roosters, cows and pigs."

"Okay. I get it. If I didn't love Michael so much, I would've packed up. He makes it bearable."

Nothing would ever come between them. Their love inspired. "At least I'll be visiting more often."

"You'd better. So, when are you going to forgive Leonardo and communicate with him like a grown woman instead of hiding like a weasel?"

She'd lived in peace from her friend's meddling for the past week and now Cass had determined to lay into her. "Never came to mind. We aren't suited."

"Or," Cass stretched out the word for several seconds, "your ginormous pride won't let you be happy. Face it, you wanted to be the one to throw yourself on the tracks for the sake of righteousness."

The truth stung, but she wouldn't confirm. "He should've told me before he did it."

Cass nodded. "I'm sure he's sorry now. And after you talk to him about it, he'll probably only sometimes ever do it again. You have to train him to your ways, girl.

Just like you have to yield to some of his." She held up three fingers. "Love, communication and compromise."

"Not with Leonardo."

"You have a problem of stepping in your own way, my friend. If he loves you, which I know for a fact he does, he'll come around."

The girls stomped into the room with their shiny Mary Janes and plaid uniform dresses, looking too adorable for words. Kamilla followed them into the kitchen, hoping their idle chatter would take her mind off losing the only man she'd ever truly loved. One day it wouldn't hurt so much to think about him.

Today is not the day.

Kamilla had been double-crossed. By her best friend of all people. Passing out from a rapid heart rate wouldn't help. Kamilla turned her back on Leonardo, striding out of the barn, only to see the taillights of Cass's vehicle as she tore up the path.

Cass had enticed her with a promise of seeing a fresh litter of puppies and a foal. She should've known her weakness for babies would get her caught up in a trap one day. Balling her fingers into a fist, the sound of crinkling came to her attention. She unfurled her hand to find the folded piece of paper her traitorous friend had slipped her.

She read the note twice and still couldn't believe what Cass had done.

My dearest Kam,
I love you, but I'm tired of arguing with your stubborn ass about Leonardo. I got his number from your phone and grilled the hell out of him.

He's a good man. A great one for you, but you already know it—that's why you're fighting so hard against him. Give him a chance, you deserve to be happy. If he hurts you, I'll hunt him down and shoot him in the ass with Michael's tranquilizer gun.

Had she fought any potential relationship they could've had? Fear. The one thing she couldn't tolerate had weaseled its way into her. What if things didn't work out between them? Or the peace they'd found with each other didn't hold? Maybe one day he wouldn't like her anymore. She rarely lived her life on "what ifs," but with Leonardo it seemed inevitable. His unpredictability set her on edge, when she sought stability in all aspects of her life. Particularly when it came to her heart.

"Casey told me to mention that there are tiny animals inside, waiting for you to get mushy over."

Startled at the sound of the deep voice that had whispered erotic words while buried deep inside of her, she braced herself to turn and face him. When she did, the world dropped away until only he remained. Head bent and hands stuffed into the pockets of his jeans, he almost resembled a man who could possess humility. Damn she'd missed him.

Instead of barraging him with the millions of questions racing through her mind, she headed to the opening of the barn. His scent teased her as she passed him, and she resisted flinging herself into his arms. Was she ready to be with a man like him? A strong man who would want to protect her at the slightest sign of danger and fight her battles for her? Could she maintain her independence if they got together, or would he always attempt to dominate?

He pointed to an area in the far right of the large space. Lying on a mound of hay, a golden retriever had four adorable puppies feeding ferociously from her. "Oh my goodness, they're so adorable."

"Your friend said you shouldn't pick them up if they're nursing. I should stop you at all costs if you tried."

The image broadened her smile.

He walked around her, obscuring her vision of the little darlings. "Look, Kamilla. I'm sorry. I was wrong to go behind your back and approach the Singletons without talking to you first." He inhaled, held the breath for a beat and then released it. "I wanted to protect you."

"Did you even think about coming to me?"

His head twitched to the side, reminding her of a robot. "Maybe for a moment, but it never sounded like a good idea."

"At least you're honest."

"Always."

She'd never known him to lie. Yet another fantastic quality he possessed. She'd never acquired the skill of holding grudges. "I accept your apology."

The brightness of his smile made her heart leap as he stepped closer with his arms outstretched.

She held up both hands. "What are you doing?"

"Getting you back in my arms, where you belong. I've missed you and I want us to start dating."

She blinked up at his candor. "What happens when—" she shoved his shoulder "—and I say *when* because you're impossible sometimes, you go all caveman and try to fight my battles for me?"

He grasped the back of his neck. "I can't promise it won't happen again. No one will ever hurt the woman I love and get away with it, but I'll try to remember to talk to you about it first."

She shook her head, cheeks burning with the effort not to smile at his amorous words. Pleased at his willingness to try to change. "That's not good enough."

"It's the best I can do. I can promise to be faithful to you. Listen to you. And I'll even let you win an argument or two."

"You're a mess, Astacio." Her laughter broke free as she rushed to him and wrapped her arms around his waist. He stood frozen for a moment before crushing her into him.

"What else?" she prodded.

"I'll remember your birthday and our anniversaries, like today, when you made me the happiest man in the world."

Her heart melted. The man knew how to sweet-talk a woman. "And."

"I'll be less vociferous when we're making love."

"I never knew you could be so chatty." She looked into his eyes with what she hoped showed her love for him. "I don't mind so much, though. Tell me you love me again."

"I love you. More than I ever thought I could. I went out of my mind with worry not knowing where you were. Please don't do that to me again."

"Well, I can't promise—"

He stopped the words she'd thrown back in his face with a kiss. A passionate melding of open mouths and tongues getting reacquainted until she struggled for breath.

"I love you, too." Kamilla panted as she looked up at him, seeing her future in his eyes.

"I figured as much."

She stiffened her back. This man would drive her to drink with his arrogance. "How?"

He lowered his head, nuzzling the side of her neck. She groaned with pleasure.

"You ran away."

"So?"

"You're a fighter. Even when you know there's no chance of winning, you'll take down as many as possible before you fall."

Again with the magical words.

"For you to run away meant you were afraid."

She scrunched her mouth to the side. "Of what? You?"

His loud burst of laughter filled the barn. "Never me. Of your feelings."

How had he pinned her down so easily? She reached up and stroked the back of her fingers along his cheek. "I'm no longer afraid, so don't think you'll be getting rid of me anytime soon."

He rested his forehead against hers. "To the middle and beyond."

She couldn't love him any more than at that moment. He'd remembered her preference of being in the middle of a relationship. She had a feeling they'd get to the end. Together. "And beyond."

Epilogue

"To Astacio, Levere and Williamson Law Firm's one-year anniversary. May they have many more." Everyone took a sip of champagne after Miguel's toast.

Leonardo held Kamilla closer to his side. "There should be a Gordon in the name."

Kamilla rolled her eyes. "I'm not coming to work with you. Two years was enough."

"I thought it was because you love being a family lawyer."

She nodded. "That too."

Her smile elicited his stomach to flutter and gave him no choice than to kiss her supple lips. He'd never get tired of having her in his arms.

The clearing of someone's throat brought them back to the party. Leonardo turned a scowl toward the intruder, then changed his expression to a smile when he saw the Singletons.

Mr. Singleton shook Leonardo's hand with an enthusiastic clap on the back and kissed Kamilla's cheek. "I can't tell you how happy I am to have you representing us. It's been a wonderful and profitable year. Your advice on the Wellington merger really saved us money. And we can't forget your defense when it came to Rossman Jewelers. The government would've tried to destroy everything we've worked for if it hadn't been for you."

He gave the couple a genuine smile. "It's what we're here for."

"Keep up the good work."

"We will. Enjoy the party."

His woman grinned up at him. "When did you become a people person?"

He studied her face. Not a trace of mischief shone in her eyes. He'd never qualify himself in that category, but being with Kamilla had made him better at dealing with others. "Since the moment I wanted to be with you. I knew kindness was the only way to get you to like me, so I changed."

She placed a hand on her chest as her smile broadened. "I'm a miracle worker."

Laughter from the depth of his chest had him arching his back. "Yes, sweetheart. You are. Thank you for being you."

He tugged her out of the room and found an area that nobody occupied. Hands trembling, he reached in his breast pocket and removed an envelope. Was she ready?

Would she decline? No. He wouldn't think in the negative. Optimism and hard work had delivered everything he'd ever wanted. Including the only woman he'd ever loved. He held out the envelope without the nervous tremors shaking it. "Here."

"What's this?"

"Open it."

Her gaze zipped between him and the envelope a few times before she gently tore it open. It took her a minute of scanning the sheet before she looked up at him. "This is a contract to be a partner. I don't understand."

"Yes. You'd have a percentage of my shares and since your last name would be Astacio, that's if you wanted to exchange Gordon for mine, or even hyphenate it, we wouldn't have to modify the company name." He'd had a better planned speech than he'd delivered.

"Exchange Gord—" The letter fell to the ground when she cupped both hands against her nose and mouth, stifling her gasp as she noticed the solitaire diamond he held out to her.

"Kamilla Gordon, I love you. Every day brings me more in love with you. I knew you were special the first day I met you, Harvard pin and all. I can't fathom my life without you in it as my friend, my lover, my keeper, my partner, but most importantly my wife. Will you marry me?"

Removing her hands from her face, she revealed a smile that could rival the brightest star in the galaxy as her head bobbed with affirmative enthusiasm. "Yes."

That was all he needed to place the platinum pear-cut diamond on her ring finger before swooping her into his arms and holding on tight. He'd never let her go again. She possessed more of his heart than he did, and that's the way it would be for the rest of their lives.

He loosened his grip on her and stared into her glimmering eyes. "I love you so much. My life is for you."

She held his face between her hands. "As mine is yours."

He sealed their agreement with a kiss that promised forever.

* * * * *

Soulful and sensual romance featuring multicultural characters.

Look for brand-new Kimani stories
in special 2-in-1 volumes starting March 2019.

Available May 7, 2019

Forever with You & *The Sweet Taste of Seduction*
by Kianna Alexander and Joy Avery

Seductive Melody & *Capture My Heart*
by J.M. Jeffries

Road to Forever & *A Love of My Own*
by Sherelle Green and Sheryl Lister

The Billionaire's Baby & *The Wrong Fiancé*
by Niobia Bryant and Lindsay Evans

Get 4 FREE REWARDS!

We'll send you 2 FREE Books plus 2 FREE Mystery Gifts.

Harlequin® Desire books feature heroes who have it all: wealth, status, incredible good looks... everything but the right woman.

FREE
Value Over
$20

YES! Please send me 2 FREE Harlequin® Desire novels and my 2 FREE gifts (gifts are worth about $10 retail). After receiving them, if I don't wish to receive any more books, I can return the shipping statement marked "cancel." If I don't cancel, I will receive 6 brand-new novels every month and be billed just $4.55 per book in the U.S. or $5.24 per book in Canada. That's a savings of at least 13% off the cover price! It's quite a bargain! Shipping and handling is just 50¢ per book in the U.S. and 75¢ per book in Canada.* I understand that accepting the 2 free books and gifts places me under no obligation to buy anything. I can always return a shipment and cancel at any time. The free books and gifts are mine to keep no matter what I decide.

225/326 HDN GMYU

Name (please print)

Address   Apt. #

City   State/Province   Zip/Postal Code

> Mail to the **Reader Service:**
> **IN U.S.A.:** P.O. Box 1341, Buffalo, NY 14240-8531
> **IN CANADA:** P.O. Box 603, Fort Erie, Ontario L2A 5X3

Want to try 2 free books from another series! Call 1-800-873-8635 or visit www.ReaderService.com.

---

*Terms and prices subject to change without notice. Prices do not include sales taxes, which will be charged (if applicable) based on your state or country of residence. Canadian residents will be charged applicable taxes. Offer not valid in Quebec. This offer is limited to one order per household. Books received may not be as shown. Not valid for current subscribers to Harlequin Desire books. All orders subject to approval. Credit or debit balances in a customer's account(s) may be offset by any other outstanding balance owed by or to the customer. Please allow 4 to 6 weeks for delivery. Offer available while quantities last.

Your Privacy—The Reader Service is committed to protecting your privacy. Our Privacy Policy is available online at www.ReaderService.com or upon request from the Reader Service. We make a portion of our mailing list available to reputable third parties that offer products we believe may interest you. If you prefer that we not exchange your name with third parties, or if you wish to clarify or modify your communication preferences, please visit us at www.ReaderService.com/consumerschoice or write to us at Reader Service Preference Service, P.O. Box 9062, Buffalo, NY 14240-9062. Include your complete name and address.

HD19R

SPECIAL EXCERPT FROM

HARLEQUIN®

Savion Monroe's serious business exterior hides his creative spirit—and only Jazmin Boyd has access. Beautiful, sophisticated and guarding a secret of her own, the television producer evokes a fiery passion that dares the guarded CEO to pursue his dream. But when she accidentally exposes Savion's hidden talent on air for all the world to see, will he turn his back on stardom and the woman he loves?

Read on for a sneak peek at
Forever with You,
*the next exciting installment in
the Sapphire Shores series by Kianna Alexander!*

Savion held on to Jazmin's hands, feeling the trembling subside. He hadn't expected her to react that way to his question about her past. Now that he knew his query had made her uncomfortable, he kicked himself inwardly. *I shouldn't have asked her that. What was I thinking?* While his own past had been filled with frivolous encounters with the opposite sex, that didn't mean she'd had similar experiences.

"I'm okay, Savion. You can stop looking so concerned." A soft smile tilted her lips.

He chuckled. "Good to know. Now, what can you tell me about the exciting world of television production?"

One expertly arched eyebrow rose. "Seriously? You want to talk about work?"

KPEXP0319

He shrugged. "It might be boring to you, but remember, I don't know the first thing about what goes on behind the scenes at a TV show."

She opened her mouth, but before she could say anything, the waiter appeared again, this time with their dessert. He released her hands, and they moved to free up the tabletop.

"Here's the cheesecake with key lime ice cream you ordered, sir." The waiter placed down the two plates, as well as two gleaming silver spoons.

"Thank you." Savion picked up his spoon. "I hope you don't mind that I ordered dessert ahead. They didn't have key lime cheesecake, but I thought this would be the next best thing."

Her smile brightened. "I don't mind at all. It looks delicious." She picked up her spoon and scooped up a small piece of cheesecake and a dollop of the ice cream.

When she brought it to her lips and slid the spoon into her mouth, she made a sound indicative of pleasure. "It's just as good as it looks."

His groin tightened. *I wonder if the same is true about you, Jazmin Boyd.* "I'm glad you like it."

A few bites in, she seemed to remember their conversation. "Sorry, what was I gonna say?"

He laughed. "You were going to tell me about all the exciting parts of your job."

"I don't know if any of what I do is necessarily 'exciting,' but I'll tell you about it. Basically, my team and I are the last people to interact with and make changes to the show footage before it goes to the network to be aired. We're responsible for taking all that raw footage and turning it into something cohesive, appealing and screen ready."

"I see. You said something about the opening and closing sequences when we were on the beach." He polished off the last of his dessert. "How's that going?"

She looked surprised. "You remember me saying that?"

"Of course. I always remember the important things."

Her cheeks darkened, and she looked away for a moment, then continued. "We've got the opening sequence done, and it's approved by the higher-ups. But we're still going back and forth over that closing sequence. It just needs a few more tweaks."

"How long do you have to get it done?"

She twirled a lock of glossy hair around her index finger. "Three weeks at most. The sooner, the better." She finished the last bite of her cheesecake and set down her spoon. "What about you? How's the project going with the park?"

He leaned back in his chair. "We're in that limbo stage between planning and execution. Everything is tied up right now until we get the last few permits from the state and the town commissioner. I can't submit the local request until the state approval comes in, so…" He shrugged. "For now, it's the waiting game."

"When do you hope to break ground?"

"By the first of June. That way we can have everything in place and properly protected before the peak of hurricane season." He hated to even think of Gram's memory park being damaged or flooded during a storm, but with the island being where it was, the team had been forced to make contingency plans. "We're doing as much as we can to keep the whole place intact should a bad storm hit—that's all by design. Dad insisted on it and wouldn't even entertain landscaping plans that didn't offer that kind of protection."

She nodded. "I think that's a smart approach. It's pretty similar to the way buildings are constructed in California, to protect them from collapse during an earthquake. Gotta work with what you're given."

He blew out a breath. "I don't know about you, but I need this vacation."

Don't miss Forever with You
by Kianna Alexander, available May 2019
wherever Harlequin® Kimani Romance™
books and ebooks are sold.